PASSION'S CHALLENGE

"Kiss me, Magheen. Kiss me as a woman should. I don't want to think you're a little girl." Daniel spoke softly as he threw out the challenge, and Magheen wasn't one to ignore a gauntlet.

She kissed him.

The warmth of his lips was caressing, enticing. She was shocked at his boldness and would have withdrawn, but his arms tightened around her and she could feel the gentle strength of his muscles as he pulled her closer.

Magheen put her arms around his neck, drawing him even nearer. She began to tremble then, and Daniel held her tightly, as though to ward off any intrusion. His mouth nipped at her ear and neck, curved moistly along her jawline and then gently nibbled at her lips.

His hands explored and roamed, and Magheen moaned from deep within her throat at the intensity of his touch. She ached all over, needing even more than he was giving, craving all he had to give . . .

ZEBRA'S GOT THE ROMANCE
TO SET YOUR HEART AFIRE!

RAGING DESIRE　　　　　　　　　　(2242, $3.75)
by Colleen Faulkner

A wealthy gentleman and officer in General Washington's army, Devon Marsh wasn't meant for the likes of Cassie O'Flynn, an immigrant bond servant. But from the moment their lips first met, Cassie knew she could love no other . . . even if it meant marching into the flames of war to make him hers!

TEXAS TWILIGHT　　　　　　　　　　(2241, $3.75)
by Vivian Vaughan

When handsome Trace Garrett stepped onto the porch of the Santa Clara ranch, he wove a rapturous spell around Clara Ehler's heart. Though Clara planned to sell the spread and move back East, Trace was determined to keep her on the wild Western frontier where she belonged — to share with him the glory and the splendor of the passion-filled TEXAS TWILIGHT.

RENEGADE HEART　　　　　　　　　　(2244, $3.75)
by Marjorie Price

Strong-willed Hannah Hatch resented her imprisonment by Captain Jake Farnsworth, even after the daring Yankee had rescued her from bloodthirsty marauders. And though Jake's rock-hard physique made Hannah tremble with desire, the spirited beauty was nevertheless resolved to exploit her femininity to the fullest and gain her independence from the virile bluecoat.

LOVING CHALLENGE　　　　　　　　　　(2243, $3.75)
by Carol King

When the notorious Captain Dominic Warbrooke burst into Laurette Harker's eighteenth birthday ball, the accomplished beauty challenged the arrogant scoundrel to a duel. But when the captain named her innocence as his stakes, Laurette was terrified she'd not only lose the fight, but her heart as well!

Colorado Jewel

GATE BRANDT

ZEBRA BOOKS
KENSINGTON PUBLISHING CORP.

ZEBRA BOOKS

are published by

Kensington Publishing Corp.
475 Park Avenue South
New York, NY 10016

First printing: April, 1989
Printed in the United States of America

To James

Chapter One

Early September, 1878

Daniel Calcord lifted a sun-brown hand to shield his eyes as he scanned the range of mountains in front and on either side of him. Like pillars reaching for the sky, the mountains rose every bit as majestically as the poets raved.

Daniel wished a poet were here, right now, to witness the anger of the late morning sky at this intrusion into nature's solitude. How poetically would the man wax then? The only indentation in these grim surroundings was this lonely, corded road that wound and wrapped itself around the peaks of power and danger.

Fall was early this year, and the aspen were already in a deep red-gold state. Blue spruce dotted the sides of the mountains, dying off at the point of timberline.

And the sky was a deep, dark cloud. Early September or not, Daniel would wager a fortune that snow was on its way. If his gamble paid, he would be in Leadville before night and the snow fell. If not, he and his men could be snowbound for weeks.

He cursed the urge that had him throwing caution to the winds and choosing Mosquito Pass over Weston Pass, the route a sane man would have taken. Mosquito Pass was the shortest distance between Alma and Leadville, but not the safest, as Daniel was learning. What was a couple more days compared to weeks of snowbound solitude?

Tugging his Stetson lower to protect his bare face from the bite of the wind, Daniel brushed his heels against the flank of his mare and urged her to go faster.

The heavy wagons behind him rolled with a steady precision. Laden with equipment and foodstuffs to last him and his men the winter, they were slow and cumbersome. But this winter needed to be spent at his camp and with his men working his mine, and not in this forlorn, windswept country.

The mine was a new investment for Daniel and his partners. The assay tests clearly had showed promise, and Daniel had been bored with his sedate life in Denver, bored with the bank in which he was a partner, weary of his law business. Daniel had been anxious to begin a new venture, and a year spent in Leadville, Colorado, had sounded appealing at the time. Somehow, in his mind, beginning a new venture was equated with adventure, not with dusty, windswept roads, nor with the threat of freezing to death from the onslaught of an early winter.

The sun had peeped out momentarily that morning, but only on the barren top of the pass, and only to be obscured by the arrival of dark clouds overhead. By noon the wind was howling savagely, bringing in the change of seasons. But a brief respite was on its way, for in the far distance, nestled into a valley between ridges, could be seen the curling smoke from the chimney of the halfway house. Called halfway, though in reality it was a bit beyond this mark, it was meant to be the halfway spot between Alma and Leadville. Just beyond the house the road could be seen to descend rapidly into a thick forest.

The drivers of each of the six freight wagons saw the smoke and immediately could be heard clucking their tongues and cracking worn leather reins over the heads of the draft animals, urging them to a faster gait. Hunger was deep inside each man; it had been many hours since the predawn breakfast.

The wagon train pulled up before the stock corrals, and a huge, thickset man with a red beard and jovial face watched their arrival from the barn door. He wore a plaid shirt and suspenders and a fine, black bowler hat, trimmed with a gray silk ribbon. After each driver saw to his own horses, making sure each had plenty of water and hay, the giant of a man stretched himself and moved toward the large two-story building that advertised, "Moels served and beds offered fer a dessent price."

Daniel had already heard the standing joke in Leadville, that the cooking was better than the spelling, thank the good Lord.

"Good day," the way-station keeper said briskly, his brogue heavy with a Scottish accent. "I didn't think we'd have another freight train through today, not with the storm and all."

"I thought to beat the storm," Daniel answered easily as he climbed from the back of the mare and tied her to the corral, near the mounds of hay. "I hope you've hot food waiting on the stove. We're hungry, down to each man of us, but we've not much time. Can you fix us up?"

"Aye, we've plenty of hot food. My name is Erastus Mac-Gregor, but most folks call me Rastus." He held out his hand and Daniel took it.

"Daniel Calcord. And these are my men." He motioned to the three who stood behind him, having by now finished caring for their horses. "Joe Simmons, Dutch Saunders, and Harvey Benson. The other men are teamsters from Denver. They'll be along shortly."

Erastus MacGregor grunted a genial greeting before turning his attention back to Daniel. "Course, even if ye get oot a' here quickly, ye've a deal of traffic ahead o' ye. Another freight wagon came through this morning, loaded down to burst the springs. And the stage is afore ye too, packed to the brim she was, what with men and baggage and even a wee lassie inside."

Daniel stopped in his tracks, scowling heavily. "Should that concern us? Are they so slow?"

"Aye, that wagoneer don't have the sense to know when he be overloadin'. Greedy soul, wanted to haul all of Denver to Leadville and make an easy fortune. I wager most of his goods be lost over the mountain before the day ends. And the passengers on the stage took a vote and decided to continue on their way. I tried to tell 'em of the danger, but ye know what fools men can be. I wish they'd have taken into account the woman. She weren't even dressed fer winter, let alone fer the snow which is comin' in." Rastus gave a shrug of his huge shoulders and led the way inside the house. "At least it's Tom Cooper who's driving; he's the best Wall and Witter has to offer."

9

"Damn!" Daniel cursed loudly. "Is there no way around them?"

"Not on this stretch of road, there's not."

"That could hold us up for hours."

"Days, more like. As heavy as that wagon was, it won't cross six inches of snow, let alone the six feet that's comin'."

"We have the right of way, Mr. Calcord, since we're the fastest," Dutch interrupted. He was a small man, and since he held his round-brimmed hat in his hands, his bare pate was obvious. A heavy growth of gray, well-trimmed beard covered the lower half of his face. A glowing black mustache curled up on either side of his nose.

"That ye have," Rastus agreed. "But first, ye've got to git around the wagon to claim it. And there ain't a passin' spot on this road, not until ye're practically inside the Gulch anyway. No, I think ye be wisest to hold up here and let the wagon and stage fight it oot between themselves. My money's on the stage. I've seen passengers git so hot under the collar at followin' a slow freight wagon that they've climbed out, roped the top of the stage, and passed the freight wagon on two wheels."

Daniel eyed Dutch, Joe, and Harvey at this blatant tall tale, and all four men laughed.

The meal was a hot venison stew with biscuits and loaded with gravy. The men ate hungrily and quickly and, in spite of Erastus's words, were quickly again headed toward Leadville. Little did it matter that the stage and a wagon train were ahead of them, Daniel was too wary of being stuck at this halfway house for the winter with only his men and Rastus's tales for company. If necessary, he would push and prod until every wheel was turning at top speed.

The descent was every bit as dangerous as it appeared. The mountain encroached on the width of the road, leaving nothing but a narrow, winding track that barely hung on to the edge. The wagons heaved from side to side, and it took a good driver to keep the horses on a straight pathway and far enough from the threatening edge to be safe. The pace was greatly slowed now, and the first snowflakes of the season began to fall gently. The road became a series of switchbacks, narrow, alternating turns for descending the steep side of the mountain. Snow began to gather and build along the road.

Daniel instinctively guided his mare nearer the slope of the mountain.

The road curved into its deepest pitch, and somewhere ahead could be heard the harness and groaning of the stagecoach. Every once in a while Daniel caught a glimpse of it below, on the outer curve of the narrow road. The top-heavy coach swayed from side to side, and the outside passengers hung on for dear life itself. Just ahead of the coach was the slow-moving freight wagon. MacGregor was right; the wagon was loaded far above its capacity. Reaching Leadville would be a long, tedious journey.

Almost as quickly as the thought ran through his mind, a surer one crept in. He well knew how dangerous an overload could be on a steep descent such as this one. The driver of the wagon was tugging on the brake handle in an effort to keep the wagon from overtaking the horses. Even from this distance, Daniel could see it was a difficult job.

The stagecoach kept a respectable distance from the wagon but its swaying grew deeper now from the force of the wind. Tom Cooper barely kept it from spilling over the side of the mountain. Passengers were hollering and cursing at the driver. Once Daniel saw a bonneted head of auburn hair peep from within, only to be withdrawn quickly when the wearer saw how close to the edge they rode.

Pieces of luggage slipped from their moorings and hit the road behind or beside. Some of them crashed down the mountain and broke into small pieces when they hit bottom, a good seventy-five feet below.

Daniel breathed a sigh of relief as Tom Cooper, true to his reputation as the best driver Wall and Witter Stage Lines had to offer, straightened out the coach and brought it to the center of the road.

Daniel's relief was short-lived as he saw the brake handle on the wagon ahead of him sheer off and the wagon pick up speed. A sudden cry of terror sounded as one of the horses was hit and crushed by the now out-of-control wagon. The frenzied fear spread to the horses of the stage, and the lead animal reared, breaking the shaft. The stagecoach horses were now freed to run in their terror. The freight wagon, driver, and one remaining horse plunged over the edge of the mountain.

11

Wild-eyed, the four stage horses whinnied and screamed, running down the road, dragging Tom Cooper behind. He had refused to let go of the reins.

The stage gave a lurch just as the outer passengers jumped free, and it toppled over the side of the mountain. Eerie screaming came from inside. With a swift kick to his mare, Daniel was quickly around the bend and the tragedy was out of sight. Another turn and another, and he was in the midst of the men who had jumped free.

In the distance he could see that Tom Cooper had slowed the horses and was leading them back to where the passengers stood. Down the mountainside, the coach was trapped on its side by a thicket of huge ponderosa pines. How long it would hang there was anyone's guess. A good hundred feet beyond it lay the freight wagon, broken and splintered. The fall was too far for the man to have survived.

The coach door was slowly pressed open, and a man climbed out, balancing himself on the side of the coach. The man was young, and a greenhorn, Daniel recognized instantly. His voice opened to yell for help, but the coach rocked slightly and his words came out as more of a croak than a plea.

Daniel reached for his rope and tied it around his saddle horn. Tossing the other end down the mountain, he rode down it to reach the coach.

The greenhorn wore a Western-style shirt, obviously expensive and obviously made in Philadelphia. Two rows of shiny brass buttons marched up either side of the broad front. The hat was a dead giveaway. Broad and round of brim, it was far too neat and spotless to be anything but brand-new. In a voice breathless with fear, the man hurriedly explained, "Reverend Pickett's dead and the girl's near dead. Got a nasty gash on her head and blood all over the place."

"How many are in there?"

"Six, not counting the reverend or the woman."

"Can you haul yourself up by my rope? And the others? Are any of them too injured to manage?"

He shook his head and had to grab at his hat to prevent its falling. "The boys and I can make it, but how will you get the woman to the top?"

"I don't know that yet, but go, get up the mountain before

12

this damned thing falls clear to hell."

One by one, the men climbed out and hauled themselves up Daniel's rope to the road. The men above gave what help they could, but it was very little. The third man was stout and strong, and he carried Reverend Pickett's body over his shoulder. Tying the rope around his waist, he pulled himself up with strong hands, using his feet to walk up the side of the mountain. The last two men brought the unconscious girl with them and gave her over to Daniel.

Daniel noticed several things about the injured woman at once. First, she was dressed in a threadbare traveling cape that had seen better days. And he bet the cape weighed more than she did. Very slight she was, and very bloody. And ridiculously young to be traveling alone. And with a damned frilly straw hat on her head! Flowers strewn all over the brim, as though she were on a May Day picnic instead of traversing dangerous mountains. Tugging it from her head, he let it dangle by its ribbons down her backside. Sweeping thick auburn hair aside, he inspected the gash. The wound was deep and nasty. Without proper care, she would die. And if he jostled her too much taking her back up the side of the mountain, she might just die anyway.

He had nothing clean enough to use for a bandage. Bracing himself against the open door of the coach and holding her slight weight against his chest, he reached beneath her skirt and tore a long length of petticoat. This he wrapped around the wound in an effort to at least staunch the bleeding.

The wooden stage creaked, and Daniel realized his moment of decision was near. There was no time to make safer arrangements for taking her up the mountain; he had little choice. Tying the rope around his waist and clutching the girl tightly to his chest, he gave the nod for the men to begin hauling him up. His body scraped the mountainside, and he felt cut in half by the tightening cinch at his waist, but he held her as still as possible. Her face matched the color of the falling snow. He bent his cheek so he might feel a waft of breath and be reassured she was still alive.

When he reached the road, there were hands to take her from him and hands to help him to his feet. And other hands to see to his torn skin.

13

"Be careful with her," Daniel ordered curtly. "Don't jostle her too much."

"She's barely alive," Tom Cooper remarked indifferently as he turned his head and spat chewing tobacco onto a nearby rock. The stage driver was wearing his injuries lightly. His face was only lightly scraped, but bloody skin hung from his hands and arms. Apparently Tom Cooper had refused before this to relinquish reins to frightened horses and was more than accustomed to riding on a dirt road by the seat of his britches.

"She won't survive the trip. The jostling will kill her," Cooper continued in his matter-of-fact voice. Another brown and yellow stream of fluid hit the rock.

"I know that too. Damn! And what do you suggest we do with her? She's your passenger. And your responsibility."

"Not mine. Was you who risked yer neck to save her. I suggest we get going before this snow gets any deeper and we're all marooned here."

"The girl won't survive the ride."

"Probably not, but she won't survive here either. And the snow will be so bad in a few hours no one will make it back here for her before she dies. Best thing to do is to take her with us."

"Dammit, man, I'm not loading her on to a wagon just to watch her die! There's not a spare inch for her to lie in!"

"Then you stay and watch over her. My responsibility is to get what passengers I can to Leadville, and get them there I will! Well, why not? Why can't you stay and watch over her? You've enough supplies to see you safe for a long time. The old toll-taker's shack is about a hundred yards ahead of us. You'll be fine until a rescue party can be formed."

"Just what I need, an invalid female on my hands," Daniel muttered, knowing all the while he had no choice. "All right. Do you know her next of kin?"

"I ain't never seen her before today," Tom Cooper answered, spitting on the ground. "Fitzgerald is the surname she gave when she bought her ticket."

"Fitzgerald? Ain't that Irish?" Joe interrupted. His brows rose and an avid interest entered his eyes. "Ain't there some talk about Lil Amundson expectin' a new girl? An Irish girl? P'raps this is the one."

Speculation spread among the men, and each one moved closer to get a better look at the woman. They were an unruly lot, the seven drivers and twelve passengers. Their clothing was dirty and dusty from constant use and the day's travels, all except for the greenhorn. Each man needed a shave, except Dutch, who never let a day go by without trimming and waxing his pride and joy, his mustache.

They were disappointed that they couldn't see more of the girl, not with her hair covering her face and the bandage obscuring all else.

"Wal, I hope the little lady gets well soon," boomed a passenger. "We can all get to know her just a bit better then."

And all the men laughed suggestively. Daniel looked perplexed until Dutch informed him, "Lil's got the best house in Leadville. Darlin' Lil's we call it. Spending yer money there's always a pleasure."

Comprehension dawned on Daniel, and his head turned to get a better look at her himself. Lil's was one of those houses, huh? One of the better ones, he hoped. He hated to go to the trouble of saving this woman's hide to have her fate be one of the nastier whorehouses that followed mining camps. But later was the time for thinking of that.

"When the rest of you get aboard, spread your weight evenly," Daniel ordered. "You're a lot of extra weight we hadn't planned on. That'll make it easier to descend this steep mountain, though we're damned near there now. Dutch, you take care of things at the mine. I'll be there as soon as the woman and I are rescued. Hopefully, before the week is out. And see to it I'm not left waiting too long, Tom Cooper. I've better things to do than play nursemaid."

"What about my luggage?" protested the greenhorn loudly.

Daniel scowled and waved an impatient hand in the air. "Go ahead and go after it, my good man. Though I warn you, we'll not wait for you to climb the mountain before the wagons leave. And what good your baggage will do your frozen corpse is beyond me. Dutch, I need food, blankets, a lamp, and oil. Have we anything else to make an invalid more comfortable for a few days?

"Joe, you help me carry her to the shack. I want her kept as steady as possible. Get a blanket. We'll put her on that and keep her still."

Dutch rounded up the supplies, and he and Harvey Benson carried them, leading the way through the rocky terrain to the shack. By the time Daniel and Joe arrived with their patient, the wooden-frame bed was spread thick with blankets. Daniel set her there and pulled a blanket to cover her. Making her comfortable would have to wait until they were more settled.

The other men followed. Sparing a half-hour, each man pitched in to help Daniel and the woman settle in the crude shack. Enough wood to last three days was chopped. Water was hauled from the creek that flowed behind the shack. A mountain of supplies was carried inside and stored. Daniel's mare was settled in the lean-to behind the shack.

The toll-taker's shack was a remnant of the old days when the man who carved the road out of the mountainside had the right to charge travelers for their use of it. Small and musty from disuse, it did have a stone fireplace and a ceramic bowl and pitcher for water.

Daniel stood at the door and waved the men off, watching as the wagons began their steady descent. A few more miles and the road would straighten out and the steepness would gradually lessen. Leadville would be just beyond. The snow was knee high now, but before they hit Leadville, the snow would be up to the axles and the men chilled through to their bones.

God alone knew how long it would be before they or anyone came back for him and the woman.

Wind caught at the door, and Daniel had to brace his full weight against it to close it. The chill air swept in and played with the smoke from the fireplace, sending wisps of it throughout the small room. The door closed, Daniel turned and rested against it. His eyes wandered over the room, finding it shabby and dirty, and he wondered how he would keep himself occupied for the next few days.

A moan from the bed caught his attention as the girl struggled to turn onto her side. Her coat and boots caught on the blankets, and that ridiculous hat impeded her. Daniel had never played nursemaid before and had no idea where to begin. The very idea was appalling. All he knew was how uncomfortable he would be between itchy blankets with all his clothing on.

Crossing to the fireplace, he tossed more logs onto the fire and settled a teakettle filled with icy water against the burning wood. Then he searched through the pile of supplies for sheets and a washcloth.

Holding them, he stood beside the bed and studied his patient. Her face was flushed, and the torn petticoat surrounding the wound was dappled with blood.

He wondered how to start and found it ironic that, for the first time in his life, he was reluctant to undress a woman. But then, all the women had undressed and been cooperative, obliging even.

His fingers went to the buttons, and years of experience came to the fore. The coat opened, he lifted her slightly to remove it. Then he quickly unfastened the ribbons of her hat from around her neck.

As the strands of ribbon slid against her skin, her neck rested on his arm, and her long hair trailed silkily over his fingers, barely touching the blankets. He noticed her face, for the bandage did not obscure her features. Dark lashes and brows complemented the deep auburn of her hair. The brows were a finely arched line, her nose, small and pert. Her lips were barely opened, pearly white teeth just visible between them. The combination of flushed lips and cheeks and pale white skin was striking. Daniel hadn't seen a woman to match this one for beauty, not since he was last in New York. In the profession she had chosen, she had a great future, especially in Leadville; he would wager his fortune on that. The only remaining mystery was the color of her eyes.

His fingers went to the intricate buttons of her high-topped black boots. Those were items he had not often dealt with before and took a bit of doing before they were removed.

Black, woolen stockings came next. They slipped from her feet too easily, as though they were sizes too large for her. She was simply dressed but neat, more like a schoolteacher than . . . than a woman of pleasure. Her starched white blouse was ironed to a fine crispness. The collar rode high on her throat, giving her almost a royal dignity. A bit of lace down the front buttonline was her only enhancement.

A plain, black woolen skirt taped across and down narrow hips. A black belt cinched the tiny waistline.

Her garb couldn't have been plainer, or neater.

17

Beneath all this, she wore a white cotton chemise and bloomers. Shaped only by the two straps holding it up, the chemise was tied down the front and between her breasts with baby-blue ribbons.

Most of the women he knew wore silks and satins, all heavily trimmed with laces and bows. Most especially women of her profession. They were the kind of women Daniel knew best. Any others didn't interest him. He hadn't the time or the inclination to find a wife. Women of her sort provided all the comfort a man needed.

The kettle whistled. Daniel rose and mixed boiling water with tepid water in the washbasin, and with a cool washcloth began to wash the girl's face and hands.

The small size of the shack was a benefit now, for the heat from the fireplace was spreading and warming the entire room.

Carefully, he unwrapped the bandage and began to gently cleanse the wound. The cut on the crown of her head had jagged, gaping pieces of skin, and bloody strands of hair clung there. Once the girl keened at the pain he was causing, but his voice and soothing words calmed her. Finally, he tied a clean bandage around her head, and when his hands ceased to torment her, the girl fell into a more natural sleep.

Daniel's hunger was growing painful. Setting a cast-iron pot over the fire, he placed a chicken in water to simmer gently and make broth for the girl. With luck, tomorrow she would be awake and hungry. For himself he would add vegetables and biscuits. Tonight he was too hungry to wait. A simpler meal of jerky and coffee would have to satisfy him.

He chewed the tough meat while his taste buds watered at the smell of strong coffee. One cup was all he could handle, he was practically asleep on his feet. Spreading his bedroll on the floor next to the girl's bed, he climbed in, clothing and all, and was asleep almost instantly.

Chapter Two

Daniel wakened reluctantly. A gentle sobbing kept hammering away at his consciousness, but Daniel tried to ignore it. He couldn't be done with sleep yet. Not as weary and aching as he felt.

The keening came again, and this time Daniel's eyes opened slowly. The only light in the small room was a golden glow from the embers of the waning fire.

Once more the eerie gasping sounded, as though someone were shivering in pain. A chill premonition swept over Daniel and he sat up, tossing his covers aside. Instantly he was on his feet and going to the bed.

His palm reached up to test the temperature of her forehead.

Beads of heated moisture covered her face and neck. Fear swamped Daniel at the thought of how tenuous her hold on life would be if the fever raged hot and high for too long. He hadn't come this far with her just to sit idly by and watch her die.

Grabbing two armloads of wood, he tossed them onto the fire. The water in the kettle was still hot, as it was nestled among the warm embers. This he poured into the pitcher, again mixing it with tepid water to the temperature he approved.

The fire blazed and the room warmed quickly.

With the cool cloth, Daniel wiped the beads of moisture from her face and neck. His fingers lowered to her shoulders and arms, and he realized the fever was indeed high, causing her to sweat all over.

He would have to bathe all of her to bring the temperature

down.

His fingers shook as they lowered to the ribbons of her chemise and lightly tugged. The garment separated and fell away from her breasts, giving him an open display of their full beauty.

His body reacted strongly to the sight of her, and he cursed himself for daring to think that way of such a sick woman. Drawing a deep breath, he lifted her still form from the bed and rested it gently against his chest. Stripping the chemise from her shoulders and back, he felt full, rose-tipped breasts burning into his skin.

Settling her full length onto the bed, he untied the bow around her waist and tugged the bloomers from her still form, trying not to see her as anything other than a very sick woman.

He dipped the cloth in water and sponged over her shoulders and high, full breasts, down her slender lines and across pale hips and thighs. A puff of fine, red hair rested in the triangle between her legs.

She was lovelier than he had ever imagined.

Again he tucked her between muslin sheets and covered her with blankets. Her breathing was raspy, and Daniel recalled what his mother used to do. He poured more hot water into the pitcher and tucked it beneath the bed where the steam would rise and ease her soreness.

Throughout the long night Daniel rose frequently and sponged her to a cooler temperature. Just before dawn he fell asleep and did not waken until the sun was high and bright. He recoiled at his own carelessness. Her fever had not abated a whit, and the trembling of her lips had increased in fervor.

Again Daniel ran the dampened rag over her form. Tilting a cup to her lips, he fed water between them. Most of it ran down her chin, but a little went inside and was tasted. The girl's tongue crept out for more.

The day seemed endless. The girl's skin alternated between hot and sweating and clammy and shivering. Daniel had to stand over her much of the day just to keep the blankets on her and a bit of fluid down her.

Evening crept in slowly, and by night she seemed to fall into a deep sleep. Daniel saw to his own needs and returned to her side, sponging the heat from her once more. Her skin was hotter than before. He was afraid to sleep, afraid that if he did, he would sleep till morning and not know if she needed him. "You will not die," Daniel said grimly, unaware that he had spoken aloud until the girl turned her head in feverish delirium, seeking the source of the harshly spoken words.

Her tongue snaked out and licked dry lips. Daniel tucked a fresh rag between her teeth and she gently suckled. Her shoulders relaxed and her breathing became softer, more regular.

Taking a sigh of relief, Daniel scooted down on his rough pallet and thought to rest for a few moments. When he woke, the room was in deep darkness, the chill spreading evenly across the floor and up the coarse, wooden walls.

"Dammit," he cursed low. He had slept too long.

He rebuilt the fire. Low on wood, he had to go outside in the bleak winter night to fetch more from the pile his men had left. Loading his arms full, he reentered the shack and kicked the door shut behind him.

A low moaning from the bed alerted him that something was wrong. Dropping the wood in front of the fireplace, Daniel hurried to his patient. She was thrashing from side to side. Daniel sat on the bed beside her and steadied her shivering, the cool sponge doing its soothing work.

"Ma, I'm sorry . . . It's Teeling . . . oh, Mama . . . And Seumas . . . and Rory . . . The Devils took them . . . They took the boys away . . ." The accent was pure Irish, down to the rolling of her r's. Each word was heavily punctuated with a heartfelt sob. Straining against Daniel's hold, she tensed her whole body and tried to throw him from her.

"Oh, no, you don't, Irish! You'll damn well hold still and calm down, or I'll sit on you!"

Instantly the girl relaxed her stiff shoulders, and her head followed the direction of his voice. In a very prim and proper speech, she demanded, "And who do you think you are, to be cursing at me, you son of an English devil?" Her voice trailed off, and a frantic note crept in the small noises she was making in her throat. "Paddie . . . Paddie . . . I need you. I'm not as strong as you are. I'm so alone . . ."

The soothing sponge was doing its work, and her voice drifted off until Daniel could almost imagine he hadn't heard

21

a word from her. The fever subsided momentarily, and he urged the wet cloth between her lips. Eagerly she took it.

All night Daniel soothed her with cool sponging. She raved unintelligible words in her fever, and Daniel would soothe her with the cool cloth until she calmed down. Moments later, or so it seemed, she began her delirious speech all over again.

The names she spoke were all men's names. Daniel was feeling very proprietorial toward his little patient, or else why did he detest another man's name coming from her lips? And so many names? He recalled Joe's talk of the new Irish girl at Darlin' Lil's, and his stomach churned. So she was Irish, and so everything fit Joe's conjecture. And so she had known men before now. He ought to be pleased, oughtn't he? That was the sort of woman he always claimed he preferred, wasn't it?

So why did the thought of another man seeing her as she was now, in her bare, beautiful state, bother him so much?

That is what you get for saving a female's life, Daniel, my boy, he thought grimly to himself.

For years he had avoided entanglements, and he had done that by keeping a strict aloofness. After the harsh lessons learned at the hands of his family, Daniel was a loner. Trust no one but yourself, need no one but yourself, that was his creed. His mother and father thought to buy him with promises of a great inheritance; all he had to do was toe their line. He found earning his own fortune easier, and a damn sight more rewarding, than sucking up to a family of miserable hypocrites.

And in spite of the fact that this Irish girl was a beauty, he had no intention of breaking with his creed. A loner he would remain. He might visit her once in a while, if he could stand to see her with other men. But get entangled with her? Never.

Oh, but she was a beauty, he thought once again, his eyes resting on her. And like a breath of fresh air with her pure skin and bright hair. Oh, yes, she would make a fortune in Leadville.

He thought he would just lean his head against the bed-frame for a moment or two. Just long enough to relax himself. Not to sleep, just to rest for a while. He had barely slept these two nights past.

The oiled cloth covering the windows kept the sun from fully penetrating the room and waking Daniel. The first thing he noticed was the silence. The room was cool again, but not unbearably so. Taking a deep yawn, he lifted his head and stretched his shoulders. His eyes opened on the Irish girl.

Emerald green was his first thought. He should have known those eyes would be deep green and large, and filled with an innocent curiosity. The black fringe of her lashes swept downward in an exhausted movement, opening a second later so she might study him again, more clearly.

He thought of the two days and nights just passed and averted his head so she might not see how unkempt he was. Daniel was a fastidious man, and embarrassed at being seen so. Running a hand through his unruly hair, he rose to his feet and crossed the room to stoke more wood into the fireplace.

Green eyes followed him. Before he ever turned to the fire, an impression of him was burned into her mind. He was tall and lean, not a bit of fat on him anywhere. He moved quickly and easily, as though he was a man accustomed to much physical action. The black hair was slightly curling around his ears and neck, and his face looked dark and masculine. He badly needed a shave. On either side of his mouth were deep grooves. He looked every bit as rough as the Rockies themselves. The linen shirt he wore was opened to the waist and revealed the black, curling hairs which tapered with his narrow waist. Gray breeches were tucked into black riding boots. He was not dressed as most of the other Westerners she had seen were. No, he looked more like an Englishman in this garb. Wariness crept into those eyes. After the last few years, she knew better than to trust any man who was English.

Weariness swamped her, and the eyes drooped closed.

When Daniel turned back to her, she was asleep.

Another night was upon them before she woke again.

Daniel had managed to shave and to change into clean clothing. The time he had for himself, now that her fever was broken and Irish needed little care, was to the point of being luxurious. The small room smelled of stew, and the fire glowed warmth. A pot of coffee percolated on the hearth.

Slowly Irish roused, her eyes flitting open gradually. Daniel stood at the hearth and watched her as she began to recognize her surroundings. The green eyes moved from the wooden timbers of the walls to the rough-cut lumber of the table and chairs. They found him standing by the fireplace and grew wider as he moved toward the bed.

Would she be coy or clever or warmly inviting, Daniel wondered. He had never been in this position with a woman of her sort and wondered how she might show her gratitude.

"It's time you woke," Daniel spoke warmly. "Two days you've been out of your head with a fever. I began to wonder if you would ever recover."

"Two days?" she questioned, the Irish in her speech lilting her voice. Suddenly her whole body shuddered. "All I remember is riding in that horrible stagecoach, next to that horrible cliff, and thinking we were sure to go over the edge, we were."

"You did."

Irish squeaked from somewhere deep within her and clutched her hands to her chest. "Is that God's truth?"

"It is. The coach was stopped by a stand of ponderosa pines long enough for you and the other passengers to escape."

"All of us?"

"All except Reverend Pickett. He died instantly."

Her eyes closed briefly, and she made the sign of the cross over herself, mumbling words Daniel recognized as prayer. This woman certainly had strange habits, considering her profession.

"You injured the crown of your head during the fall. You were unconscious when we took you from the coach. The fever settled in that night."

Gingerly, her hand went to her head and felt the rough bandage. "And the others? Where are they?"

"They went on to Leadville. The snow was threatening, and we thought it best if they left before we all were marooned here."

"Oh," she spoke slowly. "So you've been caring for me yourself?" Her head moved ever so slightly, as though to look

24

for someone else in the midst of the woodwork. Her eyes flitted to every nook and cranny of the tiny room. "I mean, you took care of me all alone?"

"Irish," he spoke softly, "it's just the two of us. I stayed behind to care for you. You would not have survived the ride down the mountain."

"Oh." Her eyes lifted and he saw uncertainty there. "I do thank you, Mr. . . . Mr. . . ."

"Calcord. Daniel Calcord."

"Mr. Calcord, I realize I owe you a great debt of gratitude. I only hope I haven't been too much of a burden . . ."

"You have been a great deal of trouble," he responded unhesitatingly. "More than I ever bargained for. Caring for a woman whose only injury is to her head is one thing. You dared to go and develop a fever on me. If I knew something about doctoring, we might have fared better. As it is, feel lucky you're alive. I thought for a while my care would kill you if the injury and fever did not."

She smiled wanly at this brisk dismissal of her thanks. For the first time she relaxed in his company. "I think, Mr. Calcord, you gave me the very best care of which you were capable. And I truly am grateful. Perhaps one day I may return the favor."

"Not too soon, I hope. I like my scalp the way it is, and I curse loudly when I'm feverish. You would be shocked." He gave a disarming smile. "Of course you heard me curse once, and gave me what for for daring to do it!" he teased.

"Did I?" Her hand went to her head, and she struggled to reach a sitting position. "I don't remember."

"Here, don't try to sit up." Daniel's hand went to her shoulder, and she recoiled from the intimacy of his hand on her bare skin.

Comprehension slowly dawned on her face as she dared to look down on the hand. Daniel removed it. Irish glanced up at him, again glanced at her shoulder, and finally, bravely, took a quick peep beneath the blankets.

She groaned.

He tried to look sheepish, but it came out more of a grin. "I'm sorry to embarrass you, Irish, but someone had to sponge you to get the fever down. And as I'm the only one here . . ." His hand motioned around the shack. "I was the

25

one who did the dirty work."

She glared up at him and saw his wicked grin and leering eyes following her shape beneath the blanket. Thrusting her chin forward and holding her head high, she rapped, "God strikes dead those men with beady, nosy eyes on their faces, peering at a person's private parts, you ill-mannered, posing son of the devil!"

Daniel couldn't help it, he roared with laughter. He expected any reaction from her but that. No coyness, no fear, no arched brows inviting him nearer; no, she gave him bravado. Words chewing him out like an ornery pubescent boy. He laughed louder, infuriating her more and bringing more irate words down on his head. Oh, she was sure to be a success where she was headed. A woman who could give as good as she got was rare anywhere.

"Calm down, Irish!" His eyes sparkled with humor. "You'll get your fever back, and I'll have to sponge you again. Only this time I think I'll think of those green eyes and blushing skin and make damned sure I enjoy it more!" The dark brows winged wickedly. "I was too worried about you surviving to notice what I wiped, but I don't think I need feel so guilty again."

Irish gasped at his bluntness, her face blushing hotly, furiously. Four brothers she had, all of them older than she, and long ago she had learned the best way to handle them was to be the one dealing out the fury. Not by blushing and flushing like a little girl!

"Mr? . . . Mr. Calcord, if you will turn around . . ."

"Oh, no, Irish. I didn't suffer so myself so you could hurry from your bed and get sick all over again. Lie down, you're safe from me. In a couple more days, well, we'll see. But for now I think a meal is the most you can handle. How about stew? I finished the chicken yesterday, so you're stuck with venison. I can't promise how tasty it is, but I do promise it's hot."

He was right. Even if she managed to climb out of bed, she was too weak to stand, let alone dress herself. And then she would be in an even more embarrassing position.

Besides, she was hungry.

He was still grinning wickedly at her, angering her all over again. Just like Seumas used to do. Well, maybe he had a heart as big as Seumas's and meant nothing by it. "Thank you, Mr. Calcord, I *am* hungry."

"Nope, don't try to move. I'll feed you tonight. Tomorrow's time enough to prove your independence." Bending his arm beneath her head, he lifted her and tucked another pillow behind her so she might sit up to eat. From the kettle on the fireplace, he scooped vegetables and meat into a bowl, lavishly covering them with broth. Sitting on the edge of the bed, he watched her and kept on grinning. "Open wide, Irish."

She did. The stew was delicious. As she chewed her last, she commented, "Someday, some poor invalid is going to vent her frustrations out on you. I hope I'm around when that happens."

"To take care of me, or to gloat?"

"A bit of both, I think."

"More broth?"

She shook her head and gave him her most hopeful look. "What I would like is a nice, hot cup of tea. I don't suppose . . ."

He was shaking his head in response. "Coffee. This is the wild West."

"It must be if that's its idea of a civilized drink. But if that's all you have . . ."

His right hand came up and cupped her chin. His gentle smile was enough to make her stomach do somersaults. "I do have cream and sugar. I can doctor it up so you can drink it just fine."

"For a man who says he's no doctor . . ."

"Stop now, Irish, before you get yourself in trouble."

"I wish you'd stop calling me that, as though being Irish were the same as being pigeon-toed and humpbacked."

The black eyes glinted and his voice softened. "But I don't know your name, Irish. And if I referred to you as 'girl' or 'hey, you,' you'd think I was maligning you anyway. And I know you're neither pigeon-toed or humpbacked. Maybe a little squinty in the eyes . . ."

He liked her dimples and the way her eyes shone when she laughed.

She brought up a hand and held it out for him to take. His clasp was warm and snug. "Magheen Fitzgerald, of the Lein-

27

ster Geraldines."

Black brows rose. "I'm impressed. Who are the Leinster Geraldines?"

"Why, the Geraldine family, of course." Her tone of voice told him he was an ignorant fool for not recognizing the name, but her eyes twinkled merrily. "Ireland's greatest kings and queens were our forebears. And we're from Leinster County, Ireland."

"Daniel Calcord, born and bred in New York City, New York State. At the present time of Denver, Colorado, United States of America. And I can't even claim a squire or a dame among my forebears. At least I don't think I can. Not on the right side."

"To tell you the truth, claiming my relations did not do me a whit of good in New York City either. They still checked my teeth and eyes before permitting me to enter your country. I couldn't help but wonder what I was supposed to do if they didn't let me in."

"Jump overboard and swim ashore. I understand that's what others do. Now, how about that coffee?"

"I'll try it. And I promise not to utter one word of complaint."

"Have you anything to complain about so far?"

"Oh, no, Mr. Calcord," she answered, sincerity in her tone. "You have taken great care of me, and I am grateful. Any other man would not be so . . . so nice as you . . . . in the circumstances."

"Your eyes are drooping again. First coffee, and then sleep, and tomorrow we'll try to get you up for a few minutes."

She managed to drink a half cup before falling asleep.

Daniel washed the plates and banked the fire. As he crawled into his pallet, his eyes sought Irish out. Tonight she would sleep restfully, and tomorrow she would be that much better.

She was nothing like what he expected, not this Irish girl. Had she been coy and cute, he would simply have seduced her and gotten her out of his system. No, she kept him laughing and thinking. And he thought that if he crawled between the sheets with her, all warm and willing and giving, that he would never get her from his mind.

And this business she was in. She was only a beginner, he would swear to that. She wasn't used to a man using her body or looking at her body. And when she did get used to that, her eyes would lose their innocent sparkle.

Bah! He needed to stop thinking like that. Like he had something to say about what she did when she hit Leadville. Like he had some claim on her. He didn't want a claim on her, and he damned sure didn't want her having a claim on him!

Daniel was an early riser from longstanding habit, but when he rose next morning, well before dawn, Magheen was already awake and waiting for him. The sheet was clutched high around her neck, and she watched him warily, worry etched between her brows.

"What's wrong, Irish? Are you feeling poorly again?"

She shook her head. "No, I . . ."

"If you're hungry, it'll be just a few minutes. I thought flapjacks and eggs . . ." Her fingers clasping at the sleeve of his shirt silenced him and had him turning to her. His hand covered hers. "What is it, Magheen?"

"I . . . I . . . Mr. Calcord, I need some privacy . . ."

"Some privacy? Irish, we'll get you going after break—" His eyes widened and his mouth formed an "O" as he began to understand her meaning. "Oh! Privacy! That kind of privacy!"

"Where are my clothes. I can go outside—"

"And catch pneumonia? No!"

"Ooch, Mr. Calcord, I canna be waiting much longer. Please!"

"Here, I'll give you one of my shirts. It'll do for a robe for a while. I'll go outside, I need some wood anyway. There's a bucket over in the corner. When I come back, I'll string up a blanket for real privacy for you . . ."

Her face was beet red. "I'd rather go outside."

"Later," he said absently, crossing to his pack of clothing and rifling through it. He peeled out a blue flannel shirt and held it up to her. "This should keep you warm enough. Hold up your arms. That's right, don't let go of the sheet or you might embarrass me, and you know how much I hate to

29

blush. Your other arm, please. There, that's covering you pretty decently. Do you need any more help? I'll put the chair between you and the bucket. You can use that to keep you on your feet. I really think I should stay. I can turn around and promise not to peek. I'll be quiet as a mouse unless you holler for me to help."

"Mr. Calcord, if you would be good enough to leave me in peace."

"Just trying to be helpful, Irish. Watch your feet on the floor, it's cold."

"Go!"

"All right, I'm going!"

She heard him laughing all the way out the door. He was certainly enjoying himself at her expense. Ooh, how she would love to have him as her patient! She would teach him a thing or two about being weak and helpless.

Daniel waited on the outside of the door, wishing he had been heartless enough to insist on remaining. Whether or not she could make it to the bucket by herself was questionable. But he could imagine how she felt. He knew how he would feel, waking up to find some strange person taking care of all his bodily needs, and then insisting on remaining when he needed privacy most. She was handling her situation very well, but he guessed that he was about to come up against a lack of patience real soon.

The snow had stopped, but a good three feet lay on the ground. And the sky overhead was laden with dark clouds threatening to erupt again.

From within he heard the chair crash to the floor. He hurried inside to find Magheen clutching onto it, barely standing where it had turned over. The shirt had ridden up, leaving most of her shapely bottom bare.

"Are you all right?" he demanded, swinging her into his arms.

Tears welled and her head lolled against his shoulder. "I'm fine, but the chair will never be the same again. Jakers, I feel so weak and so helpless! It's maddening!"

"Give yourself time, Irish. You'll be in fighting form in a few more days. Tell me, did you finish?"

"Finish? Oh! Yes, of course, I did! I was on my way back, not to!" She flushed prettily.

He grinned, settling her on the covers. His face was so near she could feel his breath against her cheek and mouth. "That's a relief, Irish. I don't think I could withstand any more of your Gaelic curses."

His lips lightly touched hers, tingling and spreading a pleasurable warmth clear through her. Her head came up, inviting him not to stop. His tongue brushed lightly against her lips, teasing her with its playing, before he finally dropped his arms to his side. Magheen's eyes were closed dreamily and her lips barely opened. Until she realized she was the only one wanting more, for he had turned his back to her.

"How about those flapjacks now?" Even to himself his voice sounded stilted. This Irish girl was a bunch of confusing contradictions. Just now, when he had kissed her, that was meant more to soothe her than anything else. A little encouragement had her opening her mouth and seeking him. But, dammit, even her kisses weren't experienced! He had the feeling he was the first man she had ever kissed. Maybe it was the fever, causing her to behave strangely.

Hell, he couldn't take advantage of a woman who was feeling helpless after an illness.

What did he mean, take advantage? That was the business she was in, wasn't it?

Without looking at her, he spoke curtly. "We need more wood first. I'll see to breakfast when I get back. And you, you don't get out of that bed!" Shrugging into his coat, he slammed the door behind him.

Magheen slept most of the day. Daniel was in and out, mostly out. He shoveled a path between the shack and the lean-to, fetched more water, and cared for his horse. The poor animal's water was frozen so Daniel set about melting it. At least the mare had hay for food and straw for warmth and was out of the biting wind.

The physical effort of splitting wood took up most of the afternoon and took his mind off the girl. Purposely he turned his thoughts to his mine and his men. Dutch and Joe were men who had worked for him in various other ventures, and he knew he could trust them. Harvey Benson was a mining engineer and came highly recommended. Daniel realized he would have to hire more men when the mine was ready, but he supposed Leadville would have men to hire. After all, it was a city that had grown from a population of 3,000 to 30,000 in a matter of months. Those men needed somewhere to work, for they weren't all going to make fabulous wealth from a lucky strike.

By the time night closed him inside the tiny cabin, Daniel was pleasantly hungry and weary, and thought he would be better able to handle his confusing feelings about the Irish girl. The wind followed him through the door, pushing him and drifts of snow both inside. Daniel doffed his scarf, hat, and thick leather coat, hanging them on the pegs just beside the door. Venison roast bubbled on the hearth, and the potatoes were soft in their jackets, nestled among the embers.

When the coffee began percolating and sent its tempting aroma through the tiny space, Irish wakened, sitting up and rubbing at her eyes. "For such a bitter brew, it sure smells good," she commented.

Daniel was crouched on his heels, poking a stick at the fire. He turned to her at the first sound of her voice, and his expression sharpened. Her eyes were shiny with moisture and her face flushed. He rose to his feet and questioned, "How do you feel?"

Irish smiled warmly. "Much better. Tomorrow I'll be up and I can at least do the cooking."

His expression hadn't lightened since he had walked in the door, and she wondered what she had done to make him angry. Surely that kiss hadn't angered him? He had been the one to start it. Next time she would turn her head and pretend she didn't like kissing at all, even though she found it very pleasant.

The palms of his hands tested her cheeks and her forehead. "Your fever's back. You've been doing too much," he accused.

"I have not. I've been in this bed all day, and it's making me jakers. I need my clothing and my stockings and my boots, and then maybe I can begin to feel human again."

"Hmm. We'll see what you're like in the morning." He motioned to the far corner of the room. "I rigged up a blanket for you. It's not much but you'll be more comfortable with privacy."

"Thank you." She wished he would smile, just a little.

Daniel didn't talk much over dinner, mostly he limited himself to answering her questions. Yes, he left family in New York. A mother, father, a brother, and a sister. No, he didn't plan on going back to see them anytime soon. He was on his way to Leadville because he had invested in a mine and wanted to see it on its feet before he turned it over to others.

"So how does one go about getting a mine?" she queried between bites.

"Either you go digging in the ground until you find a likely spot for a mine, or you buy one someone else found and sold. That's how a person gets a mine," Daniel answered.

"But I understand silver is just lying about on the ground, ripe for the pickings," Irish told him, her eyes sparkling with interest.

Daniel dropped his fork and stared incredulously at her. "Don't tell me you've come halfway around the world to seek your fortune in a silver mine! Those stories are just that, stories! It takes a lot of hard work and a lot of equipment and men to get a mining operation going. Most of those men in Leadville have followed the gold strikes for years, and now they're following silver. And in all those years, most of them have barely made a living, let alone a fortune. That's one of the damnedest fool notions I ever heard of!"

"Well, you're investing in a mine!"

"Of course I am, in a proven mine. And I brought my own supplies from Denver, some of my own men from Denver. I even planned so far in advance I have a house waiting for me. Most of those poor fools are out sleeping in tents in weather like this. If they can't make it, how can you expect a fool girl like yourself to make it?"

"I don't know what you're getting so hot about. I'm none of your affair, and what I do is nothing to you! And I'll have you know I'm not the fool you seem to think I am. I came with money. I have lots of it. And I intend to invest it all in silver!" Hoisting her nose in the air, she turned from him.

"And how much money do you have?" he questioned silkily.

"Just how do I know I can trust you with that information?"

"You don't. Except for the amount you've already told me everything I need to know. But let me remind you, I was trustworthy with your life. And I suppose you consider that worth more than money."

"Well, of course, I do."

"Then how much?"

"Two hundred pounds, sixteen shillings and twelve pence."

Daniel did some rapid calculating in his head, glared incredulously at her, and began to laugh heartily. To add insult to injury, he finally looked straight at her and said, "And the whole damned lot of it is probably at the bottom of that ravine. How do you expect to get it, girl?"

Chapter Three

Magheen's fever flared again that night. But by the next morning, she had recovered sufficiently to be sitting up in bed, eating a hearty breakfast. By mid-afternoon, when Daniel returned from his chores, she had risen and was wearing his shirt and pants and a pair of his woolen socks. The pants were rolled up at the legs, and the sleeves of his shirt were turned under so she could use her hands and cook their meal. The crude bandage was removed, and her hair brushed to a fine, russet sheen. Her face glowed with a freshly scrubbed cleanliness.

She rose from the hearth as he entered, and flushed guiltily. "I couldn't find my clothing, so I borrowed some of yours. I hope you don't mind, but if I spend so much as one more hour in that bed, I shall scream."

Daniel wanted desperately to put her from his mind, but seeing her in his clothing reminded him how their bodies would meld together if he . . .

He had to clear his head of such thoughts. In spite of Joe's conjecture about her, Daniel had been doing a lot of thinking; too much about Irish didn't make sense, and he was damned if he was getting involved with an innocent girl. In that respect, he hoped she went to work at Lil's; then he could satisfy his urges without his conscience bothering him.

"At least you haven't confiscated my boots. I suppose they don't alter so easily, or I might have to go without those, too," he growled as he took his place at the table. "I hung your clothing to dry on the peg behind the coats. I thought they wouldn't get so mussed there. But don't bother putting them on. You're welcome to use mine. You'll stay warmer, and

35

your clothing will be fit to travel in, if we ever are rescued from this godforsaken place."

Her cooking was a vast improvement over his, and he ate two helpings of everything. All he could think was how pretty she looked and how eager she was to please.

"I don't think it's so bad being here," she said idly. "I mean, we've got enough food to last and the scenery is spectacular."

Too damn eager to please, he reiterated in his mind. That was when he decided he would fare better out of doors for the rest of their enforced stay.

The snow continued to fall for six days. By the seventh, Daniel was impatient and bored. He had tried to keep as much distance between himself and Irish as possible, but in a tiny cabin, that was difficult.

Finally, in desperation, he took off early one morning. His mare was raring for some exercise, so he saddled her and stuck his rifle in its scabbard. A bit of fresh meat would be a welcome relief from the dried foods they had been eating lately.

Snow blanketed the mountains and roads, deepening most where alpine valleys met sheer rock walls. The pine trees were white topped, and the branches heavy and low hanging. The aspen had quickly lost the last of their color and were now bare against the biting wind. The loneliness of the mountain beckoned him, and Daniel urged his mare through the knee-high snow.

The quiet was what struck him most. In all these thousands of acres, he was alone. He saw nothing else human.

Dropping in altitude, he heard a sudden, piercing whistle and followed the sound. Spying what appeared to be elk tracks, Daniel followed these for a great distance and by mid-afternoon found a small herd. For more than an hour he stalked them, marveling at the ponderous size and strength of the animals. The bull elk was twice the size of the cows, an imposing beast with huge antlers, a six pointer. The bugling came again, and the bull elk lifted his head high, stretching his antlers parallel to his back. His neck muscles were swollen with strength as he answered the call. A second bull elk appeared, but he was nowhere near the age and size of the first. He circled the cows twice, his feet stomping aggressively. When the first bull raced him in answer to his challenge, the younger bull wisely ran off.

Daniel had a clean shot at the younger bull but hadn't the heart to take it. He reasoned he and Irish couldn't eat so much meat, that is, if he managed to get it all back to the cabin. The bull had to weigh six hundred pounds, and would require two or three trips to haul back that much meat. Besides, if he buried it in the snow, it probably wouldn't be there in the morning.

In truth Daniel was thinking how vulnerable the beasts were during the rutting season. A vulnerability he was just beginning to understand, he thought ironically. He decided to settle for dried meat or a deer.

Night had fallen as he made his way back to the cabin. At least the moon chose this night to shine brightly across the miles of glistening snow. As he neared the cabin, he saw the soft glow of the fire and the smoke tendrils rising above the roof. Even from this distance he could smell the odor of percolating coffee and freshly baked bread, and his belly began to rumble from hunger.

Daniel brushed and fed the horse first, and then carried an armload of wood into the cabin. He felt Magheen's eyes on him as he dropped the wood and stripped off his outer clothing. Though she quickly averted her head, Daniel saw the sparkling sheen of anger in her eyes.

"What's wrong, Irish?"

"Nothing's wrong," she mumbled. A second later, her hand flew to her mouth and she turned to him. He could see that she had been crying. "No, I'll be telling you what's wrong! A body can only take so much worry, and by the saints, you've put me through mine! What do you mean by taking off with nary a word to me about leaving? Here I was, thinking you were dead or hurt and not knowing what to do. I searched the lean-to; I even went down to the river, and still there was no sign of you. And now, after all the living daylights have been frightened out of me, you walk in the door, fit as a fiddle, as though nothing or no one bothered you. How could you be so thoughtless?"

Daniel's mouth settled into a thin line. "Who asked you to worry about me? I'm fine all by myself. It wasn't me who got hurt and had to be taken care of! Some of us are capable on our own! If it weren't for you, I'd be in Leadville right now and not out roaming the mountains to keep from dying of boredom!" All the pent-up frustration and anger of the last few days was coming out in a rush and being tossed at her head. "I've taken about as much of this cabin and you as I can stand. And you sound like some damned harpy, nagging away where you've no say, no say at all!"

"All right, you pigheaded fool! Go out and get yourself killed and see if I care! Next time I won't even leave the cabin to search for you! You're naught but a bad-tempered lout of a man, you . . . you . . . Englishman!"

That stopped him. Of all the curses in the world, that was the worst she could think of? The scowl dissipated. "If that's the best you can do, Irish, you need lessons. And I'm the man who can give them to you."

"Magheen Fitzgerald, that is my name. 'Tis an old name and a good name, and I'm not one whit ashamed of it. I would appreciate it if you would remember that, and use it. And lessons in cursing are the last thing I need from you, you foul-mouthed—"

He grinned. "Englishman?"

"Yes, Englishman! In my book there's nothing worse. And don't you be laughing at me! Being stuck with you here in this wilderness is my cross to bear, so don't you go roaring at me about how bored you are!"

"Seems kind of silly to be bored," Daniel said silkily. "Especially when there's so many ways we can entertain each other."

With a flick of his hand, he had hold of her wrist and was tumbling her into his arms. "It seems especially silly to be listening to your nagging when I know such an effective way of shutting you up, Irish Magheen."

Her eyes flickered and doubt crept in there. "Daniel . . ."

His lips hovered above hers. "Oh, I like the sound of my name on your lips, Magheen Fitzgerald. I especially like the note of pleading that goes with it. You should have given canting and raving at me more thought, Irish. I'm afraid I'm more than you can handle. I've been at my wit's end what to do to keep my hands off you. Now, it seems, I don't have to bother."

His fingers dug into the flesh of her shoulders and brought her closer to him, so close he could feel the softness of her

38

breasts through the material of his own shirt against his skin.

"Open your mouth, Irish. Open it and kiss me as a woman should. I don't want to think you're a little girl." He spoke softly as he threw out the challenge, and Magheen wasn't one to ignore a gauntlet. Besides, the feel of his warmth and strength was pleasurable, especially after the worrisome day she had had, imagining him hurt or worse.

Magheen opened her mouth for him.

The warm moisture of his lips was caressing, enticing. Magheen opened wider and his tongue slipped inside, to taste more intimately of her. She was shocked at his boldness and would have withdrawn, but his arms tightened around her and she could feel his ribs biting into her skin, the gentle strength of his muscles as he pulled her closer.

His hands rested just below her breasts and Magheen tightened her arms around his neck, pulling him nearer. An aching was spreading through her, an ache that badly needed assuaging. His thumbs rose and brushed against the peaks of her breasts. She gasped, breaking the intimacy of the kiss. Her head lowered and watched as, through the cloth, the nipples hardened at his touch. The trembling began then, and Daniel held her tightly, warmly, as though to ward off any intrusion between them. His mouth nipped at her ear and neck, curving moistly along her jawline and gently nibbling at her lips.

The palms of his hands raised and cupped her breasts, and Magheen moaned from deep within her throat at the intensity of his touch. She ached all over, needing so much more than he was giving. His mouth lowered to one nipple and gently sucked, and his hands moved to cup her bottom and press her against him intimately.

"Daniel . . ."

"What is it, Irish? You taste so good. You feel so good. You fit me just perfectly." As if to prove his words, he molded her flesh more deeply against him and gave a rocking motion that let her know just how well they fit together. His mouth moved onto her other nipple.

"Daniel, we shouldn't—" She gasped at the intensity of deep desire flowing through her. No, they shouldn't, but there was no way she could stop him now.

"Why not?" he questioned hoarsely. But Daniel was jus

beginning to realize how far they had gone, too far. "It'd damn well keep us entertained for the next few days."

Magheen's eyes flew open at his words, and she gasped again, pushing herself free of his hold. Glaring at him, she demanded, "Is that all I am, entertainment?"

"Well, this damn well isn't a marriage proposal!" Daniel roared. He had barely gotten himself under control, and here she was, yelling at him again. He was aching for her. Hell, he felt in worse shape than that rutting elk looking for a herd this afternoon. Well, better to have her anger than regrets in the morning. And this was one roll in the hay he would regret, he knew instinctively. "What did you expect, anyway, throwing yourself at me like that?"

Her fists clenched. "I did not!"

"Ha!"

"Well, if I did, it was because you started it! I didn't ask you to go hauling me around like—like—"

"Like some woman of the streets?"

A flush began at Magheen's cheeks and spread clear to her fingertips. Gasping at the insult, she turned from him, furious.

But he had started now, and he would see this through. She would leave him alone after this and not be looking for him to come back, no matter where he went or how long he was gone.

His hand went to her jaw and turned her to face him.

"Listen, little girl, I'm a man who'll take what's offered. If you're handing out a bit of fun, that's fine by me. But don't expect me to be around too long. I've too much I've set my mind on accomplishing, and getting entangled with a female like you isn't one of them.

"So if you're out for a bit of experience and fun, I may take the time. But to be honest, initiating the inexperienced has never been my idea of a good time. I like a woman willing to take responsibility for her own pleasures, as well as mine. And you, Irish, you don't know the first thing to do. I had to tell you to open your mouth, but when you're ranting and raving, it opens plenty.

"There are rules to getting tangled up with me. If you get caught, you get caught. All by yourself. Unless you're willing to take the risk, my advice to you is to get yourself tangled up with some nice boy who'll be there if you need him. I won't be.

"Why don't you look me up when you've gained some experience? You'll probably be a whole lot more entertaining then. I like a woman who gives as well as takes. And let's face it, Irish, all you were doing a moment ago was taking."

Her face was white as chalk. She could only stare at him, open-mouthed. Daniel dropped his hand and turned away from her. Hell, everything he had said was for her own good. So why did he feel so sick inside? She had to keep her distance. If she didn't he wouldn't be responsible for what happened between them. They stood a good three feet apart, but even so he could feel her trembling.

He didn't mean to frighten her. He just wanted her to stay away from him. There was something about her that made him want her too much.

Turning away from her, Daniel rifled through his pack until he found the bottle of good Kentucky whiskey the boys had left him. Tipping one of the chairs by the table upright, Daniel straddled it and poured some of the brew in his cup.

Magheen had disappeared behind her curtain and was very carefully making no noise. Though he never looked in her direction, he knew every move she made. When she washed her face, when she removed his pants. And when she crawled beneath the blankets, pulling them as high over her head as she could and still be breathing. He knew she wanted to hide from him and, more than that, from herself.

And all he wanted was to find forgetfulness in his bottle.

It might be easier to make love to her and get her out of his system once and for all.

The pallet was hard and the room was bitterly cold by morning. Daniel had a splitting headache. Rousing himself, he tossed wood onto the fire and washed his face with icy water. While he ate some of the bread she had baked the day before, he was filling his pockets with beef jerky and wishing he could get rid of his headache as easily as he had his hunger. Fifteen minutes after he rose, he had donned his outer garments and was gone for the day. Finally, Magheen was able to crawl from bed, a little of her pride still intact.

41

Her first determination was that in no way would she be dependent on him any longer. The clothing she had borrowed from him was washed and hung to dry. In his pack they would go and stay until they rotted. Her own clothing was right where he had said it was. As she tied the ribbons of her chemise, she thought of that first morning when her fever had broken, and how embarrassed she had been to be naked beneath the blankets. And she was embarrassed all over again. Of all the rough, loud, ornery men to go and get sick on, why did she have to choose him?

With an angry movement, she tugged on her bloomers and shrugged them into place. Pulling the ribbon at the waist taut, she thought again of the night before and how she had practically thrown herself at him and he had thrown her right back. She thrust her arms through the sleeves of her blouse and began to button it, thinking all the while of all the words he had taunted her with, all the laughter he had at her expense, and her ire grew. Why, he had even laughed at her misfortune of having her baggage and all her money at the bottom of the ravine! What a cold-hearted devil he was, to be sure!

Tugging her skirt over her hips and drawing the waistband tight, she thought of the many ways she would like to punish him. First, she would show him how little she needed him. She could do just fine without him. If he died out there today and no one found his body for years, 'twould serve him right!

So he laughed at her thoughts of making a fortune from the silver mines, did he? She'd show him! And then she'd laugh in his face, just as he had in hers, and she'd love every moment of it.

Her boots were tighter than she remembered. The leather must have become wet, and the dry heat inside the cabin had probably shrunk them. She moved around the room, trying to stretch them into a more comfortable shape. Well, they would have to do; they were the only shoes she had.

Too angry to feel hungry, Magheen didn't take time to eat. She banked the fire before donning her coat. With a curt, indignant movement she yanked the woolen scarf over her head and thrust her fingers into her black gloves.

When she first opened the door, a blast of arctic wind nearly had her turning back on her task. Then the image of

Daniel Calcord and his mocking face went through her mind, and determinedly, she set out into the bitter cold.

First, she had to get her bearings. If the lean-to and the river were just beyond the cabin, that meant the road lay in the opposite direction. Thank the good Lord it wasn't snowing, she thought, and though a bit of a heat wave would greatly assist her in her task, it would also be too much of a miracle to ask for.

The road was right where Daniel had described it, and Magheen had no trouble locating it. As she walked along, she watched over the side of the mountain until she decided she either had taken the wrong direction or had gone too far. She backtracked in the direction of the halfway house. A few hundred feet along, she spied the wreckage of the stagecoach and the freight wagon. No wonder she had not seen them sooner; both were like broken bits of trees from this distance. A lone wheel gave their identity away.

A chill crept up her spine as she saw how far the coach had fallen. To think she had been unconscious in that as it fell! Most fortunate, though, that trees lined most of the side of the mountain. If she could just get enough rope to lower herself, she could reach the coach and her baggage. Thank heavens she had climbed so many rocks in Ireland; the task didn't look too formidable. The climb wasn't even too steep. All she needed was a rope . . . and then she remembered seeing two in the lean-to.

An hour later, she had returned, having given in to temptation, for she was wearing another pair of Daniel Calcord's pants. Well, if she was really going to make this climb, she might as well make it in something she could move around in, she reasoned. Tying one end of the rope to the sturdiest tree in the vicinity, she tied the other end around her waist with the square knot Teeling had taught her on one of their many climbs.

Building to a gradual speed, she lowered herself, the soles of her shoes hitting against the rocks. Laughing to herself, she imagined Mr. Calcord's face when he found she had retrieved her own possessions. He wouldn't have expected such a helpless creature as herself to know anything about mountain climbing. Thank heavens she had a brother like Teeling!

43

The rope slipped, and Magheen gasped as her hip crashed into the side of the mountain. Ooh, she would have a bruise there for sure, she thought. After this, she must be more careful and try to save her anticipation of Daniel Calcord and his comeuppance until she was done.

The length of rope still had a few feet to spare when she reached a spot level with the coach. The freight wagon lay another twenty feet to the west. With care, she could reach the coach without dislodging the rope, and that would make her return journey that much easier. The snow and cold were creeping through her thin coat and around and into the too loose waistband of Daniel's pants.

With awkward steps she carefully wended her way to the coach. Baggage was strewn everywhere. It took a long search, and she finally found her satchel buried beneath a pile of debris. By then, the sun was on its downward swing and the wind was kicking up.

Elated as she was to have found her money and belongings, she couldn't help but be worried by the return trip in the increasing cold. After all these hours outside, she was chilled through to her bones. Her feet ached with the cold, and her fingers could barely move, they felt so frostbitten, as she slung the satchel on her back and fastened the crisscross straps across her chest.

Just to return to the top of the climb would be torture. How she would find the strength to pull herself up the mountainside was beyond her imagination. She wished she had forced breakfast down her; maybe then she would have felt stronger. In all her mountain climbing in Ireland, she and Teeling had never climbed in the winter, let alone with snow up to her knees.

She braced herself and took the first step up the mountain. Luckily a boulder stood where she could rest her feet and tighten the rope for the next climb. Summoning another burst of strength, she stretched upward and pulled on the rope. Her feet scraped the mountain, and she slid down onto the boulder, her shoulder slamming against the rock. The pain sapped what little strength she had. The wind whistled past her bruised body. For a moment she imagined she heard her name being called, but weariness and despair sent her beyond caring, and tears began to roll down her cheeks.

So much for showing Daniel Calcord, she thought sadly. He would be upset at finding her body frozen on the mountainside. As he said, he had gone to a lot of work to keep her alive, but then he would probably be relieved too. He wouldn't have to put up with her arguments or her mouth, as he phrased it. Oh, why couldn't he have just liked her a little bit? she wondered, as the tears fell. And why did she feel she had to prove him wrong? He wasn't wrong, Magheen sniffled loudly; she was. She was incapable, insufferable, nagging. She had so wanted to make him regret his words. More than that, she had wanted him to see her as a woman, a woman he could learn to love.

Instead, he would now find her stiff corpse.

A more humiliating end she couldn't imagine.

Suddenly the slack on the rope disappeared as it tightened around Magheen's waist. Looking up, she saw Daniel's furious face glaring down at her from the road above.

"You crazy woman! What are you trying to do, kill yourself? Never mind! Just hang on!"

Now she thought this rescue even more humiliating than freezing on the mountainside. By the time Daniel had lifted her to the road, she was truly miserable. Her feet and hands were numb. The snow had seeped down her shirt and pants and through her coat and scarf. She didn't think she would make it if she had to walk to the cabin.

Untying the rope, Daniel let loose a tirade that threatened never to end. "You are the most aggravating female it has ever been my curse to meet. You have gone to all ends to be contrary and independent, even when you make more trouble for the both of us! The sooner I get you to Leadville and off my hands, the sooner I can begin to breathe again. Here, give me your hands. They're damn near frozen! It would serve you right if you got frostbite and lost a few fingers and toes.

"And quit that damn sniveling! Here, give me your foot and I'll toss you onto the back of my horse. I swear — What's that on your back?"

Magheen sniffled. "It's my satchel. I did manage to get my money."

"Are you so money-hungry that you'd risk your neck for that paltry sum? If you'd used your head, you would have

45

realized that just as soon as the rescue party comes, there'll be plenty of us to climb down the side of that mountain and get everyone's belongings. But you were so worried about a few damn dollars that you damned near killed yourself to make sure you'd keep them! You're a fool, woman!"

His body tense with his ire, Daniel swung himself up onto the saddle behind her. The mare seemed to know what to do by instinct and trotted toward the cabin.

"You didn't tell me that. You let me think it was up to me to get my satchel. If I'd known—"

"You'd have still gone after it. You are the stubbornest woman it's ever been my curse to know."

"I wish you'd stop harping at me." His fury was quickly curing her tears and she responded in a prim manner, "I didn't ask you to come after it. I was fine and I'd have made it fine. You didn't have a thing to worry about." The most satisfying moment of her day was when she managed to throw his own words back into his face. "You can stop nagging anytime now."

Daniel growled low. Magheen ignored him. The cabin was just coming in sight, and she knew its warmth would soon be spreading over her, through her.

"I was just resting long enough to catch my breath and— ooh!" she squealed indignantly as Daniel bolted from the back of his horse and dragged her with him, tossing her over his shoulder and hauling her into the cabin.

"Would you put me down? Blast you, Daniel Calcord! Who do you think you are to be manhandling me like this?"

She quickly recognized the raging fury in his eyes as one not to be tampered with. As he set her on her feet, she scampered from him, rubbing at her arms and glaring her ire at him.

"Get your clothes off," he snarled. She wasn't in a mood to be ordered by him to do anything, but his words made sense. She was cold. Removing her coat and scarf, she lifted her eyes to glare at him. She opened her mouth to speak, but Daniel cut her off. "Take off everything, Magheen. And I mean everything," he ordered.

Her mouth fell open. "I will not! Who do you think—"

"I don't have to think; I know." A cold fury had settled inside him, causing him to speak in a low, furious tone. The grooves around his mouth deepened with every word. "You owe me, Magheen Fitzgerald. You owe me your life, not once but twice. It's time you paid your debt."

Her eyes grew wide and she began sputtering, but she couldn't think of an intelligible thing to say.

"Now, I'm going out and I'm stabling my mare. Thank God there's some female around this place with some sense, even if it's just my horse. When I come back, I want you naked and in bed, and I don't want you making one damn sound!"

The door slammed behind him, and Magheen could only stare at it. Naked and in bed? Hah! What did he think this was, the twelfth century?

Ooh, but he was angry!

Her shoulders slumped as she acknowledged that she couldn't really blame him. He had saved her life once again today, and she hadn't even summoned up a proper thank-you for him. He was right, all she did was open her big mouth.

It didn't occur to her to be frightened of him or his threats. With four older brothers, Magheen was accustomed to the male's blustering ways, as she termed them. For all Daniel's ranting, he had always been gentle with her. But she did owe him an apology and an expression of her gratitude. She would make a pot of that miserable brew he liked so well, and, perhaps, they could have a long talk and she could speak what was really in her heart.

The cold water went shooting spirals of pain through her hands when it splashed onto her fingers as she prepared the coffee. A warm rag soothed them.

While she waited for Daniel's return, she decided to remove her boots and see how much damage she had done to her feet. All ten toes were still there, pinkening, but still very cold. Another trip to Daniel's pack rendered woolen stockings, which she pulled on before hanging her wet ones up to dry. The coffee began to perk as she sat at the table to finish her wait.

Daniel gave her a long, level stare when he entered, his scowl deepening. Shrugging out of his coat, he hung it and his hat on one of the pegs before turning back to face her. This was not the same Daniel Magheen was used to, this one was so boiled full of anger that she lost a bit of her confidence. Rising, she eyed him nervously from across the table.

"I said, naked and in bed."

Magheen's brow furrowed, and she held out her hand in a supplicating gesture. "Please, I would like to say something before this argument gets out of hand."

"Think carefully. Your mouth gets you in more trouble than your lack of sense. And that's damned near killed you twice."

"Please, don't make this so difficult. Look, I've made you some coffee. You must be as chilled as I. Please, sit down and drink it. Maybe then I can say what I need to."

"I need something stronger than coffee, girl!"

"Oh? I could put some of that whiskey you had last night in it."

Daniel rolled his eyes. "Are you stupid too?"

"Please! I'm trying to apologize!" Magheen's eyes lowered for she could no longer meet that angry glare. More softly she continued, "I admit I was wrong to do and say what I did, but I needed that money and you led me to believe I couldn't get it any other way. Still, I should not have spoken so rudely to you when you did come to my rescue, again. I lied when I said I was merely resting. I was exhausted. If you hadn't come along when you had, I would have died out there on that mountain. I had no strength left to pull myself back up. It seems I'm always thanking you."

"Then pay up." The emotion in his voice was so deep, she was surprised into looking at him. "Cóme, kiss me, Irish Magheen. I hunger for you with an ache so deep it's strangling me; yet you can go off and risk that pretty little neck without compunction!"

Longingly she listened to him. Maybe he did care, just the tiniest little bit. If only . . . but she didn't know what "if onlys" there were to face. In the end, she shook her head.

" 'Twould be wrong, Daniel. All you have to do is hold me in your arms, and my heart beats so I think it'll burst. I don't know how to stop it. I only know this strange feeling I have for you will lead me into trouble if I give in to it, and that I cannot do. I owe you more gratitude for last night, Daniel, for stopping us. What we were doing was wrong. Such intimacy between a man and a woman needs to be sanctioned by marriage."

The very word frightened the life out of Daniel. He bolted from his chair and stood behind it, staring hard at her. "I'm not the marrying kind, Irish."

Magheen gave a sad smile. "I didn't think you were. And I'm not the sort of woman to be tumbled in bed by a man I'm not married to."

"Why not, Magheen?" he spoke softly. "I promise you'd never know any man as good. Can't you feel what happens between us whenever we touch? You'd like making love with me, Maggie. You'd be so hot and sweet, you'd explode in my arms."

Magheen flushed pink at his words but kept her clear gaze on him. "And what happens when it's over and you're gone?" she asked sadly. "Do I just pretend you never existed and go on about my business?" Her head was shaking vehemently. "Oh, no, Daniel, I'm not so cold-hearted and calculating that I could do that. You'd change me forever."

"I could make you. I could touch you right now and you'd not find the willpower to tell me no," he challenged.

Tears glistened in her eyes as she softly admitted, "I know."

Daniel muttered a savage curse and turned away. He never should have let her speak one word. He should have just done what he had intended from the moment he found her on that mountain. Bring her back here and warm her up in the best and oldest way known to man. He would have felt better. Hell, he wouldn't have to disappear for whole days at a time just to keep his hands off her. Then he would be around to make damned sure she didn't get into any more trouble!

Problem was, he had let her speak. He had let her tell him she was sorry, she was grateful, and he was right, all he had to do was touch her and she would give him anything he wanted! His body jolted at the thought. Damn! Why didn't he keep her quiet? Her simple admission had his imagination running wild. But they both knew he would do nothing to hurt her, just as he would do nothing without her consent.

His eyes narrowed as he turned sharply on his heel and crossed the room to find his pack. From it he brought out what remained of his whiskey and poured a healthy sample into his coffee. When he lifted his eyes, he found her watching him and he indicated the bottle. With a grimace she refused. "Thanks, but one bad brew's more than I can take."

49

Daniel paused to listen to the lilting notes of her voice. Her expression was at once sad and somehow pleading with him to understand. The bright blue ribbon of her chemise peeped out between the buttons of his shirt. He knew every inch of what that chemise covered and how soft and pliable her skin felt in his callused palms.

If this went on much longer, he would lose his mind, for sure.

Ignoring the cup of coffee, Daniel tilted the bottle to his mouth and took a large swig. When he swallowed it, he looked Magheen in the eye and said, "I'm hungry. What's for dinner?"

Suddenly her heart grew lighter and she grinned at him. "Me, too! How about bacon and eggs?"

"And pancakes?" he questioned wistfully. "I left early this morning and had no breakfast."

"I had no appetite either. But now I could eat a horse, I'm so hungry."

"How about a deer instead? I got one today."

"Oh, fresh meat!" she said, her eyes glittering. "You just wait, Daniel. Tomorrow, you'll eat like a king!"

After supper, Magheen washed up the dishes while Daniel brought in more wood and banked the fire for the night. Slipping behind the blanket partition, she slipped out of her pants and underwear and donned the long, white flannel nightgown she had brought from Ireland. There was little enough in the pack she had hauled up, but she knew this was among the items.

The cabin was warm and still smelled of crisp bacon and coffee. Magheen sat on the narrow bed and brushed out her long auburn tresses. "My wound's nearly healed, Daniel. In another day or two, you'll never know I was hurt."

Daniel came out from behind the curtain, his face neatly scrubbed and his hair slightly damp where he had brushed it back with wet fingers. His long johns were white and followed every curve and bulge of his male body. The top was unbuttoned part way down, and black hair curled between the buttons.

"Let me see." As he bent over her, she could smell the tangy scent of musk. "You're right. It's fine now." Daniel dropped her hair and climbed into his pallet, beneath heavy woolen

50

blankets.

Through the golden glow of the fire, Daniel watched her as she continued brushing her hair. Her arms came up to the top of her head and she pulled the bristles down the long length of hair, below her waist. Her breasts rose and fell with the movement. The line of her neck was long and pretty, and too damned tempting. Daniel rolled over and stared for a long time into the fire.

A hand harshly clamped across her mouth wakened her and had her groping against the long fingers in vain.

"Hush, Maggie!" the familiar voice crooned softly, taking away the worst of her fears. The hold loosened. "There's something out there and it's trying to get in. I want you out of this bed and against the corner with a . . . You can shoot, can't you?"

"I don't know. I've never tried."

Daniel frowned. "Then prop the table against the wall and get behind it. Don't lift your head for anything."

"What do you think it is?"

"I don't think, I know. It's a grizzly, and, believe me, neither of us wants to tangle with it unarmed."

Magheen shuddered. "I don't want to tangle with it armed."

Then, for the first time, she heard it. A claw tore into the oiled-cloth window, bringing streaks of the early morning light into view. Maggie screamed at the savagery of the motion. His grunting sounded like a deep barking of a pack of dogs, and as quickly as she could, Magheen scrambled from the bed, taking a blanket and the table with her to the farthest corner from the window. Daniel was by the door, his rifle cushioned against his shoulder, taking aim.

Forepaws came to the sill and tore against the wooden timbers until the opening was wide enough for the bear's whole body. His thick, furry head was thrust inside and rotating furiously. Daniel waited until he had enough of the head in his sights before pressing the trigger. The animal growled with pain as the bullet hit, and his movements slowed but did not cease. Still growling, the beast furiously slashed his forepaws against the cabin, his head still rotating

51

angrily and his teeth bared. Again Daniel sighted the rifle, again he pulled the trigger. Six rounds were fired before the grizzly lay still.

Daniel stood, warily watching the hulk of mass that was once the bear, as though there might be life left in him yet. The barrel of the rifle still smoked.

"Daniel!" Magheen was across the room and in his arms. "Are you all right? He didn't hurt you, did he? I couldna believe my eyes at the proof of his strength! He must be in the record book of the angels, he must! I didna think creatures were made so strong nor so dangerous—"

"Will you please shut your mouth, Magheen?" Daniel groaned, dropping the gun and holding her tightly against him. His lips were against her hair, and he could feel the warmth of her womanly body spreading through his own, reminding him how glad he was to be alive, and how much he wanted to share part of that very awareness with Magheen.

His mouth lowered, and Magheen responded naturally, pressing her hips and breasts against him. Her eyes were moist and filled with confused desire. Daniel thought he knew just how she felt. His mind niggled at him to let her go, but even as conscience nagged in his ear, his hold tightened, his hands moving to her hips to press her more intimately against him. She stood on tiptoe, her arms reaching out to him, her back arched, her breasts branding him with their heat. The kiss was hot and sweet and filled with every longing Daniel had fought for so many days.

He thought he would die if he couldn't touch and taste her sweet nipples. His fingers tugged at the nape of her gown, tearing it in his haste to reach her. The softness of each breast filled the palm of his hand with heat and desire, and his mouth lowered to make her suffer a like fate. Magheen moaned, her fingers ruffling though his hair.

He ached to have her. He could lay her down on the bed, and she would be so sweet and willing and giving . . .

God! What the hell was he thinking? A bear lay dead in the room, the window was gone, and the cold was already whistling through the hole in the wall. He couldn't. Not now. Not here. Not like this. Not with this infuriating little Irish woman who made him ache so bad he didn't think he would get through another hour without taking her and loving her until she was begging for more of him.

Abruptly, he tore from her arms and turned. And there, framed in the doorway, stood a man in a leather greatcoat, a rifle slung across his chest. He was of greater than average height, his brown hair mostly concealed by the narrow-brimmed Western hat he wore. What gave Daniel the impression that he was dangerous was the hard expression on his face, the grooves of anger at the corners of his mouth. Brown eyes judged Daniel and seemed to find him wanting.

Daniel made sure his body blocked Magheen from this man's view. "Cover yourself, Irish," he spoke harshly, his gaze flitting to where his rifle lay at his feet. "We've company."

"Company, be damned!" roared their large visitor. In barely two strides he was across the room and leveling his threatening fist.

Daniel had never taken a blow of such force, he thought, as he was propelled into the far wall. Seconds passed as he recovered his wind and he could hear Magheen crying, "Stop! Paddie, you've got it all wrong!"

Paddie could care less. He knew what he saw, and what he wanted to do was beat Daniel into a pulp. His fists lifted again, but Daniel was quicker and his blow caught Paddie in the belly, rolling him back and causing him to gasp for breath.

Magheen came between them, her arms futilely trying to keep the men apart. Effortlessly she was thrust aside. Daniel didn't know what this Paddie was to her, but it was a relationship he intended to thwart. His hands went to Paddie's neck and tightened. The man pulled free, a fisted palm reaching for Daniel. The action opened Paddie's coat, and as Daniel was flying across the room, his mind was reeling.

What in hell was Paddie whatever-his-name doing wearing a priest's collar?

Daniel's head was still spinning when he felt Magheen beside him and barely heard her words, "Daniel! Daniel! Can you hear me? Oh, look at me, Daniel! I don't want you hurt! Paddie, how could you do this? Priests are supposed to be gentle and humble. How could you hurt Daniel so?"

"Me? Hurt him? For the love of God, Maggie! His hands were all over you. I'll wager he hasn't spoken a word about

53

marriage yet!" Precious seconds passed, and Daniel could well imagine Magheen blushing bright red. "No, I thought not. I recognize a bounder when I see one, girl, and this is a man who spends his spare time sniffing around a female's skirts! So don't you go telling me how a priest's supposed to act, especially when the female he's sniffing is me sister!"

Chapter Four

Daniel groaned, his head falling between his knees. He should have known, he mused, half angrily. He damned well knew Irish wasn't a woman bound for Darlin' Lil's; he had thought her too innocent all along. And sure as hell, he cursed inwardly, she would have a brother who was a priest, and that damn brother would have fists of steel.

This situation was so damned ludicrous it was almost funny.

Daniel lifted his head, and his eyes strained to focus on this Paddie . . . no, on Father Paddie Fitzgerald.

His size rivaled Daniel's own. Father Fitzgerald doffed his hat and revealed ripened-wheat-colored hair. The suede coat he removed was lined with sheep's wool. And sure enough, the priest's collar was there. Daniel hadn't imagined it. With a groan, Daniel ran a hand through unruly black hair.

What a night! First a bear and now a priest. The bear had been shot and was no longer a threat. But Daniel intuitively knew he hadn't seen the last of the priest.

A cord throbbed in the priest's neck as he watched the man who had come near to seducing his sister. Near, hell! He might have already seduced her! The corners of Paddie's mouth turned down and his fingers curved into his palms.

Daniel's eyes closed wearily.

"Paddie! Oh, Paddie, it is so good to see you!" Magheen cried, her eyes beginning to mist as she stood between the two men, not knowing which one to run to. The one stood guardedly by the entry door, and the other sat crumpled across the room from him. Daniel didn't look exactly hurt, just a bit subdued for the moment. But Paddie looked as

55

though a simple movement would have him ramming after Daniel once more. She glanced from one to the other, loving both of them and not knowing where to turn.

"Has he harmed you, Magheen?" the priest growled.

She shook her head, her voice lowering earnestly. "Oh, no, Paddie. He has taken the greatest care of me. I was hurt when the stagecoach barreled down the mountain, and he cleansed my wound. He cared for me when my fever flared. I was delirious and he barely slept—"

"Did he touch you, Magheen?" Paddie demanded, his eyes glaring at Daniel.

"Not like you mean—"

Paddie's eyes narrowed. "I mean, did you touch you . . . intimately?"

Magheen blushed bright red at his questioning. "Paddie . . ."

Daniel stood to his feet, his moment of helplessness gone. The priest may have gotten in one good blow, but he would not get another. And he would not make Magheen ashamed of the feelings that had flowed between them.

"I touched her intimately, priest. I soothed every part of her body when she was racked with the fever. And when she recovered, I touched her and kissed her more. I did not take her virginity, though if you'd been an hour later, I might have. She's a tempting piece of woman, your little sister, and damnably hard to resist."

The priest's expression grew grimmer. "In Ireland a man does not touch a woman unless he means to marry her. A man would not touch her, snowbound or otherwise, without offering her the protection of marriage. Are you married, Mister—?"

"Calcord," Magheen whispered softly.

"Mister Calcord?"

Daniel stiffened, his mouth twisting with anger. "No, I have never been married, priest."

"Good. Then I assume you are free to offer my sister the protection of your name?"

Anguished, Magheen closed her eyes.

"Do you really think her reputation will be so tarnished for having spent a few days in my company?"

"In your company, alone," the priest answered, his emphasis on the last word. "It seems to me you have no choice but to offer her marriage. 'Tis the only decent thing you can do."

Daniel took a deep breath, his eyes turning to Magheen. She stood very still, her head tilted and her eyes closed. In another moment he expected her to cry. Her gown was torn where his fingers had hungrily penetrated, and he felt his body stiffen at the remembrance of the feel and taste of her. He turned back to the priest. Looking at Magheen was too dangerous. His mind couldn't stay on more pressing matters. "I agree. It seems marriage it must be." Daniel could already feel a noose slipping around his neck.

Father Fitzgerald's eyes widened at Daniel's easy capitulation, and for the first time, a smile nearly crossed his pale lips. "The first of the banns can be read Sunday. Do you go to church, Mr. Calcord?" At the negative shake of Daniel's head, he continued, "You might attend Mass that day. 'Tis heard in the hospital chapel at seven and nine in the morning."

"Paddie, you've no need to do this!" Magheen finally found her tongue. "Daniel meant nothing. He's saved my life, not once but three times!"

"He admitted to touching you, Magheen."

"But not like that!"

"Yes, like that. That is how you see it, is it not, Mr. Calcord? When you touched her, it was for your enjoyment, was it not?"

Daniel nodded slowly. "Yes, I took great pleasure in the feel of her."

"Then the wedding stands. You'd better get dressed, Maggie. The other men will be here shortly. I hurried ahead of them when I heard the shots, but they should arrive at any moment. And I don't think Mr. Calcord wants them to see you in your current state of undress any more than I do."

"Who are these other men?"

"The search party. We came as soon as possible. You both must have expected us."

"Of course we did, Paddie—"

"Then, get your clothing on, Magheen. You are not fit to face a soul, half-naked as you stand."

She flushed at his words, and her hands came up to clutch the edges of her gown together. Magheen gasped when she

57

realized how much of her skin was left bare by Daniel's rough grasp. Crossing the room, she hid behind her blanket of privacy and hurriedly tugged her clothing on.

"And you, Mr. Calcord?"

Daniel shrugged carelessly. "It's not my usual habit to worry about dressing when I face a bear. In fact, clothing was the last thing on my mind. Have you ever faced a hungry bear, Father —?"

"Father Patrick Fitzgerald is my given name," the priest said, nodding his head.

"Well, if you stay in this country long enough to face a bear, you'll learn to shoot first and dress later. Doing the proper thing takes its place behind living. And you'll notice your sister is healthy and in one piece, and mostly because I had sense enough to worry about surviving rather than what she was wearing," Daniel growled.

"I appreciate that. I also appreciate the fact that the moment the bear was dispatched, you did begin to worry about her clothing. At least long enough to begin ripping them off her. The banns will be read Sunday, Mr. Calcord."

Daniel's mouth curved angrily, but, before he could speak a word, other riders could be heard approaching. The matters between this priest and himself, Daniel would settle later. Later and privately.

Snatching his shirt from the peg by the door, Daniel shrugged it on and began to button it impatiently. His pants hung beneath the shirt, and these he pulled on, glancing up only once and that was to see Magheen leaving the cabin, her eyes averted and her cheeks flushing bright pink.

She wore her prim and proper teacher's outfit, he thought irritably. The white shirt was no longer as spotless as it once had been, not now that she had spilled blood on it and slept in it. But the skirt was long and narrow, and her slight wiggle did a lot for the way the black cloth lay against her behind. Throwing her coat over her shoulders, she thrust her arms inside.

And that damn straw hat was again on her head. Oh, she had tucked the thick red curls in a bun on top of her head, but the hair was so unruly, tendrils hung down her neck and across her cheeks. The only way that hat would remain on top of her head was to be tied down. He would get rid of that

58

hat for her, he vowed, and buy her something decent and silky, something that sat cockily on her head and shaded her eyes . . .

What was he thinking? He wasn't married yet! But Daniel could feel the noose growing tighter.

"I'll see my sister to Leadville, Mr. Calcord." Patrick Fitzgerald didn't seem to like the way Daniel's eyes followed Magheen. "I'll find a place for her to stay and send you word where she is. During the week I'm usually on my route and don't get back into town until Saturday nights. If you need something before then, see Father Henry Robinson at the Sacred Heart Church, but not unless it is important. Father Robinson is very ill and shouldn't be disturbed. The Sisters of Charity might be of more assistance; they can be found at the hospital."

"I doubt I'll need anything, Father."

Patrick turned at the front door and faced Daniel, speaking solemnly. "I would appreciate your keeping away from my sister until I've returned, Mr. Calcord. 'Tis three weeks at the earliest before you can marry, and I would not want you anticipating your marriage vows."

Daniel's head jerked toward the priest, but before one word could be uttered, the priest was gone and striding toward his horse. Daniel couldn't hear what was said, but Father Fitzgerald had the chance to speak only a few words to his sister before Magheen's arms came up and around his neck.

Magheen was nowhere so quiet. "Oh, Paddie, I have missed you so!" Her mouth curved tenderly to her brother's.

The priest smiled and Daniel growled. So he was to be the villain in this piece? And the priest's little sister had nothing to do with Daniel wanting her so? Bah! And *he* was to be the one to pay the piper, and that by marrying the girl!

The priest mounted his horse and held a hand out for Magheen. She sprinted up behind him and hugged him around his waist. Just before Father Patrick's boots touched the flanks of the horse, Magheen turned toward Daniel and then waved.

The small group of rescuers was approaching, Joe Simmons among them, and he moved to stand beside Daniel and watch them ride off.

"You know, Mr. Calcord," Joe spoke softly, his eyes on Magheen and her brother. "I've been mightily worried these past few days. Me and my big mouth," he nodded at Daniel, knowing he would remember exactly what had been said, "for speaking of the Irish girl expected at Lil's. Of course, the first thing we learned when we reached Leadville was who the lass was and that she wasn't the Irish one expected at Lil's. No, sir, she couldn't be, could she? Not with her brother being a priest and all? But I thought maybe you still thought so, and you might make a play for the girl while you were alone here with her. And then there'd be all hell to pay. A man just doesn't go around seducing a priest's sister and not have to marry her. It sure was a relief to see you'd figured it all out before we got here. She is a good girl, she's gotta be, huh?"

Daniel took a deep breath. "Yes, she's a real good girl," he answered briskly. "Now, go get the other men, and let's haul up that baggage and load the supplies. I want to leave as soon as possible. I've spent too damn many days here, wasting time!"

"Maggie, girl, hold on tight. The road's steep and Parnell here is not as sure-footed as he used to be. He's gettin' a mite old to be carrying the two of us, though you're still nothing but a wee thing. What happened? Haven't you been eating?"

Magheen hugged her brother tighter and rubbed her cheek against his broad back. "I eat like the dickens, I do, Patrick. But, lately, things have been in such an upheaval I haven't had much appetite."

One of Patrick's hands went to his firm belly and clasped the two of hers so tightly held together. "I know, darlin'," he said soulfully. "It's been a tough time for you, losing the farm so soon after losing Ma. . . ."

"It was the boys, Paddie. They were bound to fight those devil English who came to steal the farm. And for fighting to protect their own property, they were sentenced to ten years in the penal colony. Australia sounds such a way off."

"It's the other end of the earth, Magheen," Patrick acknowledged. "But what happened? What excuse did the English use to take the farm?"

60

"We couldn't pay the tithe, Patrick. The English Church wanted ten percent more and we just didn't have it! The potato crop failed for the third year running. At least we were keeping body and soul together; that's more than most of the neighbors did. Remember the O'Briens and the Doyles? They're all gone from Leinster. Kenneth Kickham emigrated to America just before the English could arrest him. Jack Luby disappeared, and rumor has it that he's in America too, but nobody's heard from him. And the O'Learys, the mother and the four children, sailed. Mr. O'Leary was captured with the Fenians and given a life sentence in England. Mrs. O'Leary had naught to do but flee the country and try to make a living elsewhere. Only the two oldest of the children survived the journey. I saw them briefly when I landed in New York.

"Paddie, they live in such squalor! I thought things were better in America, but all I heard was talk of shanty Irish, bog-trotting Irish, no-good Irish! It fair made me ill to hear such talk!"

"Maggie, back East the Irish are taking jobs some people think belong to those who were there first. Of course we're resented. We'd probably resent someone coming along and taking our jobs and for less pay. But we Irish are tough, we've been through worse. And we'll be the better for it. Besides, in Leadville, being Irish isn't bad, there's too many of us. A lot of pride went into naming a mine the Maid of Erin or the Robert Emmet mine, the O'Donovan Rossa and the Mary Murphy."

Parnell stumbled, and Magheen gasped at the unfamiliar sensation of the animal's muscles beneath her skirt. As the horse quickly recovered his balance, she sighed with relief. Her eyes wandered to the spectacular scenery around them. They were just now coming out of the mountains and riding toward town. In the distance Magheen could barely make out a few cabins.

"I admit, Patrick, when I came here I didn't expect to find such mountains. They're so high, and there are so many of them. Surely there's not another sight like them in the whole world."

"Not that I've seen. See those? Mount Elbert and Mount Massive. The Arkansas valley is what lies between us and them.

"I was pleased you chose me to come to, Maggie. Ireland's barely a fit land for the Irish anymore, let alone a wee girl. I worried about you when I heard of our brothers' arrests, and I wrote a letter, but it couldn't have reached you before you left."

"No, I didn't get that letter, but I got your earlier ones. You remember writing about the Gallagher brothers, and their fabulous strike?"

"Course I do. We've had lots more rich strikes lately. Another bunch of the sons of Ireland found the Little Chief and mined over a hundred thousand dollars from it before selling out. There's George Brent and William Knight and George Fryer—and of course, Mr. Horace Tabor, our lieutenant governor. He made his fortune not from mining but from grubstaking."

"What's grubstaking?"

"Paying for the supplies a miner needs while he's looking for the silver. Mr. Tabor has so much money from his Little Pittsburg mine, he's building an opera house for the betterment of the town. He wants to bring culture out West. And he made a nice donation for the building of the Annunciation Church." A smile lit the priest's face as he turned his head to speak to Magheen. "She'll be ready by the New Year, and then I'll really feel like a parish priest, and not a wandering preacher."

"Patrick . . . have you ever considered looking for silver yourself?"

"Ach, Maggie! 'Tis hard work, lots of deep digging and crawling underground, and usually for nothing. A lucky strike is just that, lucky. And even if a man is that lucky, he has to find the money to build the mine and buy the pumps and pay the men. No, 'tis simple in words, but not in deed."

"Patrick, I have a bit of money on me . . . and I thought to do some investing of my own." Her eyes lit up. "Maybe I could grubstake a miner or two!"

Patrick frowned. "You're better off saving your money. You'll need it when you're married."

"But Patrick," her voice was husky with emotion, "if I got lucky, real lucky, maybe I could bring in enough money to buy the boys' freedom."

A moment of silence passed between them before Magheen spoke again. "Ten years is such a long time, Paddie. I missed the boys the moment the door closed behind them. Rory is still so serious, and Seumas is always flirting with the girls . . . and Teeling—Teeling is as ever, teasing and laughing. Life feels so barren without them. I mean to find the money to buy their freedom and bring them here, Paddie. I vow I do."

His hand clasped hers. "I'll do what I can to help, Maggie, but 'tis a fortune you're speaking of."

The trees began to thin now. Everywhere Magheen looked, she saw tree stumps, sparsely interspersed with log cabins and what remained of a once fine forest. On the doors of the log cabins were signs, some humorous, some directly to the point that lodgers were not taken there, nor was food available.

An even more incongruous sight appeared in front of them a few moments later—Chestnut Street, the main thoroughfare of Leadville. The din was a constant roar of voices and wagons. A massive collection of people and goods crammed the main road through the town. Horses and buggies, ore cars and freighters filled the snow-covered road, each traveling at a snail's pace due to the overcrowding. The vehicles jerked and bucked over the massive ruts in the road that were hidden beneath the thick crust of snow. Fine, new brick buildings were butted between tent hovels and log cabins. A thick cloud of chimney smoke hung in the air, trapped in this valley between the mountains.

Magheen clung to her brother's back and read the signs as they crossed to Harrison Street. The Clarendon Hotel, the Grand Hotel, the Tontine, the Silver Thread, the Odeon. Her eyes bulged to see the lone cabin settled in the center of this broad street. "That's Pap Wyman's. He refuses to move it. Martin Duggan, our esteemed sheriff, threatens to take it by force, and that's probably as it will be."

One of the finest brick buildings housed the mercantile of the Daniels, Fisher and Smith Emporium. Paddie informed her that at the beginning of the year it was a tent store, and now it carried a selection to rival any mercantile in Denver.

Opposite this was the Charles Boettcher hardware store and behind it was State Street. Magheen strained to see more of what appeared to be stately homes on Fifth Street, but Patrick continued down Harrison.

"What are those poles on the walks, Paddie?"

"Gas lamps. Only the best and most modern for Leadville. Besides, with the streets lit, wagons can make deliveries all day and all night long. We need the supplies. God knows how this many people crammed into a town meant for one-tenth the number will survive the coming winter. By next year we'll have the railroad, and the task of shipping in supplies will be quicker and easier."

"Where do all these people live?"

"Anywhere. The lucky few have their own cabins. Many rent housekeeping rooms, which might offer a straw mattress and a washstand. The worst of the lot rent beds for a few hours at a time. Heaven forbid they get sick; they still have the bed only for their allotted time."

Patrick pulled Parnell over to the side of the road and tugged on the reins just as a small procession of people came down the street.

"That's Ben Loeb," he pointed out. "His theater is open for twelve performances a day. Ben and his brass band parade through the city before each one of them, trying to tempt in customers."

"Twelve times a day! Does he offer beds?" Magheen joked, watching in fascination as Ben Loeb, dressed in a full-length fur coat, wearing diamonds on his fingers, and carrying a baton, strutted from one side of the street to the other, leading a marching band. The band explained a good deal of Leadville's noise.

"On occasion. Most of his band and his actors sleep on the stage floor."

"Real actors and actresses? Oh, how I'd love to see the show, Paddie."

"It's not for you, girl. They do a dance called the cancan. Directly from France it is, and never have I seen anything more godless."

"Why is that?"

"They show their underwear, girl. 'Tis not decent."

But Magheen's thoughts roamed wickedly to Daniel. She couldn't help but wonder if he would like that sort of entertainment. Her intuition told her he would. He would like all

64

sorts of nice-feeling undies . . .

"Paddie, about Daniel—"

"The matter is settled, Magheen. I hope you don't mean to tell me you have an aversion for the man? Not when I caught you playing pitty-pat in your nightwear!"

"Oh, no! I like Daniel Calcord very much. But I don't want him coerced into doing something he'd rather not do. Paddie, I don't think he wants to be married, not to me and not to anyone."

"Then he ought to have kept his hands to himself. The matter is settled, Magheen. In three weeks' time you'll be married."

Parnell was brought to a stop before a white, two-story frame house with a green shingled roof. It reminded Magheen of a gingerbread house, with its many mullioned windows and fine detail. A large front porch ran the width of the house. Gently tapering columns and multicolored beadwork decorated the porch, leaving Magheen wondering what treasures she would find inside.

Patrick dismounted and held out a hand for Magheen. Her hat threatened to tumble, and she quickly caught it, practically falling into Patrick's outstretched arms. Both were still laughing when they reached the front door, the priest's hand holding Magheen's elbow.

The door was opened immediately, and Patrick smiled broadly at the sturdy, poker-faced woman who stood there.

"Ah, Mistress Howard! Allow me to introduce my sister, Magheen Fitzgerald. And Maggie, this is one of my most devout parishioners, Anne Howard. She and her husband, Joshua, own this fine home. They provide lodging to single women, and when I told them you were here, they kindly offered to let you a room."

"Oh, yes, dear," Anne Howard spoke, her voice soft as cream. The smile that spread across her face lit up her eyes and gave her a beauty Magheen had not realized she possessed. "We were all so concerned to learn that you'd been injured in that coach accident. And then to be snowbound for so long! Oh, dear, and here I leave you standing outside when what you need is a warm fire and a cup of tea. Please, come in and give me your coats.

"Father Patrick, you can stay for dinner, can you not?"

"One of your dinners, Anne?" Paddie grinned mischievously, following her into the drawing room. "Do I look like a man who would deny himself a meal of such pleasure? Of course I'm staying. Maggie, I promise you'll be fattened up in no time, or you're not true Irish!"

The inside of the house was even grander than the outside. Delicate wooden beadwork trimmed doors, windows, and the massive staircase, which was further down the entry hall. The drawing room was directly to the left, a huge, red velvet settee and matching chairs the focus of the room. The tile flanking the fireplace was hand painted, and more beadwork surrounded the wood trim. Never had Magheen seen such opulence. Beyond this room, she caught a glimpse of plants and glass. Mrs. Howard acknowledged this to be a solarium and promised Magheen a tour as soon as they had all had their tea.

Later, over dinner, Magheen met the other ladies who shared this home. Miss Kathleen Nickerson was the elementary school teacher, a sparse, middle-aged woman who spoke warmly of her students. Carrie Hutchen was much younger and prettier and worked at Daniels, Fisher and Smith Emporium. She came to Leadville to assist in the opening of the brand-new store and remained after she met her fiancé. She and Tom Fuller, a manager of one of the mines, were to be married soon.

The Howard children were boisterous and quickly had Magheen feeling at home. The twin boys were but a few years younger than Carrie, and the evening meal rollicked with their good-natured teasing and laughter. The daughter, Annabelle, was young and sweet but knew how to hold her own with two big brothers. Anne Howard termed it "learning to survive."

"I know just what you mean," Magheen laughingly replied. "I have four big brothers of my own, and the first thing a girl has to learn is how to keep them in line. Big brothers have been a girl's cross to bear since the beginning of time."

"Maggie, I was a sweet big brother," Patrick replied, affronted.

"You were not! You were the worst of the lot, Patrick Fitzgerald. You might be a devout priest now, but I can remember when Pa had to turn you over his knee and give

66

you the strap!"

Three pairs of childish eyes lit up with interest at these words. Their God-fearing priest had once been human? And ornery?

"The worst I remember was when he convinced Jackie O'Mally that he had had the sight, and that the two of them wouldn't be caught if they went to Farmer Kennick's and stole some apples. Only the apples were green, and both lads were fair sick for a goodly spell. Ma said he stole and he lied about it and he received God's punishment. Pa said it was good he survived God's punishment, now he could survive his!"

Patrick ruefully shook his head. "I should have left you in that cabin, with that bear!"

"You must have been frightened by that bear, Miss Fitzgerald," intoned little Annabelle.

"I was so scared my toes were curling, and that's the truth of it. But Mr. Calcord, he wasn't frightened by a thing." Except by Patrick, later, but Magheen wasn't about to say that aloud. "He's such a brave man, and he saved my life for the third time!"

"And now you're going to marry him," Annabelle was really impressed with romance.

"Well, when a man saves your life three times, it's time to think maybe God meant for that man to be by your side always."

"Is he handsome?"

"The most handsome man I've ever met, in my opinion, though I'm sure Carrie thinks the same about her Tom and your mother thinks the same about your father, and you will think the same about the man you marry."

"Oh, I hope so."

"Well," spoke Father Patrick, "don't get married too soon, little Annabelle. I promised you marriage in the new church, and that won't be for a few months yet."

"Father, I'm only six!"

"Ah, is that all? Then we've time."

Later Magheen was shown to the bedroom she was to share with Carrie. Magheen was enjoying the luxury of a bath and shampoo while Carrie sat in bed, brushing her long, nut-brown hair and speaking volumes about Tom and her upcoming marriage. Tom was building a house for them not far from his mine, the Giddy Betsy.

"He's so dedicated to that mine, sometimes it's like she's a real person. But that's what I love about Tom, he does nothing halfway. The mine is how he makes his living and he enjoys it. I hope to help him. What about your Mr. Calcord?"

"Oh, he's a miner too. But I'm afraid I don't know the name of his mine or much else about him really." She longed to share sweet secrets about Daniel too, but only could say apologetically, "We haven't known each other too long." Magheen was silent for a moment. "What I need right at the moment is a job. Do you suppose the Daniels, Fisher and Smith Emporium needs some help?"

"Yes, we do," Carrie answered, ceasing her brushstrokes for the moment. "I work in shoes, but I know most of the departments are short-handed right now. If you'd like, I can inquire about a job in the morning."

"Oh, Carrie, I would really appreciate that! I do need a job so badly, and that would be perfect."

"It would be, wouldn't it? We could walk together in the mornings and at dinner. Tom is so busy, too many of my days lag long and lonely."

Two days later, Magheen found herself working in the ladies' department of the D. F. and Smith. And before the day was out, her dreams seemed to truly become a reality. Already she had had the chance to implement her plan to grubstake a miner or two, only not quite in the manner she had expected.

Mr. Smith took his break mid-morning and called Magheen over to spell him in the men's department for a few moments. While she was there, one of the seediest characters she had ever seen arrived, and in all her recent travels she had thought she had seen everything. He was thin and wiry, his stooped frame making him appear shorter than he was. His head and face were full of straggly blond hair, and his coveralls were worn and tattered. His plaid shirt barely covered his red long johns.

Immediately Magheen sensed this was a miner, and she was determined to share in the fortune he was about to make. While she was trying to decide how to go about approaching him, the miner inspected several racks of clothing. Cautiously, she came nearer, and when he picked up a blue flannel shirt to inspect more closely, she said, "Now, that's a shirt as would keep a man warm in the mountains while he's digging for silver."

The small man turned to her, his brown eyes curious and prying. "I need a warm shirt for a long trip to Denver. I guess this will do."

Magheen smiled as she took the shirt and began to wrap it in brown paper for him. "Are you going to Denver for mining supplies?" He didn't answer immediately, and Magheen was beginning to fear she had insulted him. "I'm sorry if I seem so curious, but you're the first miner I've met, other than Daniel Calcord, of course."

"You know Daniel Calcord?" he questioned gruffly.

"I do. We're engaged to be married," Magheen answered, smiling brightly. "But he doesn't tell me much about mining. My brother told me about grubstaking, however, and I am looking for a miner who is in need of a partner."

The man's head went back as he studied her. "I might be able to help. I came into a lot of money not too long ago, but it's all gone now. Oh, I did some high livin', but I poured most of it into my mine and equipment. So now, I'm broke. As a matter of fact that's why I'm going to Denver. I need to make some quick money, I do. I thought, with the lack of fresh meat around here, I'd go and buy some chickens. I have this plan for keeping them warm and alive on the trip here. I've invented a stove which will travel without turning over or needing too much fuel. I thought if I could get fresh meat back here alive, I'd have enough cash to get my mine going again."

Magheen thought about that a moment and decided, "What a perfectly brilliantly idea!"

"It is," he acknowledged. "The only problem with it is that I haven't enough cash left to buy the chickens. Now, if you would like to grubstake that, I'd be willing to share the profits with you."

"Well, I had in mind something different, but —" Magheen held out her hand, "I'll do it. My name is Magheen Fitzgerald."

"William Lovell at your service, ma'am," he answered,

taking her hand. "I think we'd do best by putting this to paper, ma'am."

"I can see you're an honest man, Mr. Lovell. I heartily agree."

"I'm sorry, Daniel. I don't know where those samples came from, but it was not from this mine." Harvey Benson was speaking emphatically, days of frustration coming to the fore.

"Those samples came from here. I know because I dug them myself," Daniel insisted hotly.

"Then this mine was salted. Those did not originate here."

"Are you saying this mine is worthless, that I threw ten thousand dollars away on it? That I *gave* ten thousand dollars to William Lovell?" Daniel's lips curled at the intolerable thought.

"You may have given the money to Bill Lovell, and he may have salted the mine; that's not my area of expertise. I'm a mining engineer, that's all. I'm not saying this mine is worthless; the samples I took indicate otherwise. There's just nothing right here, on this level, worth much. But hell, you're not deep, you've got to dig! You're on Fryer Hill, man! There's silver in all directions around you. There might be some here, too, but not as close or as easy as Lovell made you think. You might have the last laugh yet, Daniel."

"If I don't, I'll catch that no-good and wring his neck. He cost me eight thousand dollars too much. I could have had any spot on this hill for two thousand!"

"He'll cost you more before you're done," Harvey said ruefully. "You'll need more men, a boardinghouse, more time, and here's a list of additional equipment you'll have to send for."

"This will set us back months," Daniel growled, reading the lengthy list.

"I think it's an investment worth following, Daniel. God knows I could be wrong, but my instincts tell me otherwise."

"And I've little choice," Daniel growled, folding the paper and tucking it inside his vest pocket. "I've invested two years' worth of earnings from my business on this. If I quit now, I've lost a fortune. Go on with it, Harvey. I'll see you get whatever you need."

70

What a day, Daniel thought wearily as he climbed into his tub that night. A snifter of brandy sat on the chair beside him, and a fine, strong cigar was in his mouth. This was the first peaceful moment of the day, a day that had begun with a grizzly and an unwanted engagement and ended with a salted mine.

Leadville wasn't being very good to Daniel Calcord.

The best moment of the day had been finding this house to be every bit as well appointed and well located as he remembered it.

Within a mile of Leadville and within two of his mine, he wouldn't have to spend too much time traveling between locations. The house stood by itself against a mountain, just off the road a bit. In a spot where the racket of the mines and miners couldn't be heard, where a neighbor would have to exert an effort to be friendly, and where a man could live in peace and do his work. Three bedrooms were what it boasted, one for himself, one for whomever, and one for Mrs. Sawyer, the woman who would see to Daniel's daily needs.

On the main floor were a front parlor, study, dining room, and, of course, a large kitchen.

Mrs. Sawyer made a good beginning. He couldn't remember food being tastier or a house being more welcoming and more comfortable. A good housekeeper, a good brandy, and a way to make a living were what made a man happy.

So why had he consented to that damn priest's demands that he marry his sister? And why, even now, when he had real problems, did his mind keep going to her? Bah! He had just become too accustomed to being responsible for her. A few days, a week away, and she would leave his mind just like the rest of them.

Daniel relaxed in the tub and let the warmth of the water swirl about him and soothe his aching muscles.

The Daniels, Fisher and Smith Emporium opened at eight o'clock in the morning, six days a week, and closed no later than six-thirty of an evening. With winter coming on, the walk to the store in the morning and home every evening was long and cold. A good mile separated the Howards' house and the store. Carrie and Magheen learned quickly that the faster the speed, the more comfortable the walk.

Magheen met Tom Fuller her third night at the Howards'. He looked to be nearing his thirtieth year and was a nice man with a crop of light-brown hair and thick sideburns. Though slight in stature, he was used to hard work, and there was nothing small about his muscles or his strength.

What impressed Magheen most of all was his obvious love for Carrie. When she was around, she was the hub of his world. His eyes sought her in the midst of conversations. His face lit with intimate smiles meant only for Carrie, but which the twins saw and tittered at.

They shared a nightly ritual where Carrie would see Tom to the door, and he would remember something in his saddle he had for her, or he would remember a decision she had to make on the house. The two of them would go out the door and be alone for a few moments on the front porch. And it was only a few moments. To be outside on a cold winter night in Leadville for too long meant being miserably cold.

The whole family would laugh, and the boys would tease even more when Carrie returned, breathless, happy and alone, to the house. She ignored their callow remarks about lovesick girls and their swain. Annabelle smiled and followed Carrie about the house, filling the room with questions too personal to answer.

All Magheen could think of was that she had seen nothing of Daniel for over a week. He hadn't shown up for Mass and the reading of the banns on Sunday; he hadn't so much as sent her a short message that he was busy. She knew practically nothing about him or his life and, for the first time, was beginning to realize exactly how opposed to the marriage he was. Her engagement was feeling more and more unreal.

Patrick was gone all week, taking his roving church to parishioners who lived too far away from Leadville for Mass. On Saturday he would return to Leadville so he could say Sunday morning Mass from the hospital chapel, so Magheen saw little of him too.

Between working at the store and doing her parish duties, Magheen was kept busy. She helped Mrs. Howard in her never-ending quest for raising money to finish building the Annunciation Church. Monday evenings were spent overseeing the lotto game in the hospital basement. One-half of the proceeds went to the building fund. Wednesdays were for religious classes for older children. Saturday mornings classes were held for the very young children. Friday nights the parish and the hospital sponsored a potluck followed by a dance, and most other evenings were spent calling on parishioners or anyone else who might contribute to the fund.

Magheen was finding Leadville to be a town of many nationalities and diverse interests. The first thing any newcomer saw was the very visible, raucous part of a mining town's life. The bars seemed filled with continuous gaiety. Bawdy houses lined every other street in town, a house for every taste and purse, Leadville citizens bragged. Gambling was everywhere, from the bars to the hotels to the bathhouses. In the midst of all this was the constant movement of people and supplies, the ceaseless din of music, voices and conveyances.

Beneath this rough crust was the beginning of a fully mature town. The fire department imported a new wagon from Chicago and three specially trained horses to pull it. As more families settled in, schools were added, more churches raised. Even the sidewalks, which, having been initially constructed by various individual owners, didn't all conform in height or width and, in so many places, didn't even meet, were replaced by a uniform surface befitting a large metropolitan area.

Silver produced by the mines was rolling into town and being converted into cold, hard cash.

Just beyond the city limits of Leadville stretched the high range of rocky mountains and all its inherent dangers. The elements alone were threatening enough; added to these were the threat of a wild animal, a snowslide, a single moment of carelessness. Any of which could mean death.

Father Patrick Fitzgerald had spent five years traveling this route over the high country. His territory included Alma, Fairplay, Kokomo, Oro City, and Buckskin Joe, all towns high and cold and dangerous to reach. From one habitation to the next he traveled, crossing the land between tents, cabins, small settlements, and pockets of mines. Long before sunup he was mounted on the back of Parnell, and long after sundown he was still pushing the poor old horse.

His flock of believers included many non-Catholics. Men of the cloth were so rare, a good Christian, and sometimes others, took what he could and forgot the small particulars that made up the differences between creeds. Patrick looked forward to the day he would settle in one spot, but couldn't help but wonder what would happen to these people for whom he traveled and said Mass when he did. With Father Robinson so ill, Patrick would reach a far greater number of people by remaining in Leadville than by traveling as he did now.

As a young priest, fresh out of the seminary and straight from Ireland, he had been determined to convert everyone he reached to Catholicism. Now, a few years of maturity later, he would be content just to get a simple prayer out of most of them. He finally realized his real calling in life was simply to offer comfort to as many as he could of those who suffered after a silver strike and of others. The young could handle the heartbreak of disappointed expectations and eagerly go on to the next great find. But they grew older, wiser, and more frightened that time would run out before they hit the pinnacle of success. For most, such an accomplishment was not to be theirs. The families they had left in the East had gone without them for so long, they might not have a place there anymore. And the con men followed too, taking what small profit the miners might have made. What the con men missed, the prostitutes found, until they too grew older and more and more hopeless.

He left the Ten Mile Canyon behind him now. A few more miles of steadily descending traveling and he would be home. The snow was so deep here it reached Parnell in the middle of his belly, and the old horse had to prance lightly just to keep moving. Someday, Patrick thought, he would have to retire the old gelding and find a younger horse. He and Parnell had seen so much of the West together, it would be like losing his best friend. The journeys were getting longer and more difficult for him though, and this was one of the toughest. He had traveled farther and found more of the cabins vacated. Patrick could not remember returning to Leadville so late on a Saturday night before. By the time he reached town, it would be past midnight.

Seeing Maggie was like growing young again. She still giggled and laughed as she had at ten. Anything new awed her, and her eyes would widen and watch until she knew everything that was going on around her. The day her letter came telling him of Ma's death he had aged ten years. The day she came herself, he regained five.

He hoped he wasn't making a mistake forcing this marriage with Daniel Calcord, but Patrick knew human nature too well. They had been alone in that cabin for over a week, and the way they were embracing when he entered told its own story. He wasn't righteous enough to judge between right and wrong, he left that up to the good Lord, but his sister's good name deserved Daniel Calcord's protection. He thought about Daniel for a moment and decided he needed to get to know him better.

Patrick had heard of the man before he met him. A purchase of a mine and an infusion of money to invest immediately brought much notice in Leadville, especially to a priest who was looking for donations for the new church. He hadn't liked Daniel on first sight, of course. The position he had been caught in made him barely tolerable. There had to be more to the man than he knew, or else why did Magheen defend him so stoutly? And this Daniel was man enough to care for her through her injury and illness and protect her from a bear.

Yes, perhaps Patrick had been too harsh on the man. Maybe it was time to make his acquaintance. He would turn here and take the route through the hill toward Leadville, and that would lead him by Daniel's house. The pleasant thing to do would be to stop for a drink, and if Daniel were of like mind to reach an accord, Patrick might even get a meal out of this. The more he thought about it, the more the idea appealed to him.

So lost in these thoughts was he, Patrick had not noticed the pack of timber wolves stalking him until they were within thirty feet of Parnell's flanks and beginning to growl. The horse belatedly saw them, and his back reared as he panicked.

The horse took off at a run, and Patrick clung tightly to the reins, his head turning and yelling at the wildly snapping wolves. There must be ten of them, all adults, and ranging in color from pure white to gray black and everything in between.

Parnell was hampered by the depth of the snow. Patrick's hand reached into the scabbard for his rifle and pulled it free. The wolves were closing in now, nipping at the horse's rear and neck. Patrick could hear the fear in the gelding's high-pitched whinny. He lifted the rifle and got one shot off. A yelp answered him, and the rest of the pack of wolves scattered momentarily, returning wilder than before.

Parnell was crazed with terror. His head jerked to be free of all control, and his massive body heaved to gain more speed. His legs were flailing helplessly in the snow, his progress hampered by his own panic.

The wolves crept close, and took a nip of his flank. Patrick felt the shock of pain run up his leg. The horse whinnied crazily and jerked forward, losing his footing on a patch of ice beneath the snow. Patrick was thrown far by the impact, his head hitting an outcropping of rocks. Dazed, he sat up, his head spinning and his heart sick as he listened to the cries of his horse as the pack of wolves fed on him while he still lived.

Patrick managed to stand, though his left arm throbbed and hung uselessly at his side. With the same arm he had to brace himself as he climbed the nearest pine. By the time he put enough distance between himself and the wolves, Parnell was finally out of his misery.

The rifle remained on the ground, and Patrick remained in the tree, helpless, in pain and alone. Several times he cried loudly for help. In the distance he could see the smoke from Daniel's chimney rising to fill the night air.

The throbbing in his head and in his arm finally won out, and Patrick rested his head against the tree trunk and passed out.

Chapter Five

Daniel dropped the book he was reading onto the table beside his chair, his eyes moving to the octagonal clock on the wall. The time was well past ten o'clock. No one, absolutely no one, in his right mind would be out on a night such as this.

The sounds he kept hearing were caused by the wind and the trees. That couldn't be a man out there, yelling for help. For the third time in ten minutes, Daniel rose and went to the window, thrusting the heavy velvet hangings aside, and peered out into the night.

The moon was bright, and clouds were on a brisk journey across the sky, leaving fragments of mountain in shadow as they passed over. The trees rose eerily in the moonlight, their size accentuated by the angle of pale light and the black shadow of the ground beneath.

Daniel's eyes followed every curve and cranny, seeking some sort of movement in the wilderness beyond the house. Still, there was nothing. Off in the distance he could hear the baleful howling of wolves.

Dropping the drapes and tossing his book on the recently vacated chair, Daniel gave in to what he knew was inevitable. He would never sleep tonight, not while thinking of some poor soul lost in this fierce cold.

He had just pulled his rifle from the gun rack when he heard human shouts. This time the voice was not imagined and it was close. Shrugging his heavy coat over his shoulders, Daniel opened the front door and hurried outside.

Into his view was riding a heavily garbed Harvey Benson, his horse loping furiously. Across the saddle was a large bundle and even from this distance, Daniel recognized it as a man.

Harvey stopped in front of the porch, and his voice, when it finally came, was hoarse with emotion.

"It's the priest!" he cried, bounding from his animal, his hands reaching for Patrick. Daniel was at his side quickly and helped take the body from the horse with a minimum of discomfort.

"I found him unconscious, sitting in a damned tree. The wolves got his horse and must have gotten some of him too. There's a lot of blood, everywhere," Harvey gasped between words, trying to catch his breath.

Together they carried Patrick inside. By this time the commotion had awakened Mrs. Sawyer and she appeared at the head of the stairs, wearing a thick robe, her hair hanging in plaits and a kerosene lantern in her hand. Her eyes took in the injured man.

"Put him in the spare room, Mr. Calcord. I'll fetch some rags and be with you in a moment."

Swiftly she descended the stairs and headed toward the kitchen. Patrick Fitzgerald was a big man, and his unconscious body a dead weight. Daniel and Harvey were breathing hard by the time they had him on the bed.

"Oh, my God, it's his leg! Those wolves took a bite from his calf! Look at it, Daniel!"

"I can see it, Harvey. Help me with his boots. And be careful, we don't want it to bleed any more than we can help."

"I don't think that leg can be saved, Daniel."

"The hell with the leg, I'm more worried about his life!"

Between the two men, they were able to remove the priest's clothing with a minimum of movement. Mrs. Sawyer came briskly into the room, carrying a large bundle of rags which she dropped as her hand felt Patrick's head and tested the temperature of the rest of his body. "I don't think he was out in the cold too long. His fingers and toes are chilled but not as cold or discolored as frostbite would make them. But just to be safe . . . I need the water that's boiling on the stove mixed with cold water. The final temperature should be tepid. We'll bring him up to room temperature gradually, with that water. He's a fortunate man that you found him when you did, Mr. Benson."

78

"Yes, Harvey, what were you doing out here? I thought I heard something, and I was just getting ready to go for a look, but I don't know that I'd have found him."

Harvey replied grimly, "I came to speak with you about something that'll wait. Don't worry, you'd have found him all right. The pack of wolves were still feeding on his poor horse." Harvey's whole body gave a shudder. "I'll get the water."

"That leg will need a tourniquet, and his arm's broken."

"Can you take care of things here, Mrs. Sawyer? I'll ride in to town to get the doctor."

The woman stopped what she was doing and balled her hands into fists, settling them on her ample hips. "Not tonight you won't. If you think I'm spending my night worrying about a foolish man who would ride out on a night like this! I've got one on my hands, I don't need two! Tomorrow will do just as well," she pronounced with finality.

"It's two miles. I've ridden it so often I know each rock by heart. Take a good look at that leg and that arm, Mrs. Sawyer. The leg probably can't be saved, and that arm is broken at a strange angle. There may be two breaks in there. Do you know enough to help this man? And when he recovers consciousness, he'll be in a lot of pain. He'll need morphine. I haven't the stomach to sit still while a grown man suffers needless pain."

Mrs. Sawyer's mouth thinned and her eyes narrowed. Of course he was right; she didn't have enough knowledge to help this man the way he should be helped, but she didn't want anything to happen to Daniel either. "You be careful, Daniel Calcord, I've heard tales of those wolves!"

"I intend to be careful," Daniel answered, turning from the room. His face was in the shadows. "And I'll bring his sister. She'll want to be here."

After two weeks of living in Leadville, Daniel knew how to cope with the icy cold. He wore long johns and thick denim pants. Over these he layered a shirt and another shirt and a woolen sweater. His coat was made of rough suede and lined with more wool. On his hands was a pair of suede gloves also lined with wool. Around his neck and covering his mouth, nose, and ears was a scarf. On his head sat his accustomed Stetson. Only his eyes were bare. Neither the cold nor the

79

wind could penetrate through all this.

In spite of his brave words, had the moon not been lighting his way, Daniel wouldn't have dared to go. As it was, he rode quickly and surely to his destination. Doctor Palmer's home was around the corner from where Magheen lived, and he arrived there first and began banging his fists on the door.

The whole house was roused by the time the door opened to let Daniel in. He wasted no time, just succinctly explained what had happened. Accidents and more were everyday fare for Leadville, and Doctor Palmer quickly agreed to come.

"I need to get dressed and fetch my bag," he informed Daniel.

"I'll tell his sister. She'll want to come too."

The doctor agreed. "She's at Joshua Howard's house. Do you know where that is?"

Daniel nodded. For two weeks he had been avoiding her, but he had hungered for any information he could learn. He had feigned indifference when Joe told him where she lived and worked, and even that she had been asking about him, Daniel. But Daniel was too proud to go to her, too proud to attend Mass when the banns were read. He might be forced into this marriage, but he didn't have to like it. Nor did he have to cooperate.

Besides, he was a busy man, he told himself. His mine was in financial trouble, and he didn't have enough men so he did much of the work himself. He had every excuse for not calling on his bride-to-be. And now that he was forced into calling on her, his heart was thumping unbearably fast.

The Howard house was in darkness. Daniel knocked on the front door several times before he heard any movement from within. When, after a lengthy wait, the door was opened, a man holding a rifle stood there, his nightshirt reaching to his knees.

"Mr. Joshua Howard? I'm Daniel Calcord, and I need to see Magheen."

Joshua Howard threw the door wide open and motioned Daniel inside. He was thickset and balding on top. His mouth drew low, and he frowned as he studied Daniel Calcord before finally speaking his mind. "Frankly, I thought you should have been here long ago, but the middle of the night is hardly a reasonable hour."

"Daniel? Daniel, what is it?"

Daniel's eyes lifted and he saw Magheen standing stiffly at the head of the stairs, her lovely features in shadow. Daniel barely stopped himself in time from going to her and taking her into his arms to tell her his news. She would be frightened and worried, and a familiar surge of protectiveness overwhelmed him.

"It's Father Patrick, Maggie. He's been injured." At her gasp of dismay he continued. "He's at my home, and my housekeeper and Harvey Benson are caring for him. I came here to fetch the doctor and you. He's alive, Magheen. He's hurt and I'm not sure what scars will remain, but I'm confident he'll live."

The green eyes were troubled, but her moment of fear seemed to be passing. She knew she could trust Daniel with her own life and that of her brother. She nodded briefly. "Give me a moment to get a few things together, and I'll come with you."

"Maggie?" She stopped and turned back to him. "Have you anything to wear for a night such as this? I can come back in the morning for you."

"My wife will see to her clothing, Mr. Calcord. Anna has done much traipsing about in cold weather. Now, how about something to warm you up after your hard ride? Coffee, brandy? Which would warm you best? Come into the kitchen, it's the warmest room in the house at this time of night. . . ."

When Magheen came down the stairs fifteen minutes later, Anna Howard and Carrie were both behind her. Agnes Moen, the maid, had long been up and about. It was she who made coffee and sandwiches for the men.

"You'll take my horse, Magheen—" Anna Howard spoke briskly.

"I thought she'd be better on mine," interrupted Daniel. "I don't think you know much about horses, do you, Maggie? The night's already bad enough without having to learn to handle a horse. Besides, you'll stay much warmer with me in front of you."

"No, I don't know much about them," she spoke vaguely, a glistening sheen of moisture in her eyes telling of her worries, "other than they're big enough to give me the willies. Thank you, Daniel, I would appreciate riding with you. Now, can you tell me any more about Patrick?"

He carried her pack in one of his hands and held the other out to capture hers. "Yes, but as we're going, don't you think? The doctor is waiting for us, and so is your brother. If he's wakened up yet, he's bound to be in a good deal of pain. His arm is broken in at least two places."

The morning sun barely peeped over the mountains as they rode up before Daniel's house. Magheen rode astride behind him, her hands clasped about Daniel's firm middle. Every time the wind threatened to come up, she had a hard shoulder to find shelter behind. Even as bundled as she was, by the time they arrived, she was beginning to wonder if she would ever feel her toes or fingers again.

Harvey met them at the door. He looked to be beyond exhaustion as he shook the doctor's hand. "I'm glad to see you, Doc. The Father's been delirious most of the night. He's in a lot of pain; even a simple touch has him wincing. I hope you brought morphine with you."

Magheen moved silently beside the men, but when they reached the bedroom door, the doctor turned to her and shook his head. "I'm sorry, Miss Fitzgerald, but you can't come in yet. You can wait here or downstairs, but I need to see your brother alone."

"But I can help!" she insisted. "I can keep him calm—"

"Later. After I'm done treating his wounds. Why don't you make some coffee for all of us? Daniel, take her downstairs."

"No," she began to protest, but Daniel had led her by the arm and was taking her with him to the front parlor. A fire crackled brightly, giving the room warmth and Maggie another glimpse of Daniel.

"Let me take your coat, Maggie."

She handed it to him, her eyes wide and sad. "I could have helped them, Daniel, I know I could have."

"Maggie, you're too close to your brother. Setting his arm will be almighty painful for him, and you'd be bound to hurt right along with him. Let's make the coffee, and then wait here for them to finish their task. Then we'll take over the care of Father Patrick, and you can be sure he recovers."

She made the coffee and delivered it, but still was kept from the room. Daniel led her to a couch in the parlor and seated her there, sitting beside her and placing an arm around her shoulders consolingly.

"One of the most difficult lessons to learn is to face your own limitations, Maggie. One of my first cases as a young lawyer was to prosecute a woman for stealing from her employer. She stole, and I prosecuted to the best of my ability. I won the case, and she was sentenced to five years at hard labor in New York's prison system. But at the sentencing appeared her four children. She'd been stealing to feed them." His eyes closed with guilty remembrance. "If I'd taken the time to look beyond my legal profession, I might have helped her. What I did was to sentence her and her four children to hunger and suffering. I was wrong, and I should have listened to others who knew better than I. Oh, she had a lousy lawyer who didn't offer her one iota of a defense, but was I any better? Is justice really so blind that there is no gray area, no room for compromise?"

Magheen was silent for a moment. "What happened to the woman and her children?"

"I couldn't stand what I'd done so I arranged a home for the children. And then I resigned my position with the county and took on the case for her. We appealed, and two years later she was a free woman. Last I heard, she'd remarried and was living on a farm in Illinois. I hope she was happy, for if a woman ever deserved happiness, she did."

Magheen wore a puzzled expression. "Daniel, how does that fit in with my brother's wounds?"

"It doesn't," he admitted with a rueful smile. "But it gives you something else to think about."

Magheen snuggled nearer to him. "You're a tricky devil, Daniel Calcord, and, oh, how I have missed you! When I first saw you tonight, I thought my heart would burst with joy. And then I heard you speaking of Patrick." Maggie made the sign of the cross and spoke softly, "Holy Mother of God, make him well for all our sakes."

From above their heads they could hear footsteps and uncomfortable groaning as the priest's arm was set. Maggie clung tightly to Daniel, her face buried in his shoulder. Once, when all was silent above, her fingers went to his cheek, and she gently stroked the half-day's growth of rough beard. "You are always around saving my skin, you are. Now

83

it is not just my skin but my brother's too. I am such a lot of trouble for you, Daniel Calcord. I hope you never regret knowing me. I will do everything in my power to keep you from regrets, that I promise."

A muffled groan sounded, and Magheen's eyes closed in anguish. Daniel pushed her face into his shoulder and clasped her tightly, offering her what comfort he could.

When all was silent, she pulled back and looked at him. He could see the bright sheen of tears in her emerald eyes. "I didn't know you were a lawyer. I thought you were a miner."

"There's a lot we don't know about each other. I've been a lawyer for twelve years. One of my clients is a large bank in Denver, so I got into banking too. Then, the urge for adventure hit me, and I decided to try my hand at mining." His smile was warm and genuine. "I've been in a dozen adventures ever since, several of them with you."

Magheen sank nearer, closing her eyes and letting the tears spill down her cheek. "Hold me, Daniel. Hold me tightly. If I lose Patrick too, I think I will go mad with the pain."

"Shh, he'll be fine. Just remember that, and keep on remembering that. Father Paddie Fitzgerald is too tough to break."

And she did think of those words often over the next hour. Patrick's groans ceased, but the movement overhead was tormenting. Finally, when she could bear it no longer, she rose and announced, "I have to know what's happening. I can't wait here a moment longer."

"Yes," Daniel agreed worriedly. "How much more can the man take? I'll come with you, Maggie."

Mrs. Sawyer was just leaving the room when they arrived. "Doctor Palmer is just about done. I'm cleaning up the mess now. You were right, Daniel, I would have made a shambles of his arm, he broke it clear up to his shoulder! If I'd set it, the doctor would have had to rebreak it, and that would really have been torment for the poor man!"

"How about his leg?"

Mrs. Sawyer shook her head and frowned, before turning from them to descend the stairs. Magheen bit her lip as they entered the room, Patrick was so still and silent on the bed. The stench of blood was thick to the point of nausea.

Doctor Palmer glanced up once and grunted an answer to

Magheen's question. "He'll keep the leg unless infection sets in. The wolf took a good bite, but I've sewn it and it should mend. He'll be missing part of the flesh and have a hell of a scar, but he's not a man to be showing off his fine leg, is he? The arm will take longer to heal. The best I can figure is he broke it in four places, from his elbow to his shoulder. He'll never have the strength in it he should have, but he'll have an arm. He needs to be watched closely for the next few days. Watch for infection or fever. He's weak enough, either one could kill him."

Magheen was pale to her lips. "I'll watch him."

"We'll take turns, Doctor. We'll come for you immediately if something seems to be wrong," Daniel assured the man.

"He's heavily drugged now. That will keep him under most of the day. By tonight he'll be awake and uncomfortable. I'll leave a bit more morphine for you to administer, just in case. But be careful about the dose. He can't take too much."

"How about some food before you go? Or can I talk you into using my bed and getting some sleep?"

"You can talk me into breakfast, but I sleep in my own bed."

"I'll get the breakfast," Magheen offered brightly. "I can't begin to thank you enough for what you've done."

"Your thanks are all that's necessary," replied the doctor. "Now you get in there and watch that man. Mrs. Sawyer is seeing to our meal, she's hungry too."

"And she makes the best flapjacks in Leadville," boasted Harvey.

"That's good enough for me," the doctor answered lightly. "Now, Miss Fitzgerald, if anything seems wrong, you tell Daniel immediately. He'll get word to me, and I'll be here as quickly as I can. The first twenty-four hours are the most critical. If he shows no sign of a fever, he's probably home free. Keep liquids down him, and don't let him thrash about the bed in pain. If that happens, give him a small amount of morphine. If he hits that arm, he could undo our night's work."

"I'll watch over him very carefully, Doctor Palmer."

"I know you will, girl. You love him very much."

When they were gone, Maggie took a good look at her brother for the first time. He was strangely still, even his breathing barely perceptible. His features were a pale white, his lips bloodless. The bandage on his arm stretched from his elbow to his shoulder, and a sheet covered him from the waist down. Maggie pulled the blankets to his chin.

"He's lost so much blood."

She spoke more to herself than to him, but Daniel chose to answer. "He has, but he'll regain it. He's too strong to be kept down for long. Here, this chair's more comfortable for you to sit in." Daniel carried an upholstered chair closer to the bed and motioned for Maggie to sit in it. "I'll be downstairs with the other men, but I'll be back shortly."

"Please, don't come back. I've cost you a full night's sleep already. Paddie and I will be fine. I can't thank you and Mrs. Sawyer enough."

Daniel put a hand on her shoulder. "You would have done the same for me, Maggie."

Maggie's head tilted to look up at him, and she smiled ruefully. "You're always saying that, Daniel. And the truth of the matter is that I never get the chance."

"Do you want a blanket?"

"No, but you could bring me a cup of that brew before you crawl into bed."

Daniel leaned over and pressed a kiss to her temple before leaving the room. When he returned, carrying a cup of hot coffee, the doctor and Harvey Benson were gone, and Mrs. Sawyer was in her bed. He opened the door and found Magheen sitting on the bed beside Paddie, wiping his lips with a damp cloth.

A spurt of jealousy shot through him. With her every action she showed how much she loved Patrick Fitzgerald. For himself she had not even the words. Of course, he had never asked for the words, and he never would. Magheen was a fine woman, soft-spoken and gentle, the sort a man took to wife, but Daniel wasn't interested in a wife. He was interested in Maggie, all right, but not as a wife. He had thought some time away from her would lessen the desire he had for her. Well, the moment he had set eyes on her last night, he knew how wrong he was. He wanted her every bit as badly as he had during that last embrace in the cabin. He wanted her smiles, and he wanted to hear that lovely, lilting voice breathe her desires into his ear. He wanted to touch every part of her, to run his fingers over her breasts and hips, to hear her give that little gasp of pleasure as he did so. He could give her full measure of pleasure and take the same from her. He wanted to lie in bed with her in his arms, satiated, and simply hold her. He wanted to touch her soft cheeks and run his rough fingers through her thick hair and feel her become part of him.

He wanted *her*, dammit.

The cup clinked against the saucer, and Maggie turned to him, smiling. "He's resting comfortably. I think he will be fine."

"Here's your coffee. I'll get a blanket." Daniel spoke brusquely, moving to the cedar chest to fetch a striped woolen blanket from inside. He glanced at her and found her bending over Paddie, pressing a kiss to his cheek and smoothing the hair away from his face.

Daniel couldn't remember so much as touching his brother or his father, let alone kissing them. His father was stern, aloof and, as he grew older, cruel. Other than meting out punishment, he had little effect on Daniel's life.

Once upon a time he had been close to his mother, but as he grew older and more independent, she had wanted to tie him closer. Daniel wasn't that sort of man. He wanted to lead his own life, fully and without strings. But she had made more and more demands on him. And when he wouldn't give her her way, she had held out the family fortune as a temptation. When that hadn't worked, she had turned on him.

Now, twelve years later, Daniel understood the weakness that had caused her behavior. Inbred in her had been a possessiveness for those she loved. And if they wouldn't be possessed, they would be punished. So when his younger brother had begun spreading lies about Daniel, their mother had wanted to hear and believe them. Between the two, they had made Daniel's life hell.

Daniel also now understood his brother's motivation; he had simply wanted Daniel's share of the family fortune in addition to his own.

Their younger sister had felt no threat from any member of the family and had done her utmost to be uninvolved, at least as far as Daniel was concerned. She had remained close to both parents, in effect creating a family of her own. She and Daniel had seen little of each other, even before he left New York.

Maybe it was best she had married young and didn't know of this side of the family.

Finally, Daniel had left New York, and he knew now he would never go back. Let them fight over the so-called fortune; Daniel would make his own.

And so far, he had made plenty. If the mine came in, he would be wealthier than his family had ever dreamed of being.

So why was he watching a young Irish girl embrace her brother and feeling, once again, as though he were on the outside looking in?

"Maggie, why don't I wait with him awhile?"

She rose from the bed, pursing her lips as she studied him. Daniel looked drawn and weary. "No, you've done too much already. You crawl in bed and get some sleep. I'm wide awake, and I'll take care of Paddie." She placed a hand on his arm and he turned back to her. "I do thank you for your kindness, Daniel."

"Magheen . . ."

Her arms went around him, strong and supple and warm. The haven was just what Daniel needed. Maggie's lips met his eagerly, in a kiss of longing and tenderness. When they broke apart, Daniel rested his forehead against hers and smiled into her eyes. "I must need sleep desperately. The man I am, I always take advantage when a beautiful woman offers me her mouth."

His words brought a flush to her face. "That was just my way of saying thank you, Daniel."

"I like the way you thank me."

It was noon before he woke, and he could hear the sounds of Mrs. Sawyer in the kitchen, preparing dinner. Good, he thought, Maggie needed a hot meal, and she needed some sleep. The mine would simply have to wait for him for a few days, until he was sure Patrick Fitzgerald was out of danger.

Maggie was nodding off when he entered the room, a tray of food in his hands. Her eyes were huge and flickering in her face, bruises beneath them. Daniel spoke softly, "Here, I want you to eat this. Then get yourself off to bed. I'll watch Paddie for you this afternoon."

"Oh, I can't ask you to do that! You've so much else to do."

"No arguing. Eat."

She smiled wanly. "I hope you keep insisting. I'm too tired to stay awake any longer, but I hate what I'm asking of you."

"Whom else would you ask it of, if not the man you are to marry?"

Her head came up at his words, and for the first time he realized how much he had hurt her by not coming to see her. "I thought . . . maybe you wanted to . . . call off the wedding. I thought you must be having second thoughts."

Shaking his head, he said, "Eat, Maggie. We'll talk about our marriage later."

Daniel showed her to his bedroom when she had finished her meal. "There's hot water in the washstand, and I promise, the bed is warm. Sleep well, you've a long night ahead."

The room was large and masculine. An oak dresser and gently curving mirror stood in one corner, the washstand next to it. An overstuffed chair was by the window, and a low bookcase stood beside it. Only the window coverings were feminine; they were light and lacy, frilly pieces of cloth.

In minutes she was washed and stripped of her clothing. Daniel was right, the bed was warm. And it smelled musky and masculine, just like him. Her eyes fluttered closed and she slept.

When she wakened, the room was in darkness. The aroma of fried chicken spread through the house, fully waking her. Quickly she dressed and hurried into the room across the hall. Patrick was still sound asleep, looking more comfortable than he had when she left him. Daniel was seated in the chair by the bed, a book in his hands. He looked up when she entered, and set the book aside.

She was wearing another schoolteacher outfit. This time, with the white blouse was a brown linen skirt. The only adornment she seemed to possess was a finely filigreed pin which she wore at the prim neckline. But her hair was a glorious riot of red curls which she had tried, vainly, to tie back at her nape. He wanted to run his fingers through the lemony scent of her hair and feel its texture against his cheek. Daniel's imagination ran to her choice of plain underwear and the softness of her skin beneath. He had to force himself to speak calmly.

"He's fine, Maggie. Not a sign of fever. He seemed restless about half an hour ago so I gave him morphine. I do believe he's on the road to recovery. Doctor Palmer said he would return tomorrow and change the bandages and check for infection. But no fever is the best sign we can have.

"You look better too." Daniel smiled ironically at his choice of words. "I mean, you always look good, but before you slept you seemed tired. Now, you look fit to tangle with any number of brothers and fiancés."

"One is enough, thank you."

"Here, have my chair."

"I can sit on the edge of the bed. I don't think Patrick would mind."

Daniel relaxed as he spoke. "Mrs. Sawyer insists on us eating in the dining room tonight. She claims Patrick no longer needs observation every moment and that we need a break."

"She must be right. Daniel . . ."

He held up a hand. "Please, don't tell me how grateful you are again. I couldn't bear it! Let's go eat instead. My stomach's rumbling to beat Ben Loeb's band." He rose and took her elbow, leading her from the room.

Once in the hallway, she couldn't resist tucking an arm around his waist and smiling at him. "You're so good to me, Daniel."

Daniel returned her light squeeze. There would be time later to sort out the conflicting emotions she roused in him. All he knew was that, at this moment, she needed all the comfort and support he could give her. For some reason, it was important that he be the man to help her.

After dinner she returned to Patrick's side. He was tossing now, the blankets down around his waist. On his forehead was a sheen of fine perspiration. Maggie cursed the impulse that had her leaving him alone for so much as a minute and hurried to his side, pulling the blankets higher. With a soft cloth she sponged the moisture from his face and upper arms. Into a cup she mixed a small portion of the crystallized morphine and water, and this she slowly fed to him. Almost immediately he calmed and began to drowse.

When Daniel came in to say good night, he found Maggie watching her brother fretfully. The empty cup and discarded spoon told their own story. With a lithe movement Daniel was beside the bed and was feeling Patrick's forehead and cheeks for a sign of fever.

"It was the pain that made him fretful, Maggie. He's cool to touch, he has no fever."

"I shouldn't have left him alone. The way he was tossing around on the bed, he might have hurt his arm."

"I think you're right. Until he regains consciousness, one of us should be in the room at all times. I will spell you in four hours."

"Daniel, I won't let you ignore your work."

"Just until he regains consciousness." He spoke firmly, his lips compressed. "And Maggie, you won't *let* me do or not do anything." His brows raised, and he waited in vain for her to speak. "Good night."

He was as good as his word. In four hours he spelled Maggie, sending her to sleep in the warm bed he had just vacated. His attitude toward her was so cool she didn't dare argue. She felt as though she had barely slept when it was time to rouse again. Only this time, as she crept across the hallway and into Patrick's room, she heard masculine voices coming from inside.

Cracking the door open wider, she heard Patrick's voice saying, "I don't care what Maggie says! I'm sore, not dying! I don't need a watchdog. It's the middle of the night, man, and a sane person would be in his bed, sleeping, not sitting up beside a man who'd like to get some sleep himself."

"All right, all right!" Daniel responded, his palms high, as though admitting defeat. "I can understand wanting some privacy, and I'm more than willing to give it to you. Only it's up to you to explain to your sister that you chased me off, understand? But before I go, you're going to swallow a bit more of this morphine."

"I am not!"

"For a priest, you're certainly a pigheaded old mule!" Daniel fairly bellowed. "I'm not leaving this room until you've taken some, and that's my last word on it!"

Patrick was frowning heavily. Daniel glared hotly. Both men were mule-headed, Maggie thought. But apparently her brother was well on his way to recovery, so she decided to let the two of them fight it out. For herself, she would rather be back in bed.

Into the warmth of Daniel's bed she tumbled and was sound asleep in minutes.

This was one problem he hadn't foreseen, Daniel thought later as he stood beside his bed and watched her sleep. He hadn't planned on both of them sleeping at the same time, and there wasn't another bed in the house. He conveniently tossed aside the idea of sleeping on the sofa. Maggie wouldn't want him to be so uncomfortable.

He wouldn't have to disturb her, he thought cunningly. But he could hold her and keep her warm. He'd like to . . . no, he *needed* to touch her. It had been so long, and he was aching just to be intimately near her. She was so soft and so sweet to touch and pet. They didn't have to go any further than that. He would be satisfied with just a few kisses. He wasn't about to go any further than that. A couple more damn weeks was all he had to wait, and then he could do as he pleased with her. She had made sure of that by trapping him into this pretense of a marriage.

Hadn't she been the one to say her heart felt as though it would burst with joy when he came for her last night? He had been thinking that other parts of him would burst.

Doffing his clothing rapidly, he slid between the sheets and carefully drew her to him. She was wearing some of those damned undies which made his dreams so vivid lately. The buttons nestled deep in the lone strip of lace running between neck and waist were small and white.

His black eyes darkened with desire. "Why not?" he wondered. "What harm could a bit of touching do?"

Daniel's fingers felt big and clumsy as they released the dainty things. Spreading the chemise wide, he feasted his eyes hungrily on her creamy bounty. Her full breasts boasted ripe, soft skin and rosy pink nipples. He felt like a kid at Christmas who didn't know where to begin to enjoy his new treasures.

His eyes flickered up to her face, and he caught her gazing calmly back at him. Daniel actually flushed guiltily, as if he had been caught doing something he ought not to have done. His mouth twisted, and he flung away from her, onto his back, and glared at the ceiling.

Twice he opened his mouth to speak, but neither time

could he think of a single thing to say in his defense. His lips snapped shut, and he turned to face Maggie. She was sitting up in bed, waiting for him to speak, her chemise down to her waist. Strangely, she didn't seem the least embarrassed by her partial nudity. Daniel's eyes lowered and darkened, blatantly hungering for more of her. He wasn't sure how much longer he could keep his hands off her, not when she was so soft and so tempting, and so available to him.

His eyes met hers. "Dammit, Maggie! I want you so badly I ache!" he growled.

Her hand lifted to his cheek and stroked gently along his jawline. The movement brought her breast within an inch of his hand. "Don't you know I want you too, Daniel?" she questioned softly.

The words took a bare moment to penetrate. With a lithe movement he rose from the bed and slid his body alongside hers. She was captured within the strong embrace of his arms and chest. His mouth met hers, hard and firm with his purpose at first, and then gentling as she returned his ardor.

His hands cupped her breasts and all rational thought fled his mind. The way she nestled against him, her mouth raising again for his kiss, told him she was as beyond thinking as he.

She was so obviously new to the ways of love that he was touched, and so eager to please him that he wondered how he would control himself long enough to please her.

"Open your mouth, sweet. Yes, just like that."

"You taste so good, Daniel. And the way you touch me makes me feel tingly all over. Can I touch you too?"

"Oh, yes, sweetheart." His hand captured her fingers and led them to caress him intimately. "Yes, just like that," he croaked, his voice hoarse.

His mouth ran forays down her neck and shoulders, not stopping until he reached a taut nipple. His calloused hand held the offering, and his lips took it hungrily, his tongue flicking across the very tip until he could stand it no longer, and he began to lightly suckle. He feasted on one, then the other.

"Daniel, can I . . ."

He laughed hoarsely. "Nothing else tonight, sweet. I don't think I can stand the pleasure. My control's wearing thin as it

93

is . . . and I want to give you so much pleasure . . ."

"Oh, Daniel, I have much pleasure from you."

He laughed again. "That's not the kind of pleasure I was talking about. I have so much to teach you, sweet Maggie." His hands went to her hips, and she gasped at the sensations coursing through her as he rubbed her against him. He was naked, and she still had her bloomers on, but the hardness of him could have been felt through a dozen thick layers of cloth.

His fingers undid the ribbon holding her bloomers up and slowly slid them down her hips, letting them ride low, baring her belly. His big, calloused hand slid to her belly and spread wide. His hand covered most of her. The contrast of his dark skin and her paleness spread the ache deeper through him. She was his woman, and he was leaving his markings on her in the most fundamental way he could. She was his. And she would give and take, to him and from him.

Rolling her onto her back, he straddled her, his big body barely touching hers. Maggie arched against him. Her breasts had swollen from his attentions, and her nipples were hot and turgid, aching to have his lips on them once more.

His mouth moistened all of her but the nipples. He lowered himself and pressed moist kisses on the undersides of her breasts, across her rib cage, around her waist. The bloomers slid off, encouraged by his fingers. He tasted the indentation at her hipbone, tickled her belly button with his tongue, and brought himself still lower.

"Oh!" she gasped once. "Daniel! Oh! Oh! Ah! Ahh . . . Ahhh . . ."

He smiled to himself, thinking he might have predicted her response. His mouth and lips continued to tease her until she was shaking with need, a need he knew she still didn't quite understand. He wanted tonight to be perfect for her. She needed to be moist and ready for him; he didn't want to be the cause of so much as one unnecessary flinch. She was tense and ready to explode. Daniel flicked his tongue deeper, and she went over the edge.

Her body was covered with a fine sheen of moisture when he rose. She was shaking so that he wrapped her in his protective embrace, his mouth tasting her neck and ears, his breath harsh and raspy. Magheen opened her eyes to look into his.

"Now, Daniel. Please?"

He swallowed a deep, audible breath and placed his legs between hers. Ever so slowly, tantalizingly, he lowered his hips and probed about her most sensitive area, where his mouth had so recently explored. His chest barely touched her breasts, he was being so careful not to hurt her with his weight.

He entered her ever so slightly. She was made for him. He knew from that one little bit that she would fit him, "like a glove, Maggie. We fit together so well." He drove another bit, savoring each sensation and her erotic reaction to them.

"Daniel, you're teasing me!" she accused breathlessly.

He gave her a little bit more, not too much, just enough.

"I can't bear it, Daniel! Please . . ."

"Please what? This?" The temptation to fill her was almost overwhelming, but he was determined to move ever so slowly. "Or this?"

"Daniel!" She could bear it no longer, and she arched herself, bringing her hips up to meet his and taking him fully.

And now his control slipped. He tightened his hold and began to slowly love her in the oldest way known to man. His loving caresses were gentle yet thrusting. He could feel her taking all of him, giving all of herself. She was so beautiful like this. So abandoned. So desirable.

She reached for her pleasure again. And again. The taut skin softening in her face and the luminous expression in her eyes were his downfall. She wanted him and welcomed him so much that he had to give in to her. The very way her flesh gripped him had him sweating for lost control. It began with his shoulders shaking, and she held him to share her strength. It ended with the spasm of his loins and her answering movements to take all of him, to give him pleasure.

Chapter Six

Daniel was sleeping on a bed of clouds, and an angel was lying beside him, stroking his cheek. Her lips pressed kisses on his, her tongue teasing the tender inner flesh of his mouth. His hand was cupping a soft pillow as his eyes slowly opened.

"Maggie?"

She opened her mouth and leaned across to take his, swallowing the word whole. Her breast was swelling, more than filling his hand, and he knew he could wait no longer. With a lithe movement he rolled her onto her back and lowered his hips to meet hers, thrusting himself deeply inside her.

Last night hadn't been enough, would never be enough to have his fill of her.

In the soft light of an early winter morning, Daniel made exquisite love to Magheen. Slowly and powerfully he filled her until she was writhing beneath him, calling his name in that breathless voice she had when she was aroused. Using his strength and control he took her to the brink and let her slowly sink back to earth. Time and again he loved her until he could stand it no longer. And then he was the one to breathlessly whisper words of endearment and desire into her ear. His shoulders tensed, his arms bringing her that bit closer so she might become one with him, his hips thrusting with his release.

As she floated back down to earth, her whole being tingling with his lovemaking, Magheen said the most natural words in the world, "I love you, Daniel."

Answering words hovered in his throat, dying unspoken, as Maggie broke the spell by curling against his side and falling into a deep sleep.

Idly Daniel studied the ornate plasterwork on the ceiling, his chaotic thoughts tumbling about in his mind. Finally, to himself only, he admitted, "Ah, Maggie, if I could love, it would be you. If I could trust, it would be you. But don't you know love only exists in a moment like this, and never lasts beyond the physical release?"

He had imagined what it would be like to hear those words from her as she cared for Patrick, and now he knew. The knowledge filled him with an infinite sadness. So even Maggie could lie to herself. She could call it love when it was mere lust.

He knew far better than she what so-called love did to people. They became possessive and demanding, and they ended up destroying each other and everyone around them. Between the two of them, his parents had destroyed their family, and they did it under the guise of so-called love. That was a trap he would never fall into.

Oh, he would marry Maggie all right, he would even raise a family with her. "But don't call it love, Maggie. Love means you're getting beneath my skin, you're reaching to my soul, and that I'll never let you or anyone do. I can't take the risk. It hurts too much to be betrayed, to have love thrown back into your face. I know, Maggie, how well I know. It's been done to me."

The very thought of his family filled him with anger and distrust still, these many years after he had left New York, years since he had seen them. Never would he trust anyone so implicitly. Never again would he leave himself so open to hurt. Not even with Maggie. And he knew all the weapons to keep her at a distance.

Unable to sleep a moment longer, Daniel rose and crossed the room to his dresser. In his top drawer were his cigars and one of these he opened and lit. He sat in the overstuffed chair beneath his window and puffed on the cigar, his eyes taking in the grandeur of the sun rising on the eastern horizon. The early morning frost descended from the mountains surrounding them and settled in the low valley.

Daniel pondered in comfort. He knew what he had to do, what he would do. She was getting under his skin, chipping away at his independence. He didn't need her, he didn't need anybody. He had never felt the loneliness so much in his life.

97

Patrick was in high spirits, or so he pretended, Magheen guessed shrewdly. He had been laughing and joking, claiming to have no pain all morning, while she knew better. He refused the morphine, charmed Mrs. Sawyer with that teasing grin all the Fitzgerald brothers shared, even behaved decently to Daniel. But to her, he was the worst. He laughed and joked and pretended everything was just marvelous. He was so falsely cheery and tense with it, she could have bopped him on the head.

She would far rather have had his cursed honesty and seen him get well quicker. The only time all morning he had faltered was when he asked after Parnell. She could tell by the look on his face he was remembering that night.

"How about another cup of tea?"

"I'm ready to float to Leadville right now. Haven't you anything better to do than sit here and mollycoddle me?"

"No," she smiled sweetly. "Nothing better."

"What do you think of this house?" Patrick quizzed curiously. "Did you expect anything so fine? I thought your man was a miner, and a poor one at that!"

"Well, so did I. But do you know what he told me? He said he was a lawyer by trade! Can you imagine that?" Her eyes sparkled mischievously. "I know he can argue, I vouch for that firsthand."

"Arguing's to be expected between a betrothed couple. And you two, you're both cursed with minds of your own. Now I counsel a couple in your position —"

Light brown brows rose quizzically. "Are you my priest now or my brother?"

"Can your sauce, chit! I'm both, and you'll not be forgetting it."

"Yes, sir. Shall I bob a curtsy now or wait until the lecture's over?"

He threw a pillow at her and grimaced at the discomfort the movement caused him. "Go on with you! Get outside and get some fresh air. And spend some time with that man of yours."

"He is wonderful, isn't he, Patrick?" The green of her eyes shone brightly, and her brother wondered briefly at the change in her. She seemed to have grown up in the last few hours, grown into a beautiful, beaming young woman.

"It was so brave of him to fetch the doctor and me in the middle of the night," she continued. "Another man would have waited until morning, but he couldn't stand to see you in pain." Biting her lips, she managed to give Patrick a rueful smile. "I know I'm rambling. But I'm very grateful to him for what he did for you . . . and —"

"And you're madly in love with the man, darlin'. And why not? He is the man you are to marry, after all." He held his hand out to her, and, as she took it, she sat on the bed beside him. "I'm very happy for you, Maggie. If anyone ever deserved happiness, 'tis you. But I'm your brother too, and I just hope he loves you one little bit as much as you love him."

"I think he does. He's not a man of many words, but, ooh, Patrick, I think he does!"

"Then find him and give me a moment's rest. When is that doctor supposed to be here?"

"Sometime today."

"So don't come back until then. And that is your priest speaking. *Him* you must obey."

Maggie felt wonderful as she tripped gaily down the stairs. Mrs. Sawyer could be heard in the kitchen, her preparations for dinner beginning. Daniel was in his study, she could hear his chair creaking. Maggie hadn't seen him at all this morning. When she had finally wakened, he was gone from the bedroom, which she decided was a good thing since she would have died of embarrassment had Mrs. Sawyer found them out. The housekeeper might even have told Patrick, and then what would Magheen say? No, in that situation, Patrick would be her brother more than her priest, and Patrick could be very stern.

She felt the need to see Daniel, to see if the memory of last night still lingered with him too. Maggie's whole body tingled, but she was just a little bit sore with it. Still, she wanted to be held in Daniel's arms once more. Then she would be content to wait until they were man and wife to have him the rest of her days, all night and all day.

She knocked briefly on the study door, entering when he called to her.

"Hello, Daniel," she said brightly as she closed the door behind her. A tender smile was on her lips, her eyes seeking his from across the room. Daniel glanced up and quickly looked away.

"Maggie . . ." Hesitation was in his voice. Idly his fingers flipped through a stack of papers on his desk.

"Yes, Daniel?"

His dark head shook, and, in a gesture speaking loudly of frustration, he ran a hand through his hair. "Maggie, I've wasted too much time already with you and your brother. The mine is being neglected, and I've a good deal of paperwork to get through before I can get back to it. I need some time alone to work. Would you mind leaving the room now? I need some privacy."

Maggie felt momentarily stunned. He was very cool. From his stance she could tell he was upset, disappointed with her, and she didn't understand why. A bitter premonition was curling inside her. "Did I do something wrong? Are you angry with me?" Her shoulders curved forward, and her hand reached out to him, but he stepped away. As her hand dropped, her brows furrowed in confusion, and she questioned, "Did I displease you last night?"

"Last night?" Daniel's voice was raspy. He turned and looked directly at her. "Last night had best be forgotten. If I hadn't been so tired, I would have controlled myself better. You made it damn difficult, offering yourself to me!" he barked. "Have you no shame?"

She drew a sharp breath, and her chest constricted painfully. The words he spoke were true, she had offered herself to him, shamelessly. A moment passed while she controlled the rioting fears coursing through her. But he shared a part of that blame, too. "'Twas not like that, Daniel."

"Of course it was. I was there, remember? You had to get your claws in me, you had to make me want you. You had to make me want you so badly I couldn't turn you down! What were you afraid of—that I wouldn't marry you when the time came?"

He lowered his voice with an effort. "You made me lose my head, Maggie. Did you ever stop to think you might get with child from what we did? Or was that part of your plan too? Did it ever occur to you I might not want a half-Irish brat?"

She stood very still, listening intently to his every word.

"I said I would marry you, Magheen, and I keep my word.

Last night was not necessary to make sure of that. Two more banns and we can wed. Until then, don't try to own me by claiming to love me. I damn well know better!"

Maggie blinked, barely able to believe what she was hearing. He sounded so bitter, so angry. As she shook her head, she had to force herself to speak her next words. "How can you say such horrible things?"

"I spoke only the truth. Was anything I said a lie? Tell me in the clear light of the morning that you love me. Say it now, Magheen! Can you lie again today?"

A lie? He thought she spoke lies? She, who had had the value of always speaking the truth birched into her hind end as a little slip of a child? Her throat ached too badly to answer him. It was impossible to speak of her love or feelings with him as he was now. Oh Daniel, she thought sadly, what are you doing to us? I thought last night we both affirmed our love. If that wasn't what happened, then what was?

Wearily, he passed a hand over his forehead. "Please, go, Magheen. I have a lot of work to get through today."

The door closed softly behind her.

She couldn't return to Patrick's room, not yet. And Daniel's bedroom was unthinkable. Yet she had to get out of here, she had to have some time and space to herself. If she didn't, she would break down and cry here, where the humiliation of Daniel knowing how much he hurt her would cause her even greater pain.

Fetching her coat from the closet, she slipped out the front door. Behind the house was an incline to the mountain. Steep and dotted with trees, it would make a perfect place to be alone. She climbed higher and higher, trying to forget the hurt by exerting herself. As long as she was on the move, she was too busy to think.

Gradually her frantic climbing slowed, leaving her prey to her thoughts. All she felt was weary and immeasurably hurt.

She didn't know what she had done wrong. She did know she had not pleased Daniel last night. How could something that made her feel so wonderful and so loved have been so disappointing to him? How could he think so little of her? He thought her a liar and a schemer . . . and shameless!

Oh, how could she bear to see him again? One knowing glance from him would leave her feeling ashamed, ashamed of herself and her body, ashamed of her love.

And how could she marry a man who made her feel so small and horrible? How could she ever think of raising a family with him? A family of half-Irish brats, she corrected herself.

She climbed until her chest ached from the effort of breathing in the cold. From high on the mountaintop she could see far into the distance, and when a funny-looking carriage approached, she knew it must be the doctor.

Whether she wanted to see Daniel again or not, she would.

Her mood was subdued when she returned to the house, but luckily he was nowhere to be seen. The doctor was already in Patrick's room, and she set about putting her thoughts on other matters.

"Where have you been, Maggie?" Patrick questioned, frowning. The smiling girl of the morning was long gone. " 'Tis too cold to spend too long outside. Don't you have any sense?"

"She can't have too much sense, not if she takes after her brother," the doctor pronounced dryly. "Your leg seems to be healing fine. The pain in your shoulder is only to be expected. I don't know what you thought you were doing, riding late at night in this weather. You're lucky the wolves took that poor horse of yours and left you alone. It's to the good Lord's credit that the poor thing died quickly. An animal suffers just as badly from frostbite as a human, I can tell you that!

"And now that you're fit to travel, I want you in St. Anthony's Hospital where I can keep a personal eye on you. What would the folk of Leadville say if I let their priest die from infection?"

Father Patrick opened his mouth to answer, but the good doctor beat him to it. He faced Patrick as he spoke, his thinning black beard bouncing to give more emphasis to each word. "I can tell you what they'd say. They'd say the priest had an in with the Lord, and Dr. Palmer couldn't even manage to save him then! There'd be not a shred of respect left for me in this town. You couldn't have been an ordinary miner or shopkeeper. No, you had to go and be a priest. So, it's off to St. Anthony's for you."

"I'm not in fit shape to travel," Patrick growled.

"Course you're not. That's why I brought my sled. All you have to do is lie there. I'll do the real work."

"That I'd like to see," Patrick answered. "I've a feeling I'll sprout wings first."

"Ah, sacrilegious are we now? I might have known once you started recovering, you'd be impossible to work with."

"Is there room on that sled for me too?" Maggie inquired.

"Of course. Two can ride inside. I'll take the horse."

"I don't mean to put you to any trouble."

"It's no trouble. Get your things together, and I'll tie them on the sled. But I can't take my patient to Leadville on an empty stomach, either mine or his." The doctor sighed, feigning disappointment, but his broad grin gave away the lie. "I suppose we'll have to stay for one of Mrs. Sawyer's meals, especially as it smells so good."

"Maggie, is something wrong?" Patrick questioned softly. Her agitation was not missed by him.

"No," she gave a bright smile. "I just remembered I'm supposed to help Mrs. Howard with the catechism for the little ones tonight. If I'm not there, she'll have to do it all by herself and that's too much for one woman."

Not wanting to face the questions she could feel building in her brother, Maggie crossed the hall and entered Daniel's familiar bedroom. The room was as neat as when she had first set eyes on it, not a piece of clothing out of place, not a speck of dust on the dresser. The bed was neatly made, the coverlet tucked securely in at the corners of the mattress, the pillows perfectly placed. Never again would she see a four-poster without thinking of last night and Daniel. And her shame of this morning.

Unable to bear her thoughts any longer, she turned her attention to the task at hand. In a matter of moments she packed everything she had brought with her.

As she left the room, she had her back to the hall and was pulling the door closed. In her other hand was her worn valise. Turning, she nearly collided with Daniel, but his firm hands on her shoulders steadied her. His eyes searched her face and lowered to her hands. "Why are you carrying that? If it's because of what I said . . ."

Maggie shook her head. When she spoke, her eyes were no higher than his breast button. "Doctor Palmer insists Patrick go to the hospital. As long as he's brought the sled, I thought to go with them. I can't leave my job for so long."

"Maggie—"

He almost sounded frantic. Maggie lifted her troubled gaze to his. "Please, Daniel, don't say anything more. I must go. We both have a good deal of thinking to do. We've said everything there is to say."

"Am I driving you away? I don't mean to hurt you." Irrationally, now that he had gotten her to leave, he wanted her to stay.

"I know you don't, Daniel. But I'd rather know the truth now than after we're married. I've been told the truth often hurts. Please, Daniel, Patrick is waiting for me."

"What do you mean, rather than after we're married? We'll still be married, Maggie!"

"I . . . I'm not sure it wouldn't be a mistake, Daniel. I won't live a life of regrets, and I'm not sure that I won't have them with you. Sometimes I think you almost hate me."

"I could never hate you," he spoke warmly, his hand grasping her upper arm, his thumb rubbing circles into her soft flesh. She knew he was thinking of last night, only now his thoughts were pleasurable. She was becoming more and more confused.

"Maggie, stay now. We'll sort this out between us."

She shook her head in answer. "My brother is leaving. I'll go with him."

Daniel dropped her arm, his eyes growing cold. "If you're sure that's what you want," he said coolly. "But is it wise? I'm very vulnerable to you when you're near. When you're out of my sight, you'll quickly be out of my mind. Can you afford that risk if you're really so dead set on loving me?" His tone of voice made the word "love" sound contemptuous.

Her chin lifted defiantly. The auburn hair was pulled back at her nape, but soft tendrils wisped about her neck and ears. "I'll take that risk, for if what you say is true, perhaps we're better off not marrying. You make me feel small about myself. I don't think I can live a life like that."

His mouth tightened. "Suit yourself. I trust you'll let me know whether we're getting married or not? And before I'm left standing as a heartbroken bridegroom at the altar?" His tone was hateful, mocking. "Now, go to the dining room.

Mrs. Sawyer has dinner ready, and I've told her you are eating with us. Dr. Palmer has already accepted."

After dinner, Daniel went to his study and waited for them to take their leave. He wanted to ignore the whole bunch of them as they left, but that would give Magheen too much to think on. She might realize how upset he was at her abrupt defection from his home. So, over dinner, he played the congenial host, conversing easily with Doctor Palmer, even giving Magheen a moment or two of attention.

That meal couldn't have ended soon enough.

He and the doctor carried Father Patrick down the stairs and wrapped him warmly in the sled. That was when Daniel left. No matter how much he pretended, he refused to watch her speed away from his home and, for all he knew, from his life.

Now he was going to sit silently and peacefully in his study and get roaring drunk.

The harness snapped and the horse whinnied. Daniel couldn't stand not knowing any longer. He rose from his chair and thrust the velvet drapes aside and watched as the horse and sled moved in unison toward the road. Doctor Palmer sat on the seat and drove the horse, while Patrick and Magheen sat behind him. The contraption resembled an open coach but, instead of wheels, this had skis. He might have been curious enough about it to go out and inspect it closely, had it not been the vehicle which was taking Maggie away.

The sled disappeared around the corner and the drapes were tugged back into place. He would just have to get used to doing without her again, he thought. He had been without her for all these years and hadn't missed her a bit, and he would do that again. Last night had been a huge mistake, he realized now. She would haunt his bedroom with memories of her in it and in his bed, and most of all, of her loving response.

If he were a gullible man, he might have believed her words. Hell, he would have wanted to believe her words. But he wasn't gullible, he was practical and, other than to repeat last night, he had no use for her in his life.

Daniel reached for the bottle of brandy in the sideboard and settled himself comfortably in the chair behind his desk.

105

After pouring a healthy measure of the brew, he rested his booted feet on the desktop and sipped.

"My Tom says you'd best be wary of him, Maggie," Carrie Hutchen repeated for the third time that afternoon. She and Maggie were taking a lunch break in the back room at Daniel, Fisher and Smith Emporium. "He says William Lovell is as crooked as the day is long."

"But Carrie, the man returned my money and gave me a profit! He arrived yesterday with the chickens and immediately sold them all. I made twenty dollars' profit, I did!"

Forcefully Carrie shook her head. "I told Tom that, even that William Lovell insisted your agreement be in writing. He still says you should stay away from him."

"But why?"

"Tom wouldn't be specific, but he's heard a great deal . . ."

"Carrie, I don't judge a man by gossip."

Carrie's soft brown eyes widened with hurt. "Nor does my Tom, and if he says William Lovell is a shady character, it's because he really believes it. Down deep he believes it. Tom is too good a man to spread lies about another, that's probably why he did not tell me what he'd heard. But he insists you should be warned. And so, I've warned you. Do with it what you will."

"Carrie, I didn't mean to hurt your feelings, but Bill Lovell has been honest with me!"

Silently Carrie returned her attention to her lunch and Maggie did likewise. As she munched on her sandwich, she thought about what Carrie had said. Tom Fuller was a good man. But Maggie was not one to judge another person, not even William Lovell. Not after watching what the judgments of others had done to her brothers. Still, there was something about Bill Lovell that made her uncomfortable. Granted, he was small and wiry and usually in need of a good shave, but it wasn't just his appearance that made Maggie wary of him. No, it was his eyes. They were narrow and beady and watched her too closely for comfort.

"Carrie . . . your warning may be just a little too late. Yesterday, after Bill gave me back my money and my profit, he offered to let me in on another one of his little deals—"

"Oh, no! You did it, didn't you? You trusting little fool! You gave him the money and the profit? Well, you'll never see that money again!"

"Oh, Carrie, do you really think not? Surely he wouldn't run off with my money. Not when I need it so badly!"

Carrie snorted. "What do you mean, you need it so badly? Tom's found out a lot about your Daniel Calcord, too. When you marry him, you won't be needing for anything!"

Maggie's eyes dropped before Carrie could see the uncertainty in them. Paddie's accident was over a week ago and she had heard nothing from Daniel. She made the excuse that he was too busy, that the mining was more time-consuming than either of them had realized.

But Tom showed up most nights.

Daniel's taunting words were what she lived with every day and slept with every night. She loved him but he didn't love her. He didn't even want a . . . a half-Irish brat from her. And, as he cruelly reminded her, that was certainly a possibility now.

Once upon a time he had felt desire for her, but the morning after that was satisfied, he seemed to feel only dislike for her. And she still didn't understand exactly what it was she had done wrong.

Foolishly, after they had made love, she had thought everything was right and wonderful between them. She had quickly learned how wrong her thinking was. And now she felt as though she were floundering more than ever. He spoke with contempt and must feel that contempt, and Maggie didn't know how she would bear it.

"He is handsome," Carrie continued blithely. "You never talk much about him. I know I do most of the talking, and that is about Tom, but you never seem to want to speak of Mr. Calcord. I certainly never expected him to be so — so handsome and so big! And when Tom told me he was fairly well to do, I couldn't help but wonder why you never told me!"

"I didn't know he was so wealthy. I thought he was the same as you and me and Tom, a working man. I didn't know he lived in such a house!"

"Did you know he owned part of that mine?"

Maggie's eyes grew round. "No! Does he, really?"

Carrie set her cup in its saucer and glared suspiciously at Maggie. "I swear, what do you do when you get with him, if not talk?" Magheen flushed furiously and Carrie chuckled brightly, "Not that, silly, we all try that!"

"Harvey, it looks pretty damned hopeless to me! We've blasted another twenty feet down, and still the assay tests show poor-grade ore!"

Daniel and Harvey Benson were in the newly erected shaft house of the Resurrection Mine, at the west end, which doubled as a blacksmith's shop and, at the present time, an office. The plans were to build a separate, quieter office and turn this space into a carpenter's bench.

The boardinghouse was under construction, changes in its size constantly being made as more and more men were hired.

"I know it's not looking too good at the moment, Daniel, but give it some more time. There's high-grade ore below, I just know it!"

"And do you know what each day is costing?"

"I've a pretty fair idea. I know what I'm asking, Daniel, the risk is tremendous. But each day, the quality of the ore goes a bit higher. We're not even deep, not yet."

"Harvey, some of the men at the bank became nervous and wanted to pull out of this venture when we first discovered the salting. I talked them into being patient a while longer, but how much longer, I don't know. I don't even know what to tell them anymore. And that last requisition for pumping machinery . . ."

"Daniel, I had to request it now. It will take six months or better to get it here and by then, it will be spring. As we keep blasting the shaft lower and lower, our chances of flooding during the spring runoff is too great. We'll need that pump!"

"But only if we're hauling ore."

"We'll be hauling ore or I've wasted a career in this business!"

"I hope you're right. I wrote the board last night and gave them the full explanation of why we need that equipment. We both need something substantial to back us up in this. Sometimes I think I don't give up because I'm too damned pigheaded rather than smart. I hope you don't suffer from the same delusion."

"Daniel, I won't see you give up on this mine just yet. It'd be the biggest regret you could have."

"You believe that strongly, Harvey?"

"Damned right I do."

Daniel took a deep breath. "All right, another month, and then it's got to be paying at least the wages of the men."

"Fair enough. We should be doing that." Harvey slammed his hat on his head and headed back toward the shaft.

Daniel turned his attention to the paper he held before him and quickly scanned it. The hollering of many men and the hammering of picks interrupted his concentration many times as he tackled the day's pile of correspondence. An hour passed and he lifted his palm wearily to the nape of his neck and rubbed.

He had already known what arguments Harvey would use to keep the mine going. Daniel had written them down in the letter he wrote to the board, and he had known what their response would be before he wrote them. If Daniel felt the mine was a likely investment, then he had to go for it. Daniel knew his own strengths and weaknesses, his biggest failing being his stubbornness. He probably wouldn't give up looking for silver until they were all broke or he had hit it big enough to rub Bill Lovell's face in it. Just the thought of the man and the fact of his being above the law riled Daniel.

Tossing his pen on the table, Daniel rose and stretched. He crossed to the window and looked out on the barrenness left by the mines. Surrounded by hills, each of which was covered with more mines, Carbonate Hill looked desolate. The pine trees were long gone, and the slag heaps covered whatever else had been left of the vegetation. The waste from within the bowels of the earth, when raised, left the land below which it was dumped sterile and unproductive.

The Resurrection Mine was doing its share of damage too.

Down below in the shaft, the men were taking as big a risk, if not bigger. One man would hold a steel drill while his partner drove it into the rocks with a sledgehammer. After a while, they would trade jobs. When the holes were drilled, black powder cartridges were stuffed inside, and the fuse lit. If the mine was a lucky place today, all the fuses would fire. If not, some man had to be brave enough to find out what went wrong. Harvey issued orders shortly after arriving that the charges were to be counted before any man stepped near the blasting area.

The tedious work was hauling all the debris aboveground, clearing the shaft so they might go even lower.

The work was dangerous and wearying. Daniel learned that the first few days on the job when he had joined his men in drilling and blasting and hauling.

The air was foul, the lighting near nonexistent. A candle attached to a felt hat cast only shadows. One of Daniel's first purchases was a gross of oil lanterns, and these he ordered hung every six feet. Still, the candles were necessary for close work.

The mines were damp and cold, and each man dressed accordingly. It wasn't unusual for a man gone for days at a time with a lung infection. Another reason for the expansion of the bunkhouse.

Thank God this was not Daniel's life's work.

The racket of the ore bucket being lowered broke into Daniel's thoughts and brought him back to reality. In the distance he heard Joe shouting some orders below. Dutch was heating the coals, readying the materials needed to repair a break in the spare chain that raised and lowered the ore bucket.

Daniel grabbed the correspondence he had to mail and went outside to the lean-to where his horse was stabled. It was just past noon, and he had plenty of time to mail his letters, buy a few supplies, return to the mine, and be back at his house before night fell.

Somehow in the middle of this day, he thought he should find time to see Maggie. The third banns were being read tomorrow and he supposed he should see her. Not even to himself would he admit he would see her because he wanted to.

Saturdays were always busy in the store. Magheen stood behind the dark-stained oak counter in the women's department and rang up sales on the hand-cranking register. Mr. Smith bragged that even their biggest competitor, David

110

May, didn't have one of these newfangled registers yet. Maggie was too busy to care. Between wrapping the numerous sales in brown paper and making change, she didn't even have time for lunch.

Pulling her rebellious hair from her eyes for the umpteenth time that day, she smiled at Mrs. Gentry as she passed her the freshly wrapped purchase.

The bell over the door had been ringing constantly since they had opened, and now was no exception. This time it rang to announce Mrs. Gentry's departure. Other ladies were roaming up and down the narrow aisles, inspecting the various goods for sale.

Magheen glanced up to see a very flustered Carrie hurrying toward her.

"It's happened!" she moaned aloud. Many of the customers turned to stare at her. "Oh, Maggie, get your things and get out of here! I knew that man would lead you to no good!"

"I can't leave! Mr. Smith would have me for breakfast if I left him in the lurch like this. Calm down, Carrie, and tell me what is going on."

"It's that unspeakable William Lovell," she replied huffily. "Those chickens you invested in — remember them?"

Magheen's brows rose as she nodded her head.

"Well, it appears your friend's invention of a heater didn't work so well. The fumes or the cold killed the chickens. And then he had the nerve to bring them to Leadville and sell them as freshly butchered!"

Magheen's hand went to her mouth. "No!"

"I tell you, yes. Of course the first bite and everyone realized they'd been had! So a group of the women went to the sheriff's, but he's gone for the day. Now, they've gone after Bill. You know, Maggie, it's one thing to be known for salting mines and cheating the men, but when an arrogant galloose thinks he can ruin a woman's dinner for her family, he's taken on too much!"

"Oh, no, how *could* he?" Maggie moaned.

"Maggie," Carrie spoke as though to an infant. "Get out of here. That sort of man will be putting the blame on you quick enough, if I know anything of his kind! Do you feel up to facing a crowd of irate women?"

Maggie lifted her gaze to Carrie. "I must," she replied, her hand passing over her brow. "I'm as much a part of this as Mr. Lovell. I never intended to cheat anyone. You know that, Carrie. Those people must be repaid their money. I just hope he hasn't gone and gotten rid of it already!"

"Maggie, you're a fool!"

"I'll stand and face what I've done. I won't run, Carrie. Those people will be repaid every cent."

"Those people may not care to be repaid. From what I saw, they were more intent on teaching Bill Lovell a lesson he'll not forget. I just hope they stop with him."

Maggie stepped out in front of the store and watched as a procession of irate women led William Lovell toward her. Carrie was right about that, she realized. He did not intend to shoulder the blame alone. Bill Lovell was being forced to move along with a pitchfork and cast-iron skillets. This was an angry mob he had no chance of escaping.

They stopped in front of the store, and the leader of the mob, an angry woman of middle years, demanded, "Are you Magheen Fitzgerald?"

Maggie nodded, swallowing.

"This man claims you were part of a scheme to sell putrid chickens to each of us. Do you deny this?"

"No, but —"

"Did you hear that?" The thickset woman demanded of the crowd behind her. She wore her hair in plaits coiled on top of her head. Around her waist was a dirty plaid apron, and on her feet were men's boots. "She admits to being in cahoots with Bill Lovell. Are we gonna let her get away with that?"

"No!" roared the angry response.

"But I didn't know they were putrid! I would never have gone along with such a thing!"

"Did you or did you not take our money for those birds?"

"Well, yes, Mr. Lovell gave me the money, but I gave it back to him when he said he'd take another trip to Denver and get some more."

"Oh? So you admit you planned to cheat more unsuspecting persons of their rightful cash?"

"I wasn't —"

"I've heard enough!" cried another woman in the crowd. "I say we tar and feather the both of them. We'll larn 'em to cheat decent folk!"

"I want my money back!" cried yet another woman. "I've a family to feed. We already went without one meal."

"Oh, I'm so sorry—"

"Shaddup!" roared the woman carrying the pitchfork. "Well," she demanded a moment later. "Can you give us the money or not?"

Magheen turned to look at Bill, who was looking down at his boots. "Mr. Lovell, I gave you everything I had just two days ago. Surely it's not *all* gone?"

No answer came, giving Magheen all the answer she needed. Turning to face the justifiably angry women, she spoke softly, "I don't have it now, but I will pay it back, I promise you. I have a job and I can save from my earnings—"

"Did you hear that? She ain't gonna pay us either!"

"Gertie, don't be so hard on the girl! It sounds like she's been a victim the same as the rest of us." Maggie was relieved to hear at least one person had listened to her explanation, but the logic of that argument was lost amid the anger of the women.

"I say tar 'em both. We won't tolerate cheaters like 'em around here!"

Maggie felt fingers bite into her arm as she was dragged relentlessly toward the mob. The only other mob she had seen had been on her side, the side of the Irish, against the English. And then she had felt safe, until the militia came roaring in, carrying their muskets and spurring their horses through the crowd. She had begun suffocating then, just as she was suffocating now.

"No," she cried, struggling against the other woman's hold. Her hair was free of its pins and straggling around her neck. The woman's hands tore her shirt at the shoulders, and Maggie felt her fear growing then. These people didn't want justice, they wanted revenge. And it didn't matter on whom they had their revenge, they simply wanted to hurt. She broke free of the woman, Gertie, but her hair blinded her and she ran into the midst of the crowd. Other hands and other fingers came at her until she was sobbing and screaming with fear.

"Let her go!" a voice suddenly called out.

Maggie was so hysterical she didn't recognize whose voice

it was. At first the women didn't obey, but when the man reached into his pocket and pulled out some coins and tossed them onto the dirty, snow-laden street, they began to listen. Some of the women went down on their hands and knees to sift for the coins Daniel Calcord had thrown.

"Let her go and I will compensate you, now. You may do what you like with Mr. Lovell."

"We spent a dollar apiece on those chickens!" Gertie shouted. "Can you pay every one of us?"

"I can and I will, but not until you've let the girl go."

The crowd, mollified at getting its money back, calmed down. They released Maggie, and she stood sobbing until Carrie came to her assistance.

Daniel peeled off dollar bills and satisfied every claim, even Gertie's. She claimed she had bought twenty-five of the chickens. Daniel was in no mood to argue.

They even lost interest in Bill Lovell. As soon as the more militant of the women had left, Bill sneaked off, his eyes darting about him as though he couldn't believe his luck.

"Mr. Lovell," Daniel shouted at his retreating back. Bill turned momentarily, barely slowing his speed. "I suggest you stay out of town. I'm in full sympathy with the women, though I think you should be hanged rather than tarred and feathered." Bill turned and ran.

Maggie was a mess. She stood at the front of the store, her shirt in tatters, her skirt bedraggled, and her hair wildly askew. Tears ran unchecked down her cheeks. Carrie held a consoling arm about her.

"Miss Hutchen, will you fetch her coat . . . and please tell your manager I've taken Maggie home? She's in no shape to work this afternoon."

Carrie nodded as Daniel dismounted, helped Magheen onto the saddle, and climbed up behind her. A moment later, Carrie returned, Maggie's coat in her hands. Daniel accepted it and placed it over Maggie's shoulders. Reaching into his breast pocket, he handed the still sobbing Magheen his handkerchief. "Here, use this." His voice was gruff.

She accepted it and wiped her eyes and nose. Definitely she sniffled. "You're always saving my hide, and I'm always thanking you."

"If you're mixed up with people like William Lovell, you'd

better carry a shotgun at all times," he growled angrily. "How'd you meet him?"

"In the store. He made a purchase and we got to talking. He needed an investor—"

"Another get-rich-quick scheme, Maggie? Won't your greedy little mind ever learn? Or is your greedy little heart bigger than your little mind?"

Magheen sniffled. The accusation didn't surprise her any. She supposed there was some substance to it. Maybe she was greedy. Her mind whirled while Daniel continued his reproaches. "Maybe you and Bill Lovell are alike, each interested only in your own welfare. You can take a man's weakness and turn it to your profit, can't you, Maggie? You know how to hit a man when he's down and leave him stranded when he needs something from you. I should have let that crowd take you, maybe then you'd have learned a lesson. Maybe then you'd treat people as they should be treated, not used, which is all you understand!"

"What are you talking about?" she replied, finally nettled. "I've never used you or anyone. I wanted to make a profit, of course I did! That's why I gave him the money. You want to make a profit too, don't you? Or why do you bother with a mine at all?" They had stopped before a house.

"Here's your home, Maggie." The words were clipped, spoken as hard as his face looked. "You can get down now and go inside and hide. Tomorrow you can start scheming again. But remember this, next time, I might not be around to bail you out of your trouble, and you might be on your own. From what I've seen, you can't handle much of anything, let alone trouble. Take care, Magheen. I think I'm lucky to know what you're like before we speak the vows. I'll never trust you, Maggie. Never."

She slipped from the saddle and stood, watching him turn and ride off. Inside the house, she went to her room and spent the rest of the afternoon crying.

Chapter Seven

Daniel's ire was still sparking as he rode toward the center of town. Of all the people in the world for Maggie to be involved with, Bill Lovell was the last one he had expected. To find her in cahoots with that lowlife shook the almighty pride out of him. Well, maybe she and William Lovell had more in common than he thought. And just maybe that common ground was the two of them plotting to take advantage of him.

To think he had been feeling badly over the way they last parted. He had even begun to think he had been too hard on her, that maybe *he* had the problem and carried too big a chip on his shoulder.

And then he had ridden by that store and heard her name coupled with Bill Lovell's!

All those women were having at her, and all she could do was cry and try to explain the unexplainable to a bunch of women who weren't about to listen. Daniel was still shaking with the fear he had felt when he first saw her predicament. The fear for her had come first, followed by shock at her partner in crime and then anger. It was the anger that had won, and this he had vented on her in front of the Howards' house.

Daniel felt like a fool.

He had to get her out of his system. The third banns would be read tomorrow; by next Saturday they would be wed. And if he wasn't careful, the Irish chit would be running him around in circles even more than she was doing right now.

As if it wasn't bad enough that Bill Lovell had stolen ten thousand dollars from him, his own fiancée had to go and

116

join up with Lovell in his damn conning schemes!

Daniel was moving slowly now, the crowds on Harrison Street being so thick on a late Saturday afternoon that man and beast couldn't easily pass through. Outside the Comique Theater, a band was playing a song Daniel had never heard and hoped never to hear again. Scantily dressed women were turning blue from the cold as they stood by the entrance and tried to entice any miners who seemed interested to come inside. One of them, a petite blonde with curly hair, winked broadly at Daniel and crooked her little finger. Daniel rode on.

Across the street a Coliseum hawker bellowed out, "Waitress girls in the shortest clothes in Leadville!" At the end of the block was a great crowd of men and gaudily dressed women watching a trapeze performance. Another block down, a wagon faced yet another crowd. A girl was singing from the rear of it. A man in a black frock coat and wide-brimmed hat slipped through the audience, hawking his latest cure-all.

It seemed impossible for the mob to grow denser, yet it did.

Finally, Daniel realized he had spent the entire afternoon going from one end of this throng of persons to the other. So why not take advantage of the evening? Stopping before the nearest bar, the Texas House, he dismounted and tied his mare to the rail. Once inside, he found it almost as noisy as the street.

A piano stood in one corner, the sign above it reading, "Please do not shoot the pianist. He is doing his best." The poor pianist was pounding out indistinguishable notes that were barely heard above the din.

In the center of the sawdust floor were several couples dancing.

The huge oak bar stretched along the north wall. Behind the bar were shelves of kegs filled with whiskey, ale, and bourbon. Other shelves held various sizes of glasses. A sign between kegs read "Pay as You Go." Another said "50 Cents a Dance."

Gambling tables were arranged beneath the upper landing and stairs, each chair already filled with gamesters absorbed in the rattle of the dice. They were an incongruous bunch.

Most of them were dirty and bearded, still wearing the flannel shirts and baggy pants they had spent the day mining in, but a few were slicked-down cardsharps, wearing polished boots, black tails, and white pin-striped shirts and sporting gold watches.

Since he couldn't go home yet, all Daniel was interested in was washing the problems of the day from his mind. Stepping to the bar, he ordered a whiskey and tossed a coin onto the polished wood surface. The whiskey tasted vile, and he decided then and there to fork over a little money for his liquor, and maybe he would survive to a ripe old age.

As he stood at the bar drowning his worries, he glanced often into the mirror overhead and saw many of the dancing couples go up the stairs. Always there was another tawdry woman to replace the one who had left. Some of them were just girls of fifteen or sixteen. The dance floor grew more crowded and more rambunctious as the evening progressed.

It was late when a scuffle came from the gaming area. As Daniel turned to see what was happening, an ill-dressed miner got shakily to his feet, gun in hand, and threatened the dealer. From beneath the table came the flash of a pistol shot. Dropping his gun, the miner cried out and reached in anguish for his shoulder. The dealer lifted his hand, which was holding the still smoking pistol, and rested it on the table.

"Any others?" the quick-acting dealer demanded. When no one answered, the game resumed much as before, and the wounded miner left the establishment, his pockets thinner. The din returned.

And he had thought New York was strange, Daniel mused, sipping from yet another drink. Nothing could compare to the frenzied activity of Leadville.

Finally he roused himself to leave, but his stride was none too straight. The crowd in the street had thinned with the loss of daylight, but the noise remained unabated.

Daniel swung himself into his saddle, swaying slightly, and walked his mare around the corner to Second Street.

These houses were finer, the music from within nearly recognizable. A fine coach stood before one of them, and a finely garbed man descended from inside the coach and strode to the building. The front door of the house was opened by a Negro, who stood aside and motioned to the man to enter.

Daniel may have been a bit inebriated, but he had been around long enough to be familiar with this sort of house. As though to confirm his thoughts, a red light appeared in the window on the second floor.

And this might just be what I need to rid myself of thoughts of that infuriating Irish, Daniel mused silently. Irish! Where did Joe say that Irish girl was going to work? Maybe she's got hair a deep red-gold and eyes as green as a sea of grass. Maybe the sweetness of her voice sends shivers down my spine and makes me want her all the more. Maybe one Irish can satisfy me instead of the other Irish . . .

Daniel stumbled from his horse and ascended the stairs where he began banging on the front door. The same black man answered, his face nowhere near so friendly now.

"Go 'way! We don't 'low no white trash in this establishment!"

"No, no, no!" Daniel replied genially. "I'm looking for the Irish girl. Don't you have one here? You have to! Everybody's Irish in Leadville!"

The black man tried to gently coerce Daniel back through the front door. "No Irish here," he stated flatly. "Try Mollie May's or Sallie Purple's. Mebbee Darlin' Lil's."

Daniel's eyes shone brightly. "Darlin' Lil's, that's it!"

"Four houses down. And get your horse off the lawn!"

"Happy to!" Daniel answered, tossing the man a coin.

His muddled mind barely managed the count of the houses.

The fourth house was a brick two-story, with a huge front porch wrapping around it, and double front doors. White lace curtains peeped through the glass inserts in the doors, and even from a distance, Daniel could see that the house was packed with men. A pianoforte played in the background, accompanied by gales of laughter.

For the first time Daniel could remember, he hesitated. Niggling at him was his conscience and the memory of Magheen offering herself shyly to him.

The front door opened and a large woman stood there, beckoning him in. In spite of the claims made by the hawker at the Coliseum, Daniel knew she wore the shortest dress in Leadville. It was little more than a black corset, plunging above and below.

"Come on in, honey," she taunted. "My ladies don't bite, unless you want 'em to. Come on, get off that little horsey and tie him up. That's right, tie him tight so he can't get loose. Now move your feet in my direction. Keep on coming, you're nearly here."

Daniel knew she was having a good laugh at his expense, but he was too drunk to care. At the top of the porch stairs, she curved her arms into his and pulled him inside the smoke-filled hallway. A group of men watched her teasing manner, laughing at who they were certain was nothing but a tenderfoot, until one of the men recognized Daniel.

"Mr. Calcord!" Joe Simmons uttered, astonished, as he straightened and moved toward the man who employed him. "What are you doing here?"

"I came to see the Irish girl. Where is she?" Daniel spoke thickly, self-consciously, trying to hide the effect of the liquor. He glanced around the room, searching for red hair and green eyes.

"The Irish? Are you sure? I mean, you're affianced and all. Do you . . . Should you . . . "

"I'm sure. I do and I should. Now, where is she?"

The buxom blonde still held on to Daniel's arm, and now she rubbed her upper torso against him. "You mean Kate Nelligan, honey? What's the matter, you only go for Irish girls?"

"Daniel, we better get home," Joe quietly opined, thinking he might extricate his employer from what Joe knew was about to become an awkward situation. A man didn't become engaged to marry a priest's sister and then go around visiting houses of ill repute, not if he wanted to stay engaged anyway. Of course, Joe had been wondering about that engagement ever since it had been announced so sudden-like and all.

Until tonight he had always considered Daniel an abstemious man.

"No, not until I see the Irish girl!" Daniel insisted.

A trim but neatly curving woman joined them then. The white lace of her almost transparent peignoir contrasted with the deep black of her hair. Her lips were a ripe, tempting red. She lounged against the doorway leading into the parlor, bending a knee forward. She certainly knew how to present her best side to a man.

Joe's mouth slid open.

"No, not her . . ." Daniel began, about to protest that Irish girls had red hair.

What lost the battle Daniel was waging within himself was when she smiled, her blue eyes crinkling at the corners, and said in a classic Gaelic brogue, "Good evening to you, sir. You've been guzzling like a serpent the whole night, I see. Don't you think you should come inside where 'tis warm and I can make you even warmer?"

Kate put his hand in hers and tugged. Daniel followed the bewitching Gael through a parlor, which he barely noticed, and up thickly carpeted stairs. A tinkling chandelier penetrated his foggy state, as did the sounds of a door opening and closing behind them. Suddenly the din ceased its overwhelming proportions, and he realized they were alone in her bedroom.

She smiled, her fingers going to the ribbon between her breasts, which was the only thing keeping the peignoir up, and tugged. The white lace floated to the floor. Below this was a silken gown of Grecian lines, very short and slit up to her hips.

"Don't you want to be more comfortable, guv?" she said softly, moving to him and working the buttons on his coat, her face slipping to a spot very near his. Practiced hands ran the length of his torso and hips. When they would have moved to a more intimate spot, Daniel grabbed her hands and stopped her.

Blue eyes met his, and he could have sworn he read impatience there. Of course, each lost moment meant lost money.

The cursed comparisons began then. Her black hair was nowhere near as soft and fetching as Maggie's red-gold tresses. The accent was similar, but Maggie's was just a bit softer, a touch sweeter. And no eyes glinted like Maggie's teasing green ones. This Kate was pretty, but Maggie . . . Maggie was beautiful, especially when she came to him with eagerness. She was eager to learn, eager to give, eager to please. Eager to love. Daniel shook his head to clear it. He couldn't do this. In spite of that damn Bill Lovell, Maggie Fitzgerald was in his head and in his heart. After sharing that

121

earth-shaking love with Maggie, he couldn't do this for mere money. Any pleasure would be forced.

So, in spite of his drunken state, Daniel found himself thinking clearly for the first time in weeks.

He just wished he had been smart enough to figure it out sooner. His head was hurting, he was tired and hungry, and he knew damned good and well he would not make it home from this house. Leaving now and going to a hotel would make him a laughingstock of Leadville, if William Lovell hadn't already.

"What's the matter, honey? Can't you do it?" the Irish girl mocked. "Does likker make you incapable?"

"How much do you want for the whole night?" Daniel asked, seemingly cold sober now.

Kate swayed against him, smiling. "Are you sure you can handle it?"

Daniel stepped away from her, grimacing. "Hell, I don't want you, I want the bed. I'll pay you for the whole night just to sleep here. Think of it as a paid vacation."

Kate Nelligan wasn't easily insulted. She had been in this business too long for sensitivity, but her practical streak had grown by leaps and bounds. When she first started in this business, she had been a child and thought it would be just for a little while. That little while had grown into years. Now she was resigned to a life of different men every night, feeling used and old and dirty. But she would give anything for a night off.

"Three hundred dollars."

Daniel took out his wallet, peeled off three hundred-dollar bills, and handed them to her.

Abruptly she nodded. "But you can't tell Lil about this."

"That's right, and you can't say a word either."

For the first time she smiled naturally. "Wouldn't do either of our reputations much good, would it?"

"Mine would sink below rock bottom," he admitted dryly, unbuttoning his cuffs.

Kate eyed him curiously as Daniel sat on the bed and removed his boots. For the first time she saw him as a person and not as just one of her multitude of customers. He wasn't a half-bad-looking gent, either.

"Why? Don't you think I'm pretty enough?"

Daniel's head tilted as he peered up at her. Suddenly he dropped his leg and met her questioning gaze squarely.

"How you look has nothing to do with it. I came here tonight to forget someone. And then I realized I'd never forget her. No matter how much time, no matter how much distance I put between us, I will not forget her."

Lucky girl, Kate thought. I could have used someone like you in my life years ago.

"I can get us some foot, if you'd like."

Daniel was stripped of his socks and boots and to the waist. He shook his head. "Not for me, not right now. Thanks anyway. Order some for yourself if you're hungry, but what I want most is sleep. I'll eat in the morning." He dropped to the bed and was almost instantly asleep.

Kate pulled the blanket over him.

Anne Howard tied the ribbons of her gray bonnet beneath her chin, her eyes flicking over Magheen. Full-bodied lips compressed tightly as she spoke. "The things I do to get this church built! Your brother's the one who should do this sort of visiting. Soliciting donations indeed!"

"He's never had such a perfect excuse to get out of a bit of work," Magheen responded, pulling on her gloves. At the moment she was not feeling too sympathetic with Patrick. This task held no more appeal for her than it held for Anne. "His leg will take several more weeks of healing for the muscles to hold his weight."

"In the meantime it's our reputations on the line! Why he thinks he needs money from the likes of Lil Amundson is beyond me!"

"To quote Patrick quoting someone else, 'Never look a gift horse in the mouth.'"

Anna's mouth twisted. "At the very least he might have said something biblical!"

Maggie smiled. "I think he tried, but no matter how hard he searched his mind, he couldn't think of anything biblical to quote."

Anna preened before the hall mirror. "What do you think? If I wore a veil, would that be too obvious?"

"Anna, you're the envy of half the ladies in town with your

123

gray lambswool coat, you are! Everyone will recognize that, if not yourself. Besides, one of my brothers, though I can't remember which one at the moment, taught me 'twas much better to face a dreaded task with bravado than to shrink cowardly from it. He said if you act as though you know what you're doing, the rest of the world won't think twice about it!" Maggie's eyes peered about the room to make certain they were quite alone. "Besides, aren't you just the teeniest bit curious? About Miss Amundson I mean? 'Tis rumored she has diamonds hanging from her chandeliers and a great, huge ruby adorning her forehead!"

"Balderdash! She's a lot like the rest of us, growing older with each passing day."

"Jakers! Then we haven't a thing to fear, have we?"

Anna's hands ceased their task of patting her hair in place under the hat, and she turned to look at Magheen. The wee Irish was looking pretty as a picture today, all dressed up in her Sunday finery. The long blue jacket, though a little worn, clung to her slender form, the hobbled skirt of a lighter blue below it billowing around her knees. On her head was a wide-brimmed black hat with one silvery feather plume dangling, and silver ribbons holding it in place beneath her chin. She pulled on a voluminous black cape, which covered all this finery except the hat, and stood silently, waiting to leave.

Anna wished she knew what brought the sadness to that dear face and why Maggie had spent most of the night before crying. Maggie didn't seem to want to tell, and Anna had to refrain from prying. It probably had something to do with that inconsiderate fiancé of hers, she decided mutinously.

"Shall we walk," Anna questioned briskly, "or dare we risk a carriage? If we're caught in a mob of people, we could be there all day."

"I favor the walk. I feel I spend most of my days cooped up, and that's what I love about Sundays. I can do as I please."

"Then walk we shall. Just be ready to run if Marsha Gibbons should see us entering Darlin' Lil's!"

"Oh, no! I never thought of Mrs. Gibbons! If she sees us, we'll never be able to show our faces at the meetings of the Rosary Society again!"

Both women looked at each other and, at the same moment, cried, "Let's get the veils!" Still laughing, they linked arms and strode from the house.

The day was sunny and fine, only a wee bite in the air, as Maggie phrased it, "to make life interesting." The women had gone to the nine-thirty Mass, returning home in time to help Agnes prepare a late brunch for the household. When Mr. Howard heard of their plans for the afternoon, he eagerly offered his assistance, which Mrs. Howard was quick to refuse.

Their lengthy trek took them past many blocks of other homes, past cobbler's and milliner's shops and, finally, to the infamous row of houses that was their destination.

" 'Tis very quiet here."

"I don't believe many of the ladies here rise early enough to attend afternoon Mass, let alone a morning one," Anna said tartly. "In fact, Joshua told me these places don't even close down until sunup! Can you imagine that? Staying up all night and sleeping all day?"

"No," Maggie answered, glancing curiously about her.

"Here we are. Straighten your hat, Maggie."

Her bustle shaking, Anne Howard led the way up the steps. At the front door she lifted the brass knocker and let it drop twice.

Daniel's head was splitting. With a moan, he sat up, but the room spun wildly around him. That was when Daniel remembered why he didn't like to drink. A movement came from the bed, and Daniel glanced down and saw Kate Nelligan. And that was the moment when the memory of the previous night came rushing to the fore, and Daniel gave an even louder groan. The dark-haired Irish girl was practically naked beneath the sheets and even now was taking most of his half.

Very cautiously he rose. Hunched over, he padded across the room to the washstand and dipped his hands into the ceramic bowl that held the icy water left from the day before. Splashing this onto his face, he moaned the louder and reached blindly for a towel. His fingers found one hanging from the towel bar on the side of the washstand. After drying his face, he dropped his head to the towel and rested there for a long while.

He had done some daft things in his lifetime, this one being one of the most daft. Whatever he had thought he was getting into when he stopped for that first drink last night, he had gotten into something a whole lot worse.

Vaguely he remembered the Irish girl's amusement when she thought him incapable of bedding her. It was a good thing he made it a practice never to worry about his manhood or he might be having serious doubts about that now in addition to his other worries.

All he wanted was to get dressed, find his horse, and go home. He wasn't sure of the time, but he could feel it was way past time for Mass.

Oh, well, he needed to calm down after yesterday, and Maggie probably needed to calm down too. What he was tempted to do, once this blasted headache was gone, was to go find William Lovell and show him in a very physical way why he had best leave Magheen alone.

Dropping the towel, he struggled to open his eyes wide. The light hurt his eyes painfully, and he squinted, thinking about hiding his face in the towel again. Instead he lifted his eyes and searched the room for his boots and pants. The pants were at the foot of the bed, and he hobbled into them. The boots were more difficult, stashed way under the bed where Daniel had to crawl to get at them. He cursed loudly as he bumped his head on the way out.

That woke Kate, who didn't seem to be at her best in the morning either, and she mumbled a few cursing words, tossed a pillow at Daniel's head, and made him feel as though she had hit him with a rolling pin.

Daniel tucked his shirt inside his pants, wincing all the while. What a way to start the day! At least it couldn't get any worse.

What Daniel remembered as looking softly enchanting last night, in the broad light of day, merely looked garish. The chandeliers, and there were four that Daniel counted as he left the bedroom and descended the stairs, needed dusting badly. The red velvet hangings were a bit shopworn, the dark oak furniture smooth and worn from use. Daniel swore never to visit a brothel during daylight hours again, amending that to just never again.

The knocker sounded twice.

Daniel set his Stetson on his head, his palms curving the sides of the brim. He was at the final landing when the front door was opened to allow two ladies to enter. He paid them little heed until he heard the Gaelic brogue spoken in soft tones.

"Miss Amundson? I'm Magheen Fitzgerald, Father Patrick's sister. It is so nice to meet such a generous benefactor of our church! This is my friend, Anne Howard. We've come in Father Patrick's stead. You must have heard about his frightful accident of a few nights ago. He still is unable to travel."

"Yes, please, do come in," Lil Amundson spoke in her deep tones, smiling all the while. "The girl is just getting the tea ready. I do hope you've the time to join me. It's not very often I receive proper ladies from the town." Lil was dressed in a sober gray morning gown, looking unlike the madam of the night before.

"That would be very nice, thank you," Magheen responded, her guilty conscience tripping her tongue as she remembered the fun she and Anna had had at this woman's expense. She smiled, her hand reaching to untie the ribbons of her hat. At that moment she spied Daniel, who was in a dead stop on the stairs.

His hand remained on his vest pocket, as though he had been straightening the garb.

Maggie's smile faded, her expressive eyes showing only puzzlement. A moment later, she seemed to have the pieces of the puzzle together and her eyes swept closed. The color rushed from her face as she took a deep breath, steeling herself to look at him once more.

Daniel took a step toward her, his hand outstretched. "Maggie," he croaked.

Her eyes flew open, the deep green translucent through the moisture filling them. Feverishly she shook her head and stepped back, almost as though she were afraid to have him touch her.

Daniel wanted to carry her from here and wipe that expression of stupefied hurt from her face, explain to her that nothing had happened. That he couldn't make love with another woman while his head was filled with a need for her.

Of course, he couldn't say any of that, not with so many

127

prying ears.

Maggie's agitation was clear in her shallow breathing, in the jerking of her back as she turned to Miss Amundson and held out shaking fingers. "I'm so sorry," she said, her voice near to breaking, "but . . . but do you mind if I come back later? I—I can't . . ."

Daniel hurried to her side. "Maggie, let me explain."

She could only numbly shake head, the tears falling freely now. "Anne . . ."

Anne took her by the arm, her normally good-natured expression now filled with concern for her friend. Briskly she said, "We'll come back later when you feel better, Maggie. Good day to you, Miss Amundson." Her eyes flashed anger as they moved onto Daniel. "And to you, Mr. Calcord."

He trailed them down the steps. "I can explain. It's not quite as it seems."

"Nothing and *no one* is quite as he seems, Mr. Calcord," Anna responded pointedly, hurrying Maggie toward home. "I think you do need to speak with Miss Fitzgerald, but not just now. Do you understand?"

"Maggie . . . Maggie, say something!"

Her fingers covered her eyes and her head shook in answer. "Not now, Daniel! Please, not now!"

"Here, I'll get my horse. At least you don't have to walk so far home . . ."

Her answer was an anguished sob, and she hurried to be on her way long before Daniel found his animal. Anne hustled behind her.

He followed them all the way home, waiting at the corner until they were safely inside. A few minutes later, Joshua Howard stepped outside and crossed over to him. "I'm sorry, Mr. Calcord, but Magheen won't see you today. To tell the truth, she's in no fit shape to see anyone."

"I'll wait."

Joshua's eyes flickered over Daniel. "For a man who couldn't even take so much as an evening to pay his respects to his affianced, you've plenty of time on your hands now. Seems to me you're playing a mighty strange game with Maggie, getting her hopes up and letting her down with disappointment after disappointment. I'd say you don't love that girl as much as she deserves, or"—Joshua's eyes narrowed at the expression on Daniel's face — "your're afraid of loving her. That's it, isn't it? You're afraid of her?"

Daniel's head went back and he gave a gruff laugh. "Afraid of Maggie? That's like being afraid of a baby who can barely make a decent fist!"

"Or afraid of commitment and loving," Joshua answered softly, straightening his stance and removing his hat to scratch at his balding pate. "Well, I hope you're not too late in discovering you love her more than you fear her. Take my advice, and give her a chance to cool down. She's hurt now, and Anne is angry enough to string you up, should you think to come inside. And I still have a healthy fear of my wife! Good day to you, Mr. Calcord."

"Wait!" Daniel bellowed and Joshua turned to him. "What time should I come back tomorrow?"

"She goes to work at seven, doesn't get home until after five o'clock. Dinner's at six, and Maggie helps with the cleaning up afterwards. She's not free till about seven in the evening. And I think tomorrow is catechism night. She may not be free at all tomorrow, Mr. Calcord."

Daniel frowned. "Just tell her I'll be here before dinner."

Joshua nodded and tipped his hat, then headed for home.

Daniel was reluctant to leave. He glanced up, at the highest window in the house, and saw a flash of blue color.

Maggie.

The curtains fluttered as they were drawn tightly closed.

The following morning he rose early. As he traveled to the top of Carbonate Hill, he saw the low-riding clouds that gave Leadville its nickname of "Cloud City." They hung wispily over the town, touching the tops of the highest buildings.

In his office, Daniel pulled coveralls over his clothing and donned one of the felt hats with a candle atop it. A moment later and in spite of Harvey's objections, he was lowered into the shaft of the mine, where he planned to help set the charges to make the mine deeper.

With so many matters weighing on his mind, he knew only one way to settle any of them, and that was by taking action, not by sitting around and waiting for things to straighten out on their own. His efforts might help the problem with the mine, and tonight he would see Maggie and settle their differences.

She might be trickier to handle than the dynamite.

Daniel rode into town early and waited across the street from the Emporium. A few minutes past five o'clock, Magheen and Carrie came out of the store and headed in the direction of the Howards' home. Their voluminous cloaks hid most of them, but Daniel would have recognized the red tresses and that straw hat anywhere. Their skirts touched the planked wooden sidewalks, flaring widely and showing a peep of petticoat as the girls moved. The black boots they wore were sturdy and had only a touch of heel for fashion.

They were well into their steady pace when Magheen heard the steady clip-clopping of horse's hooves behind her. Surprise lit her eyes when she glanced back and found Daniel, perched on his horse, following them. Carrie turned to see what caught her attention, her hand capturing Maggie's when she recognized Daniel. "I'll go on. You speak with him, Maggie."

Maggie nodded and Carrie hurried on. As Daniel reached her, he studied her face, not encouraged by the serious expression he found there. Always before, Maggie had had a ready smile for him. Not today, though. Dismounting, he held the reins of his horse in one hand and walked beside her.

Neither spoke for a while. A residential section was reached where the sidewalk ended and only dirty ice remained. Magheen had to watch her step. The houses thinned here, and they could speak with a degree of privacy.

"Daniel . . ."

"Maggie . . ."

Both spoke at the same time, Daniel relenting in a gentlemanly fashion and saying, "You first. But I want the chance to explain about Saturday night."

Maggie was shaking her head. "It doesn't matter, Daniel. You're a grown man, and I certainly have no right to judge you. I was shocked and upset . . ."

"You were hurt."

At that Maggie gave a wan smile. "Yes, I was hurt. But I've done a lot of thinking since yesterday, Daniel, and I've come to the conclusion that I have no right to be hurt by whatever you do. Patrick was wrong to force you into agreeing to marry me, and I was wrong in allowing him to do it.

130

You wanted to marry no one, you made that perfectly plain while we were in the cabin. And nothing happened . . ."

"Not in the cabin, it didn't. It has since."

"Yes," she answered softly. "It has since. I must apologize for that too. Something went terribly wrong, and I don't understand what . . ."

"Nothing went wrong, Maggie," he spoke earnestly.

Maggie dropped her gaze to the sidewalk. "It's very kind of you to say that, Daniel, and you have often been very kind to me."

Daniel began to get angry then. She thought he spoke words only to make her feel better? Didn't she *know* how good the loving was between them? Was she stupid?

"But kindness," she continued, "is not a foundation for a good marriage."

His hand on her arm stopped her. "What are you saying?"

"I'm saying the marriage is off. I should never have—"

"The hell with the should-never-haves!" His lips thinned and the words were gritted through his teeth. "You could be carrying my child right now. We'll be married. We have to be married!"

"No, no, we don't. There is no child."

"Look at me, Maggie. What do you mean, there is no child? How do you know?"

"I . . . I . . ." Her mouth clamped shut, and the straw hat threatened to tumble in her agitation. "I just know, that's all! Get your hands off me! I'm not yours to manhandle anymore!"

"Have you . . . Have you had your monthly flux?" he demanded.

"Oh!" she gasped, slapping his hands away. Tearing away from him, she turned to glare at him from the distance of a few feet. "You ill-mannered . . . member of the landed gentry! I should have known we were too different from the very first! I would never speak of such a thing with a man! Have you no brains working in your head, to come out and ask me such a question? An indecent son of the devil, you are!"

"You'll still marry me, Magheen. I'll go to your brother right now and tell him how you've tried to break it off! He'll not let you, especially not once I've told him that I've com-

131

promised you even more than at the cabin! See what he says then!"

"Even my brother can't force me to marry against my will! And why are you fighting this so? Yesterday and Saturday you would have given anything to be free of marrying me. You never wanted it, you said so! You made that plain to me, to my brother, to my friends! So what makes you so angry now, the fact that I'm the one not wanting it now? Is being rejected so new to you that you can't stand it? Get used to it, Daniel Calcord! I, Magheen Fitzgerald, reject you! I refuse to marry you! There! How does it feel, Daniel? Does it make you feel sick to your stomach and want to run to a place where you can be alone and cry? That's what it does to me! Good-bye, Daniel Calcord, and good riddance!"

Daniel scowled, stuffing his fine Stetson back on his head, and mounted. The horse skittered backward at the rough handling of the reins. "I'm going to see your brother now. But I promise you this, Magheen, you'll be damned sorry for your words this day! I vow you'll be begging me to forgive you!"

"Never! Blast you, Daniel Calcord!" She spoke the words venomously, but Daniel was too far down the road to hear. And headed he was in the direction of the new church, not toward his mine. So he truly meant to face Patrick, did he? So well and good. Her mind was made up, and no one's pressure would change it. She would not add to her misery by marrying a man who thought so little of her he would visit a house of ill repute rather than see her.

All the long walk home, her heart ached something fierce. If only Daniel would tell her what she had done wrong.

Chapter Eight

Late October brought with it numbing cold and howling winds. Especially vulnerable were the bare mining hills to the east of Leadville. The trees had long been stripped from the earth, and the cavernous valleys acted as a channel for the wind, throwing it wild and rampant against the mines and the hills, and against any man foolish enough to be in its path.

Daniel was determined to continue with the blasting, though little seemed to be accomplished by it. He and his men took alternating shifts in the mine, warming between each shift in front of the potbellied stove in the newly completed bunkhouse.

Daniel had practically moved into the bunkhouse with the men, so determined was he to find the vein quickly. And to work enough hours to forget the red-headed Irish girl.

Each night he tumbled into a bunk and each morning, before dawn, he was downing coffee, eggs, and potatoes in preparation for another day of pounding, chiseling, and blasting. The work was hard and tiring, but the days flew by in swift succession.

The latest assay tests had come back, and the ore they were shipping was a higher quality than before, but not quite high enough to cover costs. Still, it was enough to keep the investors momentarily satisfied and the men paid.

So far, the only things warm about the winter were the miners' frayed tempers. Too many near accidents, too many defective blasting caps, too many near fights with each other and with other miners had tempers flaring at record rates.

Daniel grew leaner and tougher during those weeks. The men began to wonder what was in his mind to be going at such a relentless pace. The man he drove hardest was himself.

Even Harvey began to wonder if he hadn't pushed too hard to keep the mine open. Daniel could sell and recoup at least twenty percent of the investment. If they kept going and failed, he and the other investors might lose everything.

On Saturday nights, the men went into town and to visit the saloons, the gaming halls, the brothels. Daniel returned to his home and completed the reams of paperwork he had neglected all week. Even from this distance he kept his Denver law practice going, and his clients required correspondence.

Harvey tried more than once to convince Daniel to go into Leadville with them, but Daniel always refused. He had had enough of the seedy side of Leadville to last him a lifetime.

Immediately after arguing so deeply with Maggie, he had gone to Father Patrick's rooms, searching for the priest, and had finally found him at the construction site of the new church. Daniel had set about trying to get the priest on his side in the argument. In spite of what Magheen had said, he knew she would listen to whatever her brother counseled. Father Patrick had listened, mulling Daniel's words over, one eye on Daniel all the while. Finally he had shaken his head.

"You seem to be in the habit of saving either my life or Magheen's. For that I owe you a debt of thanks," the priest had begun carefully. "But if Maggie's made up her mind, there's nothing I can do or say. She's always been strong-headed and . . . and generally she's right, Mr. Calcord. Especially about herself." Patrick's eyes had been clear and direct as they met Daniel's. "If she believes a marriage between the two of you can't work, then probably it can't. I'm sure she didn't come to the decision lightly, for I know how highly Maggie thinks of you. She's never said as much, but I believe she loves you; at least, once she did.

"Of course she's had a lot of time for thinking since then. You really didn't seem to care for her feelings a whole lot, and, it seems to me, you went out of your way to ignore her. I think you hurt my sister, Mr. Calcord. Maybe her love wasn't so deep as to survive that. Maybe she learned in the meantime that what she felt for you was not enough to support a marriage.

"Maggie deserves a good marriage and a good man. You're a good man, Mr. Calcord, that I know and Maggie knows.

But maybe you're just not right for her to marry. I'm sorry her refusal comes as such a disappointment. Somehow, I never thought you would care so much; you didn't seem to."

"I want to marry her, Father Patrick," Daniel had quietly insisted.

"I can see that you do, now. But it is Maggie's decision. Her marriage will last her lifetime, that's the kind of woman she is. She'll give her husband everything in her, undying loyalty and love. That's also the kind of woman she is. Maybe she decided you weren't that kind of man. And I'm not one to be arguing over such a serious decision.

"Maybe I was in the wrong to make it seem so important that the two of you marry. I keep forgetting that this is America, Colorado even, and that people aren't quite the sticklers they are in Ireland for doing the proper thing."

The priest had frowned and shaken his head as he turned away from Daniel. "I want whatever makes Maggie happy. And if she says you aren't the man, then you aren't. I sympathize with your loss. Magheen is very special to me too, though I admit I might be biased as she is my sister."

Daniel had listened closely, thinking all the while about the rest of his threat to Maggie, that he would tell the priest about the night they spent together making love. Father Patrick would have forced the marriage then. But when it came down to it, Daniel hadn't been able to do so. As he listened to the priest speak, it had struck him for the first time that maybe she really didn't want to marry him. Maybe his thoughtlessness had cost him Magheen.

He wondered if she had spoken the truth about the child.

It was just too damn bad he had to go and fall in love with her when it was too late.

So Daniel had returned home, determined to do whatever it took to forget her. And most days he was fine. He kept himself so busy he didn't have time to think, much less miss her. And if he grew thinner and more distant, that was part of the cure. Whenever she intruded on his thoughts, he determinedly set about thinking of matters more practical, more within his control.

Magheen had never been his to control.

So he decided that if the mine didn't strike by spring, he would take his losses and recommend that the rest of the investors do the same. He wouldn't regret coming to Leadville, he had learned too much here. A part of him would always regret losing Maggie, but nothing would really change much in his life. He would continue in his law practice much as before, sit on the board of directors of the bank just as before. In all, he would live his life much as before.

And since he had never known a life with Maggie, how could he ever regret losing what he didn't understand? But she would regret losing him. By God, she would!

What other man could make her tremble so in his arms? Or give her so much pleasure?

Then he remembered her pain. He would give the whole of that damned mine if he could walk away from Maggie and think of her smiling and teasing as she used to do, instead of seeing her pale from the pain he had caused her.

That was his biggest regret.

"Oh, Patrick, it's perfect!" Magheen cried as they walked through the rectory. Plaster walls were being erected, the plaster coming from the first gypsum deposit found west of the Mississippi River, in a small Colorado town named Loveland.

"That's what I thought. I've always wanted to live in a house just behind the church. Imagine, Sunday mornings and I can walk to Mass and not have to ride ten miles. I'll be spoiled, I swear I will be!"

"A spoiling you deserve, Paddie. Whenever I think of your injuries and how close you came to dying . . ." Her whole body shuddered with the remembrance.

"The Good Lord didn't see fit to take me yet, Magheen. He slowed me down some" — Patrick gestured to his stiff leg and grinned — "but not enough to notice."

"He's keeping you off the circuit."

"And maybe 'tis meant for me to do more good here." Patrick was in high spirits, grinning, teasing and gesturing to every wonderful new improvement he spied. "Did you see the stove? Can you believe the size of it?"

"Can you cook yet?" Maggie questioned, raising her brows. At the negative shake of his head, she laughed lightly. "Then what good it does you, I can't imagine."

"I'm to hire a housekeeper, Maggie. Me. Father Patrick

Alan Fitzgerald is to have a housekeeper to care for him and his rectory. After ten years with no one to care for me but my horse, I now can *hire* someone. It almost makes me feel like a real priest." He crossed to the wide panes of the front window and glanced outside. "Come here. Look at this view."

Magheen crossed the room and stood beside him. "It looks like a yard bare of all except scrap wood and dirt to me."

"That's because you have no imagination, Magheen! This yard, come late summer, will be full of blooms and greenery. I've been thinking of a gazebo. A small, intimate place like that would be beneficial for personal talks with my parishioners. What do you think, Magheen?"

"I don't know what to think, Paddie. The only time I knew you to construct anything, you missed with the hammer and hit your thumb. The doctor was amazed at how self-confident you must have been to hit so hard. But you never built a thing again." Magheen turned slightly so she might peep at him. A smile tilted the corners of her mouth. "Or were you thinking I might build it for you?"

Patrick laughed at her mischievous expression. "No, no, I daren't ask for that much of a miracle, Maggie. But what I was thinking was that you might come here and be my housekeeper. Since I am to have one, you know, it might as well be you. Then you can give up your job in that store, and I'll be able to sleep nights without worrying about people like that William Lovell pestering you again."

"Oh, and I'd like to be your housekeeper, Paddie, but I need my job. I still owe Daniel for all the money he put out for me that day"—involuntarily she shivered—"with all those angry women. I've only made one payment on it. And I've still three brothers who need their fines paid so they can become free men." Her face fell. "You know, it strikes me that I was far better off before I came to Leadville than after. I came here with money in my pockets, and I've since lost that and am now in debt. I'm thinking I'm a great fool, Paddie."

He looped an arm about her shoulders and squeezed. She had tried to be the same laughing, teasing Maggie, but didn't quite make it, he thought. She was missing Daniel more than she would admit, even to herself. Patrick had been tempted to question her about him, about why she refused to marry him, but had decided against it. She wasn't quite ready yet, not if her eyes still held so much sadness.

And owing Daniel so much money was definitely depressing. William Lovell should have covered the loss, Patrick considered. He understood how much she wanted her brothers' freedom. He wanted it so badly he could taste it himself. And that freedom was becoming more and more remote.

"I can pay a housekeeper. Maybe not as much as you're making now but—"

"I could do both jobs," she answered, her eyes widening as she spoke. "That would help."

"No, you can't. You've your hands full with the one. I won't have you losing more weight than you already have. What are you doing, starving yourself to save the Howards some money? Don't worry, they can afford to feed you. What you could do, though, is move in with me and save your rent money."

Her whole demeanor brightened at the suggestion. "I may just do that, Paddie. Tom's nearly finished with his and Carrie's cabin. They'll be marrying soon and she'll be moving out. The Howards have a newlywed couple interested in the room and my moving in with you would be the perfect solution. Oh, and the couple's name is Foy. Eddie and Rose Foy. He's an actor, Paddie, the first one I ever met! And so nice! Rose sings with her sister at the Tontine. I'd like to go and hear her sometime. I fancy she sings beautifully, just like Ma."

Two days later, Magheen was working in yard goods, her fingers sampling and showing the fine, recently imported silk to one of Daniels, Fisher and Smith's most valued customers. " 'Tis only eighty-five cents a yard, Mrs. Gillan. Think how beautiful the blue will look on your daughter when she makes her Confirmation. I definitely think the blue silk is your best choice."

"Maybe," the woman responded after holding the material up to the light. Mr. Gillan was one of the wealthiest men in town, and his wife's appearance confirmed that fact. She was dressed in the latest styles from New York, the patterns taken right from the pages of *Collier's* magazine. Her cream-colored dress of finely woven wool was tiered and gathered behind in a bustle. The frilly overskirt was short, barely covering her hips and accentuating the bustle. Around her neck was a tie that matched the varied green color of the ribbon trimming the overskirt. Her crowning glory was the tiny, flat-brimmed hat decorated with one small plume and much netting. Maggie would have loved to own such a hat.

"I'll take four yards of it," Mrs. Gillan answered after much consideration. "And some of that fine lace for the petticoat. The skirt should be very full, don't you think?"

"Yes, I do," Maggie responded.

As Maggie wrapped the parcel, Mrs. Gillan sidled closer to the counter and lowered her voice to speak confidentially. "I think you should know, Miss Fitzgerald, there's been some talk in the ladies' circle that you're moving into the rectory with your brother. You know, several of the ladies in the church are still adamantly angry over your involvement with" — she paused and her voice became a sultry whisper — " 'Chicken' Bill." Her eyes flashed, and a tittering laugh escaped her lips. "Did you know that's what the whole town is calling him now? I find it quite humorous, though he was a most nasty person if I ever saw one. But they don't think you showed good judgment to become involved with him. Nor do they think it right that the church be required to support you as well as Father Patrick."

Smiling sweetly, Mrs. Gillan accepted the package from the stunned and silent Irish girl. She spoke once more before leaving. "Of course, I defended you. How could you have known that William Lovell was nothing but a liar and a thief? Mr. Gillan calls him a con man! Of course, *we* know you weren't in on his schemes! It's a pity others aren't so broadminded." Shrugging her shoulders, she sighed. "But I thought you ought to know what they're saying, my dear. It won't do your brother a bit of good to make his parishioners angry."

"Don't you listen to a word that troublemaker says!" Carrie insisted loudly, later that same day. "You just tell your brother and he'll set her straight."

Maggie did not dare to repeat Mrs. Gillan's words to Paddie. She simply told him she could not move in with him, and offered to share a room with the Howard's young daughter.

"But dear, you'll be so uncomfortable there!" was Anne Howard's response.

"Not as uncomfortable as in the street. Or rooming with Miss Nickerson. You've already given your word to the Foys, and I won't ask you to break it."

"You *can* move in with Father Patrick," Anne insisted. "After all you've done for the church, no one has any right to object. Besides, it's his home, he has the right to have anyone he chooses live there."

"It's his first home. I won't be the one making it less than perfect for him, Anne."

Anne had to bite her tongue to keep from pressing the issue. "Well, if you insist, of course you're welcome to share her room. But I warn you, Annabelle is frightfully messy, and all she does is ask questions. You won't enjoy it."

But the matter was swiftly settled, and Maggie moved into the child's room.

A few days later, through the mail, she received a curt letter from Daniel, returning the money she had sent as a down payment on what she owed him.

"Give it to the church!" the note read. "I'll tear it up if you try to send me anymore." A nasty response that got her dander up first, then had her promptly running into Annabelle's crowded room and tossing herself on the bed, to give in to a good cry.

Little Annabelle heard her from the hall and came in the room. She crawled on the bed beside her, touching her tentatively on the back. "What's the matter, Maggie? Did you hurt yourself? Can I see it? Maybe I can kiss it better?" Her missing front teeth gave her words a whistling effect.

Maggie sat up, the tears falling down her cheeks, her hair wildly askew, and hauled the little girl into her arms and hugged her tightly. Annabelle felt soft and warm and real. Sniffling, she responded, "You know how angry you get with your brothers? Well, that's how angry I am with a man! A cursed, proud, hard-headed man!"

"What's 'ard-headed?"

"It means stubborn as a mule or, as in this case, as stubborn as Daniel Calcord!"

"Ooh, him. He's big," Annabelle whistled. "He's bigger than Teddy and Freddy." Pursing her little bow mouth at the thought of her twin brothers, she gave a sigh. "When I get mad at my brothers, I tell Ma. She takes a strap to them sometimes."

"I can't see your Ma strapping Daniel. But"—her eyes lit up wickedly—"I know what I can do to set him on his ears!"

140

"Won't he look sort of funny, on his ears? How does he do that, Maggie?"

The very next day, a weary Daniel returned to his home and ate a late meal. He was tempted to ignore the pile of correspondence that awaited him. He wanted to crawl into bed right away although he didn't think he would sleep anyway. He had had trouble sleeping in his own bed ever since Maggie and he had made love. Pouring himself a generous whiskey and water, he sat behind the large oak desk.

Thumbing through the mail, he set piece after piece aside as not being of prime importance. The letter with Maggie's return address caught his eye, and he immediately dropped everything else, eagerly tearing it open.

"Dear Sir," it read impersonally, setting Daniel's hackles up right away.

"Father Fitzgerald and I wish to thank you for your very generous donation. After a great deal of thought, we have decided its best use would be to set up a foundation for the recovery of fallen women. As you surely know, once a woman has fallen from grace she has a difficult time returning to God. We like to think of you as having the fate of all womankind in your charitable thoughts. We sincerely thank you for being the first to contribute to such a worthy cause."

Daniel read it, reread it, and reread it again. Then, breaking into soft laughter, he sought his pen in the cubbyholes of his desk and paper from the drawer and penned a mutually impersonal note to Magheen. She may not be speaking to him, but she was writing! The tiredness fell from him like a dark shadow.

When Magheen received his note, she tore it open.

"Miss Fitzgerald," she read. "I am in complete agreement with you and your brother's plan. I am very fond of fallen women and will do whatever I can to aid the cause. Please let me know if there is anything I, personally, can do. I am enclosing an additional amount to be used to further our mutual mission in life. Sincerely, Daniel Calcord."

She didn't want to laugh but laugh she did. And she replied, "Dear Mr. Calcord, you have such a benevolent nature! Who would ever believe it? So far your monies have helped three of the fallen. 'Tis truly amazing how simply having enough to eat can take a woman out of the business, though not neces-

141

sarily back into church. We fallen ladies owe you a true debt of gratitude. I shall enter your good name in the Mass Sunday, and I, myself, shall pray for your soul."

Heh, that ought to get him, she thought as she folded it in the envelope.

There followed more notes.

Dear Miss Fitzgerald:

Your reference to being one of the fallen came as somewhat of a shock to my innocent self. This letter is late in coming as I have spent the last three days on my knees praying for the salvation of your soul. God is not an intimate acquaintance of mine, but, I believe, he listens to me once in a great while. Please accept this donation as further proof of my regard for the fallen women of this world, one in particular.

Sincerely,
Daniel Calcord.

P.S. How does a man go about meeting these fallen women?

Dear Mr. Calcord:

Thanks to your generous donation, more of the fallen have found grace! In fact, so many have found our Lord that I can only tell you how to meet the *recovered* fallen. And that is by attending Mass. Sunday mornings at nine-thirty in the hospital chapel.

You will recognize the recovered by the aura of saintliness that hovers over each of them. Many of them have truly become saintly.

Sincerely,
Miss Fitzgerald

But no answering letter came. She waited two days and wondered if he had been offended by her little joke. Come Sunday though, he was there, in the small hospital chapel, in the third pew across the aisle from her.

Her heart began to pound when she noticed him and saw how handsome he looked in his black frock coat and starched white linen shirt. The buff-colored vest was buttoned with brass, and the small pocket held a watch and fob. On his head

142

was the dearly familiar Stetson of which he was so proud. She could feel his eyes on her throughout Mass and was sorely tempted to turn around and gaze on him too.

Paddie was so shocked to see Daniel among the congregation that his voice faltered as he spoke. Everyone attending Mass turned around to see what could possibly be wrong, their eyes following the direction of the priest's gaze. Their attention slid from Daniel to Maggie. She could have sunk beneath the pew in her embarrassment except that Daniel looked even more uncomfortable than she felt.

Maggie had to bite her lip to keep from laughing out loud.

Afterward, they met in the wide hallway that ran the length of the hospital and ended in front of the chapel. Each acknowledged the other's presence, waiting until the hall emptied of the curious onlookers before making more than the most routine comments. Maggie's brows raised and her eyes twinkled merrily. "I thought you had an incurable aversion to church, Mr. Calcord."

"I did, Miss Fitzgerald, once." He spoke as formally as she. "But when I learned fallen women attended, I was miraculously cured. Tell me, is Mrs. Willborne really one of the recovered fallen?"

Maggie looked shocked. "No! Heavens, what made you ask that?"

"Oh, she had one of those auras about her head. You know, something that shines and shimmers, like angels have."

"Don't try to flummox me, Daniel Calcord. We both know that was her hat! And don't go around using the words 'fallen women' too often, the ladies in the Rosary Society think I'm bad enough as it is. They wouldn't understand my teasing."

Daniel looked crestfallen. "You mean there is no Society for the Recovery of Fallen Women? What happened to my donations?"

"They're being used to build a gazebo."

"A gazebo?"

"At the rectory. It's long been one of Paddie's dreams."

"Oh. Somehow I never thought of him wanting a gazebo. Next he'll be growing flowers or some other such foolishness," Daniel answered gruffly. His eyes rested warmly on her, taking in her Sunday-best appearance, her loveliness. He never noticed the shabbiness of the gown or the age of her coat and

143

hat. All he could see were her eyes and the beauty of her smile. "And you're hardly what I expected of a fallen woman. You look young, beautiful, and innocent."

This new Daniel had her flushing with the sincerity of his compliments. When he exerted himself to be charming, he was charming indeed! "I believe you're the only person who knows exactly how fallen I am. And I do thank you for not telling Paddie," she added earnestly. "He would have been so disappointed in me!"

"What we did is between us, Maggie. I'd not breathe a word to a soul. But it hardly makes you fallen. It merely proves you're a woman, and a loving woman at that."

Magheen couldn't meet his eyes, nor could she believe she was carrying on such an intimate conversation with a man. Not even with Daniel. Her eyes flickered shyly over him. "I'd best be going. Anne, Joshua, and the children will be waiting for me. We walk home together from Mass every Sunday."

"I'll walk —" he began eagerly and forced himself to speak more slowly. "I mean, if I may, I'll walk with you a while." At her nod, he offered his arm and escorted her through the thick wooden doors and down the stone steps of the front entrance.

The Howards were waiting for them. Anne's expression was a bit mutinous at seeing Daniel, but Joshua was all pleasant words and greetings. The boys had gone on ahead, and Annabelle stood with her hand in her mother's and quietly listened to the adults speak. At the first lull in the conversation, she eagerly came out with, "Do you really sit on your ears? I've never seen anybody do that, but Maggie says it's so! Would you show me how to do it?" The words tumbled innocently from her childish mouth.

"Hush, Annabelle!" her mother frantically whispered, tugging on the girl's hands and pulling her behind her skirt.

"Is that what you said, Maggie? That you'd set me on my ears?" Daniel questioned, laughter lurking in his voice.

"I did."

"And apparently you said it around little Miss Big Ears. Come here, Annabelle, and let me tell you how a woman sets a man on his ears."

The child sidled closer to him, reluctantly releasing her mother's hand. Daniel crouched beside her and spoke in a very low voice. "All Maggie has to do is crook her little finger, and I get set on my ear. But it's a trick a man only performs for a special woman, and he never tells anyone else about it, because if he does, then she throws him for a loop! And then, he's done for!"

Annabelle's eyes were wide and bright. "Maggie can't throw anybody!" she retorted skeptically. "You're telling me a fara-diddle, aren't you?" Her hair bounced as she turned spritely and questioned of Maggie, "Are you sure his head is hard? It looks just like Pa's, only his hat is much nicer 'cause it's bigger. Pa needs a bigger hat to cover his head, 'specially where his hair is falling out." A tongue snaked out to lick at her upper lip. "If his head," she continued, pointing to Daniel, "is so hard, why doesn't he give *his* hat to Pa, and then maybe his head will get softer from the rain? Or Pa can give him *his* hat!" she spoke hopefully.

Daniel looked at the bowler hat on Joshua Howard's head with acute distaste. Since moving from New York, he had become a Westerner through and through. His eyes swung to Maggie as he stood to his full height. "Hard-headed now?" he grinned. "And just what do you think you are?"

"Reasonable, logical . . . right."

"Just like all the women she knows," Anne added sweetly.

"I think they're implying we're a couple of fools, Daniel."

"Not fools. Just not quite the superior beings you think you are," Anne answered her spouse, grinning. Turning to Daniel, she assumed her most prim manner. "Would you like to come to dinner, Mr. Calcord?"

"I would indeed, Mrs. Howard."

"I trust that you have reformed since we last met and are now a suitable member of society. At least suitable enough to be around my children?"

"I am a pillar of hard work and moral integrity. I only lapse every once in a while. And I'm sure you'll tell me when I do."

"It will be my pleasure," she responded, her demeanor hoity-toity. A moment later, her brows lowered and she smiled confidentially, "But before you become too moral, tell us about that Kate Nelligan who works for Lil Amundson! Is she really Irish? Do you think her black hair is natural?" Anne sounded much like her daughter at the moment. "And make it quick. I don't want the boys to overhear us gossiping!"

Daniel glanced at Maggie, who didn't seem to think Anne

was in the least humorous, before answering seriously, "I don't know much about her except she's truly Irish. I didn't believe that at first because . . . she didn't have red hair and . . . and I was too inebriated to think straight. But then she opened her mouth and out came a stream of Irish speech, or at least speech which nearly resembled what I've come to think of as an Irish accent."

His words came ruefully now, though he spoke more to Maggie than to the others. "I was looking for a red-headed Irish girl who had the charm of Irish faeries. I found a coarse, dark-haired woman from Ireland, who was very grateful for a night's respite from her chosen work. I paid her very well, Maggie, but only for letting me sleep my drunken state off, for nothing else."

"A very pretty speech, Mr. Calcord. But how do we know—" Anne Howard was interrupted midstream by a series of shooting, raucous explosions that shook the mountains surrounding them and rippled to the very ground on which they stood.

Daniel was shocked into stillness for only a moment, his dazed expression turning to one of comprehension as he understood what must be happening.

"The mine! Dear God, the mine is exploding!"

Swiftly he turned and ran back toward the hospital where his horse was still tethered. His booted feet dug a path through the crusted snow as the others watched.

"I'm going, too!" Maggie announced, turning back to Anne and Joshua. "I'll be home when I can, but maybe I can be of some help!"

"We'll all go. Joshua, you and I would be better off getting a wagon and filling it with food and supplies. Maggie, we'll meet you on the hill."

But Maggie was already gone, hurrying toward the mining hills on the east side of Leadville. The road was steep and already filled with many other townspeople heading in the same direction. As she joined the throng of men and women clambering up the grade toward the mines, a fire wagon passed them. The four horses were overloaded with heavy equipment and some four thousand feet of hose. Yet they still clipped along at a rapid pace.

Soon men on horseback and in carriages filled the dusty

road. An ambulance hurtled past. Dirty snow kicked up the mud beneath, threatening to mire those walking.

Even at this distance, the black, billowing cloud of smoke obscured the once blue sky. As Magheen neared the hill, flames shot out and identified the mine which had exploded as being very near to Daniel's Resurrection Mine, if not the Resurrection itself.

Maggie's legs moved more quickly.

A huge crowd was gathered at the mine by the time Maggie reached the summit. But finally she could see that the mine under fire was the Old Abe, the mine just north of the Resurrection.

A breath of relief escaped her only to be swallowed as yet another explosion rocked the mountain. Maggie tumbled to her knees, toppled by the weight of the man next to her. The crowd seemed to swoon as most of them joined her on the cold ground. Cries of terror filled the air while Maggie fought her way to her feet, her eyes seeking the source of the explosion.

An injured miner had been tossed from his stretcher during the most recent explosion and now lay on the ground, keening with his pain. His carriers recovered their balance and stood, gingerly replacing his broken body on the stretcher. They moved along, hauling him to the bunkhouse behind the Resurrection Mine, which was now doubling as a hospital.

Maggie could hear the injured miner moaning about the four other men trapped below.

God help them, Maggie prayed, crossing herself.

Flames burst from the timber-lined mouth of the Old Abe. In that moment, Maggie recognized how much danger all the mines were in from this fire. They were so closely packed on the hillside that any of them could catch fire from the flames and burn for hours.

As if to confirm her thoughts, a flaming wooden shingle from the Old Abe's shaft-house roof broke off and went flying toward the Resurrection and its timbered buildings.

More screams rent the air. Then Daniel was there, standing over the wooden floor where the shingle had lit, his frock coat in his hands, and using it to beat out the flames on the shingle. When that threat was overcome, he turned his attention once more to the Old Abe and the thought of four men, dead or alive, deep within its bowels.

Maggie crossed herself again.

Chaos was everywhere. The firemen were bellowing at the crowd to back away. The police department tried vainly to enforce their orders. The hose was stretched and unreeled as two of the firemen climbed aboard the wagon to man the pump. As a steady stream of water gushed out, the crowd moved back.

Maggie turned away, unable to bear the gruesome sight any longer, and threaded her way through the crowd toward the bunkhouse. As she opened the door, she was unprepared for the sight and sounds of the suffering inside. Men were deeply burned, and their shock had them crying aloud with pain.

"Damnation!" roared one of the wounded. His whole body appeared to be bandaged, even to a covering over his eyes. A thickly covered white hand lifted as the man continued hoarsely, "I told Walker McClean I only counted six charges when there ought to have been seven! He sent us back down there anyway! There was no talking to him. Not to him, by God! He asked me if I thought I had all day to wait for a faulty charge! And I told him I had the rest of my life! And then he threatened my job!"

"Damn the owners and their managers! McClean should have been the one to go below if he was so determined to risk lives! Where is the damned man, anyway? What has he to say for himself in this?"

Another, weaker voice opined; "He's run, that's what he's done! He'll not stick around to see what his carelessness has caused."

Yet another voice cried, "I say we strike, that would show them! Too bad it's come too late to help those other poor damn fools!"

Magheen could sympathize only too well with men who had been under the thumb of others with more power and money than they. She and her family had suffered from that same affliction all their lives. It seemed, even in America, power and wealth spoke more loudly than right and wrong. And now four men were dead, or near dead, and another seven badly injured.

Mine owners, managers, bankers, the wealthy. They seemed to be America's equivalent of the arrogant English.

"Dr. Palmer, what can I do to help?" she offered as she

approached him.

He barely spared her a glance. "Get these men calmed down and lying on their beds if you can. I can only handle one man at a time. Strip their clothing from them and clean their wounds. Use this salve, it's better than plain water. If any of their clothing sticks to the skin, don't pull it, call me. And don't offer to help if you haven't the stomach for it. I haven't time to pick you off the floor too."

When Anne arrived with supplies, she and another woman set up a kitchen, making hot coffee and sandwiches for the firemen and others outside who worked to control the fire.

Magheen set about gently rubbing salve over various parts of men's bodies. The red and running sores were somewhat soothed by her attentions. Several of the men had injuries from falling timbers; one of them might have even broken his arm. Only Dr. Palmer could tell for sure. The men were filthy from their day's work, and all of them needed a bath to soak in. All Maggie could do was try to make them more comfortable.

With a steady voice she tried to cheer the men. Over her dress was a white cotton apron, but it would be ruined by the time this day was done. Soot, dirt, and blood were stains that would not wash out.

The ambulance wagon backed up to the door and, beginning with the most badly injured, took the men, two at a time, to St. Vincent Hospital. The good sisters were better able to provide care for the men.

When the last of the injured was gone, Maggie turned to help Anne and the other ladies. Several women were inside now, some pumping water from the well, others taking filled coffeepots outside and returning with empty pots and tin cups.

For the first time in what seemed hours, Maggie took a deep breath and glanced out the window. From here she could see the entrance to the Old Abe mine. The timbers barely held. A steady creaking warned of their inclination to buckle and swallow the opening. The water that was still gushing over the fire began to turn to ice as the day waned.

Suddenly, one of the firemen shouted, "Listen! Is that a voice?"

A great stillness enveloped the mountain. The waiting

seemed interminable.

"There it is again!"

One by one, the women left the bunkhouse and stood on the porch, listening. Silent prayers flowed through Maggie's mind as she hoped for the fireman to be right.

"See! What did I tell you? At least one of them's alive!"

A cheer rent the crowd, which was immediately shushed by a policeman. "How can anyone hear if you're screaming?"

Mining accidents were all too common in Leadville, but no one took them lightly. Any man here could be tomorrow's victim. They may have formed a curious crowd, but each man and woman was praying and hoping this day would end happily.

"He can't get out alone! He's stuck down there!"

"Someone will have to go get him!"

Instinctively, Maggie's gaze went to Daniel. She knew him so well, and knew he would risk his life if he thought he could save that man. Holding her breath, she saw Daniel roll up the sleeves of his white shirt and loosen it from about his waist.

Was it only this morning that they had laughed and talked after Mass?

Hail Mary, Mother of God . . .

Chapter Nine

Maggie stepped forward, as if she would hurry to Daniel's side. A hand came down on her arm, and she turned, surprised, to see Mrs. Sawyer standing beside her.

"He's bound and determined to go inside after those men, and what you have to say will just weigh on his mind further. Let him go, miss."

"No!" Maggie answered vehemently. "I don't want him going in there! 'Tis too dangerous!"

"He's got to be the man he is. You'll not change him, no matter how hard you try."

Maggie turned her head, her eyes following Daniel, watching fearfully as he crossed nearer the threshold of the mine. I don't want to change him, she thought mutinously, but I don't want him to die either! I love him too much!

A deep gasp left her lips as the white of Daniel's shirt disappeared into the mine. His black frock coat was wound about his head and mouth, and to protect his arms he carried a longer, fireman's jacket.

The timbers swayed and creaked once more; the crowd was strangely silent. Moments passed, though they seemed more like hours. Bits of dirt tumbled over the opening from the hill above, echoing with a scratchy, eerie sound as they landed on the rocks below. A dry tumbleweed blew across the timbers, catching on a jumble of rocks west of the mine, meshing there with other dusty weeds.

Magheen's heart beat painfully in her breast as she waited and watched.

The creaking grew louder. The crowd gave a gasp as the timbers bowed forward. Each sway seemed to increase in

151

momentum. Then, with the suddenness of a lightning bolt, the wood buckled and splinters flew everywhere. The rough-hewn timbers split in the center and crashed into the ground, spewing rocks and mud everywhere.

"Get the shovels!" shouted one of the firemen.

Quickly the opening of the mine was covered by men frantically digging with picks and shovels and anything else that would fit into their hands. The fire seemed to be extinguished now, only smoke drifting through small openings left by the falling timbers and rocks.

For a second, Maggie was paralyzed with fear. Then, catching her skirt in her fingers, she ran to the opening and joined the men, kneeling beside them while she tore at any loose bits of dirt with her hands.

"I hear something!" shouted one of the men.

"A death rattle, likely," answered another man.

"Shut up and dig. Henry's right, I hear something too," came another answer.

"Here! Here! I'm through!" came the exultant cry as the first man managed to dig clear through the rubble and find a small opening of the mine.

Soon the small inlet was swarming with men and shovels. Maggie was pushed aside, but she was content to let others do what they were better able to do. Her fingers were raw from her efforts, and the painful beating of her heart echoed loudly in her mind.

"Hey! Hey, I got me something! Help!"

"Whatcha got, Frank?"

"A coat of some kind. God, it's him! It's Daniel wearing the coat!" Frank cried. "Come on, give me a hand. He's either dead or out cold. Either way, he's a dead weight."

"He's got someone with him," shouted Henry. "I'll be damned if that lucky devil didn't save a man, nohow!"

"Neither of them is lucky unless they be alive!" retorted Frank.

Dear Mother of God, Holy Mother of God, Magheen prayed. Please save Daniel. He's a good man, the kind we need to keep on earth for as long as you'll allow us. The sort of man who gives to others, who builds and leaves something solid and better behind for the next generation. Please, Mother, don't let them have him. I want some years with him first. I want him and his babies, I want to share a future, I want to dream with him. Hail Mary, I promise to raise our children in the church, to teach them to love you and Our Lord always . . .

"He's breathing!" Henry shouted exultantly to the crowd. "And so's Tom Mason!"

Maggie ceased her fervid, silent praying at the words and opened her eyes. Daniel had been dragged from the inside of the mine, his frock coat still wrapped around his head, and was lying in the dirt, face down, right where the men had dragged him. On his back clung the body of another miner. Apparently, before he passed out or was knocked out, he had found Tom Mason.

"Daniel," she whispered, hurrying to his side. Henry and Frank were lifting Tom Mason from him, but Maggie could see that Tom was already coming around. Daniel was very still, too still. Maggie knelt down, her gaze taking in all of him, even the black soot that covered him from head to foot.

"Help me turn him over," she ordered. The men did so as gently as they could. "Oh, Daniel," Maggie sobbed softly on seeing his injuries. A timber had caught him along the side of his head, gashing deeply beside his eye and cheek.

"He's lucky he's still got an eye," remarked Frank.

"He's luckier to be alive," said another of the men.

"We need to get him to the bunkhouse. Can you get a stretcher?"

"Right away, ma'am."

Daniel was carried inside and gently placed on one of the beds. Anne fetched a bowl of warm water and soap, and she and Maggie stripped the coat and shirt from him and began to wash him.

"Go on with you," Mrs. Sawyer announced to the nosy miners in general. "How can we get anything done with the bunch of you gawking about? Go, get out of here now. Git, I say!" Very few men were brave enough to defy Daniel's housekeeper, so the bunkhouse was quickly emptied, though the men waited within earshot of the door.

Dr. Palmer studied the wound and pronounced grimly, "Nasty wound that. It'll leave a scar. But the worst is if he doesn't wake up in the next few hours. Not a lot I can do

153

about head wounds. A man either survives or he don't. That's up to him."

"You mean he can still die?" Maggie questioned fearfully. She had thought he was safe and secure in her care.

Dr. Palmer nodded. "Clean him up, and we'll move him to the hospital. The nurses can care for him better there."

"No! I'll care for him!"

Through soot-encrusted lashes Daniel could barely make out Magheen's facial features. He felt her tears running onto his face, though, and for the first time believed she loved him. She wasn't after his money or freedom or anything else, she simply loved him. He opened his mouth and tried desperately to speak, but no words would come out.

Anna held a wet rag out to Magheen. "He's bound to be parched . . ."

"I'll clean him and feed him water," Maggie quietly insisted.

"He needs to be in the hospital," Dr. Palmer reiterated.

Daniel was pressed against Maggie's bosom as she pressed the cool rag to his lips. Relief came to his dry, parched throat and lips. Heaven couldn't be better than this, he thought dreamily.

"I'm calling for the ambulance. I'm sorry, young lady, you're not responsible for him until you're married. And until then, what I think best goes."

"I don't want to go to any damned hospital," Daniel croaked. "I want my own home, my own bed."

"He's awake!" was the cry that began at the front door and echoed down the hillside, clear into the limits of the town. "Awake! Awake! Daniel Calcord's awake!"

"How about it, Daniel? Are there any more men alive down there?" Hank asked bluntly.

The words he tried to speak caught in Daniel's throat, and Maggie fed him a touch more water.

"I found all four men, only one alive," Daniel responded wearily. "The air's poisonous down there. And even as I ran, the timbers were falling." His voice came more rapidly now, as though a nightmare plagued him. "I couldn't get them all."

"Shh, Daniel," Maggie soothed. "No one's faulting you. One man, and alive, is more than anyone expected. Why,

154

you nearly died yourself!"

"That's true enough," Anne added. "You made a miracle as it is, there's nothing else to fret about. Here, now, lie back and let me see that wound—"

"I'll see to the wound. I'm the doctor!"

"Then, stop your jawing and see to it. All you can do is ramble on about hospitals and ambulances—"

"Daniel's going to the hospital. It's the best place for him."

"I'm not going to any damned hospital. I'm going home. You'll come with me, won't you, Maggie?" His hand gripped hers tightly, and she nodded.

Anne, Mrs. Sawyer and the doctor looked among themselves. Even the miners standing in the doorway looked uncomfortable. Magheen Fitzgerald was the priest's sister and a good, moral woman, in spite of her questionable association with Bill Lovell. Of course even in that fracas it was Daniel who had come to her rescue. So the man must love her. Besides, they were engaged, even if the last of the banns hadn't been read yet. A matter that had caused quite a bit of speculation in the town.

"Yes, I'll come with you," she responded firmly, her fingers entwined with his.

"Then give me my shirt and let's go home."

"I haven't finished cleaning your wound yet," Anne argued.

"Maggie will take care of that at home."

"If you insist on going home instead of to the hospital, the least you can do is get there by way of the ambulance. And not too much jostling around, understand?" Daniel nodded, and the doctor turned to Maggie and gave her a threatening glare. "And do you understand, miss?"

"I promise he'll stay in bed and won't have to move a muscle. I'll watch over him."

With this the doctor had to be satisfied. The black ambulance wagon was summoned, and a great fanfare was made of Daniel being carried by stretcher to it and Maggie joining him inside for the ride to the house. Doctor Palmer took Mrs. Sawyer in his one-horse carriage and led the way.

A crowd of curious onlookers followed, Daniel's and Maggie's problem with their engagement and the reading of the banns being the great entertainment of Leadville at the moment. A lot of speculation had passed among the towns-people concerning the abrupt cessation of the banns, and now the people were hoping for more and even better gossip, or else why would Daniel have insisted Miss Fitzgerald accompany him?

Once inside his home, in the comfort of his bedroom, and with the doors closed securely behind him, Daniel finally allowed the doctor to attend his wound. The salve was soothing and cool to the touch. The bandage covered the right side of Daniel's forehead at a sharp angle, barely touching his eye. It gave him a rakish look, or so Mrs. Sawyer claimed as she and Maggie trooped buckets of warm water into the room and dumped them into the gleaming copper bathtub.

Once alone, Daniel stepped gingerly into the tub and allowed his weary body to relax. He couldn't wash his hair because of the bandage, but having clean, fresh skin gave a lift to his spirits. The comforting warmth nearly made him fall asleep.

Doctor Palmer was, by now, on his way to the hospital to work his skills on other victims of the disaster, a thought that brought further relief to Daniel. He breathed in the odor of chicken and supposed they would have stew for dinner. Mrs. Sawyer always fixed either chicken stew or soup when she was worrying about something. And he supposed she was worrying about him. She liked to have something to worry about.

Maggie entered after lightly knocking on the door. In her hand was an oil lamp, for the day was already waning, and over her arm rested a thick towel. "I warmed this by the fireplace. Come on out of that tub, before you fall asleep and drown."

Daniel's brows raised. He had thought about requesting a cigar and brandy to become even more comfortable, but he supposed Maggie was right. As weary as he was, he would fall asleep in the bath water.

"All right. Leave it on the chair."

"No, I'm going to help."

Daniel quirked an eyebrow. "You're staying? In case you haven't noticed, my girl, I remove all my clothing when I bathe."

"I noticed" was her prim answer. "But I'm here to be of help. And, in spite of how healthy and male you usually are, at the moment you're especially weak. Just try standing without my help if you don't believe me."

"If you think I'm crawling out of there while you stand by and watch . . ."

"In case you don't remember, Mr. Calcord, I've seen all of you. I don't recall being easily shocked by the sight."

"No?" he sneered. "Then why the Mr. Calcord? Leave the towel, and I'll call you when I'm dressed," he ordered bluntly.

"You're too weak at the moment. Don't be shy, Daniel, you're very attractive in your bare state."

Daniel blinked twice, unsure if he cared for the unemotional way she expressed such a personal opinion. "Thank you. And I offer you the same compliment. However, I can damn well get myself dressed!"

She gave him her look that said, "Men!" dropped the towel on the chair, and turned from the room. He knew she went no farther than the other side of the door. And of course the room did spin wildly when Daniel tried to rise. He grabbed onto the side of the tub as his flailing hands and arms splashed water across the wooden floor.

He didn't even hear her return to the room. All of a sudden she was there and the towel was around him. Maggie snickered something about his maidenly modesty but, at that moment, he couldn't have cared less. With careful coaxing, she got him to step from the tub and guided him to the edge of the bed. In his top drawer she found a nightshirt, and by the time she returned to his side, he was feeling more himself. He took one look at the nightshirt and bellowed for his clothing. "I'm hungry and I plan to eat a decent meal."

"You can't make it down or up the stairs by yourself, and I'm not carrying you. Neither is Mrs. Sawyer. So if that hare-brained notion is uppermost in your mind, get rid of it," she ordered bluntly.

"I'll eat in my dining room or I won't eat at all!"

"You'll eat in bed and beneath the blankets. And if you're a good boy, I'll feed you."

"What do you think I am, six years old?"

"That's how old you're acting. Now, why don't you lift up your arms so I can tug the nightshirt over your head . . ."

His eyes narrowed. "Maggie, you're enough to drive a man to drink."

"And you're enough to make a woman swear off men! First, you go willy-nilly into that mine, without a care for even the hair on your head—"

"I covered my head."

"And now you're insisting on behaving just as foolishly, by not taking care of yourself, and you dare to say I could drive you to drink! Daniel Calcord, if you aren't in bed in the next five minutes, I'm walking home. I'll not stay and see you treat yourself so carelessly one more moment. You're behaving like an obstinate, mule-headed . . . *male!*"

"And you're behaving like a shrew, Magheen!"

Her head reared back, and those emerald eyes grew dark with temper. How many times had she heard those words from her brothers when they wanted to manipulate her? She hadn't been fooled then; she wasn't now.

"Then, as shrewish as I am, you cannot want me around! I bid you good eve, Mr. Calcord. I trust next time we meet you'll be in a far more amenable mood!" With a flounce she turned and moved toward the door.

"Maggie! Wait!" Daniel bellowed as she left the room.

Maggie stood outside the room, wanting only to collect her temper before she went downstairs. Mrs. Sawyer was in enough of a state without Maggie giving her more to worry about. As though anyone needed to worry about Daniel Calcord! That huge, obstinate galoot of a man! What Maggie was tempted to do was to get her umbrella and take it to his ears. And she would have too, if he hadn't been wearing a bandage. He didn't deserve anyone caring or worrying about him. Not Mrs. Sawyer and certainly not herself.

He was calling for her again, and for two pennies she would go back into that room and give him a few choice words which would set him on his ears! And why not?

Just as her fingers turned the knob, a crash sounded and a most dreadful moaning came from beside the bed. Maggie rushed back inside the room and found Daniel on the floor, the towel down about his ankles.

"What did you do now, you foolish man? Haven't you a

158

brain working in your head?" Maggie cried as her arms went around him and helped him upright. Together they staggered back to the bed.

"You were right," he answered breathlessly. "I'm as helpless as a day-old kitten."

"I told you . . ."

His palms went to either side of her head, bringing her to face him. "Don't leave me, Maggie. You promised! You're right, I haven't the strength to make it downstairs, and I won't even try. But stay, Maggie, you promised me!"

"Of course I'm staying! Did you think to be rid of me so easily? All I was trying to do was to get this fearful temper of mine under control before I did you some *real* harm. A body can only take so much from ill-mannered, bad-tempered brutes the likes of you!"

Daniel gave a gruff laugh. His warm brown eyes turned gentle as he spoke, and his thumbs stroked the softness of her cheeks. "No, I mean stay tonight with me. I don't want to be alone. I won't touch you, not in any romantic way. And I don't mean to compromise you. But . . . Maggie, today I faced my own death. I came around and there you were, just like an angel, holding me. I need you, Maggie. I need you by me. I need your warmth and your caring. Say you care, say you care whether I live or die. Say it, Maggie."

"Of course I care," she cried vehemently, her voice coming out in a sob. "I care so much the thought of you dying inside that mine today nearly ripped the heart out of my body. How could you think otherwise? Didn't I tell you in the only way a woman knows how to tell a man?" She was sniffling now. When Magheen got angry enough, she couldn't stop the tears. "I love you, Daniel Calcord. I love you so much it hurts. And you, blast you! You act as though you couldn't care less about me or about yourself!"

"Now, don't get riled again, Magheen," he soothed. "Why don't you go get us both a bowl of that chicken stew—"

"Soup," she sniffed.

". . . soup, and you can feed it to me." His eyes closed with weariness, his nostrils flaring as he breathed deeply. "I don't think I have the strength to do even that." He relaxed against the pillow, his head drooping to one side. As Maggie took her hand from his, his grip tightened to keep her near, and the deep brown eyes flew open. "Maggie, if I fall asleep, will you promise to stay? I need to know you're here. I need to know you're beside me and I didn't drive you away. I never meant to hurt you. That woman at Darlin' Lil's, she didn't mean anything."

"You must be delirious with hunger and to be asking my pardon. Don't you know I'd forgive you anything, and you don't even have to say the words? Now, beneath the blankets with you. If that head wound doesn't get you, pneumonia will. And it will be all my fault for letting you sit here in the cold, jawing instead of getting warm." She tucked the blankets about him, noticing for the first time the way his eyes were glazed with moisture. Checking his forehead, she could find no fever.

"I'll be back in a moment with your soup. Is there anything else you need? Would you like some tea?"

"I hate tea."

"I forgot," Maggie replied, smiling slowly. "Then would you like some of that horrible brew you call coffee?"

"Maggie, I'll settle for the soup and you."

"Hmm. Somehow I don't think you'll always be this easy to please."

"I hope not. I intend to take up the bulk of your thoughts, your time, and your efforts. You've been warned."

"And so I have," she said softly as his eyes closed for the final time.

Soup, coffee, tea. All would wait until Daniel was rested. Maggie pulled the oak rocker next to the bed and made herself comfortable. He looked so vulnerable in his sleep, she thought. The lines around his eyes were gone and even his mouth was gentled.

Thank the Good Lord Daniel survived this day.

Knowing Daniel, there would be more fretful days like this one. He was a man who took life and lived it to the fullest, accepting all the joys and most of the risks of living. Until today he had steered clear of risking his heart by loving. Even if he hadn't spoken the words, Magheen felt him beginning to love her. He might not recognize it as love yet, but she did, and that was enough. One day he would be strong enough to admit it.

She had all the time in the world to wait for him.

Mrs. Sawyer came in a while later, and Maggie told her to save the soup for another time. The housekeeper returned with a blanket to make Magheen more comfortable.

By the light of the oil lamp, Maggie settled down to read a book by an author she had often heard of, but never read, Charles Dickens. Her limited budget didn't extend to books, but Daniel's apparently did. She'd found *Great Expectations*, leather bound and gold leafed, in his library, and Maggie would have wagered it had never been touched.

The evening waned into night as Maggie sat engrossed. Finally, her eyes burning from the dim light, she lowered the wick so as to be nearly invisible and rested her head against the hard wooden back of the rocker and slept.

Sometime during the night, she became aware of Daniel hovering over her, his fingers busy undoing the buttons of her white blouse.

"Daniel! What are you doing up from your bed?"

"Getting you ready to crawl in beside me. It's too cold out here and I've plenty of room," he coaxed.

"Have you gone daft? You look ready to collapse where you stand. I'm fine where I am. Now *you* get back in bed."

"Not without you. Don't be so shy, Maggie. I have no nefarious plans to seduce you. But by morning you'll be stiff and cold and miserable if you try to sleep in this chair all night."

He was right and she wanted nothing more in this life than to be close to him. The blouse slipped off her shoulders easily enough, and the buttons of her skirt practically fell open. "I just want to hold you, Maggie. I just want to know you're with me."

"I'm with you, all right," she answered, rising from the chair. "Poor fool you, Daniel Calcord. See if you ever get rid of me again. Scoot over, I take up a mite more space than you've left me."

As Daniel accommodated her, Maggie slipped beneath the blankets and was instantly assailed by the scent and warmth of him. In spite of his weakness, his hold was strong and firm. He settled on his side and she did likewise, so their bodies fit together like two spoons. She was drowsing off to sleep when she felt his fingers slip between the ribbons of her chemise, seeking the softness of her breasts. One quick tug on the ribbons and the chemise spread open, leaving both her breasts bare to his caress.

To Maggie's disappointment, he had been telling the truth. He had no nefarious plans to seduce her. After giving a low growl of satisfaction at the soft, sweet feel of her skin, he was asleep, while she remained awake half the night.

When the pounding on the door came, Maggie thought it was just a dream. She snuggled deeper against Daniel, stretching so his fingers might encircle her breasts yet again. The pounding sounded once more, but it was Daniel's low-spoken epithet that fully wakened her.

"Cover yourself," he growled. Rising from the bed, more quickly than an injured man had a right to, Daniel pulled on his trousers and began buttoning them.

The pounding came once again, just as Daniel shrugged into his shirt. The door was thrust open and Father Patrick stood in the doorway, looking more like an irate brother than a Catholic priest. His eyes quickly scanned the room, coming to rest on a barely awake Magheen, whose eyes peeped over the wool blankets and whose hair was still strewn wantonly over the pillow. The scene alone damned them; Daniel pulling on his clothing, Maggie still in bed and wearing who knew what.

"Paddie, 'tis not what you think —"

"What I think? What the whole town thinks, you mean! 'Tis common knowledge you spent the full night here!"

"Of course she did. She offered to care for me —"

"An offer you took her up on? Have you no care for a decent woman's reputation?"

"Oh, Paddie, 'twas not like that!"

"You dare say that to me? You say that while you lie in the bed of a man who's not your husband?"

"You should not be shaming her, Father," Daniel said quietly. Too quietly. Brother or no brother, no man was going to speak to Magheen like that. No man or priest was to be allowed to make her feel shamed for loving him in the most natural way possible.

"Maggie has done nothing wrong. She's a warm, caring woman who offered comfort to the man she loves, and in that, there is no sin." Daniel reached down for his boots, placing them in one hand and his hat in the other. "Now, I suggest we finish this conversation over breakfast and give Maggie a chance to make herself decent."

At his choice of words, Father Patrick grew red with fury. "I mean decent enough for the public," Daniel sighed. "Underneath all those blankets, she's still wearing her camisole and bloomers. I did not have my wicked way with your sister last night, Father, though I will not promise as much for the future."

"You'll not be seeing her again, Mr. Calcord," Father Patrick stated as the men left the room.

"I mean to speak with you about that, Father . . ."

Maggie's first instinct was to be peeved that the two men had left the room discussing her. Her! When she was the one most directly involved, they spoke as though she weren't even there, as though she didn't even matter.

Then she thought about Paddie's temper and Daniel's temper and the gossip that was surely spreading about town by now and decided to take her sweet time getting dressed. Let the men figure this one out. Daniel was expert at saving people from themselves, and Patrick was inspirational enough. Let the two of them decide what to do.

No one was in the dining room when she entered. Used plates and empty cups were scattered about the table and the serving dishes were empty, proof that the men had been there and eaten, and apparently in rather hungry and convivial moods. Not a drop of blood was to be found. Anywhere.

Raised voices could be heard coming from the study, and Maggie realized they had merely postponed their argument until after they had eaten. A rather strange thing to do since both of them had such fierce tempers, she considered. Now would come the bloodshed. Squaring her shoulders, she crossed to the double oak doors leading to the study. From there she could hear the words "ten paces," "aim," and "fire."

Oh, no, she thought wildly. Those dear fools! They're not to fight over me. I love the both of them, half-wits though they be most of the time!

Determined to avert their foolishness, Magheen swung wide the doors and stood, hands on hips, in the doorway. Daniel was fondling one of what appeared to be a huge collection of long firearms. She could see the place of honor it normally held on the wall. Daniel's eyes gleamed with pride as he spoke. "And this one was used by my grandfather in the Civil War, a Sharps breechloader. Impressive, isn't it?"

Paddie took the rifle and sighted it through the window. He held the firearm as though it were made of pure gold, whistling at the smooth feel of the wood. "I've never seen anything so grand as this. You've quite an armory, Daniel."

"I've been collecting these guns for years."

Some argument, Maggie thought irritably, unsure whether to be pleased or not that they had become fast friends. Perhaps they didn't even remember the reason they were having this little talk.

Finally Daniel noticed her, turning and looking a bit surprised at her arrival. "Come on in, Maggie. I've been showing your brother my collection. You never told me he was so keen on arms, or I'd have had him over weeks ago."

"Fine man you're marrying, Maggie," Paddie offered, lowering the rifle from his eyes long enough to acknowledge her presence. "Smart too. Mind if I borrow one of these once in a while, Daniel? Just to do a bit of target shooting with, you know. I like to shoot, but as a priest, I haven't the blunt to afford expensive hobbies. I can see how this one grabs you, though, and won't let go."

"Sure. Hey, how about right now? I can set up a target in back and we can while away the morning. By tomorrow I have to be back at the mine, and I'd rather show you how to load that one than let you work it out on your own. If that's the one you want to try, that is. The Sharps can be a bit tricky."

Paddie's eyes lit up. "Now's a fine time, Daniel," he crooned eagerly. "Oh, and Maggie, you'd best be getting back to the Howards' house. They're worried about you. I told them you could take care of yourself, but you know Anne, she frets over the simplest things," he said, sailing past her and down the hall. Paddie was in an obvious hurry to test the rifle. "And tell her about the banns, would you? It's the only thing I know of to satisfy her."

"What about the banns?"

Daniel was following Paddie. He stopped long enough to

give Maggie a kiss on the cheek. "The third banns will be read at the nine-thirty Mass on Sunday. And we'll be wed the following Saturday, my girl. That ought to please Anne Howard and all the other gossips in town too!" He grinned broadly before admonishing Paddie to wait for him.

They'll be pleased? Maggie thought sourly. What about me?

Mrs. Sawyer came out of the kitchen, wiping her hands on her apron and was just in time to hear Daniel's last remark. "High time if you ask me! You two have shilly-shallied around long enough!"

Maggie's mouth was wide open with indignation. "He didn't even ask me! He told me!"

"Course he did. You aren't about to tell him no, now are you? If you did, you'll never hold your head high in this town again!"

"Maggie!" Daniel bellowed from the back door. "Look in my desk drawer and find the cartridges, will you? Oh, never mind! You'd probably never recognize them anyway." His voice grew nearer as he returned to the hall, smiling at the two women. "What a fine man your brother is, Magheen! I thought all priests were stuffy and patronizing. Not Paddie!" Still smiling, he rifled through the drawers until he found what he sought, then lifting his hands high, he displayed the linen cartridges to the two women, who could only stare. "Got it!" he said happily, and then he was gone.

Maggie looked at Mrs. Sawyer. Mrs. Sawyer frowned, biting her lower lip. "Men!" both women exclaimed in unison.

Chapter Ten

November 1, 1879

My wedding day. Bittersweet, yet so delicious.

Fourteen months and nine days have passed since my brothers were sentenced to the penal colony in Australia. The English put them there to remain for their lifetimes. Their only hope is what money I can raise in America, and if I can buy their freedom with that money.

I have forgotten why I came to America in these last weeks. My life seemed to be taking such a wondrous turn with Daniel Calcord that every other consideration has been thrust from my mind.

I cannot forget my roots, nor my destination, nor that Daniel is one of the preferred few, an Englishman.

I doubt that he would understand my perplexity. I doubt that Daniel has ever faced failure in his life. And I doubt that Daniel would ever understand why my brothers were convicted of a crime, let alone the heinous crime of high treason.

I have considered at length. A woman is supposed to go to her husband with him having all knowledge of her. She is supposed to trust him with her life. I do trust Daniel with my life, I just don't know that he would understand what motivated my brothers, nor what motivates any self-respecting Irish man and woman to fight against English tyranny.

I don't know what Daniel would think of me if he knew of my past, and I have learned, with all my soul searching, that I am too much of a coward to find out.

He has accepted Paddie and, for that, I am thankful. I cannot expect as much forbearance concerning three convict brothers and the huge amount of money needed to buy their freedom.

Dear God, forgive me for what I think is an enormous deception. I will not tell Daniel of my three brothers. I will find a way to free them that will not involve my husband.

I mean to be a good wife to Daniel, to do everything in my power to make him happy.

But, dear Lord, I remember too well Daniel's cold response to the thought of my having his child.

He termed our child a "half-Irish brat."

He was angry, true, but so often words spoken in anger have a ring of insightful truth to them. Daniel thinks ill of the Irish, of my people, and God forgive me, I love him in spite of that.

With Your grace, dear Lord, may I have his child. And may he love that child, half-Irish brat or no, as much as I surely will.

And I promise that any monies needed to buy my brothers' freedom will not come from Daniel. I will not take from him to better my family. That money I will earn on my own. Neither my family nor I will cost Daniel one penny.

From some other source that money will come, and Daniel need never regret his vows to me.

Please, Lord, bless this union in spite of my sins.

"Magheen! What are you doing writing in that notebook when you should be getting ready?" Anne Howard demanded impatiently, pausing at the door to Annabelle's room. On entering, she seemed to fill up the tiny room as her bosom heaved with her exertions. "Everyone's waiting to go to the church and you're up here dabbling in that silly book. Here, give that to me." She snatched the diary from Magheen's hands and tossed it onto the chiffonnier. "You'll muss your dress, sitting in it on the bed like that. A bride is not supposed to sit. She's to stand and smile simperingly and look sweet."

Maggie grimaced. "How disgusting!"

"Of course it is, but traditional. You haven't even put on your veil!"

"I thought I would do that at the church."

"Balderdash! You'll do it right here. Daniel's such an anxious husband-to-be he'll be waiting for you at the door to the hospital, and it's bad luck for him to see you until the moment you reach the chancel. So you'll wear the veil and try your utmost to keep him from seeing more of you than is humanly possible. Here, give me that!"

Maggie had picked up the veil from the top of the bureau and was holding it so the length didn't touch the floor. At Anne's words, she handed the older woman the creamy tulle, and Anne proceeded to place it on Maggie's head. The lace was intricately sewn in a rose design, and a cordon of red rosebuds tumbled free, down Maggie's sides as it was unrolled.

Her fine, auburn hair was tucked into a thick bun behind her head, and the veil was clasped to her hair just above the roll with combs and another rosebud. The length of it covered the train of her dress, and Anne pulled the shorter, top layer over Maggie's face where it reached down to gently caress her bosom.

The creamy white bridal gown was fitted of satin-faced cloth that arched over her hips and flared gracefully in folds at her feet. Starched lace framed her slender neck. The bodice was slitted in front, the narrow opening reaching to the top of her breasts, displaying just enough skin to entice the groom. Between the breasts dangled a rope of fine pearls, Daniel's gift to her on the occasion of their marriage. The satin clung lovingly to each and every curve, creating a picture of grace as she was a picture of elegance and beauty.

"Here, I fetched my gloves for you. They'll do for the something borrowed."

"Annabelle gave me her blue handkerchief for the something blue." Maggie smiled at the remembrance.

"The veil is old and the gown is new . . ." Anne ticked off by rote.

"I do thank you for lending me your veil, Anne. It's so precious, I don't know how you can let it from your sight."

"I won't. I plan to be with you every moment. Now" — Anne stood back to admire her handiwork — "are you ready?"

Momentarily, Maggie's deception flitted into her mind. With a flick of her head, she tossed the worry aside, smiling and nodding at Anne. Whatever the cost, she would have this marriage. She loved Daniel too much to do otherwise.

And when the day came that she could afford her brothers' freedom and Daniel would meet them, that was the day she would begin to worry. By then she hoped to have made him so happy that he would love her enough to forgive any amount of deception.

Joshua called, and the two women hurried down the stairs and out the front door, into the waiting carriage. Annabelle and her brothers were before them, each eager to begin the ceremony.

A scant ten minutes later the carriage was pulling up before the hospital and the occupants were alighting. The boys were on their best behavior, and when they were, their manners were impeccable. Even toward a delighted Annabelle.

Magheen wore a cloak of soft gray, the hood providing protection for the delicate lace of the veil.

The day was darkly overcast, and the early morning seemed more like late afternoon. Maggie hurried inside where the gas lamps cast a soft glow down the corridors and across the walls. As she and the Howard family neared the chapel, they found Daniel pacing impatiently in the hospital corridor. Beside him was an elegantly dressed Harvey Benson.

Anne clucked her tongue and rolled her eyes heavenward. "I knew it," she intoned.

Daniel's eyes raised and found Magheen, their soft brown caressing her even from this distance.

"You are beautiful," he breathed.

"And so are you," Maggie answered softly, meaning every word. Beneath the black cutaway was a waistcoat of gray piqué and trousers of a darker, striped gray. On his head was a black silk hat, and he carried suede gloves of the same hue.

"Go away, Daniel!" Anne barked. "Don't you know it's bad luck to see the bride-to-be before she walks down the aisle?"

"I wasn't sure she was coming," he responded, the eyes dark and serious now. "You backed out once before, Magheen."

"Mr. Calcord," Maggie responded, her lips pursing, "you won't get out of your promise to marry me so easily. Now, go inside and wait until we're ready."

The white of his teeth seemed to sparkle at the teasing tone in her voice. He placed his hat in Joshua's hands. "Don't be long. Even your brother's tapping his toes with impatience."

"Give us only a moment more, Daniel."

"And have the pianist begin the music," Anne called after

him as he and Harvey returned to the chapel.

The music sounded a moment later, and Anne grinned mischievously at the bride. "I've never seen anyone quite so anxious to lose his freedom. It's a good thing he snatched you up when he did, or you might have thought twice about yours."

"Let's get this ceremony over," Joshua growled. He had taken the ladies' coats and Daniel's hat, and hung them in the vestibule. "Before you know it, everyone's going to lose their patience and leave the chapel to us alone."

Anne grinned saucily at her husband before turning and telling the boys to go inside and find their seats. At a very sedate pace she entered the chapel and proceeded down the narrow aisle. Her deep-blue velvet gown was set off by the single red rose in her hands. Behind her strode Annabelle, wearing a miniature gown that was a duplicate of her mother's. In the basket the child carried a bundle of bright straw-flowers, more fitting for a young girl than roses. Magheen entered on Joshua's arm. She carried a small ivory-bound prayer book and a single long-stemmed red rose.

At the door Magheen faltered, for the little chapel was filled to capacity. Then, garnering her courage, she stepped forward more firmly, only the tightening of her arm as she gripped Joshua's giving away her trepidation.

As they stood before the candle-lit altar, Joshua gave her to Daniel. Daniel's hands were warm and comforting as they pressed over hers. From the first moment he touched her and Patrick began speaking the words of the marriage ceremony, Magheen was more certain of herself. She responded in soft tones to Daniel's vows, an intimate smile curving her lips as she relished every word he spoke.

In many ways he seemed more nervous than she, Magheen thought. Perhaps for a man the moment seemed more fraught with fear and responsibility than for a woman. No, she amended. Nothing could feel more awesome than she felt at the moment.

She would wear her responsibilities well, she vowed. Daniel would never regret this day, no matter how many brothers she sprang on him.

Harvey reached into his vest pocket for the plain ring of gold. Inside were the bridal couple's initials and the date.

"I now pronounce you man and wife," Paddie beamed loudly. A bit more softly he uttered, "You may kiss the bride, Daniel."

"I've been wanting to do that all morning." Daniel grinned broadly, lifting her veil and dropping it to the back of her head.

"Mind you don't miss now," Maggie teased softly. "I'd hate to be embarrassed before all these fine folk."

Daniel stifled a laugh. But it was with a challenging glint in his eyes that he lowered his head and took her lips with his. The pressure he exerted was demanding yet gentle at the same time. Maggie closed her eyes and pressed her body close to him, relishing the taste and strong feel of him.

Daniel was the one to draw back. With a shaky laugh he touched his palms to either side of her head and whispered softly, "Maggie, Maggie . . . Maggie . . ."

Her eyes fluttered open.

"Don't look like that, Maggie, or we won't make it through the reception."

"How do I look, Daniel?"

Paddie coughed self-consciously. Lifting his head to the congregation, he announced, "Mr. and Mrs. Calcord have invited their friends to a reception at the Colorado House." His eyes widening brightly, Paddie added, "Daniel bought out the bar!"

"You did, Daniel?" Maggie grinned.

"I did. I had no time to prepare for a farewell to my bachelorhood with a dinner, so this will make up for it."

"Does that mean we have to stay late? Or can we get away . . . soon?"

Daniel arched an eyebrow. "Why do I think I'm getting a demanding bride?"

"Perhaps because you are," she answered saucily. "I think I can handle you."

"I hope so, Daniel. Oh, I do hope so!"

Her eyes held an unmistakable invitation. Daniel was wooed and won all over again. "Maybe we can get away. Soon."

"How soon?"

Laughing, Daniel took her hand in his and led her and the

crowd from the small chapel. Joshua handed Daniel Maggie's cloak and hood. She waited while he donned his own.

"To the Colorado House!" Daniel shouted, swinging himself inside the carriage, just behind his bride. With a lithe movement he was beside her and hauling her into his arms. "You teasing wench," he accused. "I've waited too long to get you alone."

"You corrupted me," she responded, her arms linking around his broad shoulders. Soft lips gently rained kisses across his jaw and forehead, down his nose, and teasingly across his lips. "I've been plotting to get you alone for a long time too . . ."

"As long as I've been plotting?"

"Longer," she replied emphatically. "I was thinking about this when you were ignoring me . . ."

His hands gripped her shoulders, and Daniel looked into her eyes. "I was never able to ignore you. I tried, the Good Lord knows how I tried. But from the first moment I saw you, all I could think of was how you'd feel to the touch—"

"Daniel, you *were* touching me! Remember? I was knocked out from the fall of the coach—"

"I remember, sweetheart. I remember far better than you. You were lying in my arms, still and quiet, as you've never been since, and I was slowly stripping the clothing from your back. Baby, until you've seen skin as soft and sweet as yours slowly being rendered bare, you've no idea of the thoughts going through a man's mind!"

"You didn't even know me then!"

"No, that came later. All I knew at first was how tempting you were. And all I could wonder was how I was going to keep my hands off you."

"You did a pretty good job of that," she accused.

"Until one night when you came to my room and sweetly invited me—"

"Shhh!" Maggie whispered fervently, her cheeks blushing a rosy red. " 'Twasn't like that!"

"It wasn't? Then why do I seem to remember you offering your breasts to me—" Whatever else he would have said was muffled beneath the palm of Maggie's hand.

"Don't you dare embarrass me any further, Daniel Calcord. I've married you now, and that's my cross to bear, but you'll not be making me blush every time you open your mouth."

"But I'm only speaking the truth, Maggie, me darling!" he mocked in her Irish accents.

"Hush, you son of the devil!"

"Oh, Maggie," he teased, kissing her until she could only moan in submission. His tongue flickered fire against the corners of her mouth. She breathed in the scent and feel of him, wanting this moment to go on forever. "I liked the way you offered yourself to me, Maggie." His voice was husky against her ear. "Each night I've gone to my lonely bed and you've been there to haunt me. You and those lovely breasts and those delectable thighs . . . and the way you moan my name when I'm bringing you pleasure, my Maggie."

She gave a muffled laugh. "Oh, Daniel, you make my heart pound so hard it'll burst! I can't help the way I am."

"I know. That's what makes you so delightful."

"The way I feel right now, I'll make you an old man long before your time."

"Try, Maggie!" he dared bravely. "I'll love the battle."

The carriage slowed to a stop, and Daniel had no choice, in the name of decency, but to release his bride. Stepping lightly from the carriage, he turned to assist Magheen. Joe Simmons was their driver, and he reached Daniel's side just as Maggie was setting her feet on the well-trod path that was named Chestnut Street.

More carriages, horses, and guests on foot followed them from the hospital. Others were waiting for them already. Not everyone who wanted to attend could fit into the small chapel.

At the other end of the street were freighters waiting to be unloaded, their drivers shouting profanities at stubborn mules and snarling teamsters as all movement in the street came to a standstill. A long line of wagons filled the road, for they were arriving at all times of the night and day.

The late morning sky was dark and gray. By afternoon, Maggie thought, snow would be falling, and the roads nowhere near so hospitable.

The fine, newly built Colorado House was one of the first structures in Leadville to be constructed of red Colorado brick. From the top of its shallow hipped roof hung the American flag. Arched windows lined each of the three floors. Brightly colored awnings stretched over the sidewalk, hung from the top of the first floor, protecting passers-by from inclement weather. The double front doors were topped by a half-round window and framed by two white pillars.

Altogether, this was a lavish hotel in which to hold the reception. Especially considering some of the guests.

Merchants, bankers, and mine owners mingled with carpenters, cooks, miners, brewers, and lawyers and their respective wives. Though everyone was dressed in his or her Sunday best, not everyone's Sunday best was equal.

The Gallagher brothers and their wives were garbed like the millionaires they were, while Frankie Wollery wore his Sunday-best coveralls. At least his coveralls were clean. Mike MacPherson and Soapy Stiles seemed to have forgotten what cleanliness smelled like. Maggie had cause to wonder where the nickname "Soapy" came from.

Joe Simmons and Dutch Saunders came, as did the newly married Carrie and Tom Fuller. Miss Nickerson, the spinster schoolmarm, arrived later with Mrs. Moen and Mrs. Sawyer. All of the ladies who belonged to the Altar and Rosary societies came with their husbands, several of them towing their children behind. Walter McClean and Tom Mason were late, arriving with the other survivors of the Old Abe disaster. Even Gertie Duggen, leader of the mob that had threatened Maggie, came.

The only pall on the celebrations was that the mine owners and businessmen of the town sat on one side of the hall, while the miners and other laborers sat on the other. Daniel supposed some discord was to be expected. The disaster at the Old Abe mine was fresh in everyone's memories. This was the first time since that had happened that both miners and mine owners were brought together. The solemnity of the occasion seemed to be the only thing that prevented a few nasty comments being followed by fisticuffs.

The new Mr. and Mrs. Calcord sat at the front table, just below the stage. Red velvet draperies were drawn across the stage and hung at the windows, looped with gold-tassled swags. Huge chandeliers of brass swung from the high ceiling. The comfortable seats were made of the finest horsehair, and on the arms of the chairs were carved angels.

Henry Gaw furnished aged Columbine beer from his brewery for the reception, Horace Tabor supplied the best imported champagne money could buy, the hotel provided meals for the guests, and the ladies each brought their specialty sweet.

Harvey Benson toasted Daniel with the first round of drinks. After that, the task of toasting the groom slipped from one table to the next, each toast louder and bawdier than the last. Nothing seemed too good for the hero of the moment, and Daniel Calcord was that.

When everyone had toasted his best to Daniel, they began a round of toasts to the bride. And then to her brother. Later to the best man. And still later, to the darling flower girl.

The Gallagher brothers, a bit too much champagne inside them, started in with toasts meant to belittle the common mining man.

Swiftly Daniel signaled for the entertainment to begin. The free liquor might prove to be more of a curse than a blessing.

Charles Vivian, his wife, and Eddie and Rose Foy performed an enthralling scene from *Oliver Twist*. Mr. Vivian was Fagan to his wife's Oliver. Eddie Foy's baritone voice led the assemblage in a lively and rousing olio after the play. Many of the songs were as boisterous as the town of Leadville itself.

The photographer Daniel had sent for from Denver finally arrived. With his black box and tripod slung over his shoulder, he took pictures whenever and wherever he could find someone to sit still for a long enough time. He caught Mr. and Mrs. Calcord with arms entwined, sipping champagne. Later he verbally coerced them into standing for a more serious shot for posterity. The newly married couple had to be still for so long their smiles began to slip. One more, he was warned. Even he wasn't prepared for the bride to be wearing her husband's beaver hat. Maggie was more into laughter and talking than into posterity.

The later the day grew, the higher the spirits soared. The stage floor was cleared, the actors and actresses changed out of their costumes to join the other guests. Codfish McCready had his fiddle warmed and ready. His partner, J. D. Hutchinson, cleared his voice so he could hit just the right note to call the dances.

Magheen and Daniel opened the dancing to a kind of dancing she had never seen before. "J. D. will tell you what to do. Just listen to what he says," Daniel told her.

"Do-si-do?" Maggie questioned in her Gaelic accent, perplexed. "I've no idea what the poor man is singing about."

"Follow me, ma'am. I'll teach you how to do a good ol' country swing."

She wasn't sure if she was good, but she tried her best. And the dancing was lively and fun. Soon the floor was filled with other dancers, the mine owners on one side of the floor, the miners on the other. A rousing bunch of calls began in earnest then. Maggie felt awkward at the unfamiliar words and turns. She blew loose tendrils from her face and pleaded weariness. Her toes might be happily tapping away and her hands might move in rhythm with the music, but she wasn't quite used to this.

"Ah, come on, Maggie! Let's show this bunch of Coloradans how the Irish do a jig." Paddie was enjoying himself hugely. The big man wore a plaid flannel shirt and suspenders, looking no more like a priest than any of the miners in the room. "Do you remember how, colleen?"

"I remember." Her eyes flashed as she answered the challenge. "The question is, do you?"

"The real question is — can *he* play a jig?"

Before Paddie had finished speaking the sentence, the fiddle Codfish McCready held was playing in a triple beat. McCready's thick, white brows rose with every short but loving stroke of the bow, his head bobbing sprightly with the tune. Paddie grinned at Maggie and raised his right hand, his knee bending in the beginning stance. She curtsied in reply and as she rose, her feet were tapping to the irregular beat of the music. Paddie tapped over to her and the two of them indulged in the dance they had known since early childhood. The onlookers clapped with the beat, and soon some of the other Irish-born-and-bred men joined their circle. And this time it didn't matter if they were miner or owner, they were all Irishmen.

When the dance finally ended, Magheen was ready to quit. Paddie had long since done so, his leg was not perfectly healed yet. But the dancing warmed up the crowd, and they began to mingle. Daniel partnered Mrs. Sawyer, and after her, Tom Mason's wife.

Tom Fuller and Joshua Howard understood what Daniel was trying to do, and they, too, invited wives of the working

176

men onto the floor.

Maggie stood by the curtains to catch her breath, pleased to see everyone joining in the fun.

"Miss Fitzgerald?" came a familiar voice from behind her.

Maggie stiffened, just before she turned and found William Lovell skulking behind the velvet curtains. She hadn't seen him since the day the mob nearly got her, nor did she have any desire to. "What are *you* doing here? I thought you fled this town with your tail between your legs," Maggie said curtly.

"Now," he cajoled, "don't be so hard on me, girl. I did you a favor and look how you repay me."

"You did *me* a favor? And what was that? Getting me nearly tarred and feathered?"

"I went to Denver to get those chickens for you. I can't help it if the best plans went awry. You stood to make a lot of money off me," he whined.

"Instead you cost me a lot of money!"

Bill licked his lips, his eyes brightening. "That's why I've come, to make it up to you."

Maggie paused, eyeing him uncertainly, "You mean you'll repay the money I had to refund all those people who paid for the chickens?"

"Of course I will. Just as soon as I get it."

Maggie's lips tightened. "I knew it. You've no intention of being honest. You're nothing but a low-down, sneaking cur—"

"Now, don't go using that tone on me, or I won't give you the chance of your lifetime. I could make you a wealthy woman, I could."

"You're just trying to get more money off me, Mr. Lovell, only I don't have any, so go try your wheedling somewhere else."

"But I've heard you're to marry Daniel Calcord."

"We have been married since noon this day. But if you think I'm going to ask my husband for money for you—"

Bill's brows arched upward in fear. "No, no, I don't want him knowing anything about this." At the murderous look he received, Bill shuddered and, reaching into his pocket, pulled out a handkerchief and unrolled it. "Lookee here. Ain't this the most beauteous sight you ever did see?"

Maggie stopped speaking, her eyes widening in shock. She

had no idea what gold looked like, but this must surely resemble it. A huge lump of golden rock glittered in the creases of the handkerchief. Her voice squeaked as she asked, "Is it real?"

"Of course it's real! What do you think I am? I found it, but I ain't telling you where I found it unless you're willing to back me with cash."

"I told you I don't have any money."

"You can get cash from your husband. Don't tell me a pretty girl like you don't know how to get money from her old man."

"You mean take money from Daniel? Lie to him about what I need it for?" The thought was horrendous. Maggie had never even thought so far ahead as to wonder how she would get money for household accounts, let alone money to shift surreptitiously to William Lovell.

"Of course you can get the money from him."

"I will not," she answered firmly. "If you want money from Daniel, you'll have to ask him yourself. I won't do it for you."

Bill thought for a moment. "Don't you have anything? Enough for just a grubstake will do. Twenty dollars even?"

"Twenty dollars? The only way you'd be after that paltry a sum is if you had stolen the rock."

"No, no," Bill protested too loudly. "I need it tonight. I can't wait around for a better grubstake."

"There he be, Sheriff," roared an irate voice from across the room. "I knew he'd be somewhere in this town, trying to hawk my stone, like the thievin' scoundrel he is. Well, arrest him. Ain't that yer duty?" Magheen recognized the speaker as Spade McInery, one of the miners who lived like a hermit up in the ten-mile district, north of Leadville.

Sheriff Nott frowned. "Can you prove ownership, Mr. McInery?"

"Why do I need to? That man ain't earned an honest dollar in his life."

Lovell grabbed the rock and returned it to its handkerchief. He was gradually sidling away from Magheen as the two men approached. Suddenly he stopped, his whole body straightening. Magheen realized Daniel held him by the arm and prevented him from sneaking off anywhere. "What's going on, Sheriff?" Daniel inquired.

178

"Mr. McInery here claims that Bill Lovell stole that piece of gold from him."

Daniel whistled. "Quite an accusation, Lovell. And an act that's not beneath your character, I know. Come on, let's see the rock." Bill Lovell hesitated for a moment before retrieving the kerchief from his pocket. Daniel studied the piece closely. "Pretty good-sized piece, all right. Problem is, it's pyrite, fool's gold, and not worth a cent. How much was he trying to get off you, Maggie?"

"Twenty dollars."

"Did you give it to him?"

"I'm not that much of a fool."

"Good." He turned to McInery. "It's worthless, not worth the brawl it will cause."

"I don't care what it's worth, I want that man jailed for stealing it from me!"

"He wants me off his mountain, that's what he wants!" Bill retorted nastily.

"I don't blame him a bit, Lovell. It's hard for a man to turn his back with you in the same area. I thought I told you to get out of town and stay gone."

"All he did was come my way and start his thievin' again," Spade accused. "Wall, how about it, Sheriff? Are you gonna arrest him or not?"

The sheriff spread his hands wide. "I can take him in, but I can't keep him more than overnight. Even if he did steal it, if it's pyrite, it's not worth enough to keep him more than a night."

"That's fine," came the miner's gruff answer. "As long as it keeps him from followin' me. I don't want the likes of him lookin' over my shoulder."

"You don't want to be followed, do you, McInery?" Lovell accused. "Why? What have you found that you need to keep from the rest of us?"

"Shut up, Lovell," Sheriff Nott ordered, leading Chicken Bill from the hotel.

At the front door, Nott took Lovell's arm and they stepped outside. In that second a bullet whizzed past, burning into the tender skin of the sheriff's ear. Nott winced, releasing Lovell, and grabbed at his injured ear, backing into McInery who was right behind them. McInery tried to keep Lovell from escaping, but a blazing dummy of a man was tossed at them, crumpling at their feet in the open door of the hotel.

"Fire!" came the shout from inside. Buckets of water were quickly hauled and tossed across the burning effigy.

"Where's that damned Lovell?" the sheriff demanded. The palm of his hand where it still covered his ear was now coated with bright blood.

Spade McInery cursed volubly. "He got away!" In answer to another question, he spat, "Hell, no, there's no chance of catching him now." McInery gestured to Chestnut Street which was still filled with wagons and horses and a throng of persons. "He can hide anywhere. That man's no better'n a weasel, and that's an insult to the weasels!"

Daniel was crouched over the effigy. Pinned to the dummy's vest was a thoroughly waterlogged note. "Someone's gone to a lot of expense over this," he commented.

"Yea," the sheriff agreed. "Mighty fine garb for a dummy." The dummy itself was made of straw and tucked inside fine gentleman's clothing. On the dummy's head sat a beaver hat, spats were pinned between gray trousers and shoes, keeping the whole outfit together.

" 'We'll see the mine owners burn in hell,' " Daniel read aloud, " 'unless we workers be given what's rightfully due us.' It's signed, the Elephant Club."

"The Elephant Club? What the devil is that?" Tom Fuller asked.

"Obviously a union of mine workers," Daniel answered dryly.

"A union?" boomed big Jack Rose, owner of the Rosa Vista mine. "If any of my men thinks to join a union, he's fired!"

"That goes for my men, too!" echoed another owner. The owners all nodded and agreed among themselves on their side of the room, while the workers stood across from them glaring, their tempers hot.

"We need a union," said Mike Mooney calmly. "Too many lives were lost in the Old Abe fire, lives that should never have been at risk. If the owners and managers won't protect their own men, we'll have to protect ourselves."

"Aye!" "I agree!" " 'at's tellin' 'em, Mike!" were the heated responses to Mooney's words.

"You approve of this sort of tactic?" Fuller questioned.

"I'd prefer peaceful means, if they work," Mooney responded.

"What do you know of this Elephant Club?"

Mooney shook his head. "I know nothing of it, but I'm not surprised it's here. Too many of us are discontent."

"Well, the least you could do, if you're talking union, is form a decent union, not this sort of trash."

"We don't want no damned union," bellowed a mine owner, moving forward with the other owners as in a body. The miners moved forward also.

Henry Borchert crossed the room and stood between the two opposing groups. He owned the hotel and wasn't about to let hot tempers destroy it. Motioning for the music to resume, he turned to the workers and said, "I think your ladies would like a turn on the floor." To the owners he said, "As yours would. They'd all prefer to dance than to witness a brawl."

"Maggie." Daniel smiled at her. "How about it? You survived dancing with your brother. Can you survive dancing with your husband?" They went onto the floor and led the dance, an act that seemed to bring their guests to their senses. A wedding reception was no place to settle serious differences such as these.

For the duration of the afternoon, though, the separation between owner and worker was more marked than it had ever been in Leadville.

Night was falling when Daniel spoke in Maggie's ear. "If we sneak out before they see us, we'll miss the snickering."

"I'm ready."

"Good." He took her by the hand. "Let's go."

Just as they hit the front door, Joshua Howard's voice boomed from across the room, "There they go! The newlyweds think to cheat us of the best part!"

"Hurry," Daniel roared. Magheen stopped long enough to sweep her long skirts and petticoats over an arm. Then she began to run alongside him.

The happy crowd of revelers was right behind them. "We can't outrun them, so we'll do the next best thing."

"What's that, Daniel?"

"Steal Tom's buckboard," he replied, his brows lifting teasingly. The buckboard was the only vehicle along the road he recognized other than his own, which was rigged between other vehicles, a ploy, he knew, that was meant to keep them from leaving before the crowd had at them. Daniel easily lifted Maggie aboard and climbed on himself.

"They're gaining on us, Daniel," she squeaked as he snapped the reins. "Oops, too late. They've got us."

"Not yet, they don't!" Daniel stood and drove the horses into the center of the road. The traffic had slacked off a bit since the earlier part of the day.

"Stop, thief!" Tom Fuller called out. He stood on the wooden sidewalk and watched Daniel and Magheen's flight with good humor. Beside him, his arm around her shoulder, stood a grinning Carrie.

"Harvey can give you a ride home," Daniel called out, the buckboard finally taking off. To his surprise, from beneath the wagon, out came a stream of ribbons and cans, proclaiming to everyone that he and Maggie were newlyweds. The streamer clanged noisily, but Daniel merely flicked the reins once more.

"I think we've been had, Daniel. We were set up to take this buckboard."

"I think you're right. Let's take our losses and go home."

Maggie snuggled next to him. "Yes, let's do just that."

Chapter Eleven

Feathery mists of clouds whispered through the moonlight. Silhouettes danced eerily across the night sky, melding hauntingly against the mountain and the curving road just ahead.

The draft horses plodded along at a sedate pace, the buckboard gently rolling behind. Inside, Magheen and Daniel huddled together beneath a blanket of thick fur, their breath mingling in the cold air. Maggie's happy laughter often penetrated the chill silence of the night. Once in a while, Daniel's gloved hands snaked out from beneath the blankets to jiggle the reins, reminding the horses that someone was in the driver's seat.

"Home is just ahead, darling," Daniel whispered against the thickness of her hood.

She nestled deeper against him, her mouth moving into the curve of his neck. "Sounds good to me."

"Mrs. Sawyer's spending the night with the Howards."

"Her idea or yours?"

"Anne's." Maggie could hear the rueful teasing in his voice. "She spent her wedding night with Joshua in his parents' home. She says no newlyweds should go through such a nightmare."

Maggie giggled. "I'd no idea she was so noisy."

"That's what I said to her. She went off in a huff. Sometimes I just can't understand you women."

"Joshua understands her and that's what matters."

His hand covered hers. "No, what matters is that I come to understand you."

The buckboard rolled to a stop in front of his house,

183

and he jumped down to help Maggie, whose long, full skirts were very much in the way. Daniel dealt with them swiftly, taking her in his arms and carrying her inside.

At the front door he dropped her slowly to her feet, letting the intimate feel of her glide down his front. His hands went to her throat and untied the ribbon that fastened her cloak. The hood fell back, and Maggie's silky tresses tumbled free. As she looked up at him, she was laughing, and again he was enchanted. He cupped her chin, his thumb gently rubbing her cheeks.

"You're cold," he said.

"Warm me," she said.

His mouth lowered and he proceeded to do just that, his mouth slanting over hers tenderly, taking every response she offered and wanting more.

Daniel lifted his head, hating the thought of even a few minutes spent away from her. "I have to put the horses away. Wait for me, will you?"

"Where?" she asked with an impudent grin. "Here, or in the bedroom?"

Daniel's eyes glinted with sudden heat. "Wherever you'll feel the most comfortable. I promise not to be too long."

The door closed behind him, and Maggie wandered into the parlor. Here he kept his brandy. Knowing well how much he liked it and vowing this would be a night for whatever Daniel liked, she poured a snifter. Stirring the banked fire to uncover the embers, she carefully laid kindling and a log on them, before climbing the stairs, decanter and snifter in hand.

In his room she found the shirt he had worn the day before hanging over the back of a chair. Rough, leather work boots were neatly set beneath the bed, and on his chest of drawers was a pocket watch and several pieces of loose change. The washbowl was still filled with cold, soapy water from his toilet of the morning.

He had left in something of an impatient hurry, she thought with satisfaction. At the foot of the bed, her wooden trunk awaited her arrival, right where Joshua had set it when he brought it over first thing in the morning. Inside, she had the few dainty treasures she owned, a gown embroidered especially for this night and three carefully sewn changes of underwear. Her finest undermuslin and chemise she wore beneath her wedding gown.

Placing the brandy decanter and snifter on the table beside the bed, she set about turning the covers down. Then she removed her gown and hung it on a scented hanger. Petticoat followed petticoat as she gently stepped out of them. Her finely sewn chemise came next, leaving only sheer muslin covering her breasts and hips. Maggie stretched as she hung the petticoats and chemise in the wardrobe. Rifling through the trunk, she finally found the gown of fine lawn she had spent so many hours embroidering for this night.

Turning, she thought to see herself in the mirror as she replaced the muslin with the nightgown. Instead she saw Daniel in the doorway, his black eyes no longer teasing but intimately intent as they watched her. He had been watching her for a long time, she could tell. Her reflection in the mirror told her how transparent the muslin was, how her nipples strained full and rosily against the cloth. The gown would be no more enticing. And she wanted to entice him, she knew.

The gown fell to the trunk as her fingers moved to the ribbons of the chemise and tugged, baring the creamy skin of her neck and breasts.

His mouth went dry as he stood in the doorway watching her. She was sleek and beautiful, more beautiful than he remembered. Slender fingers pushed the chemise aside, revealing textured, rosy nipples. They stood firm and impudent, daring this man to touch and taste of them.

The brilliant eyes darkened and lowered. Magheen understood what he wanted of her. Her fingers worked at the waistband, unbuttoning her lace-tiered bloomers. Dropping them to the floor, she stepped free and stood before him. Her eyes dropped at the heat in his, and at the length of time it was taking him to react. He seemed to have nothing to say. If he liked her . . . if he wanted her . . .

Daniel read the uncertainty in her eyes and moved swiftly, coming to her side, his arms capturing her with their fluid strength, as secure and warmly as she would ever need. His mouth was molding hers with an insistent pressure.

She felt the control he exerted over himself, almost as if he were afraid of bruising her soft flesh. Maggie's hands threaded around the sculptured muscles of his upper arms, wanting to feel his strength as part of herself.

His mouth nuzzled her neck and searched frantically for her mouth as he scooped her up in his arms. All uncertainties fell away. The bed was but a few steps away. Daniel crossed that span and set her down, taking one long, hungry look at her before he stepped back a foot or two and smiled. "Now, it's your turn," he said huskily. The topcoat had been removed at the front door, now his cutaway followed. His fingers worked the buttons of the elegant silk shirt, but his eyes never strayed far from her face. As she watched him, her eyes were wide with intent curiosity.

He was tapered and firm with sinewy strength. Dark hair matted his chest, disappearing into the waistband of his trousers. He sat on the bed to remove his shoes and Maggie touched his back then, loving the play of his muscles beneath her fingertips. Daniel turned as the shoes hit the floor, an intimate smile on his face.

Skin as soft and clear as hers made a man want to touch and keep on touching, he thought. Wisps of her hair fell into her eyes and she brushed them aside, waiting impatiently for the rest of the show. Daniel grinned. His shy bride was certainly a sensual creature. What pleasures they would share.

He stood and the trousers came next. He shrugged them impatiently from his feet. The cold was beginning to eat at him, seeping through his skin and leaving goose pimples behind. She had done this, he thought, and he knew damn good and well she hadn't developed goose-flesh!

Maggie laughed then, scooting over in the bed and patting the mattress beside her. "We don't want you getting pneumonia, you know."

Daniel hopped in and pulled her close. "I wasn't too sure what you did want."

"Ooch, but you're cold, Daniel. Your legs are like ice . . ."

"Can you warm them up, me darlin' girl?"

186

"Now don't you go making fun of me or my accent, Daniel Calcord!"

"I'm not making fun of your accent, Mrs. Calcord. I'm just trying my darnedest to get warm."

"You're giving my thighs a chill, you are."

"But you're so warm, Maggie," he cajoled. "Come here and let's share some of that warmth. I was the one who had to go out and put the horses away. It's no wonder I'm cold." She crawled to him and snuggled in his arms. His thighs twined around hers, his eyes closing as he sighed with satisfaction. "I like the way you feel against me. Have I ever told you I like your thighs?"

"Let me think on that," she responded dreamily. "No, not that I recall. Have I ever told you that I like your thighs too? Only they tickle the tiniest little bit."

Daniel rubbed his thighs against hers again. "Do they? Do they tickle there too? But mine are hard and hairy, yours are like silk and satin and temptation," he growled playfully, rolling her onto her back, his mouth opening hungrily and swooping to capture hers.

"Ah, Maggie," he groaned raggedly. "I've wanted you for so long . . ."

"And I you, Daniel," she breathed, her lips opening to welcome him. He tasted of wine and cigars.

"Ever since the last time, Maggie." He spoke when the need for breath assailed him. "You liked it, I know, and I spoiled it for you. I'm sorry I did that, but I was afraid of letting you too near me. I never meant to hurt you. I promise to never hurt you again."

She smiled slyly. "No more Lil Amundson's?"

"Never!" Daniel vowed.

"Remember that, Daniel Calcord, for I find that I am a very jealous woman. And if I ever catch you so much as looking at another woman, Irish or not, it'll be a skillet I'll be taking to your head!"

"I'll be good," he swore. "No more nights at Lil's, no more nights with the boys, no more . . . let's see," he questioned, his eyes crinkling at the corners. "What else do I do that's bad?"

"I don't know, I haven't lived with you long enough to know. Except that you let your temper get the best of you sometimes."

"I promise to control my temper, *if* you promise to control yours."

"Are you implying I have a temper?"

"I'm not implying a thing, sweet. I'm telling you. You've got a temper on you the size of the courthouse in Denver." His teeth nipped at one swollen nipple peeking up at him. "I don't mind that so much, at least I don't think I do. If I'm going to be such an exemplary husband, there'll be nothing to get worked up about, right?"

"If you're so exemplary, why are you wasting so much of the night talking?"

He laughed aloud at this. "Damned if I know!" His hands ran the length of her body, callused fingers greedily brushing the soft skin, rubbing her nipples between his thumb and finger. He settled his thigh between hers, content to go slow and easy with this lovemaking. They had all night and every night for the rest of their lives. There was no reason to hurry.

Except that Magheen's hands were wandering. Daniel gave a sigh as he closed his eyes.

Her clasp tightened. To her, he smelled of wood, weather, and horses, and tasted salty.

"Don't you like it?"

"Like it?" he questioned gruffly. "I like it too damn much." Giving a ragged groan, he rolled her onto her back and pinned her arms over her head. Lowering his mouth to hers, he nipped at the soft swell of her lips. "And I like this . . . and this." His head lowered to her breasts and suckled. Her reaction was immediate, the nipples filled even more, reaching impudently for his touch. ". . . and more, Maggie, so much more."

His hands reached beneath her hips and lifted her to cradle him intimately. Maggie answered with a movement all her own, and Daniel gasped in purest pleasure.

"Are you sure you haven't done this before?" he questioned in a deep voice.

"Once, that was all," she replied, biting at his chin. "Don't you remember?" she questioned provocatively. Funny, the last time she and Daniel had made love she hadn't realized how she could arouse him with the use of

188

her lips. What a feeling of power the knowledge gave her. "I guess it was hardly enough to count."

"True," he breathed in her ear. "You must need another lesson. All wives should become expert . . . at this sort of thing."

"What sort of thing?"

"This," he groaned. His hand cupped her fingers and lowered them to touch him intimately, as though he couldn't resist the temptation. "Ahhh, Maggie, you're a most enthusiastic learner."

Her smile broadened and she snuggled deeper against him. "I'm getting better, aren't I, Daniel?"

He moaned. "I think I've died and gone to heaven. Only heaven doesn't smell this sweet. You'd better stop now. I can't stand it any longer." Of course, she didn't stop. And of course, he couldn't stand it any longer. With a swift movement he had her on her back, and his tongue was making a leisurely exploration of the tender insides of her mouth.

She was achingly aware of the growing demands of his body. Whimpering with pleasure, she relaxed her legs and let him slip between them. The iron hardness of him was silky smooth as it nuzzled against her, seeking the sweet heat of her passion. Maggie entwined herself about him, inviting a more intimate touch.

Daniel's whole body shuddered with harshly controlled passion. He ached to appease the wild hunger straining against him but had sworn to go more carefully this time. She might think she was ready, but Daniel couldn't take the risk. Instead, he tortured her with slow, deliberate movements as he delved slightly deeper with each thrust of his hips. Sensations flooded through her, making her response shiveringly sweet as he left her weak with wanting him.

Daniel's eyes were brilliant, his movements sure and experienced, she realized, in that moment as the earth tilted and spun wildly.

In a voice raspy with desire, she told him of her heat and need, but Daniel was achingly slow and tender in his caresses. His hand slipped low, rounding the softness of her belly, reaching the junction of her thighs. Maggie

189

whimpered helplessly as he touched her, a fire spreading through her, threatening to engulf her.

"Open your eyes for me, Maggie," he commanded softly. "I want to see how they look when I make you mine. I want to see how you enjoy being my wife."

She obeyed him, opening her eyes and watching him greedily as he lifted over her. Her body shook with need, jolting from the impact as he entered her. Fiery sensations spread, increasing with each forceful thrust. His arousal was iron hard in its unspoken demands, and she met them eagerly, her moist softness welcoming all of him.

The world spun again as his mouth closed hotly over her nipple. The fire burning inside her was spreading upward and outward. Her body heaved in his arms as she shattered into a million tiny pieces. And then he joined her in this topsy-turvy world of pleasure and passion, his heat spreading more wildfire through her.

Their hunger was too great. They made love all night long and well into the morning. The night had been a long and luxurious one, filled with exploration and pleasure. In between bouts of loving they slept entangled with each other, their bodies tingling, for the moment, with satisfaction.

The bright sun filled the room with light and warmth, in spite of the coldness of the day outside, as Maggie woke and stretched.

"Lazybones," Daniel remarked. Yawning, he settled her once again in his arms.

Maggie's hand slipped low. "Daniel . . ." she cooed.

"I take that back. There's not a lazy bone in your body. Of course, there's a bunch of exhausted ones in mine."

Biting her lower lip, Maggie teased him lightly with her fingers. "Not everything about you is so lazy," she taunted.

"You're a loose woman, Magheen Fitzgerald Calcord," he growled, nipping her ear. "What am I to do with you?"

"That's the kind you be liking, I think, Daniel Calcord. At least that's the kind you seek at Lil Amundson's."

"They can't compare to you, sweetheart. You fulfill your duties with such enjoyment."

Maggie arched an eyebrow. "They don't? And why not, may I ask?"

"Probably because they've never had *me* making love to them."

"Love?"

His gleaming shoulders shrugged. "Something akin to it."

"How humble you are, husband."

"Have you any complaints?"

"One."

"Oh, what is that?"

She grinned broadly. "This one." Her hand stroked his silken length and the gleam in her eyes beckoned.

Daniel sighed greatly as he rose over her, the corded muscles of his arms and back gleaming with the morning light. "Never let it be said a Calcord did not do his husbandly duties."

The week passed quickly. Mrs. Sawyer decided to take advantage of the newlyweds long enough to take the stage over to Fairplay and visit her brother and his wife. So Magheen and Daniel had the whole week, and the house, to themselves.

Father Patrick tactfully stayed away, and Harvey Benson came only once and that was to bring a telegram marked urgent that had arrived for Daniel. Maggie asked Daniel about it, and he said it was nothing that he needed to attend to this week. Which was exactly what she wanted to hear.

The house smelled of Maggie's cooking and the pine logs crackling in the fireplace. Each afternoon, the newly wedded couple took off and explored this private little kingdom of theirs, until their feet and fingers grew too numb with cold to stand the outdoors any longer. When they returned, Daniel had his coffee and Magheen a cup of her sweet tea. Dinner was invariably late, for warming their blood with hot drinks brought warming of their bodies to mind and that took the rest of the afternoons and early evenings.

Daniel was a generous lover, giving of himself as well as

191

taking. Magheen's pleasure was always uppermost in his mind for she made it so easy; she was such an eager learner.

During that week he learned that many of his first impressions were true. She did have a temper, though she never used it on him . . . yet, and her humor was delightful and that she did use often. She loved to laugh and tease and make him feel comfortable. He hadn't felt so happy in years. She also had definite opinions that, thankfully, usually merged with his. He knew the day was coming when they would argue, but he was confident that he knew how to sweep her off her feet and make her see his way. The other thing he learned about her was just what he first feared; she knew how to get under his skin. He thought of her too often and in too much depth. He couldn't let her touch him so deeply that he would begin to trust her. Not when he knew how painful betrayal could feel.

Maggie instinctively knew which part of himself he withheld. He never spoke of his family or his early life, rarely even trusted her with business affairs. She couldn't blame him, for she withheld secrets from him too, and was now growing wary of the repercussions when he did learn the truth. Perhaps she should have told him about her brothers, but he didn't like the Irish, let alone approve of his wife having Irish brothers sentenced to life in a penal colony. Her hopes of buying their freedom seemed more remote than ever. She was married to Daniel, the money she made should be theirs, not hers to use as she pleased. But she would save it and use it as she alone wanted, for the thought of anything else was intolerable. When she married Daniel, she had no thought of forsaking her brothers, and, right or wrong, the doubts now creeping through her mind couldn't change it.

So she would be content with what she had. If she were lucky, Daniel need never know the whole sordid truth. If not, at least she had this time and this much happiness with him. The one thing she was sure of now was that she could love no other man as she did Daniel, nor would she want to try. What she did try was to please him, to be everything he might want in a wife and more, to make it

—— F R E E ——

B O O K   C E R T I F I C A T E

ZEBRA HOME SUBSCRIPTION SERVICE, INC.

YES! Please start my subscription to Zebra Historical Romances and send me my free Zebra Novel along with my first month's Romances. I understand that I may preview these four new Zebra Historical Romances Free for 10 days. If I'm not satisfied with them I may return the four books within 10 days and owe nothing. Otherwise I will pay just $3.50 each; a total of $14.00 (a $15.80 value—I save $1.80). Then each month I will receive the 4 newest titles as soon as they come off the press for the same 10 day Free preview and low price. I may return any shipment and I may cancel this arrangement at any time. There is no minimum number of books to buy and there are no shipping, handling or postage charges. Regardless of what I do, the FREE book is mine to keep.

Name _____

(Please Print)

Address _____ Apt. # _____

City _____ State _____ Zip _____

Telephone (_____) _____

Signature _____

(if under 18, parent or guardian must sign)

4-89

so that if he did learn about her family, he might think twice about giving her up.

When he turned to her at night, she received him with all the love inside her, giving it freely and deeply, giving as much of herself as she possibly could.

No matter what happened in the future, they had this time and she would treasure the memory forever.

On Monday morning, Maggie woke to the sound of Daniel dressing. The room was still in darkness and the house seemed filled with an unusual silence. They were no longer alone; Mrs. Sawyer had returned the night before, but she apparently wasn't up yet, either.

"Do you always get up this early, Daniel? The clock reads but four o'clock."

"I've left the mine unattended too long as it is, Maggie."

"Will you be late coming home tonight?"

"I don't know. Probably." He spoke with only half-awareness of Magheen. Already his mind was racing through all the matters needing to be done today.

Maggie smiled to herself as she climbed from the warmth of the bed and reached for her woolen robe. Daniel was preoccupied with his business, another trait she had only guessed at before now.

"Where are you going?" he asked, surprised to find her at the door.

"To make some of that horrid brew you like so much. I suppose you eat heartily at this time of the morning, especially if you don't know when you'll be home?"

"I usually wait until I'm at the bunkhouse. Old Gabe cooks up more than enough for the men."

"As long as you've a wife, you'll be taking your meals here," she said on a final note, until doubt overwhelmed her and she turned back to him to question incredulously, "Unless you prefer riding that far on an empty stomach?"

"I don't want you going to too much trouble," he answered slowly, clearly tempted by the thought of warm coffee waking him gradually. "You might as well get a bit more sleep. I can wait the fifteen minutes or so it takes to reach the mine."

"It's no trouble, really, Daniel. I've got to get up soon anyway, and I'd just as soon share a few moments of peace

193

and quiet with you. Does this Gabe feed you dinner too?"

"He'd be madder'n a wet hen if I tried to come home at noon. Gabe takes a lot of pride in his cooking."

Maggie laughed lightly. "Then please, don't insult the poor man. But I'll be fixing your breakfast."

"You can sleep for hours yet."

"No, I cannot. I'm supposed to be at the store by eight-thirty. Mr. Smith takes it amiss if I'm so much as a minute late." She turned and was through the door before he could reply. He heard her voice from the hallway saying, "Black brew comin' up!" The Western accent she tried to imitate intermingled with the Irish lilt and came out a foreign language.

The coffee was perking and the bacon browning on the stove when Daniel entered the kitchen. Maggie glanced up from her labors and smiled. He was dressed in his working clothes, denim pants, and woolen shirt. Underneath he wore red flannels. Maggie had already seen those as he was dressing. In his hand was the Stetson of which he was so proud. Seeing him like this made their marriage more real, more permanent.

"Three eggs or four?" she questioned.

"Three. And hash browns, if you made them."

Maggie grinned. "You thought I wouldn't know what you were talking about, didn't you? May I remind you potatoes come from my part of the world? I can cook them any way you can think up."

"And, of course, Mrs. Sawyer showed you how to add bacon bits and onions to them."

"No, actually it was Mrs. Moen. She went through a spell of wanting to westernize me when I first arrived." Maggie gave a timorous sigh, "And then she gave it up. You don't suppose I was a stubborn learner, do you?"

"I do. I think you were the most stubborn case she ever ran into."

"But that was before she ever met you," Maggie teased.

He took a seat at the head of the table and began eating with obvious enjoyment. When he was done, he wiped his mouth and set the napkin beside the plate. Maggie rose, intending to take the plate to the sink, but Daniel's hand on her arm stopped her. "Sit down, Maggie. It's time we

194

had a talk."

She sat and waited for him to speak.

"Maggie, you don't have to work anymore. I can support us very nicely."

"But the mine's not paying yet—"

"I have other sources of income. The mine is strapping me a bit, but no more than I had planned. I can provide all the necessities, just not all the luxuries. I've never had the responsibility for a wife before. When I leave in the morning, I want to think of you at home and safe. I don't need any more worries."

Maggie took a deep breath, and her hand came up to cover his. She would dearly love to tell him all the truth, but didn't dare. So, she would settle for a wee bit of the truth. "Daniel, I like working. I like the people I work with and the customers I see during the day. You'll be gone so much, what can it matter? I'll be home before you get here, that I promise." Warily her eyes appealed to him. "Don't ask me to give up my work, Daniel. Please, not that."

He spoke slowly. "Someone else might need that job. You don't."

"Daniel, please understand . . ."

"I think I do understand, Magheen," Daniel replied as he rose. Her heart sank at the hardness of his expression. She hadn't seen the likes of it for weeks now. "You want more than you think I can provide. You're wrong. I can provide more than you have any right to expect. But you'll keep that ridiculous job in spite of your new duties as my wife, in spite of what I think and want. You'll keep on working no matter what. And just so you can have a bit of extra coin in your pockets.

"I was right about you in the first place, Magheen. You're greedy and selfish, just like the rest of your kind."

He was gone in seconds, the door closing behind him with an ominous finality. Magheen looked at the door, thinking of his last, cruel words, and felt like crying. Instead her own eyes grew hard. How dare he be so judgmental! Just who did he think he was, to be judging her, as if he thought he was one of the sainted himself? The more she thought about his words, the angrier she became. She had enough pride for three Daniel Calcords. So he thought her greedy and selfish, did he? And just because she wanted to save some money for her brothers. Purposely, she neglected to remind herself of what Daniel didn't know.

It was with a fighting glint in her eyes that Maggie climbed the staircase and dressed for work.

"Four more telegrams came after that first one," Harvey Benson said laconically, tossing them onto Daniel's desk. "It seems the board was rather impatient for an answer."

"They don't really want an answer. What they want is a miracle. They seem to have forgotten what an effort it takes to make money. They wanted the mine producing tons of silver a day from the moment I arrived. It hasn't, and now they want out."

"They're a bunch of fools, Daniel. This mine will pay yet, that I swear."

"Don't swear it to me, I believe you. That's why my response will be an offer to buy each of them out. I believe just as much as you do that we're onto a rich vein here, Harvey. All we need is the time and the money. The money I'll find."

They stood in the latest addition to the mine buildings, the finally completed bunkhouse. At the far end of the large room and partitioned off from the rest was a small, cozy spot that Daniel used as an office and that offered more quiet and solitude than the mine itself. "Have you ordered the pumping machinery yet?" he asked.

"I did that weeks ago," Harvey replied.

"Then I'll have to find the money to cover that also. Sit down and let's come up with a reasonable tender."

"They'll want a profit."

"They don't deserve a profit, not backing out this quickly. If a man puts money in an investment, he'd better be ready to ride with that investment or lose his money. I've told them time and time again this mine will pay. I'm weary of having to convince them so often. At least I've got their responses in writing. When we hit it big, I don't want them crying foul."

"You really believe in this, don't you, Daniel?"

"I believe so much that I'm willing to risk everything I own as collateral for the loan. And it had damn well *better* pay off."

The truce was unspoken but binding. Neither Magheen nor Daniel reminded the other of the gist of the angry argument that Monday morning, but neither of them quite forgot it. Daniel was remote, a bit vague about everything concerning himself or his business, while Magheen conveniently forgot to mention her work beyond the most cursory of remarks. She was cool, always smiling. And it was that that got Daniel the most. How she could behave as though nothing had happened went beyond his understanding.

Each night, as they crawled into bed, Daniel would be distant, reserved as he first took her in his arms. But he couldn't hold out. And then fight it as she would, he always managed to resurrect the hot, passionate woman he knew her to be.

Come morning, that mistrust was there again, a festering wound in their marriage. Their home was turning into a undeclared war zone, and neither was sure how long they could stand it.

They had been married for almost a month on the day Daniel rose an hour later than usual. It was Friday and Maggie was due in the Emporium a few minutes early to count her hours for the week. She was surprised to see Daniel wearing his businessman's clothing when he came into the kitchen, but did not ask why, nor did Daniel volunteer the reason. She rode into town in her usual manner, on horseback, getting a glimpse of Daniel as he rode in the other direction, toward the mine.

She was on her lunch break, taking a long walk along the sidewalks of the town, when she saw him again. He entered the building that housed the First Bank of Leadville and other offices, and disappeared from her sight. She waited for a few more minutes, until her break time was up, before returning to the store. Curiosity had the best of her but nothing in the world could induce her to question him about his strange actions this day, though she had to remind herself often of that fact throughout the long day.

"We've got trouble, Harvey." Daniel spoke loudly enough to be heard over the roar of the engines as he entered the shaft house of the Resurrection.

Harvey glanced up from where he was guiding the hoist through the workings. Motioning to one of the other men to take his place, Harvey nodded to Daniel, mouthing the words that led them outside to the relative quiet.

"What's happened?" Harvey questioned as he removed his thick leather gloves.

"I saw Fred Trumpy at the bank. They're not willing to make the loan. He gave me some song and dance about the impending threat of a strike by the miners. He claims there's some rumor going around about the Elephant Club—"

"I ain't so sure it's just a rumor, Daniel. Some of the men are getting mighty fed up with the owners and managers around here. They're tired of risking their necks for a few men who never risked anything for anybody else. And I can't say as I blame them."

"Are our men complaining?"

"Course not! Any man hereabouts would give his eye-teeth to work in these conditions. But most mine owners don't feel like you do. They don't give a damn what happens to the miners as long as they get a good day's work out of them. Fred Trumpy ought to know that. There's no risk of your men striking."

"Unless they all organize and hold a general strike," Daniel suggested.

"There's a possibility of that," Harvey admitted. "But a better possibility is that the Elephant Club won't be behind any strike around here. Scuttlebutt has it that a representative of the Mineworkers' Union in Pennsylvania is on his way, and he'll make mincemeat out of the Elephant Club."

"So Fred's right and a strike could be imminent?"

Harvey shrugged. "Could be."

"He claims a strike could cripple the Resurrection. He

doesn't want to lend money for mining until that worry is gone."

"He's right about that too. We need to produce some income and fast."

"Dammit! The risk is mine! I offered enough collateral for twice the amount I wanted."

"Does that mean we've got to shut down?"

"No, that means you operate the mine while I go to Denver for the money. I know I can get it there."

"I don't think it's a good time for you to be leaving—"

"I have to go anyway. I have a date in court next week. This just gives me twice the reason to go."

"Won't your wife be a bit upset to be left on her own so soon?" Harvey inquired, a curious twist to his expression.

Daniel scowled. "She's coming too."

"I can't go, Daniel. I've taken too much time off from work already. If I take any more time, they'll replace me."

"I've told you, you don't need to work," he snapped. "What's more important, our marriage or your damned job?"

"Don't you go swearing at me, Daniel Calcord! If you had a brain working in your head, you wouldn't ask such a thing. But I owe Mr. Smith consideration too; he's been good to me. I can't take the time off."

"Is that your final word?"

"Yes! Oh, Daniel, please try to understand!"

"I do. I understand perfectly. Why don't you go pack my bag and make sure to put my good suit in it? That's a good girl," he finished patronizingly, returning his attention to the papers on his desk.

Maggie stared at him momentarily, then realized all the talking in the world wouldn't make him understand her. Angrily she stomped up the stairs, her mouth turned down in a scowl. "And so, because of my greedy, female nature, I'm not to be trusted even with the reasons for this speedy trip to Denver. But for consolation, I'm allowed to pack his bag and without one word of thanks! Just 'do this for me, Maggie, and this, Maggie, and be a sweet little girl and go hide your head beneath the bedcovers until I send for

199

you.' Bah!"

She finished the task, expecting him to be up any moment. He wasn't though, and she realized he expected another argument. Well, it was his turn to be surprised. He was leaving in the morning? Well, she would be sound asleep when he came to bed and he would be lucky to get so much as a peck of a kiss to see him off, she thought self-righteously.

It was several hours later when he came to the bedroom. She was lying on her side, her hand hugging the pillow, the band of gold around her finger catching a glint of light from the lamp he set on the table beside her. Auburn hair was strewn across the white muslin and the green eyes were closed, but he could still see them in his mind, sparkling with anger.

The blanket slipped low and her bosom moved gently with her breathing. The ribbons of her gown were trapped beneath her form and the bow gaped open. Only a hint of fair, white skin peeped out at him. Maggie rolled over and the gown caught fully beneath her weight and tightened across her breasts.

Daniel didn't like the way his thoughts were roaming. He didn't want to want her, not tonight, not after she had refused to go to Denver with him. He wanted to show her how little he needed her, just as little as she needed him. So, why didn't she pull that damn blanket over her head?

Disrobing, he carefully scooted beneath the covers. Slowly, she inched toward him, her sleeping body seeking the source of the heat in the bed. A slender thigh came up and nudged against his backside. He turned, intending to roar angrily at her, but she stretched sleekly and the gown rode lower from her neck and higher from the hemline.

Daniel's mouth went dry. It wasn't right for a man married nearly a full month to still react this way to his wife, he tried to convince himself. But his fingers gentled her thighs, and his chest brushed against hers. Maggie sighed and slipped nearer just as Daniel's mouth opened hungrily and swooped over hers.

The green eyes opened in surprise. She had meant to be angry with him, she thought, but the taste and smell of him wiped further irate thoughts aside. She melted against im, her answering kiss heatedly fervent, her fingers seeking to pull him nearer to her.

Through the thickness of her gown, he could feel her heat and moisture. Then all thought fled as the gown rode above her hips. He entered her swiftly, his loins forcefully thrusting. Maggie moaned in pleasure as his lovemaking escalated in its fiery hunger.

She did not recognize these two people, she thought as if from a great distance. The mating grew wilder and fiercer. This was not the gentle loving Daniel had shown her before, but a fever pitch of desire she had not imagined could exist between a man and his woman. Sensations crackled and tormented like a fever burning inside her. She was wanton as she heaved in his arms, her body enticing him to an intensity to equal hers. Maggie lifted her hips to receive all of him, and his muscles clenched as Daniel flooded her with his passion.

"Do you have to go today, Daniel?" Magheen questioned wistfully, her hand smoothing the light furring on his chest. She lay in the crook of his arm, her full length stretched beside him. The night had been filled with exploration and pleasure. Her body still tingled.

"I have to, Maggie," came the slow, sated response. "I've got business in Denver, though, I admit, it will be hard concentrating when I think of you here and me miles away. I wish you would come with me."

"Don't spoil this moment, please, Daniel," Maggie said pleadingly as her fingers touched his lips. The angry words he had already spoken to her would haunt her for the rest of her life. In spite of the love they had shared last night and the many nights before this, he still thought of her as greedy and selfish. And did he still think of a child from her body as a "half-Irish brat"? That thought was the most painful of all.

"When do you have to leave?"

"Early. I need to get ready now."

"I'll fix your breakfast." She started to roll away from him, but his hand stopped her.

"Maggie . . . Take care of yourself while I'm gone. I'll

miss you."

"I'll miss you too, Daniel, more than you can imagine," she said as she leaned over to press a kiss against him.

"No more, Maggie," he groaned. "I can't take it. At this rate I'll be soon dead from lack of sleep."

"You can sleep on the stage," she answered primly. "Besides, you didn't seem to mind so much last night."

"Last night, I didn't. And not this morning either, as I recall. But at the moment I wonder . . ."

"Don't you dare say another word, Daniel Calcord. I know when you're trying to embarrass me."

"*Me!* Embarrass *you?*" he questioned innocently. "And I was never so embarrassed as when I thought I couldn't perk up for you . . ."

"Perk?"

"That's exactly what you said. Don't you remember? Daniel," he mimicked her voice, "can't you perk up a little just one more time?"

"Ahhgh!" Maggie gasped, rising beside him, her cheeks burning a bright red. "I don't remember any such thing. You're nothing but an unspeakable—"

"Cur?" he questioned innocently.

"Cad!" she threw at him, furious. "You son of the devil! Don't you go kissing me like that! Not after you've ridiculed me and made me feel terrible about myself . . . as if I'm some kind of wanton—or whatever!"

Daniel trapped her beneath him, his lips moving over her warmly. "Did I ever tell you I have a penchant for wantons? The more wanton the better, I always say." His mouth nuzzled her into a pitiable weakness.

"You'd better have that penchant, Englishman, for that's what you've made of me."

"Good," he answered with satisfaction.

Chapter Twelve

Maggie pressed open the door leading into Anne Howard's kitchen, quickly shutting it behind her in an effort to keep the cold of the day from following inside. Stomping booted, snowy feet on the brightly colored rag rug, she glanced toward the housekeeper, who hovered near the stove, and smiled. One by one she picked her fingers free of the gloves and untied her heavy woolen scarf.

"What a delicious smell, Mrs. Moen," she commented, shaking the scarf and her hat free of snow. "Nothing in this world smells quite so good as apples and cinnamon baking in an oven on a day such as this."

"Apples, cinnamon, and raisins," Agnes Moen corrected. The housekeeper had turned her attention to the tray of tea and cups on the sideboard, but she paused in what she was doing long enough to level a sharp look at Magheen. "You seem near chilled to death. Here, move closer to the stove, it's nice and hot."

Maggie did just as she was told, holding her hands over the oven door to toast them more quickly. "Pie?" she questioned, her eyes shining.

"Strudel."

"Mmm, sounds even better," Maggie teased, licking her lips and smiling broadly.

"Mrs. Howard and Carrie are upstairs in the attic, sorting through baby things," Agnes commented, her eyes resting slyly on the girl.

The words took a few seconds to register. When they did, Maggie gave the housekeeper a surprised glance. "Is Anne . . . ?"

"Nope," Agnes stated bluntly, her lips closing firmly. "Not Anne. She says she's done having babies."

"You mean . . . Carrie? Carrie's expecting?"

"I never said any such thing. I wouldn't give away Carrie's news for all the tea in China. Though how the whole world can't guess just by looking at her I don't know! She's giggling and laughing more like Annabelle than a young married woman."

"A baby," Maggie breathed. "Carrie's expecting a baby!"

"Now, don't you go spoiling her news! You let her break it to you—"

But Maggie was gone, flying up the two flights of stairs and around the corner, long before Agnes could finish the sentence. The attic room was small and airless, filled with ancient treasures. Anne was bent over a huge trunk, and beside her, on the floor, were stacks of fine baby linens.

"Carrie? Is it true? Are you to have a baby?" Magheen questioned, catching the other girl in her arms.

"It is true! I think," Carrie amended hastily, frowning. "Anne says it's so, so it must be!"

"It is," Anne affirmed.

"Well, what does Tom say? Is he excited?"

"He says he's scared. Can you imagine a grown man being afraid of a little thing like a baby? He spouts off about the responsibility and the changes in our lives . . ."

Anne grinned smugly. "Good. If he's thinking like that already, he'll make a good father." Rising to her feet, she wiped her hands on the muslin apron she wore. "We'll finish this later. I'm famished for a cup of tea. How about you ladies?"

Maggie grinned. "Well, I came for some of that strudel. I can smell it clear in town. And a cup of tea sounds heavenly!" Her nose screwed daintily toward the ceiling, her face in a grimace. "Mrs. Sawyer takes after Daniel in liking her coffee. Ugh, horrible stuff!"

"Then come on downstairs, the both of you," Anne said, tucking her hands through the girls' arms. "We can fill our bellies and have a long, cozy chat which we haven't had since you both moved out. I can't tell you how quiet it's been around here. Joshua and the boys just don't talk enough. Annabelle will make up for that one day, but not just yet. She chatters incessantly now, but says absolutely nothing! What we need, ladies, is to catch up on the latest news."

"She means scuttle, Maggie," Carrie whispered slyly.

"So I gathered," came the swift answer. "And I hope you ladies have some, for my life has been dreadfully dull these past four days."

"Dull!" both echoed.

"How can a newly married woman's life be dull?"

"By the newly married man taking off for Denver so soon."

"Daniel's gone? For how long?"

Maggie shrugged her shoulders. They were in the kitchen now, seated around the walnut table, the tea tray in front of them. Agnes drew a chair forward and settled her ample bulk in it.

"Who knows? He's got business, he says, and won't return until it's done."

"Men!" Anne clucked, and Agnes nodded her head in agreement.

"Oh, dear," was Carrie's response. "Tom went to the Resurrection Mine early this morning to speak with him. "

"He'll just have to wait till he gets back," Maggie commented, taking a dainty bite of the strudel.

"But Tom's been so worried," Carrie protested. "He said he wanted a level-headed opinion about something. He seemed to think most of the other mine owners around here would overreact to what he has to say. Tom thinks there might be trouble. I hope not."

"What are you talking about? What kind of trouble?"

"Well, Maggie . . . some of the miners have gotten together and formed an organization called the Knights of Labor."

"I've heard of them. Aren't they affiliated with the church? This strudel is scrumptious, Agnes."

"Have another piece. You look as though you could use it," the housekeeper remarked, pleased by the compliment.

"It's really a labor union," Carrie continued, "though the men meet quietly. They know the mine owners wouldn't approve."

"But surely forming a union is acceptable here? This is America! I thought a man's freedom was guaranteed!" Maggie's brows furrowed questioningly.

"Freedom of speech and religion are, Maggie. But so are the owner's freedoms. And they're free to fire anyone they want. Anytime they want. And they just might fire a man, if they learn he's a member of a union."

Carrie sipped some hot tea before continuing. "The Knights of Labor seem to be an honest organization. They're talking about a relations board to air grievances of the miners. But some of the men, mostly men from the Chrysolite and the Old Abe, don't think it's enough. Some of these men have formed another organization, one called the Elephant Club. They've met twice, from what Tom has learned, and . . . and they're talking . . . violence! They want to use guns and fire to make the owners see reason. They want their demands met immediately."

"What sort of demands are they making, Carrie?" Maggie leaned closer for, with each word, Carrie's voice dropped softer and lower.

"More money for one thing. And I can't blame them! The men at the White Dove are working twelve-hour days, six days a week. It's inhuman, is what it is! And for less than three dollars a day. Why, that's almost one-third less money than any other mine around here pays."

"It is horrible," Maggie agreed quietly. The last time she had heard this sort of talk, it had come from her brothers and the other Fenians. That was about money too, but even more about human rights. No matter how low-born the man, he deserved his dignity. And then the culprits were the English rather than the mine owners. Already Maggie could feel her sympathy rising for the miners' cause.

"Well, it seems the owners of the Chrysolite are now demanding the miners take part in a medical plan they've devised," Carrie continued. "They want the miners to pay a weekly premium to cover themselves in case of disability or death."

"But that sounds like a good idea, Carrie," Anne offered.

"It would be, if the Chrysolite paid a decent wage. Truth is, it's practically slave labor there. Take twenty cents a day from the men, and they won't be able to feed their families."

"And the fire at the Old Abe probably didn't help tempers any. Most of the men were angry that if anyone had to die, 'twas one of them rather than the owners," Maggie remembered. "They should demand more protection. They deserve it."

"Tom has said that all along. In his mine, as in Daniel's, and most of the others, risks like that aren't taken. Their men aren't overworked to the point of exhaustion and danger. But a few of the owners don't feel that way. They treat a man's life as a cheap thing, of little or no account. They'll cause trouble for all of us, they and these unionists!"

"Daniel thinks someone ought to be prosecuted for murder," Maggie commented thoughtfully. "Forcing a man to go into a mine with a lit fuse inside is tantamount to murder! Any decent man would agree to that." Dropping her forehead into her hands, she thought for a moment. Then she lifted her eyes to Carrie. "But what does Tom think Daniel can do?"

"He was hoping, being as Daniel's one of the mine owners, that he might talk to the owners of the Chrysolite—and the Old Abe, though it's doubtful it will reopen. Make them see reason, give the men fewer hours and a bit of a raise in pay, then let them pay the premium for the death and disability. Giving in a bit now might save us all a lot of headaches in the future."

Maggie's hand reached across the table and took Carrie's. "I wish he were here. I wish he could do as you ask. Perhaps he could perform such a miracle. But Carrie, I don't know when he'll return. I can send a wire—"

"I'm so afraid that will be too late. If the miners strike . . ." Carrie's deep-brown eyes grew fearful. "If they strike, they say it will be soon. The Elephant Club members, led by that horrible Jeremiah Duggen, are spreading lies where the truth is inflammatory enough. And the Knights of Labor, they're waiting for some representative from the Mineworkers' Union in Pennsylvania before they take any action.

"I'm so afraid someone may get hurt. Someone may be

killed, and for a paltry twenty cents a day!" Her hand tightened its clasp. "Oh, Maggie, I'm so afraid it may be my Tom who's hurt!"

"No," Maggie soothed. "Not Tom. Never Tom. He's been too good to his men. Besides, he doesn't own the mine."

"No, but he manages the mine, and to some men, it's the same as owning it!"

"Shh, Carrie, calm down. You getting so upset isn't good for the baby. Besides, nothing's going to happen, nothing bad at any rate.

"Why, I remember back in Ireland, the Englishmen kept insisting someone would be hurt. And the only ones hurt were the poor Irishmen arrested and shipped abroad for the heinous crime of treason. No, Carrie, your Tom and my Daniel have money and power on their side."

"Maggie, you speak so bitterly!"

"I can't help that, Carrie. I think of the power money buys, and I want to scream. Right should be right and wrong should be wrong, and money shouldn't cast a vote for either side. But that's not the way it works.

"I hope the miners at the White Dove and the Chrysolite get their demands and get them quickly, for all too soon the power of money will tell and whatever insurrection they've managed will be quelled. The miners will either win quickly or they will lose it all. At least there's no Australia to send poor men to from America!"

"Ladies," Anne interrupted. "Let's eat our strudel before it and the tea grow cold. I want no more talk of miners and owners and strikers. If things are as bad as Carrie says, we'll hear no end of them anyway. Children, clothing, and the other women are the only acceptable subjects at a tea such as this.

"You may begin, Maggie, by telling us if what we've heard about Mrs. Sawyer and Mr. Benson is true."

Maggie blinked her eyes. "What have you heard?"

"That they're courting, silly. Didn't you know?"

"Are they?" Maggie questioned, wide-eyed. "I had no idea! But now that you mention it, I *did* wonder about . . ."

It was Maggie's habit to attend early morning Mass before going on to work, even during Daniel's absence. Paddie would then meet her after work and ride home with her. Mrs. Sawyer was always delighted to see the priest, and even more so now that Daniel was gone. She worried about Magheen riding so far alone.

And, though it meant extra work, the housekeeper seemed to appreciate the extra company. Each night, after dinner, the three of them, and sometimes Harvey Benson, would nestle around the fire in the den and there play a game or two of cards before Paddie had to leave.

One evening Maggie waited in vain in the back room of the store for her brother. When he still hadn't come an hour later, Mr. Smith locked the doors and waited outside with her, both of them searching up and down the crowded street for a sign of the priest. Finally Maggie said that Patrick must have had to do something urgent so she would see herself home. Mr. Smith offered to go with her, but Maggie waved off the suggestion as unnecessary.

"It's only a two-mile ride. I've been safe all these months, and to tell you the truth, I think I simply liked Patrick's special attention. 'Twill not hurt me one night to go home alone. Thank you anyway, Mr. Smith."

"Are you sure?"

"Daniel's home is only an extra mile beyond Anne's. Please, go home to your wife and your dinner. I promise I will go straight to Daniel's house. There's nothing for either of us to fret about, I'll be perfectly fine. But," she smiled, "I must go before it's too dark to see my way."

She waved to her employer as she crossed the street and headed for the stables. There, she paid the man for feeding and keeping her horse all week.

After helping her mount the bay mare, the stableman watched her ride off, until she was headed on the east-bound road from Leadville.

The ride was pleasant. These last couple of days had grown warmer, a chinook wind blowing through the valley and melting the top layer of snow. A thin crust formed each night as the cold settled in the valley, and it was this crust that the mare's hooves crushed as she stepped lively toward home. Maggie pulled her woolen scarf higher around her neck and ears, covering her mouth with one light fold.

Once in a while she would pass someone, usually a man. And most probably, he was on his way home after a day's work at the mine. But most of the men she saw were on the outskirts of Leadville. The farther from town she traveled, the fewer people she saw.

The mines must have been closed for better than an hour by now.

The last bend before Daniel's house encircled an outcropping of rock. Maggie took this slowly. As it faced north, this side of the road was slick with ice. A barren copse of aspen and several twisted piñon trees dotted the mountain. Night was coming and bringing with it a chill wind. Maggie shivered and drew her scarf up to cover her nose.

Her eyes dropped to the encrusted snow on the side of the road. Filthy-looking stuff, she thought. Another snowstorm was needed to cover it white again. Her eyes shifted to the center of the road and, for the first time, she noticed the dark stains that made a trail toward the house. It took a moment or two for her to realize what it was she saw. Drops of blood, she thought. Blood, leading to Daniel's house?

Maggie kicked at the flanks of her mare, urging her to hurry toward her destination. From this distance she could barely make out Paddie's horse tied to the hitching pole in front of the house. But it *was* Paddie's horse.

A chill sensation slithered down her spine, and her mouth went dry. The horse, galloping faster, skidded on the ice, but quickly recovered and took the several lengthy strides required to reach the house.

Maggie slid from the saddle, and, tossing the reins over the post, ran at full speed across the porch and inside the house. Once in the front door, she began crying aloud the only word she would think of at the moment.

"Paddie! Paddie," she cried frantically, rushing from front room to parlor. "Where are you? Oh, my God, Paddie! Are you all right?"

"Hush now, Maggie!" came the answer from the top of the stairs.

Maggie glanced up and found Paddie, white-faced and his shirt stained with blood, but clearly alive and unhurt. He came down the steps toward her as she questioned hoarsely, "What's happened? Is it Daniel?"

"No, it's not Daniel," her brother soothed. "Calm down before you wake the saints with your hysterics."

"If you don't tell me what's going on, and quickly, I shall show you what hysterics are," she threatened.

"Then hush, so the whole rest of the world doesn't hear. This poor man's got trouble enough without letting everybody know where he is."

"Who's here?" she questioned impatiently.

"A man by the name of Edward Varley. At least that's the name he gave before passing out cold on me. I found him shot in the leg and back, and bleeding outside the Old Abe mine. He's in rough shape, poor sot. 'Twill be days before he can give us his story."

"I've never heard the name. Why don't I go to town and fetch a doctor?"

Paddie shook his head. "I think not. I don't know exactly who our man is either, but someone waited until the hill emptied and the men had gone home before taking a potshot at him. Before he passed out, he mentioned the Knights of Labor and named Michael Mooney."

"I don't believe Mr. Mooney shot him!"

"Nor do I, girl. But I do believe he's the man this Edward Varley has come to see. My guess is that Mr. Varley's being here has something to do with this talk of unions and strikes, and that the Knights of Labor might have sent for him. Michael Mooney is the president of the Knights, you realize. I think it's best we keep news of him from reaching Leadville, at least until we can learn who tried to kill him."

Maggie frowned. "You mean . . . you think he's from the union in Pennsylvania?"

Paddie's eyes narrowed. "Now, who have you been talking to? But yes, I think he is from the national union, and probably represents a whole lot more men than the Elephant Club and the owners combined.

"So what the problem boils down to is that we don't know who wants to be rid of him more, the Elephant Club or the mine owners. Both sides have plenty of reasons for fearing his being here.

"And someone objects vehemently, at least bad enough to try to kill him. Someone has decided to take matters into his own hands, and if that means killing a man or a dozen men . . . well, it's all the same to him."

Maggie absorbed this, tying Patrick's news in with what she had heard earlier in the week from Carrie. "Oh, I wish Daniel were here!"

"As I do. He's a man who might keep this madness from growing into insanity. There are too many hotheads in this town just waiting for an excuse to use their guns."

"So only one man knows about this Edward Varley?" Maggie questioned.

Paddie shook his head. "At least two. The man who expected him and the man who shot him."

"Well," Maggie responded firmly. "No one else needs to know. We'll keep him here until he recovers and pray Daniel gets home by then. Who's with him now?"

"Mrs. Sawyer and Harvey. Harvey did the honors—dug that ball out as clean as you please. With luck, no fever will set in, and he'll be up and around in a few days. Though, if he's up and around and trying to incite the miners, I wouldn't give you a nickel for his chances of surviving the next potshot."

Maggie shrugged out of her woolen wrap and coat and hung them in the wardrobe. "Nor would I," she agreed solemnly. "Paddie, do you think the miners are right, that they should strike if they don't get fewer hours and more money?"

"Someone's surely been talking to you, I can hear that. Yes, Maggie, I think that at the Chrysolite, the White Dove, and the Old Abe the men should be more fairly treated. But I don't know as that calls for a strike at all of the mines. There's got to be a better way to handle this. I'm afraid someone will end up by dying. Unions and strikes . . . Maggie, those are killing words."

"Yes," she said lowly. "I know they are. It seems that whenever money or power is involved, most words are killing words."

Paddie reached a hand out to touch her shoulder comfortingly. "I know you're thinking of our brothers, but at least they're not dead, Magheen. We'll get them out of Australia. We'll get them here, with us."

"But what's the good of it all, if they come here, to troubles much like the ones they faced in Ireland? What good has any of it been? America was supposed to be better, to be fairer, to give a man an equal opportunity with others! Instead it's the same. Money and power, they're all that matter."

"Not quite, Magheen. Money and power give a man a head start, but here they aren't the only guarantees to success. If a man hasn't got them, he simply must use his own brain and brawn to get them. More importantly, a man can find justice in America. Our brothers could have been Fenians here and insulted anyone they liked, but that wouldn't have gotten them a penal sentence. No, in America a man has to do something wrong to go to prison. Not just be born poor and Irish."

"It seems to me a lot of Irishmen are going hungry in Leadville."

"And a lot of them have found that wealth we were speaking of. Not only Irishmen but Swedes, Germans, and Poles. Poor men become rich men here. But nothing in this life is totally fair, Maggie, and wealth will never be spread evenly."

"All I want is a little bit of it, Paddie. Just enough to buy our brothers' freedom. I can live my life in a cottage and by happy, so long as I'm with Daniel. But I want them free!"

Mrs. Sawyer was busy caring for the patient, so Maggie fixed supper before relieving her and Harvey.

She sat by the patient's bed with a book in her hands until Edward Varley turned and twisted uncomfortably in the bed. Maggie soothed him, straightening the blankets and turning the pillow so the cool side of the cloth was beneath his head. With a warm rag, she bathed his forehead. Tilting a cup to his mouth, Maggie coaxed him to drink of cool water. Again, he fell insensible to his surroundings.

Harvey relieved her later that evening. They had arranged for the four of them to take three-hour shifts so each might get a decent sleep. Wearily she sank into the feather mattress in Daniel's bedroom.

Morning came quickly, and Maggie rose early enough to see to breakfast for the four of them, and warm some chicken broth for their patient. After doing the dishes, she was again on her way to work at the store. That evening she did not wait around for Patrick but left immediately after work for home. Tonight Mrs. Sawyer had supper started, but after such a busy day, she was grateful for any help Maggie could give.

For the next two nights, until they were certain Mr. Varley would not suffer the complications of a fever, they took shifts sitting up with him. On the fourth day, it became apparent he was recovering, and they could relax their vigilance. All of them were glad of a solid night's sleep.

By Saturday morning, Magheen was informed Edward Varley was making a good recovery, and Harvey alone would see to his needs. Their patient had so requested.

"Men have their modesty too, you understand, Mrs. Calcord," Mrs. Sawyer told her as she returned the empty breakfast tray to the kitchen. "Perhaps by tomorrow he can dress, and then you can meet him properly."

Properly? Maggie thought sourly. Everything was proper enough when he was wearing his caretakers thin with his care, but now he's worried about propriety? Her curiosity was rampant. Exactly who was the man and why was he here and who was it he wanted to see? Patrick refused to tell her any more than he had learned the first night, and sick as he was, Edward Varley was mum.

She attended Mass on Sunday and paid a flying visit to Anne and Joshua while she waited for Patrick to finish his services. At exactly noon, they were on the road once more.

"I'll be so glad to get to Daniel's home and be able to spend the whole afternoon and evening there—"

"Why do you do that?" Paddie interrupted.

"Do what?"

"Refer to your home as Daniel's? Everything is Daniel's,

214

the house, the barn, the parlor, the kitchen—"

"Not the kitchen," Maggie corrected. "That belongs to Mrs. Sawyer."

"You know what I'm saying. Why isn't it your home?"

"It is," she answered slowly, her brow furrowing. "In a manner of speaking, it is." Maggie tossed her brother an impatient glance. "You know what I mean. You must know! It's really Daniel's home, bought and paid for by him, chosen and arranged by him. Mrs. Sawyer does all that's necessary. It's like they scooted over and made room for me." She didn't mention how useless she felt after her argument with Daniel.

"Be patient, Magheen."

"I'm trying to be patient. I'll be waiting here just as long as it takes Daniel to return. I'll be the good little wife, asking no questions—"

"Ha!"

". . . minding my own business, darning woolen socks, and baking apple pie. Does that satisfy you?"

"Lie to yourself, Maggie, but not to me. If he doesn't get home soon, you'll take a broom to his head. I've seen you do it before!"

Her eyes slid askance, and she clucked her tongue to hurry her mare. "You were my brother and deserved every lick I ever got in. But Daniel's my husband and deserves my respect."

"That he does, colleen. You just remember it!"

Maggie had many an uncharitable thought about her brother, the priest, before they reached the house. The smell of aspen wood burning in the fireplace and dinner cooking in the kitchen permeated to the front hall, taking Maggie's mind from her brother's blunt remarks as she doffed her outer garments and hung them up to dry.

"Cherry pie, I'll wager," Patrick commented, sniffing appreciatively.

"You're a priest and priests don't have money to throw away gambling," she answered smugly.

"Oo-hoo! So you're getting uppity now, me gal. Have some respect for your priest."

"I am in awe of my priest. 'Tis my brother who needs watching."

"You hit below the belt, Maggie."

"Fill it with chicken. That will cure what ails you."

Patrick grinned. "I knew you couldn't resist inviting me to dinner."

"Since when have you needed an invitation?" she questioned airily, moving inside the front room and holding her hands to the fire. "Jakers, but 'tis a lovely fire," she remarked, turning around and hiking her skirt a bit to warm her backside better.

"Yes, lovely," agreed an unfamiliar voice.

Maggie yelped once at the masculine tones, dropping her skirts and quickly scanning the room. In Daniel's great, overstuffed chair, melting into the softness of the brown leather, was their recovering patient.

He was dressed in fawn-colored britches, white shirt, and black riding boots. His wan face still showed traces of his ordeal. On the floor beside the chair reclined a cane. Light-brown hair framed a face courting a roguish grin. Gray eyes crinkled at the corners as he watched Maggie's face turn a bright pink.

"I should stand up and greet you, ma'am. However, I fear that once I found my feet, they would not be so steady again. I hope you will excuse my lack of manners this once."

"Please, don't stand for me. The last thing I want to do is have to call Harvey to help Paddie carry you upstairs."

"Thank you, ma'am. That's the way I feel about it myself. My name is Edward Varley. And I assume you're Mrs. Calcord? And that it is due to your kindness that I have recovered?"

"No, sir. I am Mrs. Calcord, but your recovering is due to my brother finding you in time. Mr. Varley, this is my brother, Father Patrick Fitzgerald."

The gray eyes widened in surprise. "Father? You're a priest?" He smiled and held out his hand for Paddie to shake. "I've never had the honor of knowing a priest before."

"No? Then what faith are you?"

"I was raised in the Presbyterian church, but I've had little time for Sunday meetings, Father. I suppose you might say I'm unaffiliated at the moment."

"Ah! A challenge no man of God can resist. Another good Christian soul to save!"

Edward Varley's grin began to fade. "I'm not in the market for a new religion just yet."

Patrick smiled wickedly, much like a wolf stalking helpless prey. "Perhaps by the time we've talked a bit, you'll be ready for one."

"Can't his soul wait until his belly is full? He looks like he needs a real meal." Maggie's eyes were merry and bright.

"Well," Patrick conceded slowly. "I suppose so . . ."

"Stop teasing him so, Paddie. He looks ready to sink through the floor! Don't worry, Mr. Varley. My brother has enough souls to save with the ones he already has. You are safe."

"Thank you, ma'am. You have saved me, in more ways than one."

"Don't get so cocky, lad. I have time to change my mind yet."

But Edward Varley had caught on that the priest was a high teaser and that his sister could give as well as she got. Seriously, he replied, "I've all the time in the world, sir. Do your worst."

Which was the last thing Father Patrick expected. He hadn't the least idea how to go about foisting his beliefs onto an unsuspecting man, nor did he even want to. Paddie, coward that he was, cleared his throat. "I think you owe us an explanation first. Exactly who are you and what are you doing in Leadville?"

"I was sent for, Father. I am not a man to come where I am not wanted."

"An obscure enough answer. Who sent for you and why?"

"Father," he began and nodded his head toward Maggie, "and Mrs. Calcord, I hope you realize that what I tell you is of the utmost confidence."

"We realize men's lives are at stake."

"Then you understand why you must not repeat what I tell you. My name is truly Edward Varley, and I am a representative of the Mineworker's Union, the union in Pittsburgh, Pennsylvania.

"A man by the name of Michael Mooney, from Leadville, wrote to my union, requesting our assistance in setting up a union shop here."

Patrick nodded. "I know him. Michael Mooney was elected president of the Knights of Labor."

"The same man," Varley affirmed. "He wrote that he was concerned about the miners' rights and pay, and about a violent organization being formed here, one called the Elephant Club."

"I have heard of it."

"Well, facing the necessity of forming a legitimate union, Mr. Mooney requested our assistance. I can verify first-hand the repercussions of violent acts and companies bringing in scab labor, so his request was met promptly. I have come to offer my help. But of course, I made the mistake of writing news of my intentions to Mr. Mooney. That's how I must have been discovered. Someone found out about me and wanted to be sure I would be of no help. Someone acted to put me out of the way, Father."

"How horrible," Maggie shuddered. "But it's what we think too. Someone shot you just to prevent you from speaking out."

"It wouldn't be the first time someone's tried to keep a union from forming."

"Did you see who it was that did this to you?"

"No, ma'am. That shot came from behind. I saw nothing."

"The futility of it has me wondering. What would your death accomplish? Another union man would come along, and another and another, if necessary."

"They would have stalled the process. And time is on their side."

"You're guessing, Mr. Varley," Paddie interrupted shortly. "I don't like unfounded accusations being tossed around. Too often innocent men are the ones maligned."

Edward Varley nodded his agreement. "I intend to find out who did this, but you're right, we're only guessing at the moment. As soon as I'm able, however, someone will answer for this. I have a deep dislike of being shot at from behind."

"I don't blame you," Maggie interrupted, "but dinner's

218

getting cold. Come, sir, I'll help you to the dining room."

Varley smiled ruefully. "I'm weak enough that I'll accept your help. But I would rather be escorting you, ma'am."

"Pretty words, Mr. Varley. However, my sister is not strong enough to bear you up should your strength fail. 'Tis my arm you'll lean on. Maggie, lead the way."

Edward Varley's condition greatly improved over the next few days. His strength and appetite returned, and soon he chafed at the inaction caused by his injury.

One of those evenings Father Patrick arrived with news from the miners.

"Michael Mooney's been asking the men about you. No, I didn't say a word," he answered to Varley's unspoken question. "Mooney sent a wire to Pennsylvania, and when he learned you'd left there weeks ago, he grew suspicious. He's now accusing the mine owners of plotting your demise. I'm afraid you're about to turn into another cause for the miners to complain about."

"Perhaps we should tell him."

"Not yet. Not until you're strong enough to be gone from here. I don't want my sister involved in your doings, Mr. Varley."

"No, I suppose you're right."

"There's no supposing about it. Mr. Calcord would be very displeased to find you here, let alone involving his wife. And that's my fault. I don't plan to let this go any further."

But Patrick hadn't reckoned with Magheen. In the Leadville stables, late one afternoon, she overheard Mike MacPherson complaining to Soapy Stiles that matters at the Chrysolite mine had gone from bad to worse. The men were now forbidden to smoke or talk while on duty. Several of the foreman had already quit after voicing their objections. Walter McClean, past foreman of the Old Abe mine and the one responsible for the loss of lives there, was one of the new men hired to take over. A rumor was spreading that wages were being cut. And where was that union man from Pennsylvania, MacPherson demanded. Did one or some of the powers-that-be really commit such a dastardly deed?

A meeting was scheduled for this very night, he said, in

the remnants of the machine shop at the Old Abe mine. "It's been unused for weeks now. No one could suspect us of meeting there. But bring your gun. Just in case."

At the mention of the word "gun," Maggie went cold all over.

A strike was one thing, but if the miners used guns, the mine owners would retaliate. And a lot of good people would die.

Minutes seemed to tick on forever before the men left the stables. Maggie mounted her mare and rode hard for the house, knowing she had to do something to keep this from escalating. Edward Varley seemed to be the only answer.

He was pacing in the front room, the monotony of lonely days wearing on him as much as his injury did. He still walked with a pronounced limp, and his strength had not returned in full yet, but he claimed to be able to face a crowd of angry miners and handle them after he listened to Maggie's story.

"Can you stop this madness?"

Edward Varley ceased his pacing and looked into her eyes. In that moment he seemed transformed from the congenial guest to a stubborn man who was capable of organizing desperate men and their unions. "Is this madness, Mrs. Calcord? Or is letting other men run and ruin lives madness?"

"Mr. Varley, they're speaking of guns!"

"Sometimes guns are the only answer," he replied mercilessly.

"I can't accept that. There must be something we can do. Someone will be hurt!"

Varley dropped his gaze at the entreaty in her eyes. "I'll go to the meeting and speak to the men—"

"I'll come with you."

"No," he shook his head. "Your brother would absolutely forbid it."

Maggie gave an impatient shake of her head. "And just how do you propose to get to your meeting, if not by borrowing one of my horses? And why would I lend you one when you're so ungracious about the one request I make of you?"

Varley gritted his teeth. "Mrs. Calcord, your brother and your husband would be angry with both of us. I owe them better than that."

"You owe me better than a refusal."

She wouldn't be budged, he realized. She was bound and determined to get herself involved in this and caution be damned. Well, if that's the way she felt, then so be it. Her stubbornness was for her husband to curb, he thought.

"All right. Just don't blame me for what happens. A woman should not interfere in man's business."

"May I remind you, Mr. Varley," she spoke in her most arrogant tones, "the mine is my business. And in case you don't know, in the West we're far ahead of you Easterners in forward thinking. In the West, we women gained the right to vote while your legislatures were still arguing about it!"

He couldn't help but grin. "Ma'am, I've never heard an Irish accent so corrupted with Western slang. Sounds rather peculiar."

"Peculiar or not, I'm going with you!"

Ed Varley knew it was useless to argue with such determination.

Chapter Thirteen

Instead he gritted his teeth and said, "I'd prefer the buckboard, ma'am. And I'll do the driving."

"I think we should wait until dark to leave. There'll be too many questions if we're seen together."

"If you go to the meeting with me, how can you avoid our being seen together?"

"I meant that we might be seen by the man who is threatening your life," she answered impatiently. "And I don't believe you're being threatened by miners. You know exactly what I mean. I will go to this meeting, Mr. Varley, and I will know what's going on."

"Only if the meeting continues after your presence is known. I imagine that with you there, being the wife of a mine owner and all, the men might be wary of what they say. As a matter of fact, the real meeting may simply take place later, when neither of us is around."

"You're trying to talk me out of this, and it won't work."

Ed Varley shrugged his shoulders and turned from her. "Suit yourself."

After supper, Maggie went to her bedroom to change into clothing more suitable for riding. As she was sitting in the chair and pulling on her boots, she heard the lock to the door click and knew immediately what must be happening. No one, absolutely none of her dinner companions, had been able to meet her eyes at the meal.

Jumping up from her chair, she pounded on the door with her fists and demanded to be released. All the while her thoughts damned Harvey Benson, Edward Varley, Maudie Sawyer, and her own brother, Patrick Fitzgerald.

They were in this conspiracy together, all of them.

She had told no one but Varley about the meeting, and he must have told the others. They all had done this to her! She ran to the window and was there just in time to see the three men ride off on horseback. Even the buckboard was a lie, the devil take them!

A short time later, Maggie heard Mrs. Sawyer's voice through the door. "I'm so sorry, my dear, but you might have been hurt. It's bad enough that the men have to go, but I couldn't allow you to also!"

"Just let me out of here!"

"Not yet, dear. Not until the men return. You really have a very stubborn nature, and, just as your brother said, you'd only follow them on horseback. No, I was given orders to lock you in, nice and tight, until they return. Then you can complain loudly to us all."

"That I will do, Mrs. Sawyer!" Maggie declared, temper in every nuance of her voice.

"I know you will, dear. Now, you just have a cozy read until they return. I'd offer you a cup of tea, but the men and I agreed I should not open the door. It will only be for a few hours, after all."

"When I tell Daniel of this . . ."

"He will agree with our actions," the housekeeper replied, not sounding the least afraid of facing her employer. "I will see you later, my dear."

"No! No," she cried, her fingers frantically working the doorknob.

But the housekeeper's footsteps could be heard descending the staircase. Maggie marched up and down the room, feeling frustrated and angry, her tongue flaying every man she had met since she arrived in Leadville. Gradually her anger began to subside, and she removed her heavy boots, replacing them with house slippers. Curling in the chair, she did just as she had been told, but only because she wanted to. She opened *The Pickwick Papers,* and read from the place where she had stopped the night before.

The stories were funny, and her mood improved rapidly. One moment she was relaxed and chuckling in her chair, and the next moment she surged from that same chair, the sounds of gunfire recoiling throughout the room, though it came from a distance. It sounded as far away as the Old Abe, she reasoned.

A second later, Mrs. Sawyer unlocked the door and stumbled into the room, her face white and frightened, her mouth compressed tightly.

"I was afraid it would come to this," the older woman groaned fearfully.

"I can't see a thing from here," Maggie muttered in some frustration. She had the window curtains thrown wide and the sash opened, and was peering out into the evening twilight. "But I think the shooting's stopped."

"How many do you think? Six, maybe eight shots?"

"Yes," Magheen replied absently. "I think we should get some water and bandages ready, just in case. If they're not back in five minutes, I'll go looking for them."

"You can't!" the housekeeper screamed frantically. "Who knows who's firing the guns? And who would recognize you in the darkness? You could easily be mistaken for a man and be shot."

Maggie pulled the window closed. "Let's worry about that when we have to."

The five minutes came and passed. Gauze for bandages was located and readied, the bottle of antiseptic waiting in the kitchen. Now that she had had more time to think of it, Maggie didn't know what would be best for her to do next. If she left and went looking for them, she might miss the men. And if she stayed, she would worry more with each passing moment. So, for the moment, she remained at the house and tried to keep busy.

The wait was not long. Horses' hooves trampled in the front yard, and Maggie could hear the low droning of men's voices as they dismounted. She flew to the front door and opened it, only to hear Paddie snarl at her, "Don't ever open a door without knowing who's on the other side of it! Move aside, girl, this man's heavy!"

Maggie stood back, holding a gas lamp high so the men might find their way. Between Paddie and Harvey was Ed Varley. His feet were dragging on the floor, and his arms were thrown over each man's shoulders. His face was screwed up in a grimace, and when he saw Maggie, he grimaced more. "I told you it would be dangerous."

"Ooh," she snapped suddenly, "Get him in here on the davenport, and let's have a look at him. What happened? Where were you shot?"

"He's not shot, Magheen," Paddie answered. "He was shot at. The horse bolted and threw him, renewing the original injuries, I'm sure."

The four of them coaxed Varley onto the davenport, and Mrs. Sawyer immediately ran her hands over him to learn the extent of his injuries. Maggie stood beside them and watched quietly, the lamp still in her hands.

"So, who did the shooting?" Maude Sawyer questioned.

"It was too dark to see, ma'am," Ed responded weakly, the pain etched on his features. "We didn't even get as far as the mine. Someone knows I'm here and has been waiting for me to leave this house. He'll try again."

"That's why I'm taking him out of here," Harvey announced. "He can stay in the bunkhouse with me and the boys."

"And how do you know it's not one of them taking potshots at people?" Maggie inquired.

"I just know, that's how."

"That's not good enough. I refuse to have his life risked any further. He stays right here until he's fully recovered." Maggie glanced around her to see how her words were accepted. "All right. How about if Harvey brings some men here to act as guards around the house? We'll all be safe then, won't we?"

"That might not be a bad idea, Father," Harvey said. "I can't watch him every minute. But with Maggie and Mrs. Sawyer here to help watch and sound an alarm if need be, he'll be safe enough."

"How bad are the wounds?" the priest inquired.

"Well, the scabbing hasn't opened, but there's a lot of nasty bruising. He'll be uncomfortable for a few more days." Mrs. Sawyer shook her head. "And that leg looks like it might be gamey for a long time to come."

Patrick sighed. "I guess we don't have a choice. Bring your men, Harvey. But I don't know how you'll explain this. By tomorrow every man in town will know about Varley and the union. They'll guess just how long he's been here. Too many men will see this as your taking the union's part. You could be asking for trouble for yourself and Daniel."

"I can't let a man be murdered, nor would Daniel."

"No, he would not," Maggie agreed vehemently.

Patrick turned to his sister. "You'll go nowhere alone, and you'll not be gone after dark. I'll ride to and from town with you each day. If we're determined to do this, we'll make sure of our precautions. Do you understand, Magheen?" He waited for her agreement before continuing. "And then, when our guest here heals, he can settle this question of a union once and for all. And frankly I don't care how he does it. But for God's sake, man, settle it so my sister isn't involved."

"I'll do what I can, but remember there's more at stake than just us. I am grateful for all you've done for me."

Maggie clucked her tongue. "As though you wouldn't have done the same for any of us, though I hope you never get the chance. Do your worst, you men, turn this home into a fortress. But remind those men you set as our guards that their pistols are to be kept in their holsters. No one is to be hurt."

Throughout the night the miners stood guard at the house, rotating their shifts frequently. In the morning, when she and Paddie rode into town, two men accompanied them. One waited outside the store the entire day, and the other, she guessed, waited outside the church or wherever else Paddie was. For the next three days, she was never alone except in her bedroom. And even then she wondered if one of the men didn't wait just outside the door.

Her patience had been tried once too often by the third night of this voluntary imprisonment, and, after tossing down her napkin by the dinner plate, she marched into the parlor and stood before the fire, her hands outstretched. Her gaze lifted to the mirror over the mantel. She barely recognized her own face. Her mouth was strained from trying to hold her temper in check, and her eyes were glinting dangerously.

Where was Daniel? This mine was his problem, not hers. She had agreed to love, honor, and obey him, not take care of his dratted mine! Of course, Harvey was really doing that. She was simply participating in unforeseen occurrences, most of which revolved around one Edward Varley.

Her mind reverted to her brothers. Her savings were mounting weekly since she no longer paid the Howards for room and board. Daniel provided for her needs, and the only expenses she had were contributions to the church and to the odd miner who came into the store with a hard-luck story. In spite of the fact that she knew nothing about the men, Maggie always gave them a little bit. They were so full of hope, she couldn't refuse. She still had more money left than ever before. At this rate, it would only take seventeen years to save enough money for her brothers.

Seventeen years!

"You look as though you're having particularly bad thoughts," Ed Varley commented, limping as he joined her in the parlor. "I haven't seen a face in such pain since I saw my sister's. And she was practicing before a mirror how to tell my best friend that she loved another. I do hope you're not planning on giving your husband bad news."

"Of course not."

Ed Varley lifted his brows and gave an indifferent shrug. "I can't imagine what else could bother a woman like you."

"Like me?"

"Pampered. Spoiled."

"Mr. Varley, you can be the most unpleasant man! I don't know why you always feel this need to goad me—"

"Not always, surely? Though when I look at you, I do see a woman who has no need to work, yet takes a job from another woman who might need the earnings to feed her family. Have you ever thought of someone besides yourself, Mrs. Calcord?"

"How dare you!"

"I would dare a good deal more if it would wake a spoiled little darling like you, so you might know what others feel and think. You might learn that other women don't have life so cushy. They don't have fancy houses and food automatically set on their tables. They can't have their cocky independence and still manage to keep a family going. They live in the real world."

"Then perhaps they should learn to have cocky independence. Maybe then they might learn that only they control their own futures, that they should *not* be at the beck and call of some man! If they learned self-respect, they might gain independence. Not all of us, Mr. Varley, like to be dependent on some man. And not all men are so reliable. Are you reliable, Mr. Varley? Or did you leave a wife and perhaps some children dependent on you when you came west from Pennsylvania? Are they perhaps waiting for you now, and worried about what has happened to you? Have you thought of sending a wire to alleviate their fears?"

"I am not married, Mrs. Calcord. Nor do I have children."

"No wonder you know so much about cocky independence," she retorted smugly. "You have a good share of your own and resent it when a woman has the same."

"It is not seemly for a woman to be independent."

"Not to you, it's not. To most men, an independent woman is a threat to their self-esteem. They like the little woman hanging around, waiting for the slightest bit of attention. Women need independence, Mr. Varley. They need control over their lives, their futures, the lives of their children. Not all men can be trusted to take good care of the 'little woman.' Some men neglect their responsibilities, and they're not the ones to suffer when they do. Women deserve to make their own decisions."

"You wouldn't know a decision if it hit you in the rear," he declared boldly.

"What do you mean by that?"

"You can't decide whether to be for or against the union. You're worried about what your husband would think and say if he were here. So much for your independence! You're just like all the dependent women of the world, talking one way, acting another. I am not fooled, Mrs. Calcord."

Magheen was surprised at the vehemence in his voice. "I have always supported the union. I just can't do it openly. Such action would be against my husband."

"Words, Mrs. Calcord. Don't you ever act according to your conscience?"

228

"May I remind you that I have taken you in?"

"Your brother brought me here. You had no choice in the name of human decency but to harbor me after that. No, Mrs. Calcord, if you are a truly independent woman, you must decide for yourself if you wish to support the union or act against us. And it must be your decision, not your husband's."

"I support the belief that all men are entitled to a decent wage and treatment from their place of work."

"Then prove it." The words were softly spoken, but Magheen knew a gauntlet had been thrown. "Support the union all the way, not just with words."

Magheen's brows rose. "So that is what this is all about. You want me to do something for you, and you think I might, if you challenge me so?"

"It's not a terribly difficult task. I'm sure you can manage it."

Varley limped into the room and took a chair near the fireplace, just beside Magheen. He made sure he could see the expression on her face. "It's something I can't ask Harvey or your brother to do, they're both solid supporters of the mine owners. You're the only one with an open mind.

"I brought pamphlets with me from Pennsylvania, pamphlets describing the union and what it can mean to every man who joins it. I did not have the chance the other night to give any of them out." He leaned forward in his chair, his elbows digging into the arms. "If I can just get a few out, a few so that what I have to tell people will spread, my task will at least be begun. I trust no one else to help me. Will you?"

"Why should I?"

"Because you believe in the rights of all mankind. Because you want these people to make the most of their lives, to have the best they can. You can help them. You can prove you're an independent thinker by helping me."

Her head came up sharply. "I have nothing to prove to you."

"No, you don't. But I think you have something to prove to yourself. Take a stand this once. You may never get another chance."

"You're trying to goad me into doing what you want. It won't work. I do something because it is what I think I should do. Not because you make me angry."

"Of course you don't. But if you gave out the pamphlets, you would only be helping others make up their minds. They should know both of their choices. And which would be worse, the Elephant Club or the Mineworkers' Union? Or perhaps no union?"

"I don't know."

"Think about it then. But I need an answer and soon."

Maggie thought about it all night. This whole situation seemed much like the one she had left in Ireland. The wealthy against the poor. Perhaps they should have a union, perhaps they should have everything a union stands for.

But Daniel was her husband.

After breakfast Maggie gave Mr. Varley her answer. She thought he accepted it well enough, but as she was leaving the house for work, he pressed a couple of the pamphlets into her palm and said, "At least read them. How can you tell me no when you don't even know what we stand for?"

Maggie folded them and placed them in her reticule. Over lunch, which was a sandwich and an apple in the back room of the store, she studied what the pamphlets said. Nothing inflammatory was in them. They merely spoke of a brotherhood of miners, everyone working for the betterment of his class. If all miners stood together, the first one read, they would carry far more power than corporations and individual owners. The mines would be working for them as well as the stockholders. The second pamphlet stressed benefits other than wages the union felt all miners deserved.

All of which made perfect sense to Magheen. But there was still Daniel to consider.

Folding them neatly, she replaced them in her reticule, determined to give Ed Varley the same answer.

The severe weather of winter was settling over the valley. Traveling to and from Leadville morning and night was becoming a major chore, and a dangerous one. But as long as Patrick or the other men were willing to accompany her, she was willing to go.

Christmas would soon be here. Mrs. Sawyer was immersed with food and other preparations. Maggie had joined the church choir, attending practice twice a week.

The younger children in the catechism classes were planning a Nativity play for Midnight Mass on Christmas Eve, and, though one of the other ladies was in charge, Maggie helped with it by creating and painting the sets. Anne, Carrie, and Agnes Moen sewed the costumes. Annabelle was all aquiver with the excitement of being the Archangel Gabriel. Her brothers were two of the three kings.

Daniel wrote and said he would be back in Leadville by Christmas.

Maggie knitted mittens for each of the children in her class, slippers for Mrs. Sawyer, Mrs. Moen, Anne, and Carrie. Joshua and Paddie both would receive fine new scarves, and Daniel a sweater of Aran wool.

On December seventh, the Leadville *Daily Gazette* announced a series of articles focusing on mysterious attacks several of the miners and their families had suffered. Michael Mooney was the only miner mentioned by name. The others had asked that their identities not be used for they needed no further trouble. All of the miners involved actively supported the formation of a union.

The owners of the White Dove were interviewed in the same piece, and they said anyone participating in the formation of a union deserved to be burned out.

On December eighth, another explosion rocketed the mining hills. Though no one was hurt and the damage done was negligible, the miners had even more to think about now. The tense situation was threatening to explode just like the dynamite the men used in their work. There was no mention of this accident in the paper.

Suddenly, the series of articles on the miners was canceled by the *Gazette*. The rumor mill had it that the owner of the newspaper, Judge Carlton Forbes, had demanded they be stopped. The judge also owned several silver mines.

This act stirred up the miners more than any other. It seemed that the owners even controlled freedom of speech, a right guaranteed to all Americans.

At the rehearsal for the Nativity play that night, Mrs.

MacPherson, whose son played Joseph, made the bald statement everyone had been thinking and no one had the courage to voice. "The judge stopped those articles because the mine owners were behind the attacks. He didn't want one of his friends, or himself, implicated."

"I think so too," spoke a normally quiet Mrs. Mason. She was a young, slight woman, her light-brown hair caught behind her head in a tidy bun. "I've been so frightened since Tom's accident. He believes in the union and supports it wholeheartedly, but he can't find work with his opinion so well known. And when I spoke with Mrs. Mooney, she seemed to think that was just as well, or we might have been a target for their attacks, too."

"Aye," confirmed Mrs. MacPherson. "I spoke with her too. She told me the men who attacked their cabin were black masked and heavily armed. They warned Michael Mooney against speaking up for the union. Who else but the mine owners would have reason to do such a thing?"

All the women were silent for a moment. With the exception of Anne Howard, their husbands were involved with mining.

"I'm not so sure of that," Carrie said finally.

"Of course you'd defend them," accused Mrs. MacPherson. "Your husband is a manager."

"But that's not why. You see, I've heard some things . . . about the Elephant Club."

"Go on, Missus."

"Well, I've heard that they've threatened to go to any extreme to get the miners to organize with them, and that includes terrorizing the miners who want the Mineworkers' Union to represent them instead of the Elephant Club. Michael Mooney was attacked, you remember, and he has been most vocal about which organization he prefers."

"Where did you hear that?"

"Tom and some of the other managers were talking about it. The last accident . . . well, they say . . . it wasn't an accident. The dynamite was set off deliberately to frighten the men. And they claim the charge could have only been set by one of the miners themselves," Carrie said.

"Joshua says it's mighty strange that the Elephant Club

seems so determined to be the miners' union at any cost. Any cost, including pitting the miners against each other," Anne commented.

"You're right," Maggie said softly, glancing at the women around her. "Tom and Joshua aren't the only ones talking about the violence advocated by the Elephant Club. Now the union . . ." Her fingers delved into her reticule and pulled out the union's pamphlets. "I have these — from the union. They tell all about it, how it started in Pennsylvania and how it's grown. What it wants for its members and from its members. See, there's no talk of violence or strikes in there."

"Not yet, they won't mention them. But they will. They're the only way to make the owners see reason," said Mrs. MacPherson, her lips tightly compressed. "But I'll have a look anyway. And I'll pass them on to my man. Maybe he'll think differently after reading them. But where did you get such things, Mrs. Calcord?"

Maggie pretended not to hear the question, and soon the conversation was dropped and the rehearsal continued.

On the ninth of December, the mine owners collectively made a statement that any man who even spread rumors of the formation of a union would be fired. And the management at the Chrystolite took the first of the insurance premiums for the men's wages.

On December tenth, the miners staged a walkout. It began slowly at first, unplanned, with the early arriving miners at the Chrysolite blocking the entrance to the mine, picks and shovels in hand. More men arrived, adding to the walkout. Other miners arrived at their own neighboring mines, and when they learned what was happening, demonstrated their support by blocking the entrance to their own place of work.

Clouds settled ominously low over the hill, trapping the cold within the valley. The men wore heavy, patched coats and woolen scarves. Their fingers were swathed in thick gloves, and their hands clung tightly to their makeshift weapons. The only discernable difference in the men, other than height and weight, was in their choice of headgear, which ranged from low-browed cowboy hats to black felt bowlers.

The managers arrived and decided not to try to enter the mines, but watched from a distance, after notifying the owners of the problem. As the morning lengthened, the miners mingled with each other, sharing complaints and common fears, enjoying a rare day of power. The feeling strengthened their resolve to band together and demand better conditions.

Finally, the owners responded, with the threat to replace the men with scab labor if they were not back at work in the morning.

That was the moment Edward Varley chose. Limping his way to the topmost point of Fryer's Hill, he stood before the hundreds of men, shouting his identity and his affiliation with the Mineworkers Union. He went on to explain more calmly his presence in Leadville. Near hopeless men watched and listened as he explained how they could benefit each other.

"All you have to do is unite! The owners and their managers are powerless without their labor, and they know it. They want a peaceful settlement, just as you do. Band together and sign a petition. We'll present it to them. And the first of the demands is the organization of a labor board where you can air your grievances! You'd be surprised at how many problems are settled in this way. Reason can deal with reason!"

"And who are you to be interfering in our affairs?" demanded a burly miner with dark hair and beard. "You got no cause to be here! We don't want no Eastern interference, do we, boys? I heard all about you Molly Maguires, you and your coal mines! Hell, the East is where most of the owners come from. We do things our way out here."

"Mr. — Mr. ?" Ed Varley's expression was most pleasant, but questioning.

"Duggen. Jeremiah Duggen. And I live here and work here year round."

"What I bring from the East is experience. We've gone through this before. Have any of you? If you haven't, you're in for some nasty surprises. And if you want to keep this peaceful, you'd best learn from my experience. I've seen both kinds, the peaceful and the dirty."

"There ain't no option but to fight," Duggen insisted. "Hell, those owners won't give us a penny unless we show 'em what we're made of! Hey, boys! Are you with me?"

Jeremiah Duggen looked about himself, but saw only men who wanted enough consideration from their employers to live peacefully. He realized he had been pushing the fighting too soon. They would need more prodding.

"So what do you suggest we do?" he questioned gruffly.

"First," Varley spoke loudly so all the miners could hear, "you need to pick a group of men to act as your representatives. Those men should sit down and write a list of demands, and present that list to the managers."

"And who will take it to them?"

"Surely there's someone in town who wants justice done."

"And when they turn us down, what do we do then?"

"Then we go on to the next step," Varley answered patiently.

"Which is?" Duggen was more obnoxious with each word he spoke.

"Which is what we decide tomorrow, Mr. Duggen. For now, we'll have the men elect their representatives. We'll need a box and some paper and pencils. Can you arrange for those, Mr. Duggen?" Varley looked directly at the troublemaker. He spoke calmly, but the words came across as they were meant to, as a challenge.

Duggen flushed, but nodded briefly.

"Good. Then we'll expect you back in an hour? With the supplies?"

Duggen took considerably longer than that, but by midafternoon the vote was in. Eight men were chosen as the representatives. While the miners continued their peaceful demonstration, Ed Varley and the eight men moved into town, where they rented a room in one of the more obscure hotels. Varley picked up the tab for that. He needed a place to sleep, he reasoned, since he now had to leave the Calcord house. Though where he had been these many days was already common knowledge.

The tension in the room was high. Duggen had been elected one of the representatives, and Varley personally thought that if he continued with his aggressive behavior when dealing with the mine managers, they hadn't a chance of winning their points without a gunfight. The man was practically panting for blood.

The others were more reasonable. Michael Mooney and MacPherson were thoughtful, realistic men. Varley understood how Mooney had been elected president of the Knights of Labor. He had a way about him of handling men. He even managed to keep Jeremiah Duggen somewhat subdued.

By midnight, the list was drawn up and signed by each man. A raise in pay, a limit of eight hours to the workday, no retribution from the strike, the right to choose their own foremen, and the mine owners to pay the insurance premiums, those were the demands the men wanted. While it totaled more than they could reasonably expect, it left room for compromise.

At dawn it was presented to Mayor John F. Humphreys. By ten o'clock in the morning he had a response from the owners: No. But the mayor insisted he could get everyone to sit down to a bargaining table. Varley told him to go ahead and try, and let him know what happened.

Meanwhile, the picket line would form.

"Let's shut down the pumps," Duggen demanded. "That'll get 'em where it hurts most."

"It will get the men too," Varley responded. "Shutting down the pumps will flood the mines, and then there will be no work to come back to. Somehow, your idea does not appeal to me, Mr. Duggen."

" 'at's 'cause you think all the good ideas come out of the East!" he snarled. "Let's vote on it! Who wants to shut down the pumps?"

"Don't push so hard, Jeremiah," Mike Mooney soothed. "What's the sense in destroying the mines? We'll only be rebuilding them in a few days. We don't even need to vote on that. It's a fool's notion."

"It is, heh? Take a good look at that."

Varley and Mooney turned in the direction Jeremiah pointed. A bevy of armed men were climbing the hill toward them. In the middle of the armed guard were men Varley recognized as scab miners. The other miners lifted their makeshift weapons and moved forward, but Varley lifted his hand and stopped them from attacking. If someone had to die, it wouldn't be this early in the fight, he swore to that.

"You're to stand aside and let these men work," the spokesman for the armed men said gruffly.

"Damn ye scabs!" bellowed Duggen who came forward, pistol in hand.

"Put that gun away, Mr. Duggen," Ed Varley said calmly. "These men don't like being scab labor any more than you like them being such."

The foremost of the scabs was a shabby young man, not more than twenty years of age. His mouth was turned down in a frown, and his eyes barely lifted to meet Mr. Varley's. "I need the work, bad."

"You must," Varley agreed, motioning the others to let them through.

"What did you do that for?" Duggen demanded.

"We're not here to kill anyone," Varley explained patiently. "And that's not enough men but for a skeleton crew. Those few straggly men will not get much done down below. Don't worry, your job is safe. For the moment. But if you'd used that gun, you'd either be running or hanged, and then you would no longer give a damn. Of course, in a way it's too bad you didn't shoot someone. It would have rid me of your troublesome presence at least." Varley walked off, leaving a fuming Jeremiah Duggen behind.

Any joy Christmas might have brought was gone. The miners were angry and their wives were frightened. The picket line formed again the next morning, but this time, many of the miners brought guns. When the armed guard came, the leader took one good look at what was happening on the hill and quickly turned around to lead his men back down it. He only had eight men, and there were at least ten times that number carrying guns this morning.

C. C. Davis arrived that morning to announce he had arranged a citizens' meeting in Hallock Hall for the next morning. He invited the miners to be there.

So many showed up that the hall was filled and overflowing into the streets. C. C. Davis then announced that the meeting was adjourned for an hour and would reconvene in the Tabor Opera House. When the meeting finally began, Davis called it to order, using the handle end of a six-shooter for a gavel. It quickly became apparent that nothing would be settled with so many diverse people involved, all of them wanting to have their say. He proposed to form a committee of one hundred citizens to settle the problems. The miners listened, but when Davis proposed to appoint the one hundred, they objected. Their objection was overruled, and the one hundred were appointed. All the men were from the mining and business establishments, men like Horace Tabor, George Robinson, and W. S. Keyes, men who preferred things as they stood before the strike.

The miners walked out of the meeting.

The rest of that day and into the next, the town was unusually subdued. Maggie went to work after attending a Mass that was filled with other wives praying for the safety of their men. Few people were on the street or in the stores. The talk at the church was all about the strike and the hardship it would cause if it went on for long.

Leadville seemed like a town expecting the worst to happen at any moment. Behind doors and windows were the women and children and other persons not affiliated directly with the mines. No one could guess where this standoff would lead, only that it would bring trouble.

That afternoon, it was learned that the newspaper editors, Robert Higgins and Hop Lee, were warned to leave Leadville. Their newspapers supported the striking miners. Both editors stayed, though their families were provided protection by the miners.

As the day wore on, fewer and fewer people ventured out. Mr. Smith told Maggie to go home early, so she wrapped her coat about her and hurriedly looked for Paddie. Neither at the church nor at the rectory was he to be found, so she left him a note at the stables, telling him she had already gone home and would see him there later.

The wind decided to pick this bleak day to kick up again. Maggie had to cover her mouth with her scarf for protection. The cold of the wind bit into her legs and fingers and tore at her face, and she averted her eyes, satisfied to let her mare's instinct find the way home.

Just outside of Leadville, visibility became almost nothing. The wind brought dust and dirty snow spiraling through the air, whipping at Maggie's clothing and hair until she had to use one hand to hold her coat tight against her and the other one to hold the reins.

Through the howling wind, Maggie heard something that had the hair on the back of her neck prickling attentively. Turning her mare around, she rode into the copse of piñon pine to the north of her. On a clear day she would easily be spotted, but today was far from clear. One of the pines blocked the wind, and for a moment she could see what was coming from the opposite direction. Men on horseback, many men, wearing scarves around their mouths and carrying weapons. They rode fast and hard, the metal of their weapons glinting even in this duskiness.

There must be one hundred men, Maggie thought, her hand going to her throat. She had seen too many battles, men pitted against each other, not to know what this meant. All she could think of was protecting her friends and neighbors, warning them, somehow. Her own danger didn't seem to matter.

Maggie didn't even wait until they had all passed her. She knew of another way to Fryer's Hill, a way more treacherous in this weather, but it would get her there in time for her warning to be of help. She would have to be careful of rocks, for there was no road, barely a path. And she would have to hurry. If she became lost on her way, it would be spring before she was found. Spring, too late for her to be of help to the miners or herself.

The mare didn't like the rough terrain, but Maggie insisted, pulling the reins taut and guiding her firmly. The wind was more dangerous across uncleared land also. Twice, Maggie was caught in the head and shoulders by flying branches.

Finally she reached the barren area that heralded the beginning of the mining camps. The camps were empty, the men were all on the picket line. Just over the next incline was the road leading to Fryer's Hill. From here she could see most of the mining hills, and they all seemed to be covered with striking men. She kicked at the mare's flanks wildly, relieved to be so near her destination. At the foot of Fryer's Hill she hesitated, wondering if she was at the right place. Never had she seen so many men in one spot since arriving in America!

"I'm looking for Edward Varley. Do you know where he is?" she inquired when the mass of men surged upright, blocking her path.

"What business do you have with him?" queried one miner.

"She ain't got none. She be married to a mine owner, she be one of them!"

"No, no! I must see Mr. Varley. What I have to tell him is important. Please, let me through!"

"I think you ought to go back where you come from. This is no place for wimmen, especially not *their* wimmen!"

"No! I've come to warn him—"

But it was already too late. The few precious moments she had saved by taking such a dangerous route were wasted in arguing with the miners. Behind her, she could hear the sounds of many riders coming with steady deliberation toward the hill.

"What is that?"

"I think it's a group of vigilantes," Maggie stammered. "Please let me by. I must speak to Mr. Varley."

The miner Maggie argued with spread the news of the vigilante group loudly. Soon, other voices echoed up the hill and down the other side.

From the stance of the men, Maggie knew they were not budging. Rifles were loaded and sighted in, pistols were primed.

"Maggie!" Ed Varley was so surprised to see her here he forgot to use her proper name. He had seen the commotion at the foot of the hill and came to find out what it was about. "What are you doing here? Oh, never mind," he grumbled, reaching for her by the waist and pulling her down to stand beside him. "Stay off that horse. You make the perfect target sitting up there. Whatever possessed you to come here?"

"I saw them—the vigilantes, I mean," Maggie answered breathlessly. "So I came to warn you. But these men wouldn't let me through so—"

"You didn't tell us what you wanted," the miner said plaintively.

240

"It doesn't matter anyway," Varley answered. "We're ready for them."

"Oh, be careful! They mean business, I swear by the holy saints that they do!" Magheen spoke hysterically, her efforts and the worry wearing her down.

Varley took her by the shoulders and stood her behind him. "Stay there," he ordered. To his men he spoke more loudly. "I want no firing of guns unless we're fired upon. If we're not careful, this will turn into a bloodbath. All we want is justice. Remember that and keep your guns low."

Chapter Fourteen

The vigilantes rode hard and fast at the rabble of men barricading the mines. Each of them was covered almost head to toe in varying shades of black. They were dressed to intimidate, with their rifles slung across the saddles and six-shooters in holsters hanging from their sides.

Magheen recognized none of these men, and for once was content to depend upon someone else for protection. She hid behind Ed Varley, and from there could watch and listen, without taking unnecessary risks.

Ed Varley was joined at the front of the miners by Mike MacPherson and Mike Mooney. The three of them stood clearly as the miners' representatives. The group of vigilantes stopped abruptly, the horse of the first man barely missing Ed Varley.

"This is your only warning," the leader of the vigilantes spoke in a deep, raspy voice. All that could be seen of him was his eyes and the bit of beard stubble that appeared above his kerchief. He addressed Varley directly. "Get these men back at work by Monday morning, if you value your life or theirs."

"Or what?" Varley demanded.

"Or else, greener! These guns mean what they say." He spoke more loudly now, addressing the rest of the men. "If you aren't back at work by then, we'll use these guns to get you off this mountain and out of Leadville. Hundreds more men are willing to ride with us. The question you must ask yourselves is, Do you want to die?" With one last glaring look at the unkempt rabble of miners, he made a gesture with his hand that caused the other vigilantes to turn and follow him down the mountain. As swiftly as they had come, they were gone.

Varley turned to Mooney and MacPherson. "I take his words as a threat to you and your families. I won't blame you if you change your minds about the actions you're contemplating. This business could get nasty."

"I'm not running from the likes of them," Mooney declared.

"Nor am I," agreed MacPherson.

"Then I suggest we take precautions. Your families are not as safe as we are here. They haven't the manpower protecting them."

"I'm not convinced they meant more than to frighten us. I recognized one of the men as Jefferson Silver, a deacon in the Evangelical church."

"Deacon or not, he must think mining has nothing to do with saving his soul. Those men sound like the kind who will do anything they think they'll not be held accountable for. And that includes hurting women and children. Now, let's get volunteers to guard your homes. And you, Mrs. Calcord," Ed Varley spoke curtly to her, "we thank you for trying to warn us, but you should have stayed out of this. Go on home now. You've no need to be any further mixed up in this than you already are." Varley turned away and strode back up the hill.

Michael Mooney gave Maggie a sheepish glance. "He's right, you know. If any of those men saw you, they'll probably tell Daniel. He'll be hopping mad when he hears."

Maggie thought so too.

Dark had settled in when she reached the house. Paddie was impatiently waiting for her. "Where have you been, girl?"

"I rode to Fryer's Hill—"

"Don't you have any sense? There's men up there carrying guns and more men after them."

"I know that, Paddie. I went to warn them about those guns." Maggie removed her scarf and shook it free of snow. "I saw a group of vigilantes on the road and realized where

243

they were headed. It was too late by the time I reached the hill, but I had to try."

"Was anyone hurt?"

"No, not tonight, that is. I think all they wanted to do tonight was scare the miners. Of course there were many more miners than vigilantes. That may have been part of the reason why no one was hurt. But they certainly made their share of threats. The miners have decided to put bodyguards on the Mooney and MacPherson houses. Perhaps you ought to suggest they do that for the family of any man who signed the petition."

"You know too much about this. I want you to stay out of it," Paddie said curtly.

"I tried, Paddie. Honestly. I know Daniel would disapprove, but I couldn't stand by and do nothing, not when I thought the miners' lives were threatened, could I? The leader of the vigilantes gave the miners until Monday morning to be back at work, or else, he said."

"Dinner," interrupted Mrs. Sawyer from the doorway.

"Good, I'm starving."

"Maggie," Patrick stopped her with a light touch on the forearm. "I don't want you working tomorrow."

"Why not?"

"The Committee of Safety," even the title galled Patrick Fitzgerald because it made the council of one hundred men led by C. C. Davis sound more pretentious than the men themselves were, "announced they're having a parade down Harrison Street tomorrow. It could get nasty."

"Does Ed Varley know?"

"I sent word to him tonight. I don't know why they're having a parade unless they think to intimidate the strikers."

"How will one hundred men intimidate the strikers, when there are thousands of them?"

Patrick paused momentarily, as though he couldn't decide whether to tell Maggie all he knew or not. "Governor Robinson today gave Davis the authority to call for militia volunteers, and Davis claims to have twelve hundred men, all willing to fight against the strikers."

"Twelve hundred?"

"That's why I want you to stay home."

"But Paddie, I can't stay home. I might be needed." Eagerly she clutched at his arm. "I can wait at the church, can't I? Then if you do need me, you can get word readily enough. Please, Paddie, let me do this, at least."

"Not at the church. But you can go to Anne Howard's house. I spoke with both her and Joshua, and they feel just as I do. You shouldn't be too involved. They'll watch out for you. But take Mrs. Sawyer, do you hear? I don't want her left here alone. Who knows who might turn against us because we harbored Ed Varley? I'm not willing to take the chance."

"Of course I'll take her."

The morning was cold and clear. The crowd lining Harrison Street was somber, almost to the point of apprehensiveness. Maggie watched from the vantage of Anne's living-room window as the crowd gradually assembled. For the first time in days, the mining hills were bare of men, for they had all come into town before sunup on this Saturday morning to see the grand parade.

A brass band began it well enough, and the crowd showed signs of livening up, but the entertainment was followed by the more mundane one of C. C. Davis and his committee of one hundred men marching behind. Davis was accompanied by H. A. W. Tabor and Judge Carlton Forbes to the balcony of the Tabor Opera House, and from there, he gave a speech dedicated to the preservation of law and order.

The whole town listened in grim silence. Davis's voice rose in timbre, the stillness of the crowd more threatening as the moments ticked by. Maggie couldn't hear a word he was saying, but she recognized his gestures as bravado.

The enlisted army of citizens followed the committee. This woke the crowd, bringing taunts and jeers from the men. Maggie thought the army numbered no more than six or seven hundred men, not the twelve hundred Davis was bragging about. Most of them were astride horses and had sabers and rifles dangling from the saddles. A commotion broke out in the rear, and Maggie had to crane her neck to see retired Col. A. V. Bond, on horseback, beating one of the unarmed miners over the head with the flat of his sword.

The crowd roared in anger at this and a fight threatened, but the police swiftly stepped in and hauled the vociferous colonel off to jail. Peace was momentary. Davis tried to continue with his speech, but the crowd began heckling and jeering at him. He was called a fool and a traitor. Davis cried out that he promised justice; the crowd answered that he must be a liar as well.

Catcalls and insults were exchanged. When the crowd grew weary of this, they fell silent once more. Maggie thought the excitement was over and had turned to answer one of Annabelle's many questions when shouts of alarm spread through the crowd.

"The militia!" was the cry echoing throughout the town.

Maggie and the others flew to the window and learned that the hysterical voices were right. The official Colorado militia, in full regalia, was heading down Harrison Street, toward the center of town and the unwary miners. The blue and gray of their uniforms proclaimed that these men were not mere volunteers, but fully trained, fully armed soldiers. Wagons of ammunition and supplies followed behind them, and beyond those could be seen huge freight bans, private wagons, and a Concord coach pulled by a six-horse team. Apparently the road to Leadville was filled this day.

The commander of the militia wasted no time announcing to the crowds that the parade was over and it was time to go home. Davis protested the loudest. After all, this whole demonstration was meant to show what a powerful man he was, and he didn't relish being sent home like a whipped dog. The state militia that he had sent for was robbing him of his audience.

As he protested to the commander, loud, insulting comments were made about him by the miners. Judge Forbes answered for him, crudely, and soon a fight was breaking out between the miners and some of the citizens' one hundred. Fists pounded on flesh as dust and dirt flew in every direction.

The commander of the militia stood in the midst of the

brawl, pointing his gun heavenward as he pulled the trigger. The fighting ceased abruptly at the sharp sound of the gunfire. The commander reined his horse in near the brawlers and ordered loudly, "This town is under martial law. Now, get yourselves off to your homes. Any man I find on this street in twenty minutes will be placed under arrest. And so it will be until I say otherwise."

As the crowd dispersed, freight wagons lined up for unloading. Across the street, in front of the Colorado House, stood the stagecoach. "Maggie, isn't that Daniel?" Mrs. Sawyer yelped excitedly, her finger pointing toward the stage.

Maggie craned her neck to see, her expression brightening perceptively as she, too, recognized Daniel. He turned and assisted an older woman from the coach. Older, Maggie could see, by the telltale silver of her hair, but very attractive and elegant. Dressed in the latest fashion from New York, she carried a mink cuff that matched the mink collar of her coat.

Releasing her, Daniel turned his attention to the much younger woman who followed. Daintily shod feet touched the steps as she alighted. A gray wool capelet trimmed with black French braiding proclaimed her social status to the world. A trim pillbox hat set off her dark hair to perfection. Even from this distance Maggie could see the way she smiled at Daniel, provocatively, she thought, as though she had some claim on him.

"I wonder who they are," Anne mused aloud.

"I've never seen the older woman before," Mrs. Sawyer answered. "But the younger one is Judge Forbes' daughter. She's been at one of those Eastern schools for a couple of years now. Daniel looks like he knows them both pretty well. They sure don't look much like anybody who lives in Leadville."

"I'd agree there. A hoity-toitier young miss I've never seen! Look at the way she's looking at Daniel—like she owns him! And she's ignoring poor Dutch Saunders as if he were lower than a snake," Anne remarked warmly. "I think you'd better get out there and let her know he's your husband, Maggie. And quick, before her ideas grow bigger than her head."

But there was something in the way Daniel was acting the made Maggie hesitate. Maybe this young, beautiful woman was one of the reasons Daniel had been gone so long, why he hadn't written more often. He had been away almost two weeks and didn't seem in any particular hurry to be home. Not even now. And he did seem more familiar with the young woman than Maggie thought he ought. Maybe she was what had taken him to Denver.

Daniel reached into his vest pocket and handed some money to one of the men standing nearby. With a nod, the man climbed aboard the stagecoach and began tossing trunks and baggages to the ground. He and another man followed the four of them across the street and into the Colorado House, their arms loaded with baggage belonging to the women. As they moved, the ladies' elegant skirts swept the surface of the dirt road. The young woman looked down and motioned to her skirt, frowning. Suddenly her face brightened and she laughed up at Daniel and whatever comment he had made. Then she took her skirt in her hand, and, lifting it just a bit so it wouldn't touch the soil and still smiling, she tucked her gloved hand inside the crook of Daniel's arm.

Maggie thought how well they all looked together. All of them were obviously monied, educated, and very high class. And way out of her league.

"Well, aren't you going over there?" Mrs. Sawyer demanded. "If you don't do something, that young woman's gonna get her clutches in him . . ."

"No . . . no," she answered uncertainly. "I think I'll see him at home. Let him get those . . . those people settled in first."

"Are you crazy? Look at her! She wants him if I've ever seen a gal want a man before . . ."

"He's married to me, isn't he? What's a woman like that doing with a married man anyway?" she asked angrily. Maggie didn't wait for an answer, just headed to the wardrobe, snatched her coat and scarf, and slid them on as she flounced out of the house and down the street.

Paddie and Harvey would be waiting to take her and

Mrs. Sawyer home in the buckboard, the same way they had come to town this morning.

Mrs. Sawyer shrugged her shoulders in an eloquent gesture to their hostess as she too headed for the wardrobe and her outdoor clothing. She had to practically run to catch up with Maggie.

The journey home was made in almost total silence. Whatever was eating at Maggie, and Mrs. Sawyer thought she could guess what it was, was something the girl didn't want to talk about. Maude Sawyer shook her head, thinking that Daniel Calcord was a fool if he was flirting with that Eastern hussy when he had a fine wife like Maggie waiting for him. It wasn't natural for a man to be gone so long and not come straight home to his wife.

She was to think that thought over and over again that evening as the hours passed and still there was no sign of Daniel. They had kept dinner hot, expecting him any moment, until, finally, Paddie said, "I'm hungry. I don't know what's keeping Daniel, but can't you warm it up for him when he gets home? Do we all have to starve while we wait?"

"No, of course not, Father," Maude said briskly. "I'm sure Daniel has good reason to take so long. He wouldn't want us put out on his account. How about it, Maggie? Will you make the coffee?"

Maggie forgot to make her customary comment about that "horrid brew," Maude Sawyer realized, as the girl went silently about her chore. After dinner, she insisted Maude join the men in the parlor while she did the dishes.

"I'm not leaving you to do these on your own."

"Please, Mrs. Sawyer, I'm not fit company for you or anyone else right now. I need some time alone."

Maude Sawyer gave a sigh of understanding. Too often when she needed to think, she did so over a tub full of dishes. There was nothing like keeping busy with warm water and dishes to soothe the worries away. She nodded her acquiescence. "All right, but I don't want you feeling sorry for yourself. Whatever is going on with Daniel right now, it's you he married and you he loves. Remember that. You've no need to fear that Eastern priss any more than

249

you have to fear an old hag like me. Understand?"

Maggie gave a reluctant smile. "You take the coffee with you. I never have learned to like that horrid stuff anyway."

Maude suppressed a smile as she lifted the tray. At least the girl was sounding more like herself.

The dishes were done, the floor was swept and mopped. The kitchen was a homey room to be in, especially in the winter. The stove was kept stoked and warm all the time, and on even the coldest days, the room was pleasant to be in. The only other room in the house that could compare was the front parlor and only after the fire had been lit and going for at least an hour.

Maggie was content to remain where she was.

She was tired but too worried to sleep; Daniel might be home at any time. She heated some milk and sat on the stool while it cooled, then sipped of it. Patrick came through the kitchen and bade her good night, slipping out the back door and heading for the stables and his horse. A little while later, Harvey did much the same. Soon Maude came too. "I'm turning in, Maggie. Shouldn't you be in bed too?"

"In a few minutes."

Mrs. Sawyer compressed her lips. "If you're waiting for Daniel, he's probably spending the night in town. It's too late to come home now."

"I'm not waiting for him. You go on. I'll go to my bed when I'm ready," Maggie answered softly.

Mrs. Sawyer's footfalls sounded up the carpeted stairs, and Maggie heard the bedroom door open and close. Maggie remained in the kitchen for a few minutes, then decided to go into the warm parlor where she could really be comfortable on the davenport. Surely Daniel couldn't be much longer?

Tossing more wood on the fire, she quickly settled down, a book in her hands. A bit of reading would help her sleep, she decided, as she turned up the gas lamp. She soon nodded off, the book on her lap. Eventually the lamp burned out and the fire slowly died.

When Maggie woke up, she was shivering with cold. Intuitively she knew something had awakened her, but could not place what is was. She sensed the lateness of the hour from the chill in the room and the depth of the darkness outside. Footsteps descending the stairs alarmed her, and she realized that was the sound that had woken her. She remained very still and quiet as dim light wavered through the door, and the footsteps crossed the hall. The light entered the room, and a shadowy face appeared just beneath it.

"Daniel!" Maggie cried, startled. "You frightened the very devil out of me!"

"Sorry," he responded dryly as he entered the room. He set the lamp on the table beside the davenport, his hooded eyes studying her. The auburn hair was tousled from sleep and her bare feet were tucked beneath the gracefully draping skirt as she lay stretched out on the sofa. The emerald green eyes were hazy from sleep, and her pink lips were lightly parted.

For two weeks he had thought of nothing but hurrying home to her. In his mind she was warm and soft and loving, as beautiful as she was this very moment.

Beautiful on the outside, but what was she on the inside? His head was still spinning from the tales that had greeted him on his return.

Maggie lifted her fingers to shyly touch his cheek, but he drew away from her, averting his eyes. "What are you doing up? I thought you'd be in bed by now."

"I waited for you," she answered. A moment passed before she continued, "I saw you in town earlier. But you were busy, so I came on home. I thought you'd be here soon after me."

The accusation was quietly spoken and all the more direct for that. Daniel was in no mood to be made to feel guilty over something his wife thought. Straightening, he replied, "I thought I'd be home earlier too. But it seems that shortly after I arrived, a full-scale war threatened to break out between the miners and the militia. It was all I could do to get the miners and the management to sit down to talks by midnight." His eyes darkened with his next words.

"I had more trouble than I expected. It seems the miners consider me part of management. And the management considers that I've betrayed them by allowing my wife to harbor one of the union's leaders in my home, as well as allowing you to hand out pamphlets with union propaganda printed on them.

"By four A.M., I managed to convince both sides that all I want is a practical solution to this problem. And I want my mine operating. Precious little else has been settled, but the miners were mollified enough that they agreed to talk again tomorrow."

He waited for her reaction, and it was not long in coming. A guilty flush spread upward from her neck to her cheeks. "It's not quite as it sounds—"

"Oh, I'm sure of that," he said sneeringly. "I went to Denver in the first place because of financial pressures, and when I come back, it's to find the mine hasn't operated since I left because of a strike. And then," his voice roughened and he moved to stand over her, his stance almost threatening, "I discover my wife . . . my *wife* has been plotting with the union members and for the strike. I learned that you harbored Edward Varley, the miners' representative in my home . . . *my home* . . . And as though that wasn't enough, that you handed out pamphlets among the miners, breeding more dissatisfaction and dissension. Tell me, wife, what other good have you done me?"

Her palms flew to her cheeks. "Oh, Daniel, please! It's not as you make it sound."

"And who is this Edward Varley? What is he to you? Are you lovers?" he demanded nastily, his fingers wrapping around her wrists and hauling her to her feet.

Maggie's eyes widened. "You don't think . . . you can't think . . . why, that's utter nonsense!"

"Nonsense? Then he didn't spend the better part of a fortnight here, in my home, with my wife?"

"He—he did, but not like you seem to think, Daniel—"

"According to what I heard, it's just like what I think. I heard you even joined him today on the hill, that you stood by his side, though you hid behind his back the moment you thought you might be recognized! So thoughtful of you to worry about my reputation, though a touch late, don't you think?"

"Daniel, you must listen—"

"I've listened plenty tonight. I've listened to C. C. Davis and Walter MacClean, Seanna Gallagher, and Judge Forbes until I'm sick with the listening. They've all been full of news of my faithful wife, my dear, faithful wife, waiting at home for my return! And the last person I want to listen to is you! Now, get upstairs and pack your things."

"I . . . I'm going somewhere?"

"You are."

His anger was all the more frightening because of the taut control he held over it.

"Where?" she managed to ask.

"Can you possibly have no idea how foolishly you've behaved? Or how angry you've made so many people? Are you such a fool that you meddle and give no thought to the repercussions? There are men who'd like to kill you, and for far less than giving out unionist pamphlets! Like an idiot you're here alone, with only Mrs. Sawyer for protection. What kind of protection do you think she'll be when a pack of men break down the door and take you by force?"

"Why would anyone want to take me?" Maggie questioned, frightened by the wild anger in his eyes.

"To hang you, my dear. To be rid of you and your meddling presence forever, thereby weakening the union. I don't know what kind of a fool this Edward Varley is that he would rely on your support! God knows you can't be trusted!"

"That's not fair!"

"I don't have time to listen to this. Get your things while I saddle your horse. You'll be safe in the cabin at the halfway house for a few days, until this dies down. A hell of a lot safer there than here, at any rate. Well, go! We haven't all night!"

He stomped through the room, and she heard the kitchen door open and slam closed. Maggie sat still for the moment, stunned by the hatred she heard in Daniel's voice. What he said, what he accused her of, was horrible. Surely he knew her better than that?

253

Of course he did. By tomorrow he'll be more reasonable. He'll listen then, she thought. She only wished she were more sure than she felt. Two weeks away and it was as though he had never known her at all. He didn't seem to be the same man she'd married. She supposed she might have been a bit more cautious in her conduct while he was gone . . . but how? She did as she thought best at the time. And in everything she did, she tried to take Daniel into account. Ed Varley was here only because she couldn't throw a wounded man out into the snow! Her brow lightened at the thought. Of course, Daniel must not know about Ed Varley's wounds. He may have been told much about her actions but, apparently, not that. And she never had the chance to tell him. But once she did, he would understand.

She felt much better with this thought and went upstairs to pack her bag. In fact, she was now looking forward to some time alone with Daniel.

The sun was barely lighting the horizon when they left. The early morning was bitterly cold, and Maggie bundled herself heavily. As they climbed higher into the mountains, the sun made its appearance and the day warmed appreciably. Maggie loosened her confining blankets and tried to talk with Daniel, but he wasn't interested. He answered with the briefest of words, effectively dampening Maggie's spirits and silencing her. Once they were at the cabin, she thought, she would tell Daniel all about it then.

The cabin came in sight about noon. The first thing Maggie noticed was the heavy smoke spiraling from the chimney. "Someone's already here, Daniel. Do you think —"

"It's Dutch. I told him to come and get the cabin ready for you. I knew I wouldn't have time to cut wood and haul water."

"You mean . . . you aren't staying with me?"

He threw her an impatient glance. "I have to get back to Leadville. I told you I had meetings set up with the miners."

"You said the management and the miners were sitting down together, you said nothing about your being there."

254

"Well, if I'm not there, they'll probably get just as far as they did while I was in Denver." He frowned heavily as he spoke. "Oh, no, not this time. This time I'll sit with them, and we'll hammer out some sort of agreement."

"Well, why couldn't I just wait at the house? I'm missing work, I don't want to miss practice for the children's Christmas program."

Maggie spoke loudly, for Daniel was pulling away from her, guiding his horse to the fenced area behind the cabin where Dutch's horse was standing. He didn't seem to hear a word she said. Maggie sighed and followed silently now.

Daniel dismounted and reached a hand to help Maggie from her horse.

"As I told you, you're in too much danger in Leadville. And I can't waste the time protecting you. You don't need that damned job anyway. Let someone who needs it take it. And the children will just have to do their play without you."

Maggie bit her lip. "I never asked you to protect me. I can protect myself."

"I've seen what you can do for yourself, and it scares me. What I'd like to know is where your brother was during all this time. Does he feel the same way you do about the union?" Daniel demanded.

"I don't know. He never said." Maggie's face turned red at her words. "I don't mean I actively supported the union—"

"Never mind," Daniel said heavily. "You've made it perfectly clear how you feel about the union. I just wonder how you could have forced yourself to marry me, feeling so strongly about the working man and all. I'm surprised you'd consider lowering yourself to my immoral standards! Let's go inside. I have to get back to town."

"No, Daniel. I want to talk to you first."

"I told you I don't have time." He swung the door open and gestured for her to precede him inside. "Hi, Dutch. Did you get the supplies?"

Dutch rose slowly from the table at which he sat whittling. Dutch did everything slowly, even answering. Fingering his curled black mustache, he answered in monotones.

"I sure did. We'll be fine for over a week."

"Good. I don't want to have to hurry back. I have no idea how long this damned strike will take to settle. I can't believe the bunch of fools let it go this far. Don't worry, Dutch. I'll be back as soon as I can." He turned to Maggie. "You'll be safe here. Just do as Dutch tells you."

"But I wanted to talk to you first. There are some things you don't know."

"Maggie, don't you think we've said enough?"

"You've said plenty, I haven't even begun!"

Daniel ran a hand impatiently through his hair. "Maggie, there's nothing left to say. I didn't expect you to create this barrel of problems, but you did. And fool that I am, I should have known better than to trust anyone. Don't worry, I won't expect so much of you next time."

"If there is a next time," she threatened.

Daniel's eyes grew cold. "Oh, there'll be a next time. We're married and married we'll stay. And together. Forever. You took those vows, Maggie, and no matter how another man might appeal to you, you'll stick to them, I promise you that." Stuffing his hat back on his head, he turned and quit the cabin.

Maggie silently fumed for the next few hours. Pacing across and back in the cabin, she thought of all that she should have said and didn't. But when she next saw Daniel, she would give him a piece of her mind! Who did he think he was anyway, hauling her up here and leaving her alone in the wilds! And why should she give up her job? She and Daniel had that argument before and after their marriage. She not only needed the money, she liked working at the store. She liked her customers and the daily chitchat. Then she remembered that she wouldn't be showing up today or tomorrow, and what was left of her spirits fell. She probably wouldn't have a job to go back to, so another argument on that score was useless.

Her head lifted, and her eyes moved to the cloth-covered window where just a bit of daylight filtered through. No wonder she felt so depressed. The cabin was dirty from such lengthy disuse and needed a good cleaning if she was to remain here for any time at all. And light, she needed more light! Nothing could seem cheery in these surroundings.

By the time night fell, the cabin was clean, the table and chairs soaped and polished, and the bed covered in fine, fresh linen. Maggie made Dutch a pallet on the floor that would be much softer than the bedroll he had planned to sleep in. At first, when he realized what Maggie's intentions were, Dutch took off, claiming he needed to chop more wood. Maggie thought that was just fine, she could get more done by herself.

When he finally managed to gather enough courage to return, Maggie had a pot of stew simmering over the fire. The smell of cheese-laced biscuits permeated the room. A brightly colored cloth covered the table. In the center stood a gas lamp, a sprig of evergreen surrounding the base. Dutch hung his coat and gloves on the pegs behind the door and stood watching Magheen as she bent toward the fire.

Dipping a spoon in the stew, Maggie tasted it. Just about ready, she thought, rising to her feet. Dutch was still standing awkwardly by the door, a red flush about his neck and high cheeks. "Well, sit down, Mr. Saunders. Dinner will be served in a few minutes."

"Yes, ma'am."

Maggie lifted a brow. "Do you play cards?"

"Yes, ma'am."

"Did you bring any cards?"

"Yes, ma'am."

"Well, Mr. Saunders, it seems that may be the only form of entertainment we have."

"Ma'am?"

An improvement, she thought. Ma'am was not preceded by a yes. "Yes?" she couldn't resist.

"I usually play solitaire. I never played with a woman before."

"Have you played with men?"

"Yes, ma'am."

"We're much the same as you men, only a good deal smarter."

The black mustache heaved a bit with this answer. "Yes,

257

ma'am."

The days passed slowly. Mornings were spent doing the necessary chores. Maggie used her afternoons to roam through the outdoors as far as she dared go. She loved to walk and hadn't had the time or the freedom for that lately. Now, she had plenty of both. But winter in the mountains could be dangerous, and she always had to be careful that she didn't go too far. Dutch wasn't much for words, but he knew a lot of card games and must have taught her every one he knew over those few days.

Maggie could feel the cabin fever beginning to burn inside her. She wanted to go home, to Leadville. The Nativity play was in a few days' time, and Maggie wanted to be there so badly.

She began thinking of returning alone. Surely by now the strike was settled. Daniel had no right to keep her up here alone, with only the silent Dutch for company. If she left in the morning, she would be home by noon. Daniel's anger must have subsided by this time.

That evening, after dinner, Maggie packed her bag. Dutch silently whittled in the chair, his feet on the low hearth. As soon as he realized what she was doing, he rose and crossed the cabin to stand beside her. "You can't leave here until Daniel says so." That was the lengthiest speech she had ever heard Dutch say.

No matter. Maggie's mind was made up. "I'm leaving in the morning. I'm sick and tired of this place. I want to go home, I've got too many things to do there to sit here whiling away my time."

"Daniel said—"

"I don't care what Daniel said! I'm going home, and that's that."

Dutch lapsed into his customary silence.

In the morning, after they had breakfasted and Maggie had seen to the cabin, she fetched her pack and tugged on her coat and gloves. Dutch was nowhere to be seen. He might have offered to return with her, she thought. Surely he was just as bored as she was. Maggie lifted her pack and moved to the door.

It was locked. Locked from the outside, as she quickly

258

discovered. A board was nailed across the door to make certain she couldn't get out. She wasn't up here just to save her skin. She was a prisoner! Her fists clenched, her bag dropped to the floor, and she landed a swift kick against the thick wood of the door. She didn't harm the door one bit, but it sure made her feel better.

The gavel hit the desk once more. Daniel rose, finally having his fill of Forbes's histrionics, and took the six-shooter from Forbes's hand.

"Next time get a real gavel. The only person you're in danger of shooting is yourself. And if you don't cooperate a bit more, I may shoot you myself!"

"I should have known you'd take their side!" Forbes accused. "You and your wife, you're both the same, a couple of bleeding-heart liberals!"

"Well, Forbes, it beats being a miserable skinflint who enjoys other people's misery." Daniel leaned across the desk and glared into the older man's eyes. "Fifty cents a day! What's the harm in that?"

"I refuse to let such scum dictate my business practices. I own the mine; what I say goes!"

Daniel gritted his teeth. He was sick of this smoke-filled room, these same arguments, and these same small-minded persons who owned the mines. "I'll say this one time and one time only. I'm giving my men a fifty-cent raise. Some of the others here are inclined to, also. If you aren't, you may be the only one left who's being targeted by this strike. And frankly, I won't give a damn!"

"Just because the men in Gunnison make four dollars a day is no reason for us to pay the same."

"We're not paying the same. We'll still be paying fifty cents less. A measly fifty cents! Good God! Have you any idea what it's costing you to stay closed for this duration? A hell of a lot more than the raise would cost."

"I don't like giving in to blackmail," Forbes insisted stubbornly.

"The men voted the union in. At least it's a decent union."

"I should have known you'd feel that way, especially after your wife—"

"Don't you ever mention my wife again. You deliberately misled me. You told me nothing about Ed Varley being wounded, nor that her brother, her brother the priest, was with them all the time. You tried to ruin my wife's reputation, not only with me, but throughout Leadville! Don't think I'll be forgetting that soon, Forbes."

"I wanted to be rid of that man!"

"Why? So the men would vote the Elephant Club into power? You idiot! We'd have had a bloody battle on our hands by now."

"We'd have won," Forbes answered smugly.

"And at what cost? Sorry, but the loss of even one life is too much for me. I have to wake up in the mornings with some respect for myself. I couldn't even go to bed at night if I thought my actions had caused someone's death."

"You're too tender-hearted."

"Someday, you'll lose someone you love. Then maybe you'll begin to understand. But for now, Forbes, just understand that I'm leaving here and signing that agreement. Many of these men will follow me. And those of you who don't, you'll be facing the union on your own. You may end up paying a full four dollars a day before you're done."

Chapter Fifteen

"Daniel, honey," wailed the plaintive voice from the bedroom doorway. "You've been late every night this week." It was his mother, looking elegant as always, her silver hair braided in the French style and anchored with a sterling silver comb. Her brown foulard overdress, the latest in European fashion, was lined with a violet silk and trimmed with ribbons of the same hue. Puffed white muslin lined the sleeves. The muslin undergown was delicately flounced into several tiers and gathered with violet ribbon.

"Can't you take a few minutes to spend with me? I've come all this way to see you, and you seem to be avoiding me. Please, honey? It's been five years! I need you so, honey," she cajoled.

His pack was on the bed, and Daniel was filling it hurriedly, but now he paused and glanced in her direction. Her soft, white arms were crossed about her waist, and on her face was a smile that could melt butter, but her eyes couldn't meet his.

He had left New York to escape that petulance and the guilt she liked to use to control her family. He hadn't swallowed her games then, and he didn't now. He had forgotten the manipulation that left him questioning right and wrong, duty and deception, and had been happy to see her when she first arrived in Denver. She had been right when she said it had been many years. Then she had begun the same old routine she used before, and it had quickly worn on him. He had wanted no part of her manipulations five years ago; he wanted none now. Why couldn't she simply be his mother and accept him for what he was? Why did she think she had to go around changing him to fit what she wanted, especially when nothing remotely resembling her life was what he wanted?

At least she hadn't brought his father, a morosely silent man who cared little what anyone else did, as long as they left him alone. Daniel tried to remember to be grateful for the simple things.

He wasn't sure when he first discovered he didn't like his parents as people. They had always been good to him and his friends. Perhaps it had been when his brother first married and his mother conflicted with her new daughter-in-law. Daniel had never understood why she talked about the girl behind her back so much. To this day he could vividly recall her calling Margaret a hussy and a good-time girl, giving the young woman all sorts of doubts about herself and her marriage. And then when David displeased the parents, Margeret had caught the blame for whatever he did too. And David had let them. He had been too weak to protect his own wife. Daniel had, and that had been the first of many eye-opening encounters with the powers that be. Finally he left New York.

At first he had thought he would miss them, but the truth he discovered was that he had been too relieved to be free of their constant demands to miss them. Now he wondered at the lack of luck that placed him in Denver when his mother arrived. After this last week of her company, he began to wonder at his sanity for writing to them and telling them of his marriage at all. He should have kept his news to himself. He should have known she would want to come out and see this new daughter-in-law.

Maybe if he had stayed in Leadville, she would have gone on to California.

Moving into the room unhurriedly, her hips sveltely graceful, Mayme Calcord repeated, "We need you, honey. David has been such a disappointment to us. He was hurt by that girl's leaving him, but he took it out on *us!* As though it was *our* fault! She only did was was natural to her kind. She was nothing but a whore!"

The words were all familiar to him, and Mayme spoke them haughtily, the color rising in her face at Daniel's unaccepting expression. "She even took our grandbaby," his mother wailed plaintively.

"I thought you didn't like the child," he said dryly. "As I remember it, you accused her of getting pregnant just to trap David."

"She tried to take David away from us . . ."

Daniel turned away before he said something he had sworn not to. "I'm sorry, Mother, but I have to finish my packing. I have to get Magheen." Daniel had heard all her words before and wasn't willing to listen again.

"Your wife?" Her shoulders stiffened slightly. "I thought you didn't know where she was."

"Of course I know where she is. She's in a cabin, waiting until it's safe for her to return."

"Are you sure it's safe yet? The way I hear it, she caused too much trouble in this godforsaken town for her actions ever to be forgotten."

"It's safe now. And, Mother, she did nothing wrong. Everything she did was just as I would have wanted."

"Then somebody's been lying to you. That nice Judge Forbes told me—"

"He needs his mouth shut, and I'll do it for him if need be!" Daniel swiftly replied.

"I hope you're not letting that woman lead you around by the nose, Daniel," his mother said petulantly. "These girls today, they expect the world at their feet. I suppose she's another one, just after what she can get. I know these Catholics. She'll have a brood of children before you know it. Margaret was one and look what she did to your brother. He's a broken man, just drinks all day and all night long.

"I'll tell you right now, I've lost you once and I don't expect to again. David is a failure, and we can't trust him to take over the family business. You'll have to do it, Daniel. That's all there is to it. We're getting too old for so much responsibility. That girl better not come between

263

us."

"Learn to get along with Magheen, Mother," Daniel warned, tugging his bag closed.

"Me? Get along with her? Don't you think you should be telling her to get along with me? She's the one new to the family. How you can expect so much of me is beyond my comprehension. Just look at all this other trouble she caused here."

Daniel rolled his eyes, wondering how to handle such a woman, wondering *if* it could be done. "Get along with her," he repeated.

"Why couldn't you have married someone like that nice little Arabella Forbes we met on the stagecoach? And she's from a decent family, at least. There's money in her background and nothing questionable about her lineage. *She* doesn't come from an impoverished Irish family!"

Daniel gritted his teeth. He had had enough. What he wanted now was to get away from her harping for a few days. "I have to go now."

"Now? Oh, Daniel, can't you at least stay for dinner? Oh, never mind! You probably can't stand that . . . Mrs. Sawyer's lumpy gravy any more than I can. You're lucky to be leaving here. Maybe you'll get a decent meal for a change."

Poor Maude, Daniel thought as he quit the house.

The cold air felt marvelous on his face. He had spent the last days cooped up inside a building, trying to work out a compromise with the miners. They were taking a final vote now. If this didn't work, negotiations would begin again after Christmas. Daniel wasn't sure he would still be involved. He was willing to raise wages, and his men were willing to go back to work, no matter what the others did.

He mounted his horse and rode furiously toward the mountains, as though demons were chasing him. The wind and the cold gave him a feeling of freedom and freshness he needed badly. Over the years, Daniel had forgotten much of the bad taste his family left with him. Now, he was recalling every bit of it.

So David, the favorite, was feeling the force of their displeasure. Daniel ought to feel glad about that, especially after all his brother's manipulating, but he didn't. No, not when the price was paid mostly by Margaret. Margaret, the innocent newcomer, who married for love and watched that love die. And Daniel was sure that any love she and David once shared had died. He didn't blame her for leaving; David didn't have the backbone to stand up to their parents, and Margaret had paid the price. Margaret and apparently a child. He would have to get her address, Daniel thought, and make sure she was all right. Maybe she needed some money. She would rather take it from him than from them, he knew.

Mayme had already offered him money to return to New York and play the dutiful son. They were done with David, he had failed once too often, she claimed. Until it suited them to bring him back as a leverage against their other son, Daniel thought cynically. He would never be able to trust any of them again, and he didn't have to learn his lesson twice.

Just when he could use money most and save his mine, his mother miraculously showed up and offered him a way out of his difficulty. Daniel laughed to himself. As though he would fall in that trap again. He would go broke first.

But he didn't have to. He had gotten financing in Denver that would carry him another few months. By then, something had to pay off.

Maggie's ire was growing. She had been locked in the cabin for three days now. Her temper had become so disagreeable that Dutch avoided her whenever possible. When he absolutely had to return, he knew he was in for trouble.

She had already missed most of the practices for the Nativity play. Christmas was close; only five days away, and she would probably not to able to sing in the choir. And she was nowhere near ready for Christmas. Of course, she probably wasn't expected to celebrate it this year, she thought acidly.

Her husband had judged her and found her morals and behavior wanting. He had even accused her of having a tryst with Edward Varley!

Magheen Fitzgerald might be Irish and poor, but like the other Fitzgeralds, she was proud. What would Paddie be thinking, now that she had been missing so long? Or had Daniel told him a story, making him believe that she was as bad as they were all saying?

The person Magheen was angriest with was Daniel. He behaved like no husband she had ever seen. He accused her of ugly things, believed all sorts of lies about her, and then didn't even have the decency to listen to what she had to say about the accusations. What sort of a man had she married? What sort of a craven future were they to share when this was done? Maggie wasn't sure she could ever forgive him.

But maybe he didn't want to be forgiven. Maybe he was content to disregard her thoughts and feelings. Maybe that was the sort of empty man he was, and the kind of empty marriage he wanted.

And maybe she didn't want this kind of marriage at all.

Daniel rode into the horse corral and dismounted. Dutch was sitting on the fence, knife in hand, whittling away on a piece of aspen wood. "How's it going, Dutch?"

The man lifted a bored gaze to Daniel and drawled, "Not too bad. I haven't had a hot meal in three days, my shins are bruised where your wife took her pointy shoes to them, and I'm afraid for my life every time I enter that cabin. I've even thought about sleeping out here, but can't decide if freezing or fearing to death is worse. Other than that, everything's just fine."

Daniel's brows lifted. "She's that mad, huh?"

"She wasn't until I had to lock her in the cabin. Then all hell broke loose."

"You didn't have to lock her in! I told you, she was free to go wherever she pleased!"

266

"As long as she stayed on the mountain, you said. However, one day she got it in her mind that she wanted to go back to Leadville, and nothing I could say or do would stop her. So, when I could only think of one way to keep her here, I used it." Dutch's work-roughened fingers twirled the ends of his mustache as he glared hotly at Daniel. "I ain't never heard such curses as that woman can speak in the Irish, and I ain't never gonna again. She's your wife, you see to her. I was just damned near ready to come get you if you hadn't shown up. She's your responsibility. You can go get the bejesus kicked out of you instead of me."

"Oh, Lord, I didn't mean to make her that mad!"

"No? It sure looked like it to me. It looked like you were spitting mad yourself when you brought her here. Something's happened to change your mind, has it? Well, don't waste your time telling her. I don't think she'll listen."

Daniel sighed, knowing it was his responsibility to clear Maggie's reputation. After all, he himself had made that reputation questionable. "It turns out Edward Varley was badly wounded when she took him in. She saved his life."

"And the pamphlets?"

"I forgot about those." Daniel's eyes brightened. "Yeah, maybe I can calm her down by reminding her of those." His face fell into a grimace. "No, she deserves more honesty than that."

Dutch tossed him one last glare, hopped from the fence, and ambled over to the lean-to where his gear was stored. He was hitting the road to Leadville as soon as it was humanly possible. "Even I know more about women than that," he mumbled. "You ain't gonna handle that woman that way. You'd either better watch out for your own shins or get down on your hands and knees and apologize. I ain't ever seen a woman so mad. I didn't even know they could get that mad!"

Daniel hesitated at the door of the cabin until he heard Dutch ride off. All was quiet inside, for the moment. Daniel was glad he and Maggie had the privacy to argue this out here.

Okay, so he had been wrong about Ed Varley. She still shouldn't have been poking her nose into things that didn't concern her. Nor handing out pamphlets for the union. It was his interests she was supposed to be protecting!

But this time he would listen to her explanations, he thought magnanimously.

Lifting the board from the door, he propped it against the cabin, turned the handle, pushed wide the door, and walked inside.

The hip bath faced the hearth, and Maggie was curled inside it, totally naked. Her hair was piled on top of her head, several loose wisps at the nape of her neck. As the door was opened, she turned and looked toward it, a combination of fear and shock stilling all movement.

When she saw who it was, an arm shot out of the water, and Daniel found himself clutching a wet sponge to his chest. She had aimed it between his eyes.

"Get out of here!" she cried hoarsely, her hands working frantically to give herself at least a modicum of modesty.

Daniel's eyes gaped hungrily at this unexpected pleasure. An unwanted thought intruded, however, and he suddenly bit his mouth shut, angrily demanding, "What do you mean, taking a bath in the middle of the day? What if it had been Dutch instead of me, coming through that door?"

Maggie's eyes flashed with temper. "He wouldn't dare come through that door during the day! Nor should you have, you great overbearing, ill-mannered, bad-tempered devil! Haven't you a brain working in that soft head of yours?"

A washrag followed the route of the sponge. "Now, get out of here until I'm decent!" she screeched, wanting nothing more in this world than to face him properly. She had every intention of having this fight, but it would be a fair one and she would not be hampered by humiliating nakedness.

Daniel glanced down at his wet coat and shirt. She was

very angry, he acknowledged to himself.

He had had a hell of a time lately, first having to go to Denver and find financing for the mine, and then having to deal with that miserable strike and also his mother. He had no patience left; he had used it all in those frustrations. But a deep anger that Maggie could turn on him too, and just when he needed her the most, was burning inside him.

But he had given her provocation. What else could he expect if not a fight?

Of course, as bitter as this argument was turning out to be, matters might never be settled between them.

He would apologize, though he intended once to be enough. At the mulish expression on her face, he rather thought it wouldn't be, not for Maggie anyway.

He had a choice now, either fight or make love. The latter was infinitely preferable.

Her skin glistened with droplets of water, and his body responded tautly, wanting her silkiness to press against. But her mouth was so set. She looked as stubborn as he knew she was, but she also looked unbearably young and hurt . . . and soft.

Unbuttoning his frock coat, he tossed it onto the nearest chair, coal-black eyes never leaving her face. A smile crinkled around the corners of his mouth at the way her eyes widened and blinked in confusion at his action. His shirt followed.

"Daniel," she croaked. "Let me get out of here and get dressed. And then we'll talk."

He shook his head, smiling now. "And I'm supposed to go outside like this?"

"Put your clothes back on."

"Too wet." His smile turned roguish as his eyes plundered her nakedness. The cabin was cold and the water was rapidly cooling. Her flesh was covered with goose bumps. A rosy nipple peeked around one arm, and Daniel could see that it was puckered taut as well.

He carried a towel to the side of the tub, Maggie's wary eyes on every step he made. "Need any help?"

"Oh, go away!" she snapped impatiently. "I'm going nowhere, Englishman, not till you . . ." Her voice trailed off as Daniel reached down for her. She shrank back, as far as she could, but those wily hands were all over her.

"Get out of here!" she demanded, slapping ferociously at them. "I don't want you to touch me! Leave me alone!"

Daniel laughed gruffly, hauling her against him, getting his pants far wetter than either his shirt or coat. The floor and rag rug held puddles of water. "But I want to do far more than merely touch you, love."

"I don't want anything to do with you, Daniel Calcord," Maggie said primly, folding her arms against her chest.

"You won't even let me dry you?" he teased, sliding her bare feet to the floor so quickly that Maggie had to grab at him to keep her balance. Her smoothness glided along him, her soft breasts so at odds with the hardness of his muscles that Maggie gasped when they first touched him.

"Put me down," she demanded, her voice quivering. "I'll not share such . . . such intimacies with you! Not after all you accused me of . . ."

Daniel paid her no mind. Quickly wrapping the towel about her, he began drying her with soft strokes of the towel. Maggie stilled all movement, wanting nothing more in this world than to spurn him, but nowhere within her could she find the strength.

He sat on the edge of the bed and pulled her between his thighs, her silkiness burning his. The towel continued its torturingly slow path.

The lesson they both learned in that moment was that two weeks was far too long for them to be separated.

Rich, auburn hair tumbled to her shoulders. Daniel's gaze trapped her eyes, and he could clearly read every one of her yearnings there.

"Maggie, I'm thinking we made a mess of everything," he whispered softly into an ear. The sensation slithered along her neck and spine, melting her against him.

"I think so too," she whispered back reluctantly.

Daniel angled his mouth to speak more intimately against her, but her lips were there and he took advantage of her weakness, capturing them with his. Her whole body quivered with an age-old need, her mouth flowering open to his. Daniel's tongue delved intimately inside her, tasting all she had to give.

Sighing her capitulation, Maggie wound her arms around his shoulders and drew him closer. His iron-hard arousal pressed against her thighs as his hands molded her buttocks intimately into him. His tongue licked at her lips, sending fire through her.

"My heart's pounding so hard, it'll burst," she said on a whispering breath.

"I can hear it clear over here," he said, smiling.

Her breathing became rapid and hoarse and hot. As the towel slid impersonally over her breasts, they ached for his more intimate touch. Daniel took his time, savoring her sweet resignation as he teased her senses, refusing to uncover her even though her body strained and practically begged him for it. Maggie thought she would go mad with wanting him.

Playing the role of tempter became too much for him too, and he cupped her softly mounding breasts, pressing moist kisses over her flesh. Lifting her in his arms, he brought her to the bed and gazed down on her as he stood beside it, unbuttoning his trousers with rough, jerky movements. Kicking them aside, he joined her. His lips sought hers with a wild hunger, lowering to taste of the rosy peaks. His mouth settled there, teasing her with long, leisurely kisses.

Maggie groaned at the fierce desire coursing through her. Her hand snaked around to tempt his silky smooth hardness and had Daniel gasping at the fiery sensations spiraling through him. His desire reached a fever pitch and he lifted over her, lowering his hips to hers, entering her slowly and deliberately. His forearms were on either side of her head, carrying his weight, and he watched the fleeting expressions on her face as he moved rhythmically within her.

Her skin was soft and pink, her eyes glazed with the pleasure he tempted her with. Daniel could happily keep on like this forever, watching her as he brought her to the peak of enjoyment again and again. And again. He wanted her to beg him for release. He wanted her to learn how much she needed him, that only he could give her this satisfaction.

She was moist and sweet, a dense forest of temptation that he plundered again and again. In spite of the cold, sweat was running from his gleaming shoulders. His face was harsh in the twilight. He drove on, his forceful thrusting going deeper with each movement of his hips. He was cradled between her thighs, his hips meeting hers, their bellies mingling with the motions of this most intimate dance.

His lips parted and his eyelids lowered as the primitive enjoyment became too much to bear. One driving rhythm and another, and another, and the shuddering began at his loins, spreading out to every sensitive nerve ending in his body.

Maggie gasped and her arms clung tightly around him, her body heaving and receiving all of him. The world spun crazily about them, but they were safe and secure in this center of their own making. Daniel thrust his hips against her again and again. Maggie closed her eyes and clung more tightly, letting the world spin at its own pace.

Their passion spent, Daniel collapsed beside her, his strength gone, his mouth nuzzling at her neck. His legs felt like water. The room was cooling rapidly, and he thought he ought to toss some wood on the fire, but couldn't find the strength. Instead he put one leg over Maggie's, holding her beneath him, and slept.

The room was in pitch blackness when he woke. He was warm, but he had Maggie half beneath him, her softness cradling him still. She smelled sweet, like wildflowers mixed with the musky scent of woman, and he liked it.

He had attacked her like a wild man earlier and couldn't find an ounce of remorse in himself for it. If he hadn't, they would probably be arguing now, saying things they would never forgive each other for. No, they didn't need to talk, he decided. They needed to make love.

Never again would they be separated for so long. He didn't know how he had stood it this time. Every night, he had gone to his hotel and thought of her until he ached for her. All he could think of was getting back to Leadville and making love to his Maggie.

Only she could give him this sweet release. Never had he felt such satisfaction with another woman. But then, he had never known a woman like Magheen before.

Magheen Fitzgerald Calcord was sweet, opinionated, hot-tempered, and all woman. His woman. She might make him angry and frustrated, but any other kind would bore him to death.

His hands curved around her waist and rose to cup her breasts. She was bigger there than he remembered, and he thought he remembered everything about her. He liked the change in her. He liked anything about her.

His tongue snaked out and tasted of the soft flesh behind her ear. Her skin was as sweet there as everywhere else, and he felt himself begin to harden again.

He ought to get out of bed and make a fire. By the morning the cabin would be unbearably cold. Maggie moaned in her sleep and cuddled against him, her breasts brushing against the black hair on his chest. His arousal deepened.

To hell with the fire, he thought, rolling Maggie over. He searched until he found the same sweet forest of earlier, penetrating himself into a world of pure pleasure.

The sun was high and streaming through the cloth-covered windows when they both wakened. "Morning," Daniel said, smiling down on her.

It was late, but they had made love on and off all night long. "Hungry?" Daniel questioned, his mouth lowering to place a morning kiss on her lips. His fingers sneaked between her thighs and teased gently.

273

"I think one of us is a wanton," Maggie accused.

"No, love, *both* of us are wantons." She could hear the laughter in his voice as his breath gently wafted against her hair.

"Well, then, that's all right. 'Tis the mismatches that go wrong," she teased.

"We aren't mismatched, not in loving anyway. And I love making love to you."

Her palms flattened against his chest. "Daniel, about Ed Varley—"

"Shh, I don't need to hear. I already know you only took him in because he was injured, and you were right, I would have done the same.

"Love," he spoke hesitantly, "we've only a few days here and I'd like to spend them with you, with no talk of mines, miners, or strikes. I want to spend time together, Maggie, time getting to know my wife."

"We're going to spend a few days here? But what about Christmas and the choir . . ."

"It may be our only chance for a long time to be alone. Don't you want to?"

"Oh, yes, of course I do, Daniel!"

"Then let's do so. We've other Christmases for presents and choirs and whatever. But if we throw this time away between us, we may regret it forever."

"Oh, Daniel, I'd like that! But I do want to tell you about the miners—"

His fingers went to her mouth. "None of that talk. Just you and me, Maggie. The rest of the world can be forgotten for a time. This can be a second honeymoon, making up for the long separation."

"Here?" she laughed. "Daniel, we spent time here before we were ever married. You weren't inclined for a honeymoon then."

"Oh, I was inclined for the honeymoon, it was the wedding that bothered me. Now I can do to you what was preying on my mind back then. Now I can touch you and make love to you as I ached to do but was too stupid to admit. I should have made love to you then; we would

274

have been married weeks ago. And I'd have been doing this to you weeks ago instead of slowly losing my mind." He lowered his mouth, and his lips brushed hers. "And this . . . and this. And you," taking her hand, he placed it on him, "could have been doing this to me, months ago."

"Daniel, you're insatiable!"

"You make me that way," he growled in her ear.

Looping her arms about his shoulders, she peered into his eyes. "Poor you, Daniel Calcord, for you make me that way too."

"You sound upset by it."

"Of course I am. Everything else in my life I've had some semblance of control over, but not this, Daniel, not this great, hulking need for you."

"Ah, sweet Maggie," he groaned into her ear, and all thought of breakfast was forgotten.

He had brought fresh supplies with him when he came, so that first night, they feasted on steak and champagne and one of Mrs. Sawyer's chocolate pies. After that they ate whatever Maggie concocted. They took time for walking and riding in the afternoons, talking and making love at night.

Daniel discovered Maggie hated to lose at games. He would laugh at her, and she would toss the checkers at his head. Maggie discovered the same thing about Daniel, and she was every bit as anxious when she bested him at gin. Only she demanded money. "A penny a point, you said. Let's see, you owe me . . . hmm . . . sixteen dollars and forty-nine cents." Holding her palm out to him, she finished, "Pay up, mister. Your credit isn't any good with me."

"I demand a rematch. Only we'll play poker this time."

"Poker? I don't know how to play poker!"

"I'll teach you." At her mistrustful expression, he offered a concession. "If I teach you poker, you can teach me to play something you know. That's fair, isn't it?" He offered his hand for her to shake.

"The only other game I know is chess."

"Okay, teach me chess."

After a moment's time, during which Magheen contemplated this offer dubiously, she took his hand, saying, "Okay, it's a deal."

Maggie lost her winnings and another twenty-four dollars at blackjack. Daniel then taught her five-card draw and seven-card stud, and Maggie lost another forty dollars. She didn't carry that kind of money on her and had to borrow from Daniel to pay him.

"I'll sign a note," she said primly.

"I thought you'd say that," Daniel answered, grinning. He reached for a paper and pen. "Here, you can sign right now."

"And I think it's time I taught you to play chess. For money," she added, lifting her brows wickedly.

"For money," he conceded. "It's only fair." Daniel poured himself another cup of coffee and settled down at the table. Maggie was busy instructing him on the proper setup of the board.

"And the queen can move in any of those directions?" he questioned, clearly concentrating.

"Yes, she's the most powerful piece."

"A woman," Daniel said softly, reaching for her hand across the table. "It's deceptive how soft, yet powerful they are."

The first game didn't count. But the second and third did. Maggie was busily recouping her losses. Daniel was definitely bothered that he couldn't get the hang of the game any better than he did and kept questioning her about strategy. "I think I've got it now. Let's play another."

"I don't know," Maggie answered, a gloating smile across her lips. "I feel like I'm taking advantage of you. You're losing a fortune, you realize?"

"The sixty-two dollars is my fortune, and I'll lose it however I want." His head reared back as he studied her. She was enjoying this, he knew. "All right, we'll double the stakes."

"Double," she agreed happily.

"You stand to make a pure profit of twenty-five dollars. Not bad for a wench as badly dipped as you were when we sat down."

"You're right," she said, sighing. Her modest demeanor was meant to infuriate him, but Daniel was too busy appreciating the view he had of her pretty face to pay much attention to that. "I'll let you go first, since you seem to need every advantage you can get."

Daniel quietly smiled, moving his king's pawn forward two spaces.

Maggie clucked her tongue. "Maybe you're right and we should clear some of these pieces from the board right away." She moved her bishop's pawn forward, clearly expecting Daniel to take it.

Daniel brought his queen to the left side of the board. With an innocent expression on his face, he queried softly, "Can it be? Why, Maggie, I do believe it's a checkmate!"

Maggie hurriedly glanced down. It couldn't be! She had only had one move. She studied the board carefully, looking for a piece to move in front of the king or a space to set him in. Daniel was right; he had checkmated her. Openmouthed, she lifted her head to stare at him.

Daniel was sitting on the opposite side of the table, biting his upper lip to keep from laughing out loud. His glazed eyes and shaking shoulders gave him away.

"You set me up, didn't you?" she accused, rising.

The guffaw came out now. Coarse and loud, it boomed from one end of the room to the other. Tears of mirth were streaming down his cheeks, and Daniel clutched at his chest, he was laughing so hard. "You want to sign another note, love?" He barely got the words out, his gasping laughter choked him so hard.

"Why, you—" Clearly, Magheen didn't see a thing funny about this. She toppled the board and pieces off the table and into his lap and came after him with all the fury of a humiliated woman.

Daniel knew when it was best to retreat. Still laughing, he headed out the front door and across the yard, up the back mountainside. "You should have seen your face, Maggie!" he hooted gleefully. "I've never seen anything so funny in my life!"

Which didn't soothe her ruffled feathers at all.

"You led me to believe you didn't know how to play chess, and I'll wager every penny I've lost tonight you knew how to play all along. Didn't you?"

He grinned, backing away. "Since I was six, love. I was a champion in New York."

"You lying, deceitful—"

Maggie flew at him and he caught her, both of them tumbling in the snow. Maggie's kicks were hampered by her petticoats and skirt and soon enough by Daniel's legs capturing hers between them. "I couldn't help it. You were asking for it, love."

"Don't call me your love."

"Why not? You are. I've never seen such an irate one either." He was still grinning from ear to ear. "I've been waiting all my life for someone to pull that on. You walked right into the trap, Magheen, me darlin'."

Her struggling movements ceased. "I never claimed to be a *good* chess player."

"Which is just as well, 'cause you aren't. That's a mistake no one with any experience should make. But you sure livened up my day!"

"Blast you! I'll get you for that, Daniel Calcord. Some day, sometime, when you least expect it, I'll get even!"

"I'm quaking in my boots, love."

"So am I. This snow's cold."

"Come here and give me a kiss first, and then I'll let you up."

"I could refuse and watch you freeze to death."

"And I could warm you up in the nicest possible way." His hands snaked around to cup her rear possessively. "I'll even make the tea. Just for you, sweetheart."

Maggie smiled at this coaxing. "Okay," she responded sweetly. "Help me up, will you?"

Daniel found his feet and held out a hand to her. She took it and rose, her shoulders and chest bumping against him. Daniel's hands came around her waist to steady her, and her arms lifted to his shoulders. Her nose nearly touched his. She was grinning hugely. A cold snowball

278

slid down his back. Daniel's expression didn't change.

"And that's just the beginning, you devil."

Daniel laughed heartily at her treachery. He might deserve it, he thought, but he didn't have to let her know that. "I know of a way to shut you up, darling, a way that leaves me bereft of words too."

Tossing her over his shoulder, he strolled to the cabin. Maggie knew very well what he had in mind and wasn't about to argue.

Slamming the cabin door shut with his foot, he set her down. His eyes were glinting wickedly as they roved over her, and his fingers were already working the buttons of his shirt.

Magheen sighed, barely supressing a grin. "Again? I thought you said you'd make tea first."

"Later."

"Daniel," she said, shaking her head. "What am I going to do with you?"

He took her in his arms. "Love me, darling. Love me just as I do you."

Afterward, Daniel rolled onto his back and collapsed on the bed. "Don't move," he gasped. "I couldn't stand it."

Maggie laughed, her fingers drumming a tattoo against his thigh. "Are you sure?" The fingers sneaked nearer.

"Wicked woman," he accused, trapping her fingers with his own. Maggie rolled onto her side and cuddled closer. "We could leave for Leadville in the morning," he said. "I'm too exhausted to continue this honeymoon."

"You are? And it's only been three days. Think of the poor men who take honeymoons of a week or more."

"They have my greatest admiration."

"Aye, I admit their stamina is to be admired."

Daniel opened one eye and peered at his wife. She was the vision of innocence with her rosy complexion and sweet smile. "I think your nickname should be 'wicked wanton.' You just never get enough, do you?"

"I don't know yet. Why don't we stay here another week

and find out?"

He laughed aloud at that. "You're bluffing! I don't think I'll teach you any more poker. You're too damned good at it."

"Ah, well, it was worth a try," she replied with a smile, barely managing to stifle a yawn. "You've exhausted me too."

"I need food, woman," he growled in her ear.

"I do too," she responded, closing her eyes. "Where is it?"

"Needing to be dished up on the plates. You do that and I'll get more wood. Deal?"

"Does that mean you have to open the door? And let all the cold in?"

"I'll be quick."

"You'd better be," she said, eying him boldly. "I'll be turning into an icicle dressed like I am."

He was still laughing as he rose from the bed and tossed the blankets aside. "We'll both get dressed. Just have something hot for me when I return. I should have gotten the wood this afternoon. Only I got waylaid by some wench who wanted to teach me chess . . . instead she taught me a few other things."

The venison stew was hot and tender, the biscuits ready to bake. Maggie filled the coffeepot with water and hung it over the hearth to boil. She had just set the plates on the table when the door burst open and Daniel came in, a heavy load of wood in his arms.

"Brrr," he shuddered, the wood tumbling from his arms. Maggie closed the door behind him. "The wind's kicking up. I think another storm's blowing in. We should have left today. I wanted an extra day just for us, greedy soul that I am." He stretched his hands over the fire to warm them, watching as she continued with her work. When he spoke, she ceased her movements and turned to look at him. "If we miss Christmas Mass, how upset would you be?"

"I won't like it, but I'd rather miss Mass than gamble with our lives."

"I'm sorry, Magheen. I know it means a lot for you to be with your friends and your brother for the celebration. Even Annabelle was asking me if you'd be back before Christmas. She'll be disappointed." Real regret was in his voice.

"Daniel," she said, crossing the room and placing a hand on his shoulder. "You're my family now. 'Tis you I want to spend Christmas with."

"But Anne was telling me how hard you'd been working with the choir and all. I thought we'd leave in the morning and be home tomorrow night, Christmas Eve. Then you could have attended Mass and sung to your heart's content. I am sorry, Maggie."

"You didn't bring the storm, Daniel. I would like to be there for Christmas, but if I cannot, I cannot. At least we're safe, and together. That's what counts."

He watched as she took the biscuits from the hearth and set them on the table and ladled the stew onto the plates. The other news couldn't wait any longer either. "Maggie," he spoke hesitantly, "my mother is in Leadville. She took the railroad from New York to Denver and came back with me on the stage. She's waiting for us at home."

The stew pot trembled in Maggie's hands. "Why didn't you tell me sooner? She came all this way and was left alone? What must she be thinking of us? We should have gone back immediately, not spent idle time like we have!" The cast-iron pot threatened to spill and Daniel steadied it, taking it from her hands and placing it on one of the warm stones around the hearth.

"I needed time alone with you."

"But how rude, Daniel!"

"She'll still be there when we get back."

"Is she the older woman you helped from the stage?"

"Yes."

"She is beautiful," Maggie enthused.

"She is."

"Oh, Daniel, how lucky you are! I wish my parents could be here and meet their new son . . ." Her hands flew to her cheeks and her eyes shone at her latest thought. "Daniel, she'll be my mother too! Tell me about her, what she likes, what she does! Oh, I do so want to get to know her!"

"Ah, well, she . . . she likes to paint. She's good with her hands, makes clever crafts, things like that."

"She sews?" Magheen questioned, perplexed by his obscure answers.

"She prefers to buy her clothing, Maggie. She's very social, entertains all the important people my father needs to impress, that's what she's really good at."

Maggie thought this over for a moment. "And your father, why does he have to impress anyone?"

"It's part of his business. He's a banker in New York."

"Oh. Is it a big bank?"

"Pretty large, yes."

"Daniel, do they *own* the bank?"

"The family owns the bank, my grandfather started it." Her eyes widened. "Is your family very wealthy?"

"The rest of them are. Maggie, when I came to Colorado, I was penniless. I had my education but I wanted to earn my own money."

She nodded. "I can understand that. Pride is a devilish thing to have, isn't it, Daniel?"

"I wanted to be free of my family. I wanted to be on my own."

"Of course you did. It must take very special parents to have let you go so far away and for so long." Maggie's expression grew wistful. "But why are you telling me this now?"

"Maggie, she wants me to return to New York with her. I've told her no, but I know her and she won't stop there. She'll try to get you on me too. I've created a life for myself here, I don't want any part of New York. Besides, I'm not very close to my family, not like you and Paddie."

"I wouldn't ask you to do anything you don't want to do, Daniel. You ought to know me better than that. Besides, I didn't like New York very much, and New

York didn't like me or the other Irish either, I can tell you that." Her expression grew hopeful. "Oh, Daniel, it will truly be wonderful having parents again! I promise to treat them as if they were my own."

"I know you will, Maggie. Just be careful. Remember . . . they're not really your parents."

"But they will be, I know. I am so looking forward to knowing them, Daniel."

"I know you are, but . . . just be careful, will you? Sometimes you trust too much, no one deserves that much trust."

"I don't understand, Daniel."

"I know you don't. But my mother may not be what you expect. In fact . . ." Daniel hated to say anything more. He didn't want to speak against his mother, but he couldn't be sure how she would treat Maggie. He didn't want to make her wary of them before she ever met them. What if they loved her? What if they actually liked having her for a daughter-in-law?

"If there's no snow by morning, we'll leave here then. We should be able to get to the house even if it starts snowing later in the day. If there's snow on the ground, we'll have to wait here and celebrate Christmas alone, just the two of us."

"I'll feel horrible if your mother is alone for Christmas. She knows no one."

"She knows Mrs. Sawyer and the Forbes family. She'll be fine."

"Yes, Mrs. Sawyer will take good care of her. She'll have her feeling right at home soon enough. You don't have to worry about your mother with her there, Daniel."

Daniel was more worried that Maude Sawyer would get fed up with his mother and quit, but he wasn't telling Maggie that.

The snow began late that night. By the time morning came, there was no doubt that they were traveling nowhere for the next few days. "I'm sorry, Maggie. I shouldn't have pushed my luck so far. If we'd left before yesterday, you'd be home. You'd see your brother tonight and sing in the Mass in the morning."

"And instead all I've got is you for company," she said, smiling intimately on him. "Tell me, are you too exhausted to cut down a tree for us? I can make a few ornaments from ribbons and candles . . ."

"I've got the fixings for a punch."

"I'll bake an applesauce cake, the kind you like, filled with raisins and nuts."

"I might even let you beat me at poker. After all, it is Christmas Eve."

"How about letting me win at chess instead? Same stakes as yesterday? I want my money back."

Chapter Sixteen

The snow let up late Christmas night, but it was the twenty-eighth of December before the roads were passable. On the morning of the twenty-ninth, Daniel and Magheen left the cabin and descended the mountain. Through the low-hanging clouds they could see the town of Leadville spread out in a panorama before them. Long lines of lumbering freight vans and other wheeled vehicles were on the road ahead of them. While they had been snowbound midway up the mountain, so had the freighters, but on the other side.

Now, the road to the town was jam-packed with these wagons, riders, and a lone Concord coach, making the journey unduly tedious. In spite of the joyfulness of the season, the drivers and passengers were out of temper with each other. More than once during the day of slow travel, Magheen heard unsavory curses flung between men.

The wheels of two freight wagons interlocked as one irate driver attempted to pass the other on this narrow mountain road. Both wagons might have fallen down the mountainside, but the first driver had enough sense to swerve into the mountain, cracking the reins hard so the horses would pick up speed. When the danger was passed, the first driver bounded from his wagon and went for the throat of the other man. This slowed the rest of the traffic, and soon other teamsters were intervening in the fight. It was an hour before the tedious journey continued.

Darkness had fallen by the time they arrived at Daniel's home. Together they rode into the barn, Daniel leading the packhorse behind his. Maggie unsaddled her mare while Daniel did the same to his gelding. He had begun unloading the packhorse when Maggie joined him.

"You brought back the remnants of that fruitcake?" she questioned, eying him in disbelief.

"It was too good to throw away."

"Why does it seem as though we're bringing back more than we took with us?"

"I've been wondering that myself. Maybe Dutch packed more than I told him to—"

"Don't go blaming me for your problems," Dutch quipped, ambling through the barn door. He was slight and stoop-shouldered, his gait awkward. Through the waxed mustache, he smiled at the look of surprise on their faces. "I've been watching from the kitchen window. Thought I'd wait long enough for you to unsaddle, then I'd make my appearance." His brows lifted questioningly. "Looks like the two of you have settled your differences."

"Not all of them," Maggie responded coolly. "And if you ever think to lock me in anywhere again . . ."

Dutch held up his hands. "Not me, ma'am! I'll quit my job first. I decided I wasn't hired to risk my neck, and I was nothing but a fool to do so. Next time, I'd let you escape. I'd rather face Daniel here."

"Are you implying I'm not as dangerous?" Daniel asked, affronted.

"I ain't implying a thing. I'm stating a fact. And another fact I'm stating is that if you don't get in there and get Maude's ruffled feathers soothed, you ain't gonna just lose a cook, you're gonna lose your mining engineer as well. Harvey ain't taking kindly to the way your ma is treating her. She's no servant, he says."

"He's right," Daniel affirmed, his face set. "Here, finish this and I'll take care of Maude. Maggie, you wait here with Dutch for a few minutes."

"But, Daniel—"

"Just do as I say for once," he answered impatiently and a moment later was gone from the barn.

"That man! He's always bossing me around as if I were nothing more than a child," she sulked.

"Didn't you take a vow to love, honor and *obey* your husband?" Dutch questioned.

"Yes, I did," Maggie admitted slowly.

"They weren't just words, girl, they were promises."

"You're right, of course. Here, give me that bridle. I'll hang it up."

"Don't go giving me that long-suffering look. You know as well as I do that you're to obey Daniel. You should have remembered it at the cabin, instead of kicking in my poor shins so that I can barely walk."

"I vowed to obey Daniel, not *you*."

"I noticed," Dutch grumbled.

"You even cost me my job," she accused.

"For the last time, none of this was my idea. Besides, you don't need no job. You're Daniel's wife, that's work enough."

Magheen thought of her measly savings account and snickered below her breath. "A lot you know."

The horses were rubbed down, fed, and fresh hay was tossed in their stalls, but still Daniel hadn't returned. In the tack room, Maggie sat on a high stool and watched Dutch take a bridle from the wall and begin to polish it. The small room gave the impression of clutter, but closer inspection soon disabused that notion. The walls of the tack room were covered with hanging equipment and tools, all neatly arranged and in order. Even the workbench was free of clutter. Dutch's fingers worked the cloth in a rhythmic motion, until the bridle was smooth and supple, gleaming from his careful attention. When Dutch finished one piece of equipment, he moved on to the next.

"How long have you worked for Daniel?" she questioned during a quiet moment.

" 'Bout six years now."

"You must have met him when he first came from the East."

287

"No, but a few months after that. Long enough that he'd set up his law practice and was busy."

"He's a good man," she said softly.

Dutch lifted his gaze to her. "He is that. One of the best I've ever met. One of the brightest, stubbornest, but one of the best as well. He's a man to whom right is right, and right is what he does. Not many men like that anymore."

It was the longest speech Magheen had ever heard from Dutch, she should have known it would be about Daniel. How his men felt about him was apparent in the respectful way they spoke with him, treated him and in the length of time they remained with him. Her fingers touched the back of Dutch's hand, making him pause in the motions of his task. "He is a man to admire, and I will try to be a more obedient wife."

Dutch gave a gruff laugh. "At least you said try. I know what a challenge it will be to you to be meek and mild."

"Not meek and mild, I said *obedient.*"

"Same thing. And you're too much like him, too stubborn for your own good."

Maggie had to laugh. "Maybe that's just what Daniel needs."

Dutch grinned suddenly. "Maybe it is."

"Maggie," Daniel called from the door. "Come on inside and meet my mother. Dutch, don't you stay out here too long. It's too cold and you'll freeze to death."

"Not in here I won't. And if I get cold, I'll light the stove."

But Daniel had Maggie by the hand and was hurrying her inside.

"Is everything all right, Daniel?"

He turned to her and spoke absently. "Yes, it's fine. Maude was a little upset about something, but she's over it now. She's just been worried about you and the length of time we've been gone. She's ready to murder me, I think. Let her know you're fine, will you?"

"Of course I will," she answered, entering through the back door which Daniel held open for her. Maude Sawyer and Harvey Benson were seated at the kitchen table, their fingers entwined across the top. When Daniel and Maggie entered, they flinched guiltily and quickly withdrew their hands.

"Maggie," Maude said, relief in her tones. Rising, she hugged the girl in her comfortable embrace. "How are you? I can't tell you how worried we've been. You were gone so long you missed the Nativity play and Mass." An accusatory glare was turned on Daniel.

Magheen hastily intervened. "Daniel . . . I mean, *we* thought it best if I left Leadville for a while. Some of the men were very angry with me. They thought I was taking sides with the miners, you know."

Shrugging, she continued, "Then it snowed and we couldn't get home."

"I heard what some of the men had to say. This town certainly has a lot of fools," Maude replied, her eyes looking coolly at Daniel as she spoke the blunt words. "Now, tell me, have you eaten? How about some tea or coffee? I've a pumpkin pie in the oven."

"I could use something more than pie," Daniel replied.

"Me too, I'm starving. But I would love a piece of your pie for dessert. No one bakes like you do, Mrs. Sawyer."

"Oh?" The older woman straightened her spine at this compliment, her eyes once again shifting to Daniel. "I'm glad someone likes my cooking."

"How about if we eat in the den? That way you can meet my mother, Maggie. She's been asking about you."

"Oh, I'd love to meet her," she answered, her hands smoothing her skirt in a self-conscious gesture. "Do I look all right? Perhaps I ought to go and change."

"You're fine as you are."

"I'm dirty from all the riding, and I smell like horses."

"You've roses in your complexion from the chill of the ride. And we both smell like horses," he answered, laughter in his voice. "She wants to meet you now. You can smell like lilacs tomorrow."

Maggie thought of the small, impeccably groomed woman she saw alighting from the coach and frowned. "I don't know if this is such a good idea."

"I do. Believe me, how you dress tonight isn't going to make one bit of difference in her opinion of you."

"I hope you're right," she commented softly, following him from the room. Maggie missed the knowing looks exchanged by Maude and Harvey as Daniel spoke, or she would have been more worried than she already was.

"Mother, this is my wife, Magheen Kavanaugh Fitzgerald Calcord," Daniel announced proudly, "of the Leinster County Geraldines, once the ruling family of Ireland. Maggie, meet my mother, Mayme Calcord, of New York City." His hand beneath her elbow drew her forward.

Mrs. Calcord turned from her position in front of the fire, straightening as Daniel spoke. Her face remained unsmiling as the introductions were made. Mayme Calcord was just as Maggie remembered, small and graceful and pretty. Her silver hair was pinned on top of her head, and several rings flashed on dainty pink fingers.

Maggie summoned an uncertain smile; in the back of her mind were remembrances of her loving mother welcoming a stranger into the family with hugs and kisses. Suddenly she felt alone. Not everyone was as loving as her mother, she had to remind herself. That did not mean she would not learn to love this stranger as well.

"Daniel's spoken so much about you, but never once did he mention how pretty you are," Mayme chirped. "Why didn't you tell me, Daniel? Don't you think she's pretty?"

Magheen flushed at the awkwardness of the moment. She didn't want reluctant compliments forced from Daniel. Besides, if she didn't know he found her attractive, especially after the last few days, then she was a fool.

"I do, Mother," he answered softly. "I think she's very pretty, and also very tired. Let's sit down. We've had a long day and we're both tired."

He took the overstuffed chair facing the fireplace while the two women shared the davenport. "You look worn as well, my dear," Mayme was all concern as she drew Maggie into the conversation. "Tell me, was it a long journey?"

Maggie answered, and the conversation turned to where she and Daniel had been and how the weather kept them so long. "It was a beautiful Christmas Day," Maggie enthused. "The snow was deep, creating a white fairyland in the mountains. Just like in the tales of old, I could almost see beautifully gowned faeries in the twilight, little people scattering among them." Her eyes glowed as they rested on Daniel. " 'Twas quite the nicest Christmas I can remember."

"Well, I wish I could say the same for my Christmas," Mayme commented, her eyes lowering to where her hands smoothed her skirt. "I don't know many people in town and felt like a complete outsider at the service . . ."

"Ooh, I was sure my brother would greet you!"

"Your brother?"

"Father Patrick," Maggie nodded eagerly.

"My dear," her mother-in-law trilled. "I attended the Lutheran service with that lovely Arabella Forbes and her father. After the service we went to one of the hotels for brunch . . . I couldn't see putting poor Mrs. Sawyer to more work than she already had, what with her—her suitor and all his friends constantly around. The food was quite dreadful, nothing like what I'm used to. Poor Arabella was mortified, but we managed to get through the day. Still," she sighed, "what's a holiday with none of one's children around?"

"I'm so sorry. Of course this is a new town, and you must have felt quite dreadfully alone. We'll try to make up for it, I promise."

Daniel frowned, reaching for the bottle of brandy on the table beside him. Maude came in the room then, in her hands a tray heaped with fried chicken, potatoes, beans, and biscuits. Maggie rose and crossed the room to help her fill the plates. "It looks delicious, Mrs. Sawyer."

"Is it more of that chicken we had for dinner? Be careful, dears, it's quite tough. Though I will have a piece of your pumpkin pie, Mrs. Sawyer."

291

Maude stiffened at the insult and glared hotly at Mayme. "Maybe it's your false teeth and not my chicken!"

"Looks good to me, Maude," Daniel interrupted before a full-scale war ensued. Maggie's eyes moved from one woman to the other. "I'll have three pieces of the chicken. Yours is the best I've ever eaten."

"Oh?" his mother questioned archly. "Can't your wife cook very well? I would have thought she'd be a more than adequate cook. She must have learned some cooking skills, coming from such a large family. It was large, wasn't it, dear? Don't all you Irish come from families of nine and ten children?" Sighing, she uttered morosely, "I suppose that's the most I can hope for my son now."

Maggie was shocked into silence by her mother-in-law's attack. Then, softly, she said, "Actually, there are five children in my family, though my mother lost three young ones. Yes, we would have had a large family, if they had lived, but my mother had enough love in her to handle that many. How many children do you have, Mrs. Calcord?"

"I was more than a breeding machine," came the indignant response.

"So was my mother. She was very much loved, and, though she is dead now, you shouldn't be questioning her choices. Not in front of me, anyway." Maggie left no one in doubt that she did love her mother very much. For the first time since Maggie had met her mother-in-law, Mayme Calcord had nothing to say.

But Magheen was confused. Mrs. Calcord called her by an affectionate name, dear, and spoke very pleasantly. So, why did she have this uneasy feeling within her? She felt more and more uncomfortable as the moments ticked by. And why did her mother-in-law's artless statement about large Irish families offend her so much? Maggie was proud of Irish families, of being Irish. And Mrs. Calcord was only showing an interest in her background and family, which was more than Daniel had ever done.

As she sipped her tea, the conversation resumed, turning to news of friends Daniel and his family had in New

York. Maggie tuned the conversation out, admiring the elegant way Mrs. Calcord handled herself, even the way her little finger curled at the cup's handle as she drank her coffee. Her small feet were firmly planted on the floor, and long, graceful nails toyed idly with her necklace. She looked fragile in white lace, Maggie decided, wondering how she might look in it.

"Maggie," Daniel said, interrupting these musings.

"Oh, I'm sorry. I was daydreaming."

"You're tired," Daniel said as he rose. "And so am I. It's time we were both in bed."

"But I never had an answer," his mother objected.

"I'm sure Maggie has no objections to shopping with you tomorrow."

"Good." Mayme sat forward and spoke enthusiastically. "I want to buy a wedding gift for you and Daniel, and I'd like to buy something personal for yourself, maybe a dress for the new year? Or something more intimate? I trust there's someplace decent to shop in this town?"

"Well, yes. There's the Emporium. I worked there until . . . I married." Maggie's voice trailed off. She was going to miss her work and the people there sorely.

"You worked there? My dear, there's no reason for a member of our family to seek work. If Daniel can't support you—"

"Mother—"

"See? I knew you should have stayed in New York with us! I can't imagine this poor girl having to go out to work—"

"It wasn't like that," Maggie objected.

Daniel rose and crossed the room, his hand taking Magheen's elbow. "No, it wasn't," he bit out gruffly. "But of course, that is the interpretation you would choose. Good night, Mother, we shall see you in the morning." He practically pushed Maggie toward the stairs.

"I'm sorry—"

"Why? Because my mother thinks I can't support you? What did you think your insistence on working made everyone think, and not just my mother? As I said before,

I can support you."

In the bedroom, Daniel released her and crossed the room to look out the window, at the same time unbuttoning his shirt with rough movements. Was he this angry over the thought of her working, Maggie wondered, not understanding why this could be so. She watched him a moment longer, before turning around and unfastening her own clothing. His belt clattered to the oiled wood floor as Maggie was drawing her nightgown over her head.

They had a pleasant evening, she thought, if one discounted his mother's artless words. Certainly nothing bad happened to make him act this way.

Crawling into bed, she pulled the blanket up to her chin and watched while he finished undressing. He joined her a moment later, lying on his back and staring at the ceiling.

"Daniel, what did I do wrong?" she asked when she had tired of the sullen silence in the room.

"You didn't do anything wrong," he snapped.

"Then why are you acting as though I did? How can I please you if you don't tell me what I did wrong."

"Maggie," Daniel finally answered, rising on his elbow beside her. "It's not you. My mother has the knack of enraging me, and I don't know what to do about it. She seems to like twisting words and making insults out of them."

"I noticed she's not always the most tactful of women."

"Ah," Daniel moaned, rubbing his hands over his eyes. "That's the understatement of the year."

"Can I help?"

Daniel smiled briefly and shook his head. "Not with my mother. I've wrestled with the problem for years. I'm almost convinced there is no solution. Of course . . . you can help in other ways." His hand reached for the oil lamp and turned it out. The moon shone brightly, illuminating the room with a soft glow. The mattress sagged and Maggie found herself held in a strong embrace.

"We don't need that gown," he whispered, his fingers

tugging it over her head. Their bare bodies touched intimately as he cradled her, her auburn hair spreading across the pristine sheets and twining in the tangle of arms and shoulders. She watched him wonderingly at this instant change of mood.

"Ah, Maggie, I don't ever mean to hurt you," he said, lowering his head, and his mouth gentled hers.

Daniel wanted to explain what he was feeling, but he wasn't certain he understood it himself. All he knew was that he had to try. "When I saw my mother in Denver, I was thrilled to see her. Five years is a long time, and I still have many good memories of my childhood. And then suddenly, five years' separation wasn't enough. I was a grown man, but she acted as though I'd never grown up, as though I deserved nothing of her respect. I was a man with my own life, my own responsibilities, and she thinks I should forget all these just to go back to New York with her and take care of her responsibilities.

"All she thinks about is what she wants, what she needs, just like before.

"When I left New York, it was because they left me in no doubts that my brother was the favorite, the one to take over for them. So I came out here and made my own life. Now they're not so sure David is right for the job, and they want me to come back. The problem is, I'm happy here. I don't want to go back. And I was more than happy to spend Christmas alone with you in the cabin."

"She sounded so lonely, Daniel."

"Hell, if her children had been so important to her at Christmas, why did she leave David and my father behind? Because they're not that important, that's why! Her words were simply something to use to make me feel guilty, something to try to control me with."

His eyes were dark and confused as they looked down on her. "In case I never tell you again, Maggie, remember this. I need your honesty, your loving. I know you'll say what you mean and not leave me guessing as to why you feel slighted or unhappy. I don't have to wonder about what I've done wrong; you'd have flattened me with your tongue already! You're more real to me than that world I grew up in. I don't want that world; I'll never want that world. Not even if that damn mine explodes into smoke by morning."

Maggie frowned. "Daniel, I don't understand . . ."

"I know you don't. You've spent your life dealing with the likes of Paddie, who's direct with you, honest, sometimes to the point of pain. You can't comprehend a relationship called 'love' which is more wicked for being based on deception. My mother wears a sweet smile and all the time is plotting how to make me, or someone, behave in the manner in which she wants. She's very sweet and simpering with her insults; you don't even realize you've been insulted until long after she's spoken.

"Daniel, she does love you." But even as she spoke the words, she realized his mother didn't love him in the way Maggie thought of love. Mayme Calcord's was a possessive love. Daniel would never receive full approval unless and until he did as she wanted. By choosing to be his own person, he was failing in her eyes.

Maggie thought of her own parents and of how proud they would be when each of her brothers chose his own way in life. How could Daniel's mother think she had the right to dictate Daniel's choices? Or judge the way he lived? He was a fine man. Why would she try to make him feel any less than that?

If she truly loved him, which would come first, his needs or hers?

"Does she love me, Maggie?" Daniel echoed her unspoken thoughts. "Or am I just another possession to be used when it's convenient and tossed aside when David's more the son they want?"

She shook her head slowly. "I'm not sure I understand what we're talking about, Daniel."

He smiled ruefully. "I know. I think that's one of the reasons I love you so much. You're so damn innocent you think all relationships boil down to love, and maybe they do, but it's not always the same kind of love, not always a

296

good kind of love."

Her arms looped around his neck. "I understand that I love you, Daniel Calcord."

"And I don't know how I've lived this long without you, Mrs. Calcord. Have I told you how you make the day brighter?"

"I'll remind you of that the next time you're mad at me."

"You know . . ." he growled against her ear as his palms cupped the fullness of her breasts and his thigh rubbed between her own, "there's a lot to this loving stuff."

"Daniel," she whispered, feeling close to him as never before. Maybe now was the time, she thought. He was beginning to trust her, surely? What he once said about fathering a half-Irish brat, that was but his temper speaking.

Haunting the recesses of her mind was the derision in his voice and manner as he spoke the words.

"I . . . I have something to tell you . . ."

"And I have something to show you," he growled.

As usual, his forwardness made her laugh. "I've seen *that* before. Funny little thing, it is too, the way it changes shapes and sizes."

"I love it when you talk sexy," he growled, nibbling on her ear.

Her news, the parents, tomorrow, all were forgotten in the passion heating between them. When the loving was done, Maggie curled up in his arms and could almost imagine they were still in the cabin. He was already asleep, and she was dozing off when she remembered what she had wanted to tell him.

Her news would have to wait another day.

"Oh, dear! Must we ride in that thing?" Mayme Calcord eyed the buckboard warily and from a distance.

"Well, if you'd like, we can ride to town on horseback," Magheen offered.

Mayme's eyes closed dramatically. They flashed open

297

angrily, and at the same moment her mouth did. "Oh, that son of mine! He really pays no attention to appearances, does he? First you and now this! He really likes to pull unpleasant surprises on me. The very least he could do was have a carriage, but no. He acts as though people don't judge him by what he drives."

Tossing the skirts of her voluminous traveling dress over an arm and grabbing the seat with the free hand, Mayme hauled herself aboard.

"First you and now this?" The words had been blurted out so artlessly that no one would have thought they had been carefully thought out before uttering them. Or was it a not too subtle way of letting Magheen know exactly what her mother-in-law thought of her? Maggie's hands were too full of reins and her mind too full of contradictions to demand either an explanation or a retraction yet. She wasn't sure she ever would. What good would an unpleasant confrontation with his mother do Daniel?

It was impossible to maneuver the buckboard through the rough dirt streets of crowded Leadville, so Maggie pulled it alongside the Howards' home and left it there. Agnes Moen was the only one home at the time, and Maggie declined the cup of coffee she offered. "We'll be back later," she called out to the older woman who was now closing the door to keep the chill weather from seeping inside the house. "Tell Anne and the children hello for me."

"I would have loved a cup of coffee, but I'm certainly not taking mine with the housekeeping staff. Aren't any of you people well bred enough to know what's proper and what's not?" Mayme snapped as they walked toward the center of town. "I wanted to get Daniel a nice gift, and I certainly don't intend carrying heavy packages clear across town. What you need is a boy to fetch and carry for you. They're not very expensive," she added dryly. "I'd imagine even Daniel could afford one of those."

"Daniel is a very successful man, Mrs. Calcord." Maggie wanted to clear this matter up immediately, thinking that Daniel's mother would be much happier when she knew the truth. She referred to her mother-in-law by the formal name as the woman had never even hinted at what Maggie should call her. "You seem to have a wrong impression—"

"I don't think so. It's very obvious to me that Daniel belongs with his family in New York. He's not accustomed to living in these straitened circumstances. It's you who have the wrong impression." Mayme's chill blue eyes met hers directly, her mouth tightening perceptibly. "As a child, Daniel had every advantage, everything a child could want. He was taught to expect the best life had to offer. He had nannies, the best of friends, private schooling, anything his heart desired. I don't believe Daniel has forgotten the pleasure of having all that. What I can't bear is to see how far down in the world he's gone. Why, that Mrs. Sawyer told me he was up before dawn to go to work at his mine. As though that were necessary! She talked as though he did menial labor! My Daniel!

"What Daniel should do is admit he needs our help and come home to New York with us."

Maggie bit her lip. "Daniel doesn't want to go to New York," she said softly. "And he's man enough to know there's more to life than material possessions."

Mayme Calcord frowned haughtily. "Of course you'd think so, or at least say it, you, who've never had anything. You don't know what it is to have wealth; you know less about my son. I don't know how you induced him to marry you, but I wasn't fooled by all that talk of Irish royalty in your family. You set a trap for him and you snared him. Let's see how long you can keep him."

Maggie was stunned by the verbal attack. With anyone else she would have just walked off and never have anything to do with them again, but this woman was Daniel's mother, and she had a responsibility to at least try to love her.

"Daniel married me because he loves me," she answered surely. "He's not a man to be trapped by anyone, not me and not you. He will not return to New York with you."

"We'll see, shall we?" Those pretty painted lips smirked

with satisfaction. "And now, where is this—this place where you worked?"

Maggie shook her head, appalled at the thought of a gift from this woman. "We really don't need—"

"My dear, the gift is not for you, it's for Daniel. He is my son, And I will buy the largest, most expensive gift I can find, so that neither you nor Daniel will find fault with my generosity. Daniel will keep my generosity in mind, no matter what happens between the two of you. I'll even look for a pretty peignoir for you, so Daniel can see what an attempt I'm making for my new daughter-in-law. I've been through all this before. He won't find fault with my behavior, I promise you."

Maggie hadn't the slightest idea what to say to this woman. Apparently reason wasn't what she wanted. They stood beneath the newly painted sign of red and gold letters that read Daniels, Fisher and Smith Emporium, looking at window displays Maggie hadn't seen before. Clothing of bright green and red were interwoven on a bed of cotton snow and silver snowflakes, bringing to mind the joyousness of the season. But the woman beside her reminded Maggie of all that was bitter and hateful in the world. All Maggie could think of was how to get away from her, at least for a while. "I have to see my brother," she said hastily. "I don't think you need me for anything, do you?"

"Oh, I shan't be needing you. I've survived stranger places than Leadville on my own. Though what Daniel will say when he learns you deserted me, I don't know," Mayme Calcord clucked brazenly.

Magheen gaped at such open hostility. "You can tell Daniel anything you like."

"I will, dear," Mayme answered, turning and entering the store.

Magheen briskly moved through the streets until she reached the corner of Seventh and Poplar, the site of the new church. Her mind still whirled from the impact of Mayme Calcord's words. Daniel was right, all she was interested in was getting what she wanted. Whether others wanted it or would be hurt by her actions didn't seem to matter. How could anyone be so selfish? Maggie wondered.

Stopping before the stone steps, Maggie looked up and realized the new church was nearly completed. Even the remnants of the construction were cleared from the site. Maggie hurried up the stone steps and pulled on the door. With ease, it swung open and Maggie followed it inside. Several laborers glanced at her momentarily before resuming their work. They were removing scaffolding, ladders, and other equipment. Some of the men appeared to be doing general touch-up work. Other than that, the inside of the church was completed too.

The altar was a simple box covered in white cloth. Behind it hung a huge crucifix. The wooden pews had upholstered kneelers. Maggie knelt in the first of the pews and bowed her head. For several moments she let the peace of the house wash over her before she could consider her mother-in-law more calmly.

What this woman would mean to her marriage, she couldn't imagine. She did wonder if the rest of Daniel's family was like Mayme, and was suddenly grateful for the goodness of her own family. Her father and brothers were real men, living as they believed. They were good men too, caring more about right and wrong than wealth. She could only hope that what she and Daniel shared was solid enough to get them through this.

In the world she knew, a family was for sharing love and trust, and a new member would be welcomed with open arms. Every newlywed couple had its share of burdens, and the rest of the family should relieve those, not add to them. That was the way Magheen had been raised, the way she believed.

What sort of family did Daniel come from for his mother to behave in this way?

And if she was not welcome, what of this child she carried? She couldn't even be sure that Daniel would accept a "half-Irish brat," let alone his family

She needed someone to talk to, but not Paddie. She

301

was his baby sister, and priest or not, he had a temper and a very protective nature. Maggie didn't think he would understand this kind of family any more than she did. People like this just didn't live in the same world.

Besides, she would feel that she was betraying her husband if she spoke of this to anyone they both knew. All she could do was get through the next few days as best she could, and hope Daniel's mother left. Soon.

Maggie wrapped the woolen scarf around her neck and braved the cold of the day. The sun was high and bright, but her breath was no more than a fog of cold as she stepped briskly down the stone steps and sped on her way. In front of the National Bank, she heard a voice calling her name. Turning, she saw Edward Varley hurrying toward her.

"Mrs. Calcord! Maggie!" He was smiling as he reached her. "I know you well enough, don't I, to call you Maggie by now?"

"I think you do, Mr. Varley," she answered easily. Maggie liked this man. He hadn't always been the most tractable person to know, but he behaved as his conscience told him and that was something she had recently learned to appreciate.

"You can call me Ed. You did once before." The pause in his speaking was a bit awkward, and Ed tried to cover that by removing his derby. "I wanted to say good-bye. I'm leaving on the stage in the morning and taking the train back to Pennsylvania in a few days."

"Already? You mean your work is done?"

"No, the work's not done, but it is begun. The men know what to do now and I'm of no further use here. My home is in Pennsylvania, not Colorado. An agreement has been hammered out with the mine owners; that's a start. And the Elephant Club has disbanded, so there should be no immediate threats to the union's existence."

"So, you are free to leave?"

"Yes. I wanted to thank you for taking me in when I was wounded. I know what you risked, not only the good will of the town but your husband's anger as well."

302

"He would have done just as I did."

"Well, we didn't know that at the time, did we?"

"I did."

He smiled at her confidence. "Yes, perhaps you did. You both seem to be the sort of people who make up their own minds and follow them, no matter what the rest of the world may think."

"And you are that kind of person, Mr. Varley. You didn't come all this way because someone else thought it right for you. You came because you thought it right."

"You saved my life twice, Maggie. That I won't forget."

She couldn't prevent the sudden grin crossing her lips. "In spite of the fact that I am married to a mine owner? That I am one of THEM?"

"In spite of that," he agreed, grinning hugely. "I also learned from you that we're all human, miners and owners. I'm not so sure about the corporate boards, however."

"Nor am I, Mr. Varley." At his expression, she corrected herself, "Ed."

Setting the hat back on his head, Ed took both her hands in his and gazed deeply into her eyes. "I'll probably not be seeing you again. I want you to know that I think you're one of the finest women I have ever met in my life. I want you to remember that always."

"Why, thank you," she stammered, her heart touched. "I am glad to know that, in spite of my independent ways, you can still find it in your heart to like me. I'm glad to have known you too. I thought unionists were a different sort of men, more destructive. I learned that you simply care about the miners themselves, not even so much the right and the wrong. I admire that."

Gently he squeezed her hands, and then, as though he couldn't stop himself, he hauled her against his chest and kissed her on the forehead. "Have a good life, Magheen Calcord. You deserve it." Releasing her, he ran back in the direction he had come from, quickly disappearing into the crowd. Maggie gazed after him for a long while before resuming her walk. Lifting her eyes toward the Emporium, she paused momentarily. Mayme Calcord stood just outside the door, beside her was the young woman who had traveled on the stagecoach with her.

Mayme wore a curiously satisfied expression as she introduced the two young women. "Magheen, my dear, I would like you to meet this very nice woman I met on the stage, Arabella Forbes. Arabella, this is my daughter-in-law, Magheen Calcord. Arabella is Judge Forbes's daughter, and a delightful young woman."

Arabella Forbes was more than just delightful, she was beautiful and elegant, and a woman who came from the same world as the Calcords, Maggie quickly realized.

Her jet-black hair was intricately coiffed and held in place with jeweled combs. A fur cape and matching bonnet topped a day dress of fine rose wool. The voluminous skirt took up almost half the width of the sidewalk. Dainty hands were kept warm in a muff of matching fur.

Standing next to these two women, Maggie felt dowdy and plain. Maybe she should pay more attention to keeping her unruly curls confined, she thought, and perhaps pay more attention to her style of dress. Her everyday fare of blouse and skirt must be growing tedious to Daniel, especially as he was used to such women.

"I thought we'd have tea," Mayme continued briskly. "Is there a decent place in this whole town in which to eat?"

How did she get herself into this? Magheen was to wonder again and again over the next two hours. More importantly, how could she get out of this?

They were lunching at the Colorado House, at Miss Forbes's suggestion, and, of course, it was a wonderful place, positively the best spot Mayme Calcord had found since coming to Leadville. That Arabella Forbes had her unequivocal approval was readily apparent. The two women talked of fashion and New York and its theater. Miss Forbes had just come from New York so she was as acquainted with it as Mayme Calcord was.

Maggie sat silently, picking at her food, until Arabella turned to her and gushed, "I met your husband on the stagecoach. Such a pleasant man, so attractive and well educated. I didn't think I'd run across anyone quite like

304

him once I left New York."

"Daniel is from New York," Mrs. Calcord reminded them. "I too think he's wasted in this forsaken little town. But we're doing our best to get him back where he belongs. Isn't that right, my dear?" Mayme smiled sweetly on Maggie who was suddenly very intent on her food.

Dusk was settling across the horizon when they returned to the house. The journey home was completed in silence. Mayme had said all she had to say either earlier in the day or to Arabella Forbes. Maggie had a splitting headache and just wanted to get home.

To make matters worse, Daniel was still gone. Harvey arrived later that night with bad news. "One of the water lines broke. Daniel said he's not leaving until he's sure there'll be no flooding."

"But the first Mass in the Annunciation Church is set for tomorrow morning. I thought he'd want to go with me."

"He's not even a Catholic, dear," Mayme interrupted. They were in the parlor and Mayme had mending on her lap, her fingers working furiously. "Can't you do anything by yourself?"

Harvey sighed. "He'd like to be here, I know. But if the mine washes out, so does the work of the last four months. And we're close to hitting a vein, Maggie, I know we are."

"More than hopefulness is required to make money, Mr. Benson," Mayme said primly.

Harvey plopped his hat on his head and turned toward the kitchen and Maude Sawyer. How Maggie could stand being cooped up with that woman was more than he would ever understand.

More than Maggie could understand either, but she was determined to do the best by and for Daniel that she could. For that reason she invited Mayme to Mass in the morning. With another curt comment the older woman refused.

Maggie went to bed early and was up before daylight, getting ready for Mass. She felt as excited as if it were her own church, surely as excited as Patrick himself must be. A church of his own was something he had worked for all his life.

Maude was waiting for her in the kitchen, garbed in Sunday finery. With a grimace she said, "You didn't think I'd spend the whole day here with that woman, did you? I heard her refuse to go, so I'm going."

"I should have asked you."

"Under normal circumstances I'd have refused. But with that woman in the house, I'd convert if it got me away from her."

Chapter Seventeen

A brand-new year, Maggie thought excitedly, her slender form bouncing as she perched on the wooden buckboard seat. Eighteen-eighty, a whole new year, a whole new decade, a whole new beginning.

Harvey wrestled with the reins, Maude sitting next to him. On her other side was Magheen, looking across the breadth of the Arkansas valley toward Mount Elbert and Mount Massive.

The horses plodded through the main street in Leadville. The marquee at the Opera House advertised Jack Langrishe and company in *Two Orphans*, a production Maggie had been wanting to see. Pap Wyman's, at the intersection of State Street and Harrison Street, was closed at this early hour. The Saddle Rock Café was open day and night but was empty of customers this early New Year's Day morning. The Odeon Variety Theater advertised "girls in short skirts and bare arms," but none were to be seen as they passed.

The only sign of a new decade was the grand Annunciation Church. Maggie couldn't have been prouder if she had build it single-handedly.

Of course another sign of change just might be in the way Harvey and Maude exchanged soul-searching gazes, their hands entwined. They never said a direct word to Maggie, but she was beginning to think that the stories told by Anne and Carrie just might have a grain of truth in them. Sooner or later, a wedding would take place.

On holidays, even the teamsters seemed to take a rest and

the streets were opened to idle traffic. With the exception of the churches and, later on in the day, the saloons, nothing was open.

She and Maude had already hitched up the horses and were on their way to town when Harvey caught up with them on horseback. "Daniel can't leave the mine yet. He said to tell you he's sorry, but the mine has to come first. He said you'd understand."

"I do," Maggie responded cheerfully. "He took too much time off at Christmas." Shrugging lightly, she gave a smile. "I did want him to share in Paddie's joy, though. In spite of their being such different men, they really like each other, you know."

"I know, Maggie. Here, scoot over and I'll drive. Let me tie my horse to the back of the buckboard first. What happened to Daniel's mother? Didn't she want to come?"

Maggie and Maude exchanged glances and Maude mumbled, "She said not."

Harvey looked from one to the other, his brows raising. "You left her behind for the whole day?"

"We did ask her to come with us," Maggie defended. "What were we supposed to do, one of us stay home with her and miss all the fun?"

"Leaving her behind wasn't the nicest thing either of you've ever done, but it was one of the most sensible," Harvey grumbled, rattling the reins. "She must have so much money that the Easterners she knows don't much care how she behaves. Out here, we're more particular and she'd have to earn friendships, not buy them."

The church was already filling when they arrived. Paddie, beaming with pride and happiness, stood at the front door and greeted his parishioners. For his sister he had a kiss. "Can I interest the two of you in a baptism?" he asked of Harvey and Maude. "You're here about as often as many a bona fide Catholic. I'd throw in a wedding for nothing."

"We may just take you up on that, Father," Harvey responded, grinning.

The second pew was reserved for Paddie's relations and closest friends. In the front row were the town's governing fathers, among them Horace Tabor and his wife, Augusta. It was rumored that Tabor himself had donated a good deal of the money to build the church, just as he had for so many of the other churches in town. He wasn't even Catholic.

Paddie's sermon was one of gratitude for the generosity of parishioners who had enabled the construction of this grand church. "I suppose one day I'll stand up here and lecture you on the sins of drinking, lewdness, and unforgiveness. But, for right now, you look near perfect to me." The whole congregation laughed. Little was as well known in the Leadville area as Father Fitzgerald's high expectations for his parishioners, and his sermons showed that.

Afterwards, a potluck dinner was held in the basement of the church, and most everyone remained to enjoy the day. The children heard stories, then games and drawing centers were set up for them. The adults talked and danced to a lively fiddle. The opening of the new Catholic church was an affair everyone in Leadville took part in, no matter what religion they were.

At two in the afternoon, Dutch Saunders arrived and came looking for Harvey. "The pump's broken again," he said, nodding to the ladies. "We need you bad."

"You go on," Maude said, in her matter-of-fact manner. "Maggie and I can go home alone. Don't worry about us. Just take care of yourselves."

"Will you be needing any food?" Maggie questioned of the men. "We can cook . . ."

"Thanks for the thought, but we've plenty. When I left this morning, Gabe Printz was cooking up a storm. He's probably got enough by now for the next three weeks," Harvey laughed as he spoke. Growing serious he said, I'd appreciate it if you ladies left now. I'll just worry about you getting home if you wait till dark."

"I don't know if I'll like being married to a miner," Maude clucked, sighing. "I think he wants to ruin all my fun, and I don't even know which comes first, the marriage to the mine or to the wife."

"Oh, that's wonderful news," Maggie cried exuberantly, hugging first Maude, then Harvey tightly. "I wondered if he'd ever ask!"

"You should have wondered if she'd ever say yes," Harvey grumbled. "I've been trying to talk her into it for weeks now."

"After one marriage, I thought I was plumb wore out. It took a lot of thinking to agree."

"I know what you mean," Maggie agreed softly, her eyes twinkling.

"Don't go giving me that," Maude reprimanded her curtly. "You and Daniel haven't had time to wear each other out. Besides, you're near perfect for each other. You're each just as hard-headed as the other. I know it, even if the two of you fools don't."

The men helped pack the remnants of dinner and walked with the ladies to the stables where the buckboard and horses were stalled. For a few moments on the road, the buckboard followed closely behind the men; then the horses took off in another direction up the mountain, and the buckboard plodded along its slow way.

Mayme Calcord confronted them the moment they walked in the front door, demanding to know where they had spent the day.

"I told you about the opening of the new church," Maggie replied reasonably, hanging her coat in the wardrobe. Maude Sawyer was sneaking out the door and into the kitchen. "Mass was at nine-thirty this morning, just as I told you"

"I didn't expect to be left on my own all day!"

"This was my brother's day. I would not have missed it for the world," Maggie responded softly.

"You'll wish you had, I promise you. Daniel won't appreciate your rude treatment of his mother."

"If your feelings are hurt, I apologize. But my brother is very important to me too. You were more than welcome to come with us."

"I haven't felt welcome since the moment I arrived! You and that housekeeper . . . You've gone out of your way to keep Daniel from me. The two of you are thick. Don't think I won't tell him about it."

"Why don't you tell Daniel about it right now, Mother?"

He was leaning carelessly against the doorjamb, his coat hanging over his arms. He had just come in from the mine and looked tired. Maggie knew from the dull light of his eyes and the weary stoop to his shoulders that the day had already been long enough. Now was not the time for this, she thought, but there probably was never a good time for such complaints.

"Those two women took off early this morning and left me alone all day," she carped shrilly. "I might have wanted to go with them, but they didn't even bother to ask me."

"Is this true, Magheen?"

"I told her about the opening of the new church last night. She refused then, and when she wasn't up in time, I assumed she still didn't want to go."

"You don't like me," Mayme accused. "You've never liked me! You've gone out of your way to make me feel unwelcome — And after the expensive gift I bought you . . ."

"I repeat, if your feelings are hurt, I apologize. But nothing and no one was keeping me from sharing this day with my brother. If you need to vent your anger on someone, your son is here. Until you are done, I will be in the kitchen with Maude." With as much dignity as she could muster, Maggie turned and left the room. It seemed a shame to leave a weary Daniel to cope with his mother, but she was his mother and he probably stood a better chance of reasoning with her than anyone.

Mayme vented her anger against Magheen for a long while. Daniel was looking bored with it, as though her complaints were all something he had heard before. Finally, Mayme glared at Daniel and smirked hotly, "You think I made all this up? That girl has you twisted around her little finger. She's running you, and like a fool, you dance to her tune. Don't you even care that she's cuckolding you?"

"Be careful, Mother, I've about had enough of you!"

"Oh, are you so blinded by her that you don't care that she's kissing men all over town? That most of the town saw her yesterday?"

"What the devil are you talking about?"

"I saw her in town yesterday, kissing Edward Varley, that's

what I'm talking about!"

"You're lying!"

"I'm not! Ask anyone. Ask Arabella Forbes! We both saw your wife in the arms of another man!"

Raised voices followed Magheen into the kitchen. There, the stove was keeping the room warm and the tea kettle was whistling on top of it, blotting out all foreign noises. Maude glanced up at her entrance. "Sorry, but I didn't want to stick around and listen to her. Who's she tangling with now?"

"Daniel's with her."

Maude's brows rose as she straightened. She had been slicing bread, but this made her stop. "I don't know how you could have walked out on them. Don't you realize she's saying all sorts of nasty things to Daniel about you?"

"I imagine so," Maggie answered, pouring water over the tea leaves. "But my conscience is clear. I need not tell you how relieved I was that she was still abed when we left this morning. I was afraid she might change her mind and ruin a perfectly good day. I think another day with her might have been the end of my temper. At least she's not my mother, but if she were, I would not appreciate Daniel's interference. So I shall not interfere." Her mouth was set determinedly as she finished speaking, "And if she weren't talking about me, she'd be talking about someone else."

"Aren't you the least bit worried what she'll say to Daniel?" Maude asked, incredulity in her expression.

"As long as he doesn't repeat it to me, no."

"She means trouble, Maggie."

Maggie sighed. "I know she does, and I don't know what to do about her. If Daniel sides with her—"

"Then he's a fool!" Maude cried hotly.

"She's his mother," Maggie responded softly. "He loves her. He can't always like her, not the way she behaves, but the love is always there."

"Maggie, you two have had enough trouble between you—"

The door creaked open and Daniel stood in the doorway.

312

"Maggie, I'd like to speak with you. In our room. Now."

"I'll be up in a moment," came the reply. Maggie was steeping her tea and not about to be intimidated by him. "I'm fixing a cup. Would you like one?"

Daniel ran an impatient hand through his hair. "I'd rather have a whiskey, a good, stiff one, but I can get that myself. On second thought," he mumbled, closing the door behind him, "I might have two or three."

Maude's mouth gaped open. "I wonder what it was she said."

"Plenty, I'd guess," Maggie responded tautly.

"Hmm, I wonder if Harvey's mother is alive."

Maggie laughed grimly. "If she is, take second thought about the marriage. I've known this woman two days, and already she's given me nothing but trouble. How it will end is anyone's guess. Tell Daniel I'm upstairs, will you?"

She was comfortable by the time he arrived. Her boots were exchanged for slippers, her cup of tea cooling on the table beside her. She sat in the chair beneath the window and proceeded to do her mending.

"Why can't you at least make the effort to get along with my mother?" Daniel demanded through gritted teeth, shutting the door behind him. "Did you have to leave her alone here all day? Can't you imagine what it would be like to be in some place strange and new, knowing no one?"

"I asked her—"

"She overslept," he responded.

"She gave me to understand that she didn't want to go."

"Are you sure, Maggie? Or are you going out of your way to be nasty to her?"

"What do you mean by that?" Maggie spoke softly, determined to hold on to her temper.

Daniel seemed just as determined to vent his. "I mean she gave you a peignoir set yesterday, which you refused. What was she supposed to think of that? And then, when she wanted you to choose a gift for our wedding, you refused again. You left her alone in the store, with no idea of what you wanted or needed! If Arabella Forbes hadn't come along then, she would have been completely lost. I didn't think you

313

could be so selfish. Because she's my mother, I would have thought you would give her more consideration. What's the matter, Maggie? Are you jealous of her? Jealous of her money and background? I told you I could provide all you needed and more. Don't you want to believe me?"

This last hit a sore spot. Maggie flushed angrily as she rose from the chair, the sewing tumbling about her feet, her hands clenched in fists. All her good intentions had flown out the window. "Do you honestly think I could envy a woman like that?"

"What do you mean 'a woman like that'?"

"A woman so shallow and selfish she cares nothing for anyone else, a woman who thinks life begins and ends with material possessions and who manipulates her family to get her way!"

"Does your envy pain you so much that you have to make up statements like that? Try being truthful for a change," he taunted.

"Truthful? What would you know of the truth, being raised in a family belonging to *that* woman?"

"Leave my family out of this."

"I'll say what I like, just as you've said what you like about my family and my country. I did not want a peignoir set, purchased by your mother, nor did I want a wedding gift from the likes of her, but I never said so. I have gone out of my way to be nice to her."

"You've no need to lie, Magheen. My mother made perfectly plain the kind of treatment you handed out to her."

"You got a good earful, didn't you? Blast you, Daniel Calcord, I was beginning to trust you, fool that I was! No longer. You take the word of a woman you know as well as you know her over mine? Is it easier for you than admitting the truth?"

"Trust? What do you know of trust? Or truth, for that matter? An elaborate tea service is in my dining room, the bows still on it. The least you could have done was to have thanked her for it. But no, not with your small little mind."

"Your mother has made it plain what she thinks of me and our marriage." Maggie stormed, trembling with anger.

314

In all her imaginings, she had never envisioned a scene such as this. She expected Daniel to at least ask her what happened, not to assume every word his mother spoke was the truth. It seemed he had chosen between them and his mother was the one chosen.

"I will not thank her for a gift given in such animosity. She thinks to buy you. Well, you may be for sale, but I am not. She is the most selfish woman I have ever met in my life. She would do nothing from generosity or love, everything she does has an ulterior motive and I'll have none of it, or of her!"

"Or of me either, I suppose?"

"Not if you take her side."

"She was right about one thing, bad breeding always shows."

Magheen tilted her head and glared at him. "Probably it's the only thing she's ever said in her life that has a bit of truth in it. *Your* bad breeding is showing."

"I thought you were a better woman, Magheen. I didn't think you would stoop to such behavior simply because you were jealous."

"It is not jealousy I feel for either of you; pity is. I pity you because she's using you and you haven't the wits to see it. Most of all, I pity you for what you're throwing away. I pity you for the lack of values you've succumbed to, for the price she deemed you worth—"

Daniel clenched his fists and roared at her, "Don't you ever say such things like that to me again! I expect courtesy, and I expect you to behave with courtesy toward my mother."

"I have always behaved courteously, just not obsequiously."

"Use any words you choose," he spoke coldly. "Just see to it that my mother is hurt no further. She's a far better woman than you any day. At least my father has never had to worry about her having lovers, let along meeting them in public!"

Maggie was stunned by these words. "What lies has she been telling you now?"

"Lies? Did you or didn't you meet Ed Varley in town yesterday?"

Maggie hesitated a second too long. "I did."

"You don't deny meeting him?"

"Why should I? I met him. In public. On the street. In broad daylight. In front of your mother!"

"And you kissed him! Have you no shame at all?"

The attack took her breath away. So this was the cause of Daniel's anger. Jealousy over her innocent meeting with Edward Varley. Once before he had thrown accusations out and never listened to her explanations. And even though they had made up for that misunderstanding, he had still not apologized.

"None," she answered, the emerald eyes glittering with anger. "I meet any number of lovers in broad daylight, that way I can skip going to brothels late at night, unlike some people I can name."

"Of course you would bring that up," he spoke coldly. "I can't tell you how much I regret the folly that led to our marriage. It's too bad your lover didn't come along before you took the plunge. You might have saved us both a good deal of regret." He turned to leave the room, and suddenly Maggie was struck with the realization of how horrible this argument had become.

"Don't go, Daniel," she said in a rush. "This should not have gone so far. I did not mean to insult you or your mother, but my temper—"

"I think we've said everything that needs to be said. I'll be moving into the bunkhouse at the mine for the time being. My mother can move into town so you needn't be bothered with her. Harvey will come by to check on you and Maude every day."

"Daniel, don't leave," she begged. "If you walk out now, the bitterness of our words may be all that remains. We may never settled this."

"I thought we'd settled it. Our marriage was a mistake, at least on that we agree."

"I never agreed."

He passed a weary hand across his brow. "I need some time, Maggie. I'll be in touch in a few days." He was gone as quickly as he spoke, the door closing softly behind him.

Maggie spent a miserable night, cursing her unruly tongue. Why couldn't she have done what she knew was important, and that was controlling her Irish temper?

Because she had never watched her tongue in her life, she admitted to herself. Because she said exactly as she pleased and had never had a Daniel to answer to before. Oh, why couldn't his mother have been someone she could love? And why couldn't *she* have been someone his mother loved?

Or was Daniel right and was she the one in error, petty and jealous of his mother as he claimed?

She swore that in the morning she would make amends to her mother-in-law, swallow that horrible pride that threatened her marriage.

But in the morning Mayme Calcord sailed down the stairs, and into the kitchen, a smirk on her rouged lips. "I knew Daniel would see through you," she crowed to Magheen. "I knew you wouldn't be able to hold him."

Maggie took a deep breath before speaking. "Please don't make this any more difficult than it is. I would like to once again apologize if I did anything to hurt you. I've—"

"You've lost him, that's what you've done," Mayme smirked gleefully.

"Maggie," Maude spoke sharply, "don't do this. You have nothing to apologize to her for. When Daniel comes to his senses, he'll know that."

"Daniel wanted us to like each other, Maude. I should have been more patient."

"Don't bother now," Mayme chirped. "I have what I was after. Daniel will join me for dinner this evening at the hotel. I expect that's where he'll be spending his evenings until we leave. And at least the hotel can offer decent fare."

Magheen just wanted this horrible nightmare to be over quickly. She was no longer angry with Mrs. Calcord; she had vented her anger the night before. But she was sad that everything should end as it had.

Her stomach was churning as it so often did these days. If this scene continued much longer, she was afraid she would have to leave the room. Quickly. And then Mayme would know there was a whole lot more to crow about.

"Do you want me to take you into town?"

"Don't bother. Daniel said he'd send a man and a carriage for me." Sharp eyes looked Maggie up and down. "He never got a carriage for you, did he? You never rated as much of a lady, that's why."

"You foolish old woman . . ." Maude began, her shoulders stiffening.

"Please, Maude, don't," Maggie begged, placing a hand on the housekeeper's arm. "We don't need any more ugly scenes."

"That's right, Magheen," Mayme boasted. "Cut your losses while you can. I've won."

"And there's the carriage," Maude announced, a smile on her face for the first time that morning. The rolling noise made by the high wheels was unmistakable. "I'll tell the driver where your luggage is."

Mayme nodded haughtily. "At least you packed. I would have thought you too good to even do that for me."

"I'd do anything to see the last of you."

"Too bad you won't have your job for much longer."

"I don't want this job for much longer," Maude pronounced as she headed for the door.

"Would you like breakfast before you leave?" Maggie asked Mrs. Calcord.

"No. I want to leave as soon as possible."

Magheen nodded serenely. "Good-bye, Mrs. Calcord."

"Yes, it is good-bye, isn't it? I don't think we'll be seeing each other again."

"No, we won't," Maggie agreed firmly. She remained in the kitchen until she saw the carriage rolling away, Mayme Calcord's luggage stacked on top. Then she went to her room where she remained for the rest of the day.

Harvey came to dinner that night, and the next night too. The new equipment had arrived at the mine, and Daniel and the men were busy installing it.

"I don't know when he'll have time to come home, he's so busy," Harvey explained, his eyes shifting from Maggie to Maude.

Maggie nodded silently, her attention on the mending she

318

held in her lap. Yesterday had been spent soul searching, and few acceptable answers had been found. She might have handled Mayme Calcord better, but the end result would have been the same. The woman did not want her for a daughter-in-law, and as long as her opinion was so important to Daniel, their marriage stood no chance.

Daniel said he would return in a few days so they might settle affairs between them. To Maggie that meant only one thing, the end of their marriage. She had no idea of American laws, but Catholic laws were the same the world over. Even if Daniel could legally end this marriage for him, she was tied by church canon forever.

One thing was certain; she was not about to stay in this house and go slowly mad with so little to do. Tomorrow she would ride into town and see if there was a chance of getting her job back.

Maggie rose early and saddled the bay mare. She stopped at the Howards' fine house and had tea with Anne. Annabelle was full of happy questions, which Maggie did her best to answer. Anne watched her closely but kept her mouth firmly shut. Whatever was going on between Daniel and Magheen was their business.

From there Magheen rode to the Emporium. Mr. Smith said he was sorry but he had already filled her job. Before she went back to Daniel's house, though, she decided to visit her brother and turned down Harrison Street to get to the new rectory.

And there, tethered before Lil Amundson's place, was Daniel's black horse.

In that moment Maggie realized how broken her marriage was. Nothing would take away words spoken in bitter anger; nothing would make things as they once were.

Emptiness swamped her. In a moment, she thought, she would break down and cry. Pulling on the reins, she turned the mare around and headed back through town and up the hill to Daniel's house. She couldn't face Paddie now, nor did she know when she would be able to.

She didn't want to give him more grief, and what she had to tell him would do that. What she needed to do now was make her plans carefully, and not tell Paddie until it became absolutely necessary. And to think that two days ago had been one of the happiest in his life.

She also had to face her other problem: how she was going to raise her child by herself.

All she could think during that lonely ride home was how bitterly Daniel must be regretting the marriage.

She needed to talk to someone, someone who could advise her. Someone who was impartial. But who?

An early afternoon fog was creeping in, shrouding the house as it loomed before her. Paddie was right; she had never accepted this house as a home. She was still a stranger here, she thought sadly.

Maude appeared at the door, drying her hands on a towel. "You've been gone long enough. Harvey and I have been worried about you." A smile lit her eyes. "He told me Daniel was asking about you this morning. Maybe by tomorrow he'll be cooling down and at least come home for supper. Wouldn't that be grand? Then you and he could get some of this straightened out."

Magheen nodded faintly, moving up the stairs. What could they say to each other now, she wondered, leaning against the bedroom door. More recriminations, more arguing? No, she was done with the arguing, with the ugliness. If Daniel ever looked at her again as he had the other night, with hatred in his expression, she thought she would die. No, she couldn't face that just yet. One day, maybe, but not too soon. Not when she was still hurting so badly over his visiting Lil's.

She needed to get away from here, to find some time for herself. She couldn't go to Paddie's. That was the first place Daniel would come looking for her, and she supposed he would come looking. He would feel some responsibility.

The thought struck her that if she went to Denver, she could find a priest there to counsel her. Maybe she could get a job to tide her over while she was there. She would have time for thinking, and for planning.

There was the child to consider now. A half-Irish brat, she reminded herself bitterly. Thank the Good Lord she hadn't had a chance to tell him about the baby the other night.

Lifting a corner of the feather mattress, she took her savings and carefully counted the bills. A few she placed in her reticule, enough to cover the cost of the fare and a few days' lodging. The rest she concealed among pieces of her clothing in her small traveling satchel. Tomorrow when she left, she would hide it in the money purse she suspended from her waist beneath her skirt.

She found it ironic that the money intended to be used for freeing her brothers was buying her own freedom.

Later that night, she penned notes to Daniel and Paddie. They would be worried, so she did what she could to alleviate that worry. She needed this time alone, she reiterated in each note. She would be in contact with them in a few days, she said. She left a longer letter for Maude. The housekeeper had become a good friend over the last few weeks, and Maggie would miss her. She hated to go without speaking a word to her, but she knew Maude would try to talk her out of leaving. She might even get to Daniel before Maggie could board the stage. No, Maude would have to settle for a letter too.

The stage left for Denver at noon. With luck, she would be on it and spend that night in Central City. The new route went north through Kokomo, Recen, and Wheeler, the area known as the ten-mile district, then east to Georgetown, Central City, and Blackhawk. By tomorrow evening, she would be in Denver.

"In the last two months we've dug the main incline out another hundred feet and begun a fourth level of production. The shipment of ore this month should reach twenty-five tons, not a bad amount for the dead of winter. But the best news of all is that the grade of ore is increasing with each shipment and each drop in the incline," Daniel reported briskly. "We're on the track to proving you right, Harvey. How does it feel!"

"Finally, as though I knew my business. I was beginning to doubt it for a while there. Damn good is how I feel!"

"Don't go feeling too good. You know your business all right, the ore's good, that I'm convinced of, but who the hell is it who wants to sabotage this operation?"

"You're talking about the fire yesterday?"

"I am. I admit it looked like a careless accident, but I'm convinced it's not. Someone deliberately set that fire."

"So, who do you think did it? One of our men? And how?" Harvey shook his head. "It can't be. I have them watching each other."

"No one was watching Dick Fell."

"Daniel, he saved Norm Wheeler's life, and damn near at the cost of his own! You can't convince me he meant to hurt anyone."

"No, I don't think he meant anyone to be hurt, but I do think he started the fire and it got out of control. He was the only one who could have done it, Harvey. Think about it."

"I am thinking about it." Harvey clasped his hands behind his back and moved to the window to look out on the cold day. "All right, I admit, if it was sabotage it had to be Dick who did it. But why? I'd swear he's an honest man. Hell, he's got five children to provide for!"

"I know all that and a bit more besides. He's lost heavily at the gaming tables, Harvey. I think he's a desperate man. His second son is sick and needs an operation, but instead of telling us about it, he goes to Pap's and tries to gamble his way into a fortune. I don't know how much he's lost, but I've heard it's plenty."

"Are you saying someone *paid* him to set the fire? Who?"

"I don't know. Someone we haven't begun to suspect so far. But it's someone who's smart, has money, and who's greedy for even more."

"You mean a man already established in town?" Harvey questioned thoughtfully. "I suppose it would have to be. Only someone like that could afford to pay to have fires set and explosions go haywire." Harvey shook his head sadly. "I've seen men kill over a mine before, Daniel. It's hard to understand a man who would go so far. I don't think I can understand the kind of man who'd put wealth above lives."

"All right," he said, straightening. "Let's go to the bunk-

322

house. It's time we had a talk with Dick."

Dick was sitting on the edge of the bed, his hands bandaged where the fire had burned him. He looked up as Daniel and Harvey entered the room, his bloodshot eyes narrowing. Black bruises marred the whiteness of the flesh around his eyes and cheeks. His dark, curly hair was singed and matted with dirt and soot.

"I was just coming to talk to you," he said in his slow manner.

"Don't get up." Daniel motioned with his hands. "You need to lie down for a while yet."

"I don't deserve your consideration," he snarled. "I deserve that you should horsewhip me and leave me to die."

"What we want is the truth, Dick. Give us that and we'll call it even. But if anyone had died in that fire . . ."

"Don't!" Dick roared. "I can't stand thinking about that, thinking about how close Wheeler came to dying, how close I came to being responsible for the death of someone. I'd have had to face my maker with that sin on my soul, and what would I have said? I needed the money?"

"No one died. We were lucky this time. Next time maybe we won't be so lucky." Daniel paused a moment. "Why, Dick? Why did you do it?"

Dick couldn't meet Daniel's intent gaze. Looking down at the floor, he began to speak. "He offered me money, more money than I'd ever seen in my life at one time. I needed the money for my son."

"I know that now. You should have told me."

"Told you like I did the last time?" His head jerked up and he glared at Daniel. "You gave me an extra hundred dollars then and told me to quit drinking so damn much! Beth looked at you like you were God's gift to the world. I hated you for that, did you know? You seemed so damned high and mighty that you thought you could tell a man how to live! But I took your hundred and I paid off my bills, and Beth was so happy for a while. I hadn't seen her that happy since we married. All I've given her is a passel of kids, traveling, poverty, and now this.

"I never meant to hurt anybody. I thought I could set the

323

fire and keep everyone away."

"You saved Wheeler's life. You injured yourself in the bargain."

Dick breathed deeply. "All of a sudden I realized what I was doing, and it made me sick to my stomach. I couldn't do it. If I could have put out the fire then, I would have. But it was too late."

"Who paid you?"

"Judge Forbes."

Daniel and Harvey were both astonished. "Are you sure?" Daniel demanded.

"Of course I'm sure."

"But why?"

Dick shook his head. "That I don't know. Oh, I asked him, all right, but he laughed and told me I knew enough to earn my money and to get about it. I'm sorry, Daniel. I'm sorry I did it, and I'm sorry I can't give you answers."

"That's okay. I'll have the answers soon anyway." Daniel nodded and headed for the door. There he paused, his hand on the doorknob, and turned back to Dick Fell. "Harvey will give you your week's pay and you can go."

It was Dick's turn to look astonished. "Aren't you gonna have me arrested?"

"I would, but then I'd have your wife and kids on my conscience. I won't have that, not even for a paltry revenge. No, I'll be content with getting Forbes."

"I'll testify against him," Dick offered eagerly.

"It'd do no good. You'd have to admit to being a criminal and setting the fire first. Why would a jury take your word against the likes of Forbes? No, we'll have to get him some other way."

The door was just closing behind him when Dick piped up with, "Thanks, Daniel."

Daniel hadn't set foot in Lil's place since his fiasco of months ago, and he didn't want to now. He still felt like a full-fledged idiot when he thought about that night. But he supposed he owed it to Norm Wheeler, his injured miner, to tell his girl about the fire at the mine. Flo Harper would want to go to the Resurrection and at least see how Norm was faring.

The opulence of the front parlor was garish in the daytime rather than elegant as it had been at night. Daniel stood uncomfortably at the foot of the wide staircase and waited for Flo. A couple of the women descended the stairs, eying him assessingly. Daniel doffed his hat and wished them an uncomfortable "good afternoon." He wasn't embarrassed that he was here, but his conscience was bothering him.

If Maggie should hear of this visit, he would never live it down.

Kate Nelligan was the next to come down, and she had a broad smile for Daniel. "I've thought of you often, Mr. Calcord. Wondered if you'd be back . . ." Sidling next to him, she clutched at his arm and whispered questioningly in his ear, "I'd heard you'd married. I was sooo disappointed."

"Ah . . . yes," he said, shrugging his arm and trying to get out of her clutches. She was hanging on tight. "I married— ah . . . ah . . ."

"I heard your wife is Father Patrick's sister."

Daniel swallowed convulsively. He was beginning to wish he hadn't let Dick Fell off so easily. He should have let him come in here and find Florence Harper. "Flo! I'm looking for Flo Harper! What do you suppose is keeping that woman?"

Kate's fingers inched their way up to Daniel's throat and jaw, stroking lightly. "Flo? Why Flo? I was hoping you'd think of me. I could make you real happy, Mr. Calcord."

"Mr. Calcord!" Flo Harper hurried down the stairs toward them. She was a small woman, too young for her profession to have scarred her just yet. She was wearing a simple day dress of blue calico and high black boots. Her blond hair was crimped and pulled back from her face with a ribbon. Everything about her appearance was too youthful and innocent for anyone who didn't know to guess at her profession. "What are you doing here? Has something happened to Norm?"

Daniel finally managed to extricate himself from Kate

325

Nelligan and firmly set her to one side.

"He was injured in a fire at the mine. Don't look so worried, he'll be fine, I promise you. But he wants to see you. I think he wants to hold you, Flo. He wants to know he's still a whole man."

Flo took a deep breath. "Let me get my coat. I'll be right with you."

"And I thought you were looking for something else," Kate said suggestively to him.

Daniel grinned suddenly. "You say you're Irish, yet you can think that? Don't you know that darling, sweet, beautiful Irish wife of mine has a temper that would be taking my head off if I came here for more than Flo?"

"I thought maybe she wasn't enough for you."

"She's more than I can handle. I'm trying to be enough for her."

Kate laughed lightly. "I lose more good men to marriage. Too bad. Well, good day to you. And keep your hands off Flo, or I'll be telling Mrs. Calcord."

Daniel rode with Flo as far as the bunkhouse and, from there, walked across the complex to his office. Harvey was sitting at the desk, filing out payroll checks. He glanced up at Daniel's entrance. "Add five hundred dollars to Wheeler's pay."

"What?" Harvey cried. "We need all the cash we've got for the next shipment of supplies."

"I don't care. That man damn near died inside my mine! The least I can do is give him enough money to get his girl out of that whorehouse and get them married!"

Harvey looked ready to argue further, so Daniel barked impatiently, "This is still my mine, and that's still my money! Just do as I say, Harvey!"

"You can be the stubbornest, stupidest . . ."

"You've been talking to Maude again, Harvey."

"Damn right, I have. When are you going home and face that wife of yours? You've made enough of a jackass out of yourself; don't let it go on any longer."

"I don't intend to. I cooled down by the day after our argument. But, if you recall, we had equipment arriving, and it needed installing. And then we had that damned fire. I spent thirty-six hours straight in the mine, and I was too damn tired to listen to them squabble. Sorry, but Maggie understands that the mine has to come first."

"Maybe she does, but you didn't tell her it was the mine keeping you away. She thinks you're still angry with her over your mother."

"Not over my mother, maybe over Maggie doing a few things she shouldn't have been doing," Daniel answered dryly.

"It sounded like you believed everything that woman said to you when you and Maggie were arguing."

"What did you do, eavesdrop?"

"Who the hell needed to eavesdrop? You were shouting louder than a brass band!"

"So I don't like to watch two women fighting. Settling their battles was the last thing I needed."

"It seems I have to remind you, your mother is not Maggie's battle. She's yours. And you stuck your wife with an impossible situation, then blamed her for it."

"I know I did and I'm sorry. I'll tell her so tonight, just as soon as I see her."

"You'd better, or Maude will never let you hear the end of it. She doesn't let me hear the end of it as it is."

"Maggie is going to have to learn to keep away from Ed Varley, though."

"Varley's been gone since Maggie spoke to him. He was on his way to catch the stage, which you would have known if you'd bothered to listen."

"Well, good riddance. I didn't like the way he looked at her. He looked too damn hungry to me." Daniel slapped his hat on his head and left the office. Mounting his horse, he headed in the direction of town.

The dining room of the Colorado House was rapidly filling. Daniel stood at the entrance, his eyes quickly scanning the room, searching for his mother. He found her in a far corner, talking earnestly to one of her companions with her head bent close. She looked every bit the sophisticated, knowledgeable woman she was, and as though she had deliberately chosen her surroundings with the patterned wallpaper that matched her clothes.

White linen covered the table, the four corners of the cloth nearly reaching the floor. Crisp napkins in intricate folds were at each place setting. Bright gold banded each plate and wineglass, and the utensils were also gold. In the center of the table stood a gas lamp wreathed with pine sprays. Garlands of pine trailed gracefully to the floor along each side of the table.

While Daniel watched, his mother lifted her head and laughed happily. The man beside her straightened, and Daniel recognized him too. Judge Forbes. Across from him sat his daughter, Arabella.

Coincidences clicked together in Daniel's mind. His mother pushing him at Arabella, always speaking so highly of her and her father, the Christmas Day they spent together.

What he was thinking was almost too horrible to be true, but he knew his mother was capable of doing anything to get what she wanted. And she wanted him in New York. What better way than to make sure he would lose the mine?

First, she had set about alienating him and Maggie. Second, she had set about costing him the mine. Judge Forbes and his daughter must have proved useful for both goals. In fact the judge was probably more than happy to help.

Judge Forbes nudged her hand and motioned to where Daniel stood. As Mayme Calcord turned to her son, he could read first surprise, then triumph glittering in her eyes. And guilt. Beyond question she and Judge Forbes had plotted the fire. Her motives he could understand, but what were his?

Daniel maneuvered among the tables until he confronted theirs. The judge was lighting a cigar, seemingly comfortable with the situation. Daniel nodded at Arabella, unsure how much of this she knew.

Addressing his mother, he said bluntly, "I wouldn't go to New York with you if you managed to plot a fire that burned all the way to hell. If I see you on the street, I won't so much as acknowledge you. Go back to New York, get out of my life, and stay out of it."

"And you, Judge," he said, turning his gaze slightly. "You'd better watch every step you take, for, I promise you, I'll be right behind you. And one day I'll get you. You'll pay for the fire in my mine and the near loss of life. The first time you take one foot wrong, I'll see you hang! Hell," he said more loudly, his face jutting angrily forward, "I'll hang you myself if I have to!"

"Now, Daniel," the judge drawled. "Your mother wants you to go home with her. Surely you can understand that. It's a motherly way to feel."

"You damn near killed two of my men," Daniel accused angrily.

"No!" Mayme protested, rising. Turning to Judge Forbes she cried out, "You said no one would be hurt. You promised no one would be hurt!"

"I promised to convince him to go to New York with you. If one of the men had a slight accident, well, that's his problem. I saw that he was paid well enough for any risk he took."

"You're no better than an animal, Forbes," interjected Daniel.

"You'll never prove I did anything wrong," the judge smirked.

"Oh, I'll prove it. And sooner or later you'll pay. Tell me, were you behind the fires and explosions at any other mines?"

Forbes shrugged. "I don't know what you're talking about."

Daniel turned and walked away from the hotel before his anger got the best of him. Men like the judge should be stripped of everything they owned and have to learn what it's like to be an ordinary man, he fumed, mounting his horse.

"Daniel," his mother cried from the entry of the hotel. "I have to talk to you."

"No," Daniel said firmly. "No more words. You've done all the damage you can this time around. I'm getting out of here."

"I didn't know he planned to hurt anyone," she cried petulantly.

"A little bit of thought would have told you that, Mother. But you've never given a thought to anyone but yourself, have you? 'Do anything necessary to get my own way,' that's your motto."

"It's that girl! She's turned you against me!"

Daniel jerked his horse around and rode off at a furious pace. He should have known, even when it was all over, she would still try to blame someone else for her own mistakes.

Maude opened the door, and as soon as she saw Daniel, her expression changed to one of stunned surprise. Daniel was carrying flowers.

He felt like a fool. He had searched all over town until he found one greenhouse that had something blossoming, then he bought everything they had. He only knew he had to make up with Maggie.

"If you're looking for your wife, I don't know where she is," Maude bit out rapidly. "And I don't know why you care, not after what you had to say to her. The last I saw of her was this morning when she was going to town. And that's been hours!"

"Maude, it's six o'clock at night! It's too damn dark for a woman to be on her own!"

"I know that! I'm near ready to go after her myself. It's not like her to be gone so late." Maude was less than happy with him; that was clear from the way she kept him from entering his own house.

"Can I come in?" he snarled.

"Of course. It's your house, isn't it? I mean you own it, don't you?" Standing aside, Maude opened the door a bare inch to give the illusion of welcoming him. Daniel placed his hands on her shoulders and scooted her out of the way. "What took you so long?" she barked. "I thought you'd be here as soon as you told your ma off . . . Or did you forget to tell your ma off? You two-timing, back-biting rascal! Your ma's not good enough to wipe Maggie's shoes and you

330

know it!"

"I don't need to hear your opinion of my mother!"

"You need to hear somebody's opinion, you great big fool! I gave you an earful the last time you were here, anyway. Nothing's changed since then. Not my feelings and not your mother."

"I'm just going to wait for Maggie."

"It might be a long wait. When Harvey came, I sent him out looking for her. That was a couple of hours ago. I just went up to her room and found these notes. They're to you, her brother, and me. Her clothing is gone, all her toiletries are gone, even her books are gone. I'd say you went and did it right this time, Mr. Calcord. Your wife's gone and left you."

"What the hell . . ."

"What did you expect her to do, wait around until your ma died from old age? Like I said, Maggie's too good for your ma, and a whole lot too good for you!"

"Did Harvey go to Paddie's?"

Maude crossed her arms belligerently. "I suppose so."

"Where's my letter?"

"In there." She motioned to the parlor with her head.

Daniel entered the room and found the letter addressed to him on the mantelpiece. In a second he had it opened and was quickly scanning her words. When he was done, he crumpled it in his hand and tossed it onto the fire. "Where's yours?" he demanded.

"It's mine, and you have no business reading what belongs to me."

Daniel grimaced tightly, his eyes wild. "Are you going to get me that letter, or am I going to throw you out in this snow until you beg to give me the letter?"

Maude glared at him, for the first time satisfaction in her expression. "I wondered when you'd be back to normal. Bringing flowers, bah! Like you're gonna get out of getting down on your hands and knees and apologizing to that girl!" She felt around in her apron pocket until she found the letter and handed it to him. "Mine doesn't say much either."

Daniel looked at her suspiciously. "Either?"

"When I read my letter, you didn't think I wasn't going to read yours, did you? How else would I know what was going on?"

"You are one of the sauciest women I've ever known."

"Where are you going, Daniel?"

"I'm going to find my wife!" he bellowed.

Chapter Eighteen

Magheen lightly chipped her fingertips in the font of holy water, made the sign of the cross on her forehead and shoulders, and slowly entered the quiet inner sanctum of the Sacred Heart Church. A few persons waited for confession in a line against the far walls, Maggie recognized. She wasn't sure she had the courage to face that just yet. Doubts were beginning to creep through her mind as to the rightness of her action.

The last two days had been long and tiring. Her whole body still shook in rhythm with the rolling motion of the high wheels of the Concord coach. She had arrived in Denver less than two hours before and had immediately inquired about a hotel and the whereabouts of a Catholic church. The hotel was simple; across the street and down half a block was the Inner Ocean Hotel, but reaching the church had been more difficult. She had had to take one of the horse-drawn streetcars down Larimer Street to Sixteenth Street, and, from there, across to Broadway. She would see the church from the corner, she was told.

Her two days of traveling had given her much time to think. The coach had been crowded when she left Leadville, losing many of its occupants at various stops along the way, but gaining more than it left off at each place. Finally, weariness and boredom had set in, and Maggie had settled deep in the corner, thinking that she might have been too precipitate in her flight. But once again had come the recollection of Daniel's angry words and the sight of him entering Lil Amundson's house, and she had known she wouldn't turn back. She badly needed to speak with someone impartial, someone who could advise her.

Last night had been shared with another woman, in the uppermost floor of the hotel in Central City. The whole town had seemed to be built at twisted angles and hanging from the side of the mountain, which, judging from the stilts some of the houses were perched on, it was. The room had been tiny and cold, but it had meant a roof over her head and the additional advantage of staying still instead of rocking as the coach had. The bed had been soft with a feather filling and warmed with hot bricks fresh from the hearth.

Leaving at six this morning, the coach had arrived in Denver just after two o'clock. It had taken her this long to find her way around the funny streetcars that followed the track through the center of town. Now here she was, dusty, dirty, tired, and hungry, and as lost as she had ever been in her life.

She tried to recall who the priest was here, for she distinctly remembered Paddie talking as though they knew each other well. No name came to mind as she slowly sank into the pew, her satchel at her feet. Her mind was still mulling over the problem as her head dipped to one side, her eyes closed, and she slept.

"Saints preserve us, but I haven't had such a wee thing sleeping in my church for a month of Sundays," came the lilting voice to her ears.

Maggie thought she was dreaming. The familiar Gaelic accent, the warm humor in the voice, the breath so close to her ear had her thinking, for just a moment, that she was home in her own land, in the familiar church where she had been baptized.

Consciousness seeped in and she quickly knew better. As she straightened her head, one of the daisies decorating her straw hat fell off into her lap. Maggie glanced down at it, looking so forlorn and lonely, and up at the priest who was bent over her, and sniffled.

The big man straightened and felt in his cassock until

334

he found his pocket and the handkerchief inside. This he gave to Maggie.

"Thank you," she blurted, wiping her eyes and nose and looking around herself for the first time. "Are we alone?"

"Ah!" he cried, obviously pleased. "A fellow Irish! I thought so when I first looked on you, but a man can't always be certain. Red hair doesn't mean so much in America. And yes, we're alone."

Maggie sniffled again and continued, "I meant to go to confession, but I seem to have slept through the time. Is it very late?"

"Near five o'clock."

"Oh, you must be wanting your dinner!" she cried, rising to her feet and feeling around for her satchel. "I'm sorry. I don't mean to make you late—"

"You've come for confession?"

Magheen nodded. "I have. But I'll take a long time, Father. I have a lot that needs saying."

The priest raised his brows. "That bad, eh?"

Magheen nodded, sniffling into the handkerchief. " 'Tis terrible."

"Well, then, I think we'd better have our meal first, and then we can tend to your soul. I don't think the Good Lord would have made us quite so hungry if he didn't intend us to see to our bellies first at a moment like this. Come this way, please." He held out his hand and motioned her across the church to the back door.

Maggie looked startled. "I can come back in an hour. I don't mean to be any trouble," she insisted.

"Oh, have you already eaten?"

"Not yet, but—"

"Then you can eat with me. I loathe eating alone and this is Mrs. Curtis's night off. Besides, I haven't heard that fresh-off-the-boat accent from anyone in a very long time. You're making me homesick, girl." They were walking across the church yard, toward the rectory, when he spoke again. "I don't believe I caught your name?" he prompted.

"Oh, I'm sorry, Father. I'm Magheen Fitzger—I mean

Calcord." An embarrassed laugh followed. "The name is still so new to me that I've not acquired the habit of using it yet when I introduce myself."

"I imagine that's something that takes getting used to," he responded, holding the door to his home open for her. "My name is Father Kevin O'Gorman. Your name was Fitzgerald before?" At her nod, he continued, "There's a priest by that name in Leadville. Any relation?"

"He's my brother. He's why I came to America. Oh, I mean he is, but there are other reasons too. Only those other reasons keep getting lost somewhere along the way."

"Is that why you're here, for those other reasons?"

"No, well, not exactly. I'm here because my marriage is in such horrid trouble, and I don't know where to turn . . . and I can't ask Paddie. Well, if you know him, you know what a temper he has, and he won't be happy with me, or with Daniel for that matter! I wasn't sure what to do, so I thought that if I came to Denver I might find another priest, someone who could advise me."

"Ah, you've found the perfect man. And my first bit of advice is to sit down while I fetch the kettle. Mrs. Curtis always leaves a pot of my favorite, chicken and dumplings, on the stove on Wednesdays."

"I can't let you serve me! I'll get the kettle," she insisted.

"No, you pour the milk. The glasses are in that cupboard over the sink. Yes, right there."

"Father, that was delicious," Maggie said, sitting back in her chair and smiling for the first time since he had met her. "I didn't realize how hungry I was."

"You've been traveling since yesterday?"

"Yes," she sighed. "The modern conveniences, such as the Concord coach and its springs, are supposed to be wonderful, but I disliked every moment of the journey. I don't like being jostled around and into other people, or bouncing at every rut in a dusty road."

"But surely the journey to America was much worse?"

"It was longer and much more frightening," she acceded

as her mind wandered back in time. "Weeks of traveling on water, followed by the uncertainty of Ellis Island and wondering whether they'd even let me in the country. New York was noisy and crowded, and, Father, the Irish I saw there, some of whom I knew in the old country, seemed to fare little better there than they had in Ireland."

"At least they have hope here. They can work for a better future and maybe find it. But why, after all you've been through to find your brother, did you leave Leadville, Magheen Calcord? What happened to frighten you away from your home?" he asked finally, his eyes resting sympathetically on her.

She began to gradually tell him. As the time passed, she realized she hadn't looked at every facet of her life and how they tied together in a long time. The words flowed and she told him everything. All about her brothers, the Fenians, and her brother, the priest, from whose letters she got the first germ of the silly notion that there might be a fortune waiting for her in Leadville, all about Daniel and the cabin and his mine and his mother and his propensity for visiting Darling Lil's. She even told him of the never-met Kate Nelligan. Father O'Gorman said nothing. Yet. So, very quietly she told him of her greatest fear, the child and how Daniel would receive him, her half-Irish brat.

A couple of things were quickly obvious to Father O'Gorman, the first was that she spoke the truth, even when it was not to her credit. The other was more intuition, but Father O'Gorman did not think a man of whom she spoke so highly could help but love her in return.

"I can't explain for your husband, Mrs. Calcord. He may have a perfectly good reason for being in Lil Amundson's house, especially in the middle of the afternoon," the priest added the last words softly. "He's the one who needs to do the talking and quite a bit of explaining.

"He shouldn't have left you to cope with his mother, not alone. But I don't believe he's a mama's boy, to be clinging to her apron strings, not when he's accomplished so much in his life, not when he's built such a good life on his own. I do think he was angry at the time and needed to get over that anger. You should not have run away; he's probably worried sick right now.

"And you should know that there are many such possessive mothers in the world. You haven't been given the only one. Be thankful she lives in New York, and you don't have to see much of her."

"But Daniel may be moving back there with her," Maggie protested.

"That's only in your mind. He never actually said so, did he? He doesn't sound like a man who would throw away everything he values in the world at her beck and call. And, I suggest, when you get home and your husband talks, you do some listening. And then you need to do some talking, and he the listening. It seems to me neither of you knows a whole lot about the other. You admit your Daniel doesn't even know of your brothers in Australia, and he should. They are his brothers as well now, Maggie.

"And as for this child you're carrying, you've taken something he said months ago, in anger, and let it keep you from telling him about his own child. Now, was that fair of you? You haven't given the poor man a chance. You ran away when things got too rough instead of relying on the man you married to stand by you.

"I don't think you know your Daniel very well, but he doesn't sound to me like the kind of man who would marry you while he despised the very thing that makes you yourself, your Irish heritage."

Maggie's expression grew hopeful. "You don't think he meant what he said?"

"I do not. I don't think he would have married you if he thought he'd despise the child you would bear him. But I do think the both of you are guilty of neither explaining nor listening to the other.

"So your penance, my child, after six rosaries in which you will beseech the blessed Virgin to help you find more patience and understanding, thereby emulating her, is to go home to Leadville and tell your husband everything

338

you have told me. And then listen to what he has to say in return. I have a feeling you're both in for some surprises.

"The stage leaves at six in the morning. Can you be on it?"

Maggie nodded, her eyes dry for the first time since they began speaking.

"Good." Father O'Gorman smiled. "And tell your brother I look forward to seeing him in the spring at the bishop's conference." Leaning forward in his chair, he clasped her hand. "And give Daniel my thanks for his generous contribution to the children's fund."

"You know Daniel?" Maggie gasped.

"Everyone in Denver knows your husband, Mrs. Calcord. That's why I'm so sure he wouldn't have married you if he didn't love you very much. There's few women in this town who don't envy you. Go home and make him happy."

The Denver City Railway closed its lines at dark, so Father O'Gorman walked Maggie to her hotel and saw her inside. At four A.M. the next morning, she rose and readied herself for the return trip. Tomorrow evening she would be back in Leadville, she thought excitedly, with Daniel. And they would talk, and she would tell him about her brothers. Just that would make her feel better. Of course, so would learning about his visit to Lil Amundson's, if it was an innocent visit.

To the west of the main lobby was the dining room. Maggie sat by the window and ate a breakfast of oatmeal and toast. She was early and could take her ease, making these early morning hours probably the only pleasant time for the next day and a half. From the window she could see the northern portion of Larimer Street and its array of fine department stores. The Tabor Opera House of Denver could barely be seen in the distance, at the corner of Curtis and Sixteenth, but its stately architecture was easily recognizable, even from here. Across the street was the depot where she would catch her stagecoach in a few minutes, and next to it were the stables and smithy that served the stage lines as well as the general public.

As she nibbled on her toast, quietly watching the early morning rising of the town, a wagon came out of the stables and turned onto the street, rattling past her window. Three people rode on the wooden buckboard seat and one rode in the back. Maggie blinked twice, thinking she must be imagining things. Bill Lovell, Jeremiah and Gertie Duggen, and Walter McClean had little in common. But she wasn't imagining that they were in the same wagon, heading out of town.

A little while later when she was waiting to board the coach, she was to think it even more unusual when she recognized Spade McInery, the miner who had caused such a ruckus at her wedding reception, as one of the passengers on the stage line. He seemed not to recognize her and climbed on top to ride with the luggage. Maggie was content to crawl inside and sink against the leather cushions of the coach for protection.

More men climbed aboard, a conglomeration that reminded her of her first stagecoach travel and its dangerous end. She spoke the truth to Father O'Gorman last night; she hated traveling by coach, and recalling that other trip was giving her a queasy sensation.

The driver called out, his hands snapping the reins, and the wheels began turning. At least she hadn't conjured Tom Cooper up from somewhere in the recesses of her mind, she thought. Maggie turned her eyes to the side of the coach and allowed herself to be lulled into a half-sleeping trance.

The difference in the air became noticeable the moment the stage began its climb up the front range of the Rocky Mountains. They had been out of Golden for a few hours now and were headed into the Clear Creek district, turning north at Fork's Creek. Here, they ate a late lunch, and the driver let off passengers whose destinations ranged from Idaho Springs to Georgetown, Lawson, Dumont, Empire, and all the small mining sites in between. Anyone headed for Nevadaville, Black Hawk, or Argo remained on the stage for another hour or until Central

City was reached. Once there, Maggie climbed from the stage, aching in every bone in her body. When she reached Leadville, she swore to never get aboard a stagecoach again.

The same crooked hotel of two nights ago perched on the side of the mountain, awaiting her arrival. Wearily, Maggie made her way up the steps and into the room assigned to her for the night. Dinner was forgotten as she undressed and tumbled into bed, her whole body aching from the hours on the stage.

"Damn blast that woman!" Daniel roared.

"Which one?" Harvey inquired pleasantly. "Your mother or your wife?"

Daniel glared angrily around the drawing room, encompassing Maude, Harvey, and Paddie with that one angry look and stomped off into the dining room where he poured himself a healthy glass of whiskey. Neat. And swallowed it in one downing. Then he returned to the drawing room and glared and spit nastily, "My mother doesn't even enter into this."

And she didn't. She had tried for the past two days to see him, and finally, this morning, he had agreed. She was all apologies and tears, but Daniel was adamant. It was time for her to return to New York. If and when Daniel wanted to see her again, he would make the first move. The way he felt right now, he never wanted to see her again. As far as he knew she was taking the stage out of here tomorrow.

"She must enter into it somehow," Paddie protested. "She's the reason my sister's gone."

"Your sister! Your sister's a damn coward, that's what!" Daniel roared.

"Forgive me for interrupting," Maude said sweetly, "but I heard the argument you two had, and I don't blame her for running away. Though, I admit, in her place I would have beaned you with my cast-iron skillet first!"

"Thank you, Mrs. Sawyer," Daniel growled, mocking a

bow in her general direction. "Just what we need at this moment. A calm, cool head of reason."

Harvey shook his head impatiently. "Okay, so we know she's not in Leadville."

"We don't know that for sure," Daniel gritted.

"She's not here, not at the rectory, not at the Howards', nor with Tom and Carrie Fuller. No hotel in town has her registered. Where the hell else do you propose looking?" Harvey questioned hotly, proving even he could turn on Daniel.

At that moment a knock sounded on the front door, and Daniel bit back the angry words he had planned to level Harvey with. "Get the door, will you, Maude?"

"What's the matter? Forgot how to ask decently? A woman would think *we'd* chased that girl off the way you're behaving!" She was turning away as she finished her blunt speech, "And I was there, I know what awful things you said to her, Daniel Calcord. Seems to me you were just asking her to retaliate somehow."

"Retaliate? Is that what she's doing?" he roared, following in the housekeeper's generous wake. "Never mind, I'll get my own door! And when I get my hands on her, I'll show her retaliation!"

With that he swung open the door and glared at the newcomer. Instantly his face flooded with hope, and he held the door to a welcoming width. "Come on in, Sheriff! Have you heard anything? Do you know where she is?"

Sheriff Nott removed his hat and nodded at Maude. Stomping his boots on the porch to clear them of snow, he entered the foyer slowly. Harvey and Paddie hurried to the door as soon as they heard who was there.

The sheriff was a big man with a mouth full of chewing tobacco, a man who didn't believe in wasting time. "She paid for a stagecoach ticket to Denver. Whether or not she was on the stage nobody recalls, and the driver is still on his return trip. Won't be back until tomorrow night."

"She bought a one-way ticket to Denver?" Daniel asked uncertainly. "Are you sure it wasn't two-way?"

The sheriff nodded. "One-way. It seems she doesn't intend to come back. *If* she is on the stage. Like I said, nobody recalls her getting on."

Daniel's mouth was drawn in a thin line. "Oh, she got on, all right. I should have known that's what that stubborn woman would do." With a nod to the sheriff and a briefly uttered "Thank you," he turned and crossed to the stairs, taking them two at a time. A moment later he returned, a pack in his hand, and reached into the hall wardrobe for his outer garments.

"I'm going with you," Paddie said, buttoning his own coat.

"I don't need you. I can fetch her myself."

"I don't care whether you need me or not, *she* might."

"Just don't slow me down, preacher. I'm not waiting for you."

The morning was unbearably early and she ached so horribly that she drank hot coffee, thinking it might do something for her as Daniel claimed it did for him. All it did to Maggie was make her queasy, and she quickly pushed the cup away from her. Tea and toast settled her stomach somewhat. All she could think of was that she only needed to get through a few more hours on the stage and she would be home.

Her satchel was tossed on top of the coach with the other luggage and tied in place. One of her fellow passengers offered his assistance in climbing aboard, which Maggie gratefully accepted. She was one of the last on and had to sit between two men, one of whom smelled as though he'd just come straight from a mine. The other man wore a natty charcoal-gray suit and bowler hat, which he removed as he greeted her. Maggie smiled at him as she took her seat. She lifted her eyes to the man across from her and found Spade McInery studying her curiously. It was just a matter of time before he remembered, she knew.

"Mr. McInery, my name is Magheen Calcord. We met

in Leadville, remember?"

"Ah!" The grizzled old face lit up at the name. "Dan'el's wife! Now I recall!" He glanced curiously around the coach and then asked, "but where is he?"

"Daniel's in Leadville. I had to go to Denver—"

"Dan'el let his wife travel alone? That don't sound like Dan'el to me!"

Of course it didn't, but Daniel hadn't had a thing to say about her traveling plans. And she wasn't about to tell every passenger on this coach that she had foolishly left her husband and was right now regretting her action bitterly. So she said nothing.

The coach went into motion abruptly, and Maggie was thrown back against the seat, her delicate nose getting a good whiff of the miner next to her.

Just a few more unbearable hours, she thought, clutching her hankie to her nose, and trying desperately to find less offensive air to breathe.

The day lengthened, and the coach slowed its pace, for it was laboriously crawling higher in the Rockies. By midmorning they turned south, heading deep into the mining districts of Colorado. The man with the offensive smell left the coach early in the ten-mile district, just a few miles past Wheeler.

Most of the other men spoke of their destinations, and names such as Recen, Kokomo, Carbonateville, and Robinson were mentioned. Maggie said to Mr. McInery, "And where will you be getting off, sir?"

"Ah . . . Kokomo's fine by me, ma'am."

"I wish I were getting off that soon. Leadville seems so far away."

The men bound for Recen descended to the road, and the coach rolled again. "Kokomo's just a couple of miles ahead, ma'am," McInery said.

"It's been a pleasure to have seen you—"

"Robbers!" came the sudden cry from the front of the coach. The driver whipped the reins so hard the passengers inside could hear the sound of them beating against the six horses. Maggie clung to the man next to her for dear life as the coach picked up speed and she and the other passengers were tossed about like billiard balls inside. The road was rough and rocky. Every time a wheel rolled, the wood seemed to creak a heavy protest against such abuse.

A shot rang out and a warning was bellowed, "Stop or we'll shoot to kill!"

The reins were momentarily stilled as the driver seemed to consider this. Almost imperceptibly the coach slowed. The driver issued a curt "whoa," and the coach slowed to a standstill. Maggie found herself sitting on top of the man with the gray suit, and he was clutching the handclasp with all his strength. Awkwardly, she climbed from his lap and sat beside him, straightening her straw hat. Amazingly she hadn't lost it on the ride. Maggie leaned forward and could barely make out three men on horseback through the window, their faces covered by hoods.

"All right, get out. All of you," one of the men ordered.

The voice was vaguely familiar, Maggie thought, searching her mind for the answer. The men descended before she did, and when Spade McInery's feet hit the earth, she heard that familiar voice say, "You, McInery. Get over here."

That was when she recognized the voice. Awkwardly, she stumbled down the step and would have fallen if Spade hadn't caught her.

"Dammit!" one of the robbers bellowed, and Maggie tried to avert her head, as though that would keep Jeremiah Duggen and the other men from recognizing her. But she recognized all three of them now. Duggen, Bill Lovell, and Walter McClean, the men she had seen yesterday in Denver. The only person missing was Gertie. She could feel Duggen's eyes burning into her, but by no means was she willing to admit she recognized them.

"The rest of you, get back inside," growled McClean. "No, not you," he said to Maggie when she would have joined the others. They did as he ordered, and McClean motioned to the driver to be on his way. When the driver hesitated, McClean raised his pistol and shot it in the air,

345

just to frighten the horses and get them moving.

McInery said, "What do you want with me and the girl?

"All we want is that little piece of paper you went to Denver to get."

"How'd you know about that?" McInery demanded.

"We followed you. Just 'cause you didn't get your assay tests done in Leadville doesn't mean we don't know what's going on."

"Claim jumping, heh? Not my claim, you don't! I stashed that document afore I ever climbed aboard this stage! There's no way you're gonna find out where my mine is!"

"Course there's a way, Spade," said Lovell gloatingly. "You'll tell us. Now, come on, before we start shooting."

"I ain't telling you nothing. You're no more'n a bunch of thieves!"

"Course you will, or we'll start by shooting that pretty little thing behind you. You can look up now, Mrs. Calcord. I know you recognized us."

Maggie lifted her gaze then and faced the trio defiantly. "Daniel will—"

"Daniel ain't here," McClean finished for her. "And we are. You better think on that one, Mrs. Calcord." He raised his pistol and aimed it between her eyes. "Now, McInery, where's your claim?"

"I ain't—"

McClean pulled back the hammer of his pistol and sighted along the gun. "Now, McInery," he threatened in a low voice.

Maggie closed her eyes, and her lips mumbled a series of soft prayers.

"It's on Kokomo Gulch," McInery answered reluctantly.

"Where on the Gulch?"

"About three-quarters of the way up," he said, his shoulders drooping in defeat. "You won't find it without me. I made sure I left no markings. I've known for weeks that Lovell was watching me. I took care."

"Yes, I suppose it's best that you lead the way," Mc-

Clean said after careful consideration. Then he smiled grimly, "but we don't need the girl."

Maggie's heart stopped beating for that instant as she waited for the retort of his gun. Instead she heard Bill Lovell snap angrily, "I didn't plan on getting involved with no murder," and he swept McClean's gun from his hand. "We'll take the girl with us, and when we find the mine we'll get our money. Then we can clear out, and no one will ever find us. But I don't hold with murder, no matter what."

"You know what Forbes said—" McClean protested.

"I heard him," Lovell replied. "But I don't see him here doing the deed. Did it ever occur to you that all we're getting for this is money, not his lifelong protection? If we get caught, we go to jail for stealing. If we kill the girl, we hang. And don't tell me Forbes will hang with us. Hell, he'll be the one handing down the sentence!"

"I don't want to be involved in murder either," Duggen said. "I'm with Bill, all we need is the mine. Let Forbes take care of the legalities on how to own it. There's no way I'm killing for him."

McClean thought it over for a moment, then said, "Okay. You take McInery, and I'll take the girl on my horse with me."

"I'll take her," Lovell protested.

"Hell, man! I let her live, didn't I? I said I'll take her with me, and that's what I intend to do!"

"She left Denver three days ago?" Daniel demanded abruptly. He and Paddie had traced her as far as Father Kevin O'Gorman's.

"I walked her back to the hotel myself," the priest affirmed. "I know she had to get on that stage the next morning. She vowed she would."

"Dammit!" Daniel cursed, his hands going to his head. "That means she should have been home the day before yesterday, when we left. But she hadn't made it."

"The stage wasn't in, Daniel. She probably arrived after

347

we left and is now comfortably ensconced at home. Where we'd be if we had a lick of sense," Father Patrick said.

"I don't know," Daniel said, his brow furrowing. "Something doesn't feel right about this."

"Nothing feels right after eighteen hours in the saddle. Let's go find a room and get some sleep. By morning we'll be able to make a whole lot more sense out of this mess," Father Patrick finished.

"You're probably right," Daniel mused.

"You don't need a room. I've got two beds in the spare room. You can bed down there. Go on and get washed up for dinner. Mrs. Curtis would be insulted if I let two friends go away before sharing a meal," Father O'Gorman invited.

"If you're sure we'll not be in the way," Paddie questioned. "I'm not certain I can make it around the block the way I feel right now."

"Of course I'm sure. Now, go on, the both of you. I'll tell Mrs. Curtis to set two more places."

They were crawling into the narrow beds which sat side by side in the extra room in the rectory when Daniel spoke to Paddie. "Just in case, I think we ought to ride home by the same route the stage took. We can ask after Maggie and the stage as we travel."

"Seems like a waste of time to me. I think it's obvious she's in Leadville by now. But if it's that important to you, I'll agree."

"You were right," McClean quipped. "We'd have never found this place on our own. You hid your tracks neatly, Spade. Matter of fact, we'd probably never have guessed you'd struck the vein if you hadn't acted so funny over that pyrite. That was the first time any of us had any suspicion. And as long as Forbes was willing to pay us to tail you, well, we were mighty happy to find a way to relieve the gent of some of his money."

"Judge Forbes is behind this?" McInery demanded.

"Don't say anything—" Lovell began.

"It won't matter. The judge will make sure everything's tied up nice and legal-like. Gertie, you go on back to Leadville and tell him what we've found."

"I ain't leaving my husband with that woman!" she snarled, her eyes on Magheen.

Maggie was tied with her back against one of the support posts of Spade's cabin. He was on the other side of the post with her. They had spent an uncomfortable night, tied like that, after a ride up the canyon that had taken until well after dark. Locating the cabin in the dark had been something only Spade could have done. This morning he had pointed out the vein.

As Gertie's eyes glared accusingly, Maggie scooted nearer to the post and Spade.

"You ain't leaving your husband with anyone. You ain't got no choice. Go on, get outta here. Now," Jeremiah ordered threateningly. "I don't need no woman telling me what to do!"

Gertie's face fell. "But—but Jeremiah—"

"Get out of here before I lose my temper, woman!"

When she was gone, McInery spoke again. "When it's learned the judge owns my claim, everyone will know who's responsible for this."

"Don't be stupid, McInery," Walt McClean gloated. "Like I said, no one's gonna be in trouble. Everything's gonna be done all nice and legal-like. You're just gonna be inconvenienced a little."

"How do you plan to steal a man's claim and make it legal? Stealing's stealing, that's what!"

McClean leaned forward over his knee and smirked in McInery's face. "All the judge has to do is go to the County Courthouse and file an injunction against you to keep you from operating. He'll claim he owns the extra-lateral rights to your mine, just like he did to John Jacques' mine. By the time we let you go, he'll have filed a legal claim to the surface rights, and the courts will have to stop you from operating. All he has to do is claim that the apex of the vein rests higher up than your rights go; the courts will do the rest."

349

"That'll be a damned lie!"

McClean's smirk was even broader. "Who do you think they'll believe, you or the judge and his hired experts?"

McInery's face tightened. "If I have to, I'll get my claim back with a gun!" he threatened.

McClean laughed. "Go ahead. The judge will like that. Then all he has to do is have you killed, in self-defense of course, and he'll get the mine without any of the legal hassles. That's right, McInery, go right on ahead."

McInery's face was flushed, and he pulled angrily on his bonds. "You'd better watch yourself, McClean. You and Lovell and Duggen! I'll get the three of you if it takes me the rest of my life!"

McClean turned to the others. "Now, aren't you sorry you stopped me from killing him?"

"Stop baiting the man, Walt," Lovell ordered. "You're not helping matters. Why do you think he even needs to know what the judge plans?"

" 'Cause I want him to know we're all laughing at him!"

Maggie cringed, trying to make herself invisible. She already knew Walter McClean was a sadistic brute. Her arms and ribs still hurt where he had held her yesterday during the ride up the Kokomo Gulch. She only hoped she would get out of this alive. Her being involved would only be a hindrance to them. After all, she could give credence to Spade's story, and hers would be the only credence.

"When do we let 'em go?" Duggen asked.

"When Gertie gets back and tells us the judge says to, not one moment before," McClean said, smirking. "That's when we know for sure he's got the plan rolling and we'll get our money. We've got to keep 'em here until we see our money," he baited softly, his eyes on Maggie. "And if we don't get our money, we'll have to take our fee out in trade. Won't you like that, darling?"

"Leave her alone, Walt," Lovell snapped impatiently.

"Ah, com' on, Bill, I know you're sweet on her. Hell, we're all sweet on her, except maybe Gertie, and she'd like to push her eyes outta her head. But maybe," he sidled closer to Maggie, his eyes leering on her lips and bosom, "you'll be nice to us before she gets back? You might even like it," he cajoled.

"I said leave her alone," Lovell shouted, the barrel of his gun pressing against McClean's neck. "She's not for the likes of you. She's a married woman!"

"Hell, Bill, married women like it too! Just ask her! Look at that face! Bill, I swear she likes it well enough when Calcord does it to her!"

"I mean it!" Lovell roared, pushing the gun so it held Walt's face at an angle. "Leave her alone!"

"Okay," Walt muttered. The gun gradually lowered, but Lovell kept a close watch on him through the rest of the evening and the night.

In Recen, Daniel and Paddie pulled their horses up in front of the hotel, dismounted, and tied them to the hitching post. "I'll look in here and the stables. You check with the sheriff."

"Daniel," Father Patrick said impatiently. He'd been gone from his parish long enough and was anxious to get back. All Daniel's worrying seemed to be wasting time rather than being careful. "We know she was in Central City three nights ago. She's back in Leadville right now. If we hurry, we can be there by nightfall."

"Paddie, I know you think I'm being an old woman but—"

"Daniel! Daniel Calcord!" bellowed a voice from across the street. Daniel stopped in mid speech and turned, following the sound until he spied the heavyset man hurrying toward them.

"Dick! What are you doing here?"

Dick Fell practically ran across the dirt road, his hand smoothing out his hair. Abruptly he stopped in front of them and gasped heavily until he caught his breath. "I . . l saw Gertie Duggen . . . in Leadville," he spoke laboriously. "She was acting kinda strange, so I thought I ought to follow her and see what she was up to. If I'd a'known you was after her, I wouldn't a'bothered," he replied, still gasping heavily.

"We're not after her. We've been to Denver and are just now on our way back to Leadville," Daniel retorted.

"You mean you ain't here 'cause she is?"

"No, I didn't even know she was here."

Dick's face screwed up in puzzlement. "Hell, Daniel, I swear something mighty strange is going on. What, I'm not sure. But Gertie came back to Leadville after she and Jeremiah had been gone for weeks. Only when she came back, she was alone. And she went looking for Judge Forbes. I followed them to the courthouse, listened while they got . . . what do you call those legal pieces of paper that keep a miner from operating?"

"An injunction?"

"That's it! An injunction . . . against Spade McInery. Then they left town, the judge and Gertie Duggen. I thought they was behaving mighty peculiarly, and, as I've nothing better to do now, me not having a job and all, I thought I'd tail 'em. So I followed 'em here. They're in the hotel now.

"Something else pretty strange about this. Seems ol' Spade got himself kidnapped from the stage line three days ago. The same day as he was getting back from Denver after registering his claim."

Daniel looked at Paddie. "The same day Maggie was due back."

"Yeah," Patrick responded, all attention now. "Seems like the judge is up to no good."

"Mrs. Calcord was on that stage?"

Daniel nodded.

"Daniel," Dick Fell's voice lowered to a whisper, "when Spade was kidnapped, they took a woman too. I just come from the sheriff's, and he told me so. I never bothered to ask the woman's name. I never thought there'd be a connection."

Daniel's mouth tightened and he glanced around. "Let's get out of the middle of the street. If Gertie and the judge come out, I don't want them to see us."

Quickly they crossed the street and entered the High Country Saloon, they managed to sit beneath the broad front window. From here where they could see the front of the hotel and anyone entering or exiting.

Daniel finally spoke. "Dammit, it's got to be Magheen."

"Maybe not."

Daniel glared at his brother-in-law. "Are you willing to take the chance?"

"No," Paddie replied emphatically. "I'm not. And for that reason, I'll go ask the sheriff about the kidnapped woman. You two can wait and watch."

Moments later Paddie returned. "It was Magheen, all right, using the name Magheen Fitzgerald."

"She didn't even use her married name to buy the ticket?" an incredulous Daniel roared.

"She was angry," Paddie snapped. "Of all the crazy things to worry about! I'm sure she didn't mean anything by it."

"And I'm sure she did," Daniel answered gruffly. "But I'll settle that later. And with her. First, we've got to find her. They've had her three days?"

"Yep," Dick affirmed. "Took 'em about two o'clock in the afternoon on Tuesday."

Daniel rubbed his neck and spoke in an absent manner. "Spade went to Denver to file on his claim. He was kidnapped, along with Maggie, on his way back to the Canyon. Meanwhile, Forbes filed an injunction against McInery, though no one was even supposed to know about the claim yet." He lifted his head and spoke directly at Paddie. "It's too much of a coincidence. There's got to be a tie-in somehow. And Maggie's involved. But how?"

"Well," Dick drawled, "if she recognized the kidnappers, they would have to take her."

"Well, if we're going to find out," Paddie said, rising, "now's our chance. The judge and Gertie are just leaving the hotel."

Chapter Nineteen

"Dammit! You're nothing but a bunch of incompetent asses!" snarled Judge Forbes. His slender frame was elegantly clad in a black frock coat and pin-striped pants. At the moment, any attractiveness he had was hidden by the ugly anger blotting his face. His mustache bobbed up and down with each movement of his lips.

"What do you mean by bringing that woman here? Don't you know what Daniel Calcord is capable of doing when he finds out who's responsible for his wife being here?"

Only because the words were shouted did they finally penetrate through the hazy fog that shrouded Maggie's mind. Slowly her eyes opened, and, through the thick veil of lashes, she barely made out Judge Forbes across the cabin. Not that it mattered who was here, she no longer cared. Her back and arms ached from the day and night tied to the support post. It wasn't until Bill Lovell began to fear for her life that she was untied and allowed to stretch full length on a makeshift pallet of coarse blankets.

She knew her fever raged still, and that too was part of the reason her body shivered and ached. The cabin was cold, and at night the fire was allowed to run down. The one night Maggie spent tied to the post had been enough to give her the fever and make her throat scratch so badly that she could barely swallow. Even now she was cold. So cold that when the door opened and Jeremiah's wife entered, she shivered weakly and tried to burrow deeper into

354

the blankets. She didn't even care enough to make the effort to identify the new arrival. Her head spun wildly, and the voices became an incessant buzz in her ears. Maggie could find no warmth, and soon the effort of seeking some became too much. Her fingers relaxed their grip on the blanket, and her hand fell to the floor.

"Daniel Calcord won't stop until he's found the men who kidnapped his wife," Judge Forbes continued bitingly. "Why didn't you just let her go on her way? Who the hell told you to kidnap her in the first place?"

"Well, it seemed to make sense at the time," Walt Mc-Clean defended stoutly. "She recognized us, I know she did!"

"So what if she did? You three can light out of town anytime and Calcord won't follow you. Or at least he wouldn't have, not until you took her." His eyes scanned the room quickly and found where Magheen lay half on and half off the blankets. Even from this distance it was easy to see how ill she was. Her face was flushed with fever, and she lay as though her whole body were in pain. "Dammit," Forbes growled, "I don't like killing women, but you've managed to box us in a corner and now we've no choice."

"No!" Lovell snapped, horrified that anyone should think of killing Mrs. Calcord. She had done nothing, she was a nice lady, if a bit too gullible. But when Bill had taken advantage of her, he had never thought of putting her in this kind of danger.

Forbes turned and glared at the man. "You'll do as I say. You've already cost me the mine. Now I'll have to drop the lawsuit if I don't want to be under suspicion in their disappearances. It'd be too coincidental otherwise. And if you think for one moment that we can keep either of them alive, I suggest you think about facing Calcord. Alone." Shaking his head firmly, he finished his thought. "No, we've got to kill them both now. We can't leave any witnesses to tell about this. Calcord can't know what happened to her. As a matter of fact, it'd be best if the bodies were never found."

"So how do you propose we do it?" McClean questioned.

"A quick bullet to their heads," Forbes answered.

A bound and gagged Spade McInery protested loudly on hearing this. His booted feet violently banged against the wooden floor, and the weight of his body thumped the chair across the room. Above his gag, his eyes were wild as they glared accusingly at his captors.

"I done a lot of things I ain't proud of, but I never murdered nobody," Lovell stated bluntly. "I ain't planning on starting now."

"Jeremiah will pull the trigger."

"No!" shouted Gertie. Duggen's head came up at Forbes's words, and his eyes met his wife's as she made the protest. "You ain't leaving him holding the bag. Jeremiah's no murderer any more 'n Bill. One of you two will have to do it."

Forbes ran the tip of his tongue across dry lips. His hand rifled idly through the graying hair as he considered a moment. Turning to McClean, he spoke softly. "It's worth an additional thousand dollars if you'll do the deed."

McClean's brows shot up. "You got the cash on you?"

Forbes gave an exasperated grimace. "Who the devil keeps that kind of money on them? I'll have to go to town to get it."

"Then I'll wait to kill them until I get the money. It's not that I don't trust you, Judge; it's just that I've learned to be careful over the years."

"Why, you—" Judge Forbes didn't finish the thought. If he didn't want their blood on his hands, he had to make sure that McClean did the deed. He truly believed that as long as he didn't pull the trigger, he would still be an innocent man. "It'll have to be in the morning then. By the time I ride into town, the banks will all be closed."

McClean gave a brief nod. "Morning it is then."

Daniel's fingers tightened around the butt handle of his revolver at McClean's carelessly spoken words. He, Paddie, and Dick Fell waited just outside the cabin, beneath one of the poorly covered windows and could hear everything the men and Gertie discussed. He had looked inside once and found Maggie lying on the floor and knew something was terribly wrong. He had to do something and soon. But after listening to the men talk, he wasn't sure she would survive if he took the time to go back to town and fetch the sheriff.

He and the other men had followed Gertie and the judge up Kokomo Gulch since early afternoon. Until they had the cabin in sight, Daniel was wondering if this wasn't a wild-goose chase. They gave the judge time to get inside and settled before they crept to the window to see what was going on. The first thing Daniel had seen was Maggie. And it had been all he could do not to go roaring inside and try to get her. But whatever he, Paddie, and Dick did, they had to be sure of winning this battle. If he lost, it was Maggie's life he would lose.

"Paddie," he whispered tautly. "You get back in the trees and pick a good, tall one and climb it. You need to be able to see all around the cabin for this. There's only this one door, but a window on either side. I'm going to pull a little surprise on the judge and his friends, and I need someone good with a rifle to watch them as they come out."

"I'm going in with you. That's my sister they're talking of murdering."

"I need a man who's got good aim. I've seen you shoot and I've seen Dick shoot. Believe me, you're the only one for the job. Here, take my Winchester. You may need it. Do you think you could kill a man if you have to?"

Paddie nodded. "If I have to. But I think I can keep them in line just by maiming them."

"Just don't let any of them get away. They'll pay if they've hurt Maggie. Now, go pick your spot." Paddie hurried off and was gone from sight before Daniel turned to Dick. "I need you to go to the corral and get the animals worried. Stir them up real good. I want them damn near stampeding."

"What are you gonna do?"

"When they come looking for whatever's bothering the animals, I'll slip inside and get Maggie. You watch out for yourself, but Paddie's a good shot. He'll protect you."

"Seems to me you've got the dangerous job. How do you know they'll all come out after I stir up the horses?"

"If they don't, that's their problem. I'll shoot to kill."

Daniel waited a few moments until he lost Dick from sight. Paddie was long gone, and Daniel could only hope he had picked a prime spot. Dark was settling in and little could be seen that wasn't included in the circle of gaslight coming from inside the cabin. Crouching low, he scurried around to the side of the building and waited until Dick acted.

It took only moments for the neighing of the animals to penetrate the darkness. Daniel could hear chairs being scooted across the floor inside the cabin as the men rose and went to the windows to see what was happening. "I can't see a damn thing," Daniel heard McClean say. "But something's gotta be out there spooking the horses."

"Maybe it's an animal," Jeremiah suggested.

"Unless you were followed," McClean said to Forbes. "Could someone have been on your tail?"

"Nah. Why should anyone be interested in the two of us? I don't know a soul in Kokomo."

"You might not, but there's lots of people who know you that you wouldn't know. Get your gun, Jeremiah. We'll check out the horses. Can you watch 'em?" he asked, his head gesturing toward the prisoners.

"What's to watch? They're tied up, aren't they?"

"For a supposedly smart man, Forbes, you sure are stupid sometimes. Bill, you watch 'em."

Duggen and Walt McClean left the cabin. Daniel was rapidly forming plans in his head. If he just went in, he would be against Lovell, Forbes, and Gertie, and they all had guns. If he waited too long, the others might come back, unless Paddie stopped them. And then the ones inside the cabin would be warned. Maggie might be in more danger then.

Moving to the front of the cabin, he crouched low, intending to ram the door and go in shooting. Suddenly, an explosion rent the night sky, lighting it and the mountain it silhouetted into a huge panorama of bright bursts. The earth rocked beneath his feet, and Daniel scrambled to the dirt, just as huge clumps of earth, trees, and rocks fell from the sky and into the clearing of the cabin. He heard cursing from within and barely crawled out of the light before the door opened and Bill and Forbes came out. They ran toward the corral and headed for the mountain, which was where the explosion had seemed to originate.

So Gertie was alone. Daniel rocked to his heels and peered through the window. She waited in the wake of the open door, watching the men as they ran off. With one purposeful stride, he was at the door, smacking it hard and letting it knock Gertie off her feet and against the far wall. Propelling himself inside, he held his gun high and aimed right where he thought she should be. She was. Only Gertie didn't move a muscle. The force of the blow seemed to have knocked her cold.

Daniel took her in with one quick glance, then turned his attention to where Maggie lay so still. Kneeling beside her, he roamed his hands over her, but all he learned was that she was burning with fever. Before he could give her his full attention, he needed to make sure Forbes and the other men were taken care of. Either one, the fever or the men, was capable of killing her.

Spade McInery jerked in the chair, the words he spoke muffled by the gag tied securely around him. Daniel had his hands free in moments and, between the two of them working frantically, his feet and mouth were freed seconds later.

The old miner stretched fingers and legs painfully. "Got an extra gun?"

"Yeah, here," Daniel answered, tugging the extra one he carried from his waistband and handing it to Spade.

"Lord, Daniel, but it's good to see you!"

Daniel nodded absently. "How long has she been like

this?"

"This is the second day now. The damn bastards left her tied to the post overnight, no blanket, no heat, no nothing. She ain't used to such, you can tell. She's a lady. I tried to tell 'em so, but that Walt McClean, he said he wasn't gonna untie her until she was nice to him. Well, she called him a son of the devil and said she'd die before she was nice to the likes of him. Walt decided to see how far she'd go, so he left her all night like that. I think she'd still be there if Chicken Bill hadn't untied her hisself."

"I'll kill them all," Daniel murmured.

Several shots sounded outside the cabin and Spade hurried to the door, closed it, and pulled the crossbar down.

Daniel had Maggie in his arms and was brushing her hair from her face and neck. "She's so hot. Do you know if there's any water in here?"

"Sure do, Daniel," the old man said, coming to his side and carrying a canteen and a man's handkerchief.

"Keep an eye on Gertie, will you? I'm going to make Maggie more comfortable."

"But what about Forbes and McClean—"

"Dick Fell and Paddie are out there now. They'll not let any of them escape."

Gently he wiped beads of sweat from her forehead and face with the cool water. Her skin was ashen, and her hair had lost its fine sheen. In just these few days she seemed to have lost weight even though she had none to spare. Her head jerked convulsively as the water touched her lips, and Daniel cursed inwardly. The bastards hadn't even had the decency to give her water!

Her tongue snaked out, and Daniel moistened it from the canteen. Slowly he fed her the moisture, but she greedily sought more. "Gently, Maggie," he whispered soothingly into her ear. "You can have all you want, just not all at once."

Her eyes fluttered open at the sound of his voice. He knew she couldn't focus on him, not the way her eyes were glazed over with moisture.

Still she said, "Daniel . . . Daniel . . ."

"I'm here, Maggie. You're safe with me, sweet. Shh, don't thrash so. You're very ill."

Her fingers gripped his shirt tightly, and her eyes opened wide in an attempt to see him better. "My baby, Daniel. I don't want to lose my baby," she cried softly.

Daniel held very still, his fingers seeking hers. "Maggie . . . Maggie, you're expecting a baby?"

"Don't be angry," she whimpered. "I know you don't want . . . want my child . . ."

"How could you be so stupid?" he demanded hotly.

"I'm sorry," she said shuddering. "I knew you wouldn't like my having a child . . . not a half-Irish brat . . ."

The words roared in his ears. He had said them, he knew he had said them. Once. He couldn't remember when, how, or why, but he remembered saying them though. "Maggie, I didn't mean that!"

"Hold me, Daniel. Please."

Bullets whizzed outside. Every once in a while, Spade would send an answer of his own. Twice, someone tried to get back inside the cabin, and when he found the door locked, cursed and hurried off to seek some other shelter.

Daniel cradled Magheen to his chest. Whispering words of love and tenderness, he rocked her until she felt relaxed enough to tumble back into a safer world of sleep. Just being washed and having water made her sleep more restful, less fitful. When he was sure she slept, he set her back down on the blankets and rose to join Spade.

"Have you seen any of them yet?" he asked, settling beneath the window, beside the old man.

"I got a glimpse of Jeremiah now and again, but whoever's up in that tree got 'im afore I could! He only wounded 'em, though. Jeremiah hollered real good and dragged himself against the corral gate. I wanna get a good shot right between the eyes of that McClean. Forbes too, dammit! This were all his idea!"

"We'll get them all," Daniel promised. Glancing back at Maggie once more, he said, "I'm going out there. I want you to keep this door locked until I tell you to open it. And tie Gertie up, will you? The last thing we need is an irate female on our hands."

Dousing the lights first, Daniel gradually pushed the door open and crept out. The cabin door swiftly closed behind him, and as the bar was drawn, he scurried across the yard, keeping to the shadows.

The moon was obscured by thick winter clouds, and little could be discerned through the dimness. Daniel made his way to the corral, led there by the painful noises Jeremiah made, and crept around to the lean-to that doubled as a barn and storage shed. The sounds of a man shuffling around inside the lean-to came to Daniel's ears, and he waited patiently for the man to come out. A moment later, he did so, his arms filled with something Daniel couldn't make out in the dark. Daniel lifted his gun to the back of the man's neck and said softly, "Stop right there."

"Put that gun down, Daniel," Dick Fell hissed. "My arms are full of giant powder, and I sure as hell don't want to drop it!"

"Dynamite?"

"Where the hell do you think that explosion came from? Where'd you get that stuff?"

"Found it in the lean-to. Spade must be using it in the mine." Dick could barely make out Daniel's face, but at the look of surprise that crossed it, Dick couldn't suppress a sheepish grin. "Maybe I can't shoot, but I know my explosives. When they wouldn't come out at the neighing of the horses, I decided to blow up the mountain. And it worked!"

"Sure did. Damned near brought down the cabin as well," Daniel grumbled. "Put that stuff back, will you? It's dangerous during the day, let alone at night when you can't see a finger in front of your face."

"See that timber over there?" Dick questioned with a nod of his head. His gesture made Daniel glance toward the side of the mountain where several timbers formed a rectangle. "It's the shaft house of McInery's mine. Forbes and McClean are holed up there. I thought to blow 'em out."

Daniel was sorely tempted, but his conscience wouldn't let him kill a man in cold blood. "No, that's too much. Even for the likes of them. Where's Bill?"

"He's long gone. That man's got the luck of the Irish, or so to speak. Father Patrick missed with his shot, and Bill grabbed the first horse he could find and took off. He'll be halfway to Durango by morning."

"Damn! I wanted him."

"Well, if I ain't to blow up the mountain, just what do you propose?"

"I propose to let you and Spade wait them out and to let Paddie ride back to town for the sheriff. He can have Gertie, Jeremiah, McClean, and Forbes just as soon as he gets here. I'll worry about Lovell later. Right now I've got to see to Maggie."

"How is she?"

"Sick. In the morning I'm taking her home. She won't get well here."

"I hope she can take the ride back to Leadville."

"It's ten miles. I'll keep her as comfortable as I can. That will have to be enough."

On his way back to the cabin, he motioned Paddie from his post in the tree and gave him the news. "I'll be leaving at first light. Maggie's real sick." His head came up, an expression of pain crossing his face as he gazed on Paddie. "Did you know she was expecting a baby?"

"No! Why didn't you tell me!"

" 'Cause I didn't know until a few minutes ago."

"She didn't tell you? That doesn't sound like Maggie. She'd be pleased as punch to be having a baby. Why would she try to hide it?"

" 'Cause she thinks I don't want it."

Paddie rocked back on his feet, his lips working feverishly. "Then I think you'd better get in there and tell her you do want it! What's the matter, don't the two of you talk about anything important?" he demanded.

"I guess not," Daniel admitted quietly. "Once, in anger, I told her I didn't want a half-Irish brat. I didn't mean it, but I wanted to keep her at arm's length. She was getting under my skin, and I wasn't sure how far I could be trusted. When I said that, she sure kept her distance." His hand rubbed agitatedly across his temples before he spoke again. "Hell, Paddie, she was always so concerned about keeping her job and the money she earned that I never once thought about a baby."

"Did you ever talk about what she needed the money for? You must have noticed she never spent a cent on herself."

"Of course I noticed. She gave most of it away to miners, grubstaking them, she claimed. She wanted to make a fortune."

"Of course she did, you idiot! She needs a bloody fortune. We've three brothers rotting away in Australia, on the penal colony, and she wants to buy their freedom," Paddie said irritably. "I think the two of you should come to me for counseling in marriage. For two people who supposedly love each other, you don't do much talking. You may argue, but apparently not about the important things!"

"There are three more of you?" Daniel asked incredulously.

"Aye, Mr. Calcord. Three more of the Fitzgerald brothers, Rory, Seumas, and Teeling. And they aren't priests. They're Irishmen though, good Irishmen. Fenians through and through. And when they hear that you don't want Maggie's baby—"

Daniel bared his teeth and snarled, "That's my baby too! And don't you—or your brothers—ever forget it!"

Father Patrick's mouth loosened its anger, and his brow lightened perceptibly. "Then I suggest you go tell your wife that. And maybe you ought to tell her a few other things as well. Like you love her. Like you'll love the child, half-Irish or not. And that you'll beat her with a branch if she ever dares to run away again!"

Daniel's nod was firm. "That I'll do!"

By the time he was back in the cabin though, other thoughts were on his mind. Maggie's brow needed soothing, and a drink of cool water was offered to soothe her throat. Spade left, returning moments later, carrying Jeremiah Duggen who had been shot in the leg. "I'll just tie him to the bed so he can't cause any trouble." Gertie was already awake and tied to the post. "I'll be back when we've got McClean and Forbes. Course, cowards that they are, they'll hide in the mine until someone goes in after them."

"Don't you do it. That's what the sheriff and his men are for."

"But I've got a particular stake in settling this. That sorry excuse for a man tried to steal my claim!"

Maggie moaned, and Daniel ceased to care about McInery's mine or Forbes's whereabouts or anything else. Bringing her fever down was the only thing concerning him all night long.

Daylight was breaking when the sheriff arrived. Patrick had the good sense to bring along a doctor who informed Daniel that Maggie had been through the worst of her fever. "Of course I'd prefer it if she didn't have to be moved for a few more days, but I can see that she can't stay here. Wrap her well in blankets, and try not to jostle her too badly. She should be all right for the three or four hours it takes to reach Leadville."

Daniel followed his advice, keeping the horse at a steady, sedate pace. Every so often, they would stop and Daniel would feed her more water. What helped him most, though, was the fact that she was growing more alert, stronger. A couple of times she raised her head and asked him questions about where they were going and how long the ride would take. But for the most part she was content to curl up in his arms, braced against his chest as protection from the movements of the horse, and sleep.

Maude Sawyer saw them coming from the distance. She waited on the porch and ordered Daniel to bring Maggie upstairs immediately.

"I can walk, Daniel."

"No, you cannot," he answered sternly.

The warming pan was removed from the bed while

365

Maggie disrobed to her undergarments. She slid between the sheets, her feet sinking into their deep warmth.

"You need to be washed, child," Mrs. Sawyer reprimanded. "I don't know where you've been, but you haven't been taking care of yourself."

"I was kidnapped, Maude," Maggie responded, her eyes growing big, "by Bill Lovell, Jeremiah Duggen, and Walt McClean. You'll never guess who was behind it!"

"Maggie, don't waste your breath talking. You need some rest," Daniel protested.

Maude's eyes widened and she replied, "Who the devil would kidnap you?"

"Judge Forbes! Would you believe he was claim jumping? He tried to take Spade McInery's mine, just like he took John Jacques' mine."

Daniel hunkered down beside her at her words and demanded, "Forbes was behind that too?"

"Yes! And Daniel, he was the one who tried to form the Elephant Club. He paid Jeremiah to set it up; he even paid Walt McClean to cause those mine explosions, thinking that the miners would be willing to force the union if they thought their lives were in danger. Forbes planned to control the mines through the union, only you and Ed Varley stopped him before his plans got too far along."

"Judge Forbes did all that?" Maude questioned, perplexed. "I always thought he was a straight-shooter. He's such a stickler for the letter of the law!"

"He wasn't last night. Last night he offered Walt McClean a thousand dollars to shoot Maggie and Spade."

Maggie's mouth dropped open. "He did?"

"He did," Daniel replied firmly. "He won't be offering anybody anything for a long time. The sheriff of Kokomo has him now." Turning to Maggie, he spoke harshly, "So next time you think about running away, remember all the trouble you caused this time!"

Maggie's face fell at the censure in his tone. Leaning back against the pillow, she closed her eyes and murmured, "I'll sleep now."

"Look what you did," Maude hissed as they left the room. "She was in good enough spirits until you opened your mouth and did your damnedest to ruin them." Shaking her head, Maude huffily walked away.

Too bad, Daniel thought unrepentently as he entered the guest room and kicked his boots free. She needs some sleep and so do I. A moment later, he was crawling under the blankets and was quickly asleep.

The opening and closing of the front door woke Daniel. From the guest room he could make out the excited male voice and guessed that Harvey had arrived. Daniel made a mental note to tell Harvey to rehire Dick Fell. And give him a big raise.

Cautiously he crossed the hall, opened his bedroom door, and entered. He needed a shave, a bath, and some clean clothing. But first, he had to reassure himself that Magheen was really safe and at home. She still slept, her hair strewn across the pillow, her fingers dangling over the edge of the bed. The few hours of sleep seemed to have done her a world of good. Already there was more color in her cheeks. A few days of Maude's cooking would have her weight right back where it belonged . . . or would it? How much should she weigh now that she was having his baby? He hadn't thought about things like that before.

He would from here on out. Being married to Maggie meant giving her a lot of care and concern.

The day was late and the room was dark. Daniel stumbled to the wardrobe, stubbing his toe on the way. Softly he swore, "Dammit!" but it was loud enough to waken Maggie.

"Daniel?" she said, yawning and stretching at the same time.

"Shh, go back to sleep, Maggie."

"I don't want to go back to sleep. I'm hungry," was her response as she rolled on her side and looked at him. "Why didn't you light the lamp?"

"I don't want to waken you."

"I was already awake," she lied, yawning again, and then smiled.

He had forgotten what her smile was capable of doing to his insides. It had been so long since she had looked at him like that, as though she loved him, that he had to stop what he was doing just to watch her.

"Thank you," she said simply. "Once again you saved my life. That's three times for me and once for my brother. I don't know why you put up with me."

"Don't you, Maggie?"

Pushing with her hand she sat up in bed, her hair swirling about her head and shoulders, the strap of her chemise above the blanket. Calmly, she met his gaze. "No, Daniel, I don't. Please, tell me."

He walked over to the bed and sat beside her. Lifting her hand, he pressed it to his lips and smiled at her. "Because I love you. I love you so much that when you were gone I discovered life isn't worth living without you. You bring sunshine into my day. You make the day brighter, the week brighter, the year brighter."

"What a nice thing to say," she said, smiling again.

"It's how I feel, Maggie."

Sighing, she hung her head. "I'm sorry I left as I did. I know now how wrong I was. But at the time I thought maybe I could find someone . . . someone who could help me decide what to do."

"How could you think I'd be so upset over our baby, Maggie? I've said foolish things in my time, but most of them I didn't mean. Don't you know me better than that?"

Lifting her head, she turned confused eyes on him. "You were angry because I couldn't get along with your mother." He would have interrupted, but her fingers pressed against his lips, silencing him. "Rightfully so. I should have gotten along with her."

"She's gone back to New York, for good."

"I'm sorry. I didn't want to drive her away."

"Maggie, she made herself unwelcome. You're my wife. For some reason, she seemed to think that of no impor-

368

tance."

Maggie sighed. "And then there was the baby. I wasn't sure you wanted one. I've worried about it for so long."

"How long have you known?" At her hesitation, he pressed her fingers tightly. "How long, Maggie?"

"I suspected it since before we were married," she admitted, biting her lips.

"You told me you couldn't possibly be carrying a child then."

"Of course I said that. If I admitted it, you'd have felt obligated to marry me. I didn't want you that way. I wanted you to love me as I loved you."

"Foolish, foolish, Maggie," he groaned, pulling her into his arms. "You refused to marry me. What if I'd taken you at your word? What would you have done?"

"I didn't think that far ahead. It hurt so badly when I saw you in Lil Amundson's . . ." Her voice trailed off as she remembered the last time she had seen him there. Her body grew stiff in his arms.

"What is it now, Maggie?"

"You went to Lil's the day after our argument!"

"I did?" he questioned, searching his mind for remembrance. "Oh, yes, I did. Is that why you left?" At her nod, he continued, "I went to Lil's to get Norm Wheeler's girl. We'd had a fire in the mine that morning, and he was hurt. He kept asking for her. It was the least I could do."

Maggie groaned. "Father O'Gorman said I should have more faith in you. He was right. I am sorry I misjudged you so badly."

"Father O'Gorman, in Denver?"

"Aye. He said we didn't do enough talking. I'm beginning to think he was right."

"Funny. That's what Paddie said to me last night. He accused us of not speaking about the important things. Like ourselves."

Maggie's fingers stopped stroking Daniel's neck. "I'm afraid he's right. There's a whole lot about me I've been keeping from you. I think I should tell you now."

369

"Now? And I thought you were hungry? I'm starved! And since Harvey's already here, I imagine Maude has dinner ready." Rising, he tugged on her hand. "Come on, lazybones, get up and put your clothes on. That baby will starve with you."

"But I wanted to tell you—"

"Anything you have to say can wait until after dinner. I'll fetch some water for the basin, and you can wash first."

"Daniel," she began, but it was too late. He was already gone from the room.

Harvey came out of the kitchen the moment he heard Daniel coming down the stairs. His eyes were gleaming with excitement, and before Daniel's feet touched the bottom step he cried, "We hit it, Daniel! I told you we would! Look at this assay report." Hitting the paper with the palm of his hand, he shouted gleefully, "1,098 ounces of silver per ton! We're rich!"

"Good," Daniel responded briskly, moving into the kitchen.

"What do you mean 'good'? That's about as innocuous as 'it's about time.' Dammit, you act as though you knew this was going to happen all along!"

"If I hadn't believed it was going to happen, I wouldn't have put all my money in that mine," Daniel answered feelingly. "I'm just glad it finally has happened. That's one less thing to worry about." He filled the basin from the water kettle kept warming on the stove. When he turned around, he was smiling broadly. "Guess what? Maggie and I are having a baby!"

"That's wonderful!" Maude said.

"Great," Harvey gritted. "But nowhere near as wonderful as my news."

"That's what you think," Daniel smirked, pushing against the door with his elbow to open it. "But, to my mind, fortunes are made and lost every day, but I'm a first-time father but once in my life." On that he danced away and up the stairs.

"Hell, I've never made a fortune or lost one," Harvey

370

grumbled. His eyes lit up suddenly. "On second thought, this is my first fortune!"

"It's a good thing I'm not of child-bearing years, or I might just give you back your ring, Mr. Benson," were the words Maude chilled him with.

Maggie was out of bed, padding about the room in her chemise and knickers when Daniel returned. "Soap and water," he announced. "No baths for you yet. Not for a day or two."

"I don't know how long I can stand feeling like this. I think that cabin gave me fleas."

Daniel laughed. "It's in your mind, darling." He sat on the bed and watched as she washed and brushed her hair. "Leave it down."

Maggie did as he asked and went to the wardrobe for something to wear to dinner.

"How did you work up the courage to take the stage to Denver?" he questioned curiously. "After your last experience, I would have thought that's the last trip you'd take."

"Oh, Daniel, that was the worst thing! I kept imagining us rolling off the mountain, and all I could do was hang on to the man next to me. Poor thing, he'll be sore for weeks where I grabbed him."

"And where was that?"

"His arm! I think he thought I was hysterical . . . and then Spade and I were kidnapped. How is Mr. McInery?"

"He's fine. When we left him this morning, he was ready to tear Forbes and McClean apart, limb from limb."

"I can't blame him. That poor man was sadly mistreated."

"And you weren't?"

"Oh, they untied me soon enough. But poor Mr. McInery, they kept him tied to that chair after they took him from the post."

"Mr. McInery thinks you saved his life."

Maggie laughed. "No, saving lives, that's your specialty, not mine."

Daniel's brows raised. "Well, he thinks so. And since he does, he's made you a full partner in his mine."

Maggie grew very still as Daniel's words sank in. "Oh, I can't take that. Can I, Daniel?"

"Of course you can."

"But I didn't save his life. You did."

Daniel shrugged his shoulders. "I wouldn't have gone after Forbes if not for you. In that sense, you did save his life."

"Oh." Maggie concentrated hard, counting huge numbers off with her fingers. "Do you think half is worth . . . twenty-four hundred pounds?" she questioned eagerly.

"Hmmm, in dollars that's . . . Yes, I think it's actually worth more than that."

"Ahhh!" she squealed excitedly, tumbling into his open arms. "I can do it then. I can buy my brothers' freedom."

Daniel's expression grew perplexed. "But Paddie's free as a bird. I just saw him this morning."

"No," Maggie replied slowly, a frown growing on her lovely face as she gazed up at Daniel. "Not that brother. I once said there was much you didn't know about me."

"If you're going to spring another brother on me, I'd have to agree with you," Daniel said carefully.

"Not one brother. Three."

Daniel gave a mock shout of alarm. "Three?"

Maggie nodded her head. "And they're Fenians, in Australia . . ."

"The penal colony?"

Maggie nodded again. "Yes, but they're good men! You'd like them every bit as much as you like Paddie if you met them! I promise, Daniel. You would!"

"I don't know. It's bad enough having one Catholic priest in the family, let alone three more. And Fenians!"

"They're not priests!"

"No?" he asked hopefully.

"No, they're farmers. But Seumas once went to Dublin to learn the trade of smithy. He didn't get along very well with all the Protestants, though, and came back after a few months."

"Maggie, me darling, did it ever occur to you that I am Protestant and your brothers might not like that?"

"It occurred to me," she said, smiling intimately at him. "But we're already married, by Paddie, so there's nothing any of them would dare to say about it."

Daniel had to laugh. He laughed so hard his sides hurt. Pressing his forehead against hers, he ruefully gazed into her eyes. His hands started at her shoulders and moved familiarly down the slenderness of her body, returning to cup the fullness of her breasts. "I'm glad we're already married. I'd hate to have to fight three brothers for you, but I'd do it, if I had to. I don't want to live the rest of my life without you."

"And since we're already married," she said sweetly, "they'll have to accept you, and your Protestantism."

"You have a devious mind, darling."

"I know."

"I want to make love to you," he crooned softly.

Maggie's eyes closed dreamily, and she was still smiling. "I want to make love to you too."

"I want to right now, but I'm starving and I know you are also. Besides, Paddie is here, so my guess is it's Paddie come to haunt us."

"I think so too."

"We could plead that you're too ill," he said hopefully.

"But I want to tell him about my half-mine. He'll be so happy to hear we've finally got the money to free the boys."

"You might have told me about them months ago. I would have given you the money."

"But I didn't want to come to the marriage so encumbered! That wouldn't be fair to you!"

Daniel compressed his lips tightly. "I might have known. Well, at least you have your mine and your fortune now, so we don't have to worry about you making money ever again."

"Oh, Daniel, thank you for understanding so well! I was so afraid that you might think my brothers were criminals or something."

"With just you as a sister, I might have. But with Paddie, their brother? Never!"

Her arms wound around him tightly. "I love you, Daniel. I love you so much sometimes I think my heart will burst with it."

He held her every bit as tightly. "Don't you ever forget it, Maggie." His lips sought and found hers, their warmth at once soothing yet demanding. When they finally broke free, both were breathing heavily. "If we don't go downstairs now, we'll stay up here all night."

"I know," she said, tempting him with her eyes.

"What are you trying to do, embarrass me in front of your sainted brother? Get on, go downstairs. You'll just have to wait until we've seen the backs of our guests."

"And we can sleep late in the morning."

Daniel's eyes darkened. "As late as we like."

Mrs. Sawyer had prepared one of her delicious dinners, stuffed baked chicken and accompaniments followed by apple pie. Dinner conversation was more about the kidnapping and its aftermath. Judge Forbes didn't like his cell in Kokomo and was demanding to be returned to Leadville. "If he was smart, he'd keep his mouth shut," quipped Patrick. "Outside the jail are a dozen men wanting to get their hands on the man who jumped their mines. Legal technicalities or no, they couldn't care less. They just want to lynch him.

"Jeremiah Duggen and Walt McClean are willing to testify against him, hoping, I'm sure, for a reduced sentence for themselves."

"What about Gertie?" Maggie asked.

"Oh, she'll spend a few weeks in jail, but there's nowhere to send a woman for longer punishment. She'll go free soon enough. We're going to have to go after Lovell if we want him, though."

"He's like a bad penny, he'll turn up again."

"Guess what, Paddie!" Maggie said proudly, turning to him.

"What can it be?" the priest asked good-humoredly. He was pleased with himself, with Daniel, and with Maggie. Nothing could interfere in his happiness.

"Spade McInery made me a partner in his mine," she

374

announced. "Do you know what that means?"

Patrick's smile faded in astonishment, his surprise genuine. His eyes went to Daniel as he asked, "What does it mean?"

"It means we've enough to buy the boys' freedom. They could be on their way to America within the twelfth month!"

Patrick nodded his head in agreement. "Aye, that they could be."

"Who wants coffee," Maude asked, and the three men all said they did.

"I'll come with you, Maude," Maggie offered. "I'll put the kettle on while you're pouring coffee, and we can join the men in the front parlor."

The door was still swinging in their wake when Patrick turned to Daniel and spouted, "I told you to start talking with her!"

"I did. We talked plenty," Daniel answered innocently.

"You know what I mean. Between husband and wife should be honesty."

"I've been honest with her."

"You pretended you didn't know anything about her brothers, didn't you?"

"Well . . . just for a moment or two."

"Just for the moment or two they were being discussed."

"If you want to argue about this, I suggest we go into the parlor. I sure don't want Maggie overhearing us arguing, not when she thinks we get along so well." Rising, he carried his brandy with him into the other room.

Paddie followed, his expression one of anger. "And what's this . . . lie about her owning one-half of Spade's mine?"

"I didn't lie. She does own it."

"Blast you, Daniel, I know you own one-half of that mine, and Spade owns the other half! He told me you were the one who grubstaked him!"

Daniel finished his drink, eying his brother-in-law carefully. "All right. But this is just between us, understand?"

"I don't know about that," Patrick hollered.

"Then let me put it bluntly. If Magheen ever learns that it was me who gave her that mine, I'll know who told her. And if you ever think to get one more red cent for that church of yours . . ."

Patrick drew a hot breath. "Do you think I'm for sale?"

"No, but if you'd use your mind, you'd realize what problems I'm solving for the future. If she doesn't come up with the money, she'll spend all her efforts getting some. This way, she's got the money, she thinks she earned it, and she can put all her concentration on me—and my child."

"Hmm," Paddie murmured, "I was thinking of building a church school."

"I think it's a good idea," Harvey said. "She's the only woman I've ever seen who could be more stubborn than Daniel."

"You still should be honest with your wife."

"Of course I should. And I will. Always. Just not about this."

"Did you straighten out that business about the baby—"

"Shh, here they come. Harvey, not a word of this to Maude."

"Not on your life."

"You are two of the rottenest husbands I've ever known," Paddie whispered. "Oh, coffee! Thank ye, Maggie." Father Patrick was smiling broadly as the women entered the room, Maggie carrying the tea tray, Maude the coffee things. "Here, give those to me." Reaching for the trays, he set them on the table in front of him.

Moments later he added another tidbit to the conversation. "Isn't it wonderful of your husband, Maggie? He's pledged one thousand dollars for the new school."

Daniel choked on the hot coffee burning its way down his throat. "You ought to be so proud of him. What a wonderful man you've married." Daniel's coughing was getting worse so Father Patrick clapped him on the back. The coughing stopped, but Daniel never felt so helpless in all his life.

"And Harvey, well, Harvey's just a bit less generous,

376

but five hundred dollars is still a goodly sum. Thank you, men."

Harvey bit his tongue to keep from saying anything.

"And I must be going now," he said rising. "I hate to eat and run, but you know how busy a priest's life is. Thank ye for dinner, Mrs. Sawyer. It was delicious as usual." He crossed to the hallway, Daniel following him.

"I've been wondering, Paddie, when do priests go to confession?"

"Oh, every time I go to Denver, I see Father O'Gorman. And if he comes here, we do the same service likewise."

"It's a relief to know you have to answer for your soul to someone."

The priest grinned hugely. "We all answer to the same God, but some of our sins have a better intent than others. I hope the Lord takes that into account."

"For your sake I do too. But did you have to make it a thousand dollars? That's a lot of money."

"From what I heard you've come into a lot of money. I feel sure you and Harvey can afford it."

Daniel's grin was crooked. "I feel like I've been fleeced by a priest."

"You have," Paddie whispered, winking.

Chapter Twenty

"I never thought making love to a pregnant lady could be so satisfying," Daniel said softly, nibbling on Maggie's ear. The bed was warm and comfortable, their guests long gone and the night stretching luxuriously before them.

"And I wasn't sure what to expect from an expectant father," she teased. "Tell me, do you ever feel peculiar in the morning, or do you get cravings for strange foods?"

"Funny you should ask that. Lately I've had this craving for Rocky Mountain oysters, and usually I can't stand 'em. Do you think our shared affliction could be causing that?"

"Could be. Have you had these symptoms since before you knew about the baby?"

"Sure have, lady," he sighed. "You'd have thought that with my experience I might have put two and two together and come up with baby, wouldn't you?"

"It's all right, as long as you always get the first symptoms," Maggie teased, holding her laughter no longer. Her head was turned into his shoulder, and she nipped his flesh when he protested at the way she laughed at him. Finally he rolled over and caught her beneath him, loving the way her bare breasts felt beneath his chest and the way her hair spread over their bed, enticing him to take a handful to his lips.

"Enough talk," he said, settling her more comfortably in his arms. "You promised to tell me about yourself, remember? Earlier today?"

"But I told you about my brothers . . ."

"No, I want to know all about you. From your first memory, to the day you got on that stagecoach in Denver and I met you for the first time. Tell me about your parents, your brothers, Ireland. Don't leave anything out."

"There's not a whole lot to tell."

"Then tell me what little there is. What's it like, losing a farm to the English, losing your brothers to them as well? How about your boat ride over? Ellis Island? The train trip west? I could spend my whole night thinking up questions."

"Well, my very first memory is of Rory standing over my bed, singing an Irish folksong, and Teeling sneaking up quietly behind him, then poking him in the ribs and making him jump high enough to reach the sky. . . ."

Daniel laughed as he did often throughout that night. Her other three brothers sounded every bit as warm and human as Paddie was. That she loved her family was apparent in every nuance of her voice, every expression on her face. For a second he envied his own child, being loved wholly as Maggie was wont to do. The envy died quickly when he remembered that was the way she loved him also.

Pain was there too, when she recalled the deaths of her parents, the loss of the farm, and the subsequent loss of her brothers. He laughed at her naiveté in crossing the Atlantic Ocean and two-thirds of a continent, sure she would find a fortune at the end of her journey. "I did, didn't I?" she asked, and Daniel couldn't refute her words.

And when she was done, Daniel began. "My first memory is getting the boy next door with my slingshot. I remember it well because I was so proud of myself, first to have figured out my slingshot and secondly, because the boy was the neighborhood bully. And because my mother paddled my rear so hard I couldn't sit down for a week."

Maggie had different sorts of questions for Daniel to answer, questions about his first girlfriend, his first kiss, the kinds of girls he met while attending the university.

"That's no fair," he accused. "I didn't ask you about your previous love life."

"That's because I didn't have one," she answered primly. "Remember, we're suppose to know everything about the other."

"Everything?"

"Yes," she nodded eagerly. "That's what Father O'Gorman said."

"So have you told me everything?" he queried softly. "Everything?"

Maggie opened her mouth, then she seemed to really consider the question. Finally, she answered, "Not everything, but close."

Incurably honest, he thought, laughing inwardly. "I thought your Father O'Gorman said 'everything'?"

"He did. But not everything is worth telling."

"Oh-ho, this gets better by the moment."

Maggie arched her head to see him better. "And have you told me everything? *Everything?* I'll bet what you've neglected to tell me could take the rest of the night!"

"Okay. Let's make a pact. What you did before we were married doesn't count. What I did before we were married doesn't count either."

"Were you that bad?"

"Yes. I like the way you look at me, as if I'm perfect. I don't want to lose that."

"You won't lose that, silly. I don't care what you tell me. I'll always think you're perfect. Though," she turned her head and spoke into the night, "you do have a bit of a temper, and," she added, wrinkling her brow, "you do swear once in a while. . . . And your drinking could be just a bit more temperate."

"Anything else?" he questioned good-naturedly.

"Well, yes, there is. It's a bit delicate . . ."

"You wicked woman, don't tell me that I'm not perky often enough." Daniel rocked his hips against hers, making her gasp with pleasure.

"By the way," he said moments later, relaxing against the sheets, "all this time, when you were worrying about

380

how I'd feel about our child, our half-Irish brat as I once callously called him, didn't you ever ask yourself what sort of name Calcord is? I mean, don't you wonder where my family's from? We Calcords haven't always lived in the States, you must realize."

"I thought you were English . . ." But she knew by his teasing grin that he had a surprise in store. "So, where does your family come from, Daniel?"

"I suppose most Calcords come from England. But my father's father came from the Aran Islands, just off the Galway coast."

Magheen gasped. "You're Irish?"

"Part of me is. My grandfather married a McFee, making my father half-Scottish. My mother is a Cheatham, English by name, but her blood is probably as intermixed as my own.

"So Maggie, me darling, you were wrong. Our child will be *better* than half-Irish."

TURN TO CATHERINE CREEL — THE REAL THING — FOR THE FINEST IN HEART-SOARING ROMANCE!

CAPTIVE FLAME (2401, $3.95)
Meghan Kearney was grateful to American Devlin Montague for rescuing her from the gang of Bahamian cutthroats. But soon the handsome yet arrogant island planter insisted she serve his baser needs — and Meghan wondered if she'd merely traded one kind of imprisonment for another!

TEXAS SPITFIRE (2225, $3.95)
If fiery Dallas Brown failed to marry overbearing Ross Kincaid, she would lose her family inheritance. But though Dallas saw Kincaid as a low-down, shifty opportunist, the strong-willed beauty could not deny that he made her pulse race with an inexplicable flaming desire!

SCOUNDREL'S BRIDE (2062, $3.95)
Though filled with disgust for the seamen overrunning her island home, innocent Hillary Reynolds was overwhelmed by the tanned, masculine physique of dashing Ryan Gallagher. Until, in a moment of wild abandon, she offered herself like a purring tiger to his passionate, insistent caress!